Trapped at the Altar

JANE FEATHER

headline
ETERNAL

Cataloguing in Publication Data is available from the British Library

ISBN 978 1 4722 1322 8

Offset in Adobe Garamond by Avon DataSet Ltd, Bidford-on-Avon, Warwickshire

Printed and bound by CPI Group (UK) Ltd, Croydon, CR0 4YY

Headline's policy is to use papers that are natural, renewable and recyclable products and made from wood grown in sustainable forests. The logging and manufacturing processes are expected to conform to the environmental regulations of the country of origin.

HEADLINE PUBLISHING GROUP
An Hachette UK Company
338 Euston Road
London NW1 3BH

www.headlineeternal.com
www.headline.co.uk
www.hachette.co.uk

Trapped at the Altar

PROLOGUE

Somerset, England, August 1667

The cavalcade of horsemen rode into the narrow defile between the steep cliffs that hung over Daunt valley. The River Wye was a thin ribbon below them, sunlight dancing off its surface as it wended its way across the lush green floor of the valley.

There were six horsemen in total, wearing buff leather coats, swords at their sides, pistols holstered in the saddles in front of them. They drew rein at the narrowest part of the pass, where two men, swords drawn, stood in their path.

"Who enters Daunt valley?" one of the challengers demanded, standing easily, legs apart, his sword held between his hands. Higher up the cliff, behind two rocks, two others trained their muskets on the new arrivals.

"Chalfont," responded the lead horseman. He had his hand on his sword hilt but made no attempt to draw it. "We are come in peace with a gift for Lord Daunt."

The challengers sheathed their swords and stepped aside. "You are expected. Pass." He gestured to a youth standing to one side. The young man took off with the news of the visitors as if all the devils in hell were upon him, flying across the rocky ground with unerring footsteps, setting off a shower of loose scree tumbling ahead of him.

With a nod, the horseman led his little parade in single file through the narrow pass and down to the valley floor.

By the time they reached it, a small crowd had gathered on a square of flattened turf outside a substantial cottage. A tall gray-haired man stood in the doorway to the building, an imposing figure with harsh gray eyes, the nose of a falcon, and angular features. He was dressed plainly in leather britches and jerkin, but his linen was fine, gleaming white, the fall of lace at his throat immaculate.

The cavalcade drew rein in front of him, and the horsemen dismounted. Only then did the small figure huddled on a pillion pad behind one of the horsemen reveal his presence. "We have brought the boy, my lord Daunt." The spokesman of the little group turned and lifted the figure from his horse. The boy was wrapped tightly in a heavy cloak, the hood pulled low over his forehead, and when his feet touched the ground, he staggered a little, before righting himself with a steadying hand on his shoulder.

"The boy has been riding for four days with only a few hours' sleep during the hours of darkness," the spokesman stated, as if excusing the child's sudden weakness.

Lord Daunt merely inclined his head in acknowledgment. "Come here, boy." He beckoned.

The child shook the hood off his head, revealing a thatch of short chestnut hair. He looked at the man who had summoned him, his deep-set eyes blue as a turquoise sea. The steady gaze held defiance, but his lordship could see behind that to the boy's confusion and fear.

"Come," he said again, more softly this time.

The child stepped forward boldly and offered a jerky bow. "My lord."

"So, you are Ivor Chalfont." The Earl tipped his chin with a forefinger. "Let me look at you." He seemed to scrutinize the child for a very long time before saying, "You have much of your mother about you, my boy. I trust you have your father's courage to go with it." He looked over the boy's head to where a group of women were gathered. "Dorcas, you will take charge of our ward. He needs food and rest."

"Aye, my lord." An apple-cheeked woman separated herself from the group and came over, dropping a curtsy in the Earl's direction. "Come along with me, lad. We'll soon have you running with the boys."

Ivor Chalfont regarded her solemnly, then felt other eyes upon him. He looked behind the Earl. A pair of gray eyes were fixed upon him from the rather grubby countenance of a very small girl.

"I'll bring the boy, Dorcas," the child declared, stepping out from behind the Earl. She held out her hand to the newcomer. "I'm Ari," she stated. "And I will look after you, boy." She grabbed his hand in her small, warm fist.

Ivor stared at her, torn between amusement and indignation. How could this little baby scrap even think of looking after him? He was six. He was proficient with a wooden sword, and if he'd been allowed to ride alone instead of with the indignity of pillion behind one of his father's men, he would have managed perfectly well.

The little girl tugged at his hand. "Come on, boy. Dorcas has made sweet cakes with honey. They're very good, you'll see."

She tugged him along behind her, and after a moment's hesitation, he followed her. He had no idea where he was or why he was there, but the little hand firmly grasping his was oddly comforting.

ONE

Somerset, England, September 1684

"Ari . . . Ari, will you *please* stop climbing?" Ivor Chalfont stopped on the steep goat track leading up the sheer cliff from the river below. He looked in exasperation at the small figure climbing twenty yards ahead of him. He hadn't a hope of catching her; he knew that from experience. Ariadne was small and lithe and astonishingly agile, particularly at climbing the towering cliffs, which sheltered their childhood home in a deep Somerset gorge. He glanced behind him. Far below, the River Wye sparkled in the warm late-summer sun, running peacefully between wide green banks. Cottages were clustered on either bank, smoke curling from chimneys. A few figures moved around, working in the neat gardens or fishing along the river. The sound of hammering rose in the quiet air from a man repairing a strut on the wooden bridge that spanned the river at its narrowest point. It was a peaceful, positively bucolic sight. On the surface. The reality was quite different, as Ivor well knew.

He cast his eyes upwards again. Ari was still climbing. She couldn't really think she could escape the reality of the gorge, could she? But Ivor knew she wasn't thinking that. She understood the facts of their life as well as he did.

He cupped his hands around his mouth and bellowed, "*Ariadne*. Stop, *now*."

Ariadne heard him, as, indeed, she'd heard his every other call. Those she'd ignored, too locked into her world of furious frustration to pay any heed, but now reason and logic took over, besides which, it was never wise to try Ivor's patience too far. She stopped on the track, turned carefully to look down at him so many feet below, then sat down on a rocky outcrop to the side of the track, hugging her knees, watching as he began to climb up to her.

His shadow fell over her a few minutes later, blocking out the sun's warmth. She raised her eyes to look up at him. Ivor stood with his hands on his hips, breathing easily despite the steep climb. He was a tall, well-built man, with the strong, muscular physique of one accustomed to physical labor and life in the outdoors. His deep-set eyes were the astonishing blue of the Aegean Sea, and they surveyed her upturned face from beneath well-shaped russet-brown eyebrows with a mixture of exasperation and wry comprehension.

"There are times, Ari, when I'd happily wring your neck," he declared, kicking a stone out of the path before sitting down on a large rock.

"You and half the valley," she returned, looking back down the track to the peaceful scene below. "The elders are ready to burn me at the stake."

He gave a short crack of laughter. "Not that, exactly, but I wouldn't put it past them to lock you up and starve you into submission."

She shrugged slim shoulders beneath a thin white shirt through which the tones of her skin showed delicately pink. "They wouldn't succeed."

"Maybe not," he agreed, lifting his face to the sun, letting it graze his closed eyelids. "But they're mad as fire, Ariadne, and they don't understand why, now, you're refusing to honor the betrothal."

"I give that for their anger." She snapped her fingers contemptuously. "I'll not marry you, Ivor. There's no point in discussing it."

Ivor sighed. Ariadne was as stubborn as a mule and always had been. But in this situation, all the obstinacy of a team of mules would not win the day for her. "You may now own half the valley, dear girl, but you are still subject to your grandfather's will. Our marriage was willed by Lord Daunt before his death . . . for God's sake, you agreed to the betrothal just a few days ago. Your grandfather's will is sacrosanct; you know that as well as I do. You have lived by Daunt rules all your life. The elders will make the wedding happen one way or another."

"Forcible marriage is illegal in the laws of the land."

"In name, maybe, but not in practice. You have a duty to obey your grandfather's will, and here in the valley that is the law. Since when," he added, "did Daunt and Chalfont obey any laws but their own?"

"I'll run away."

"How? You have no money, no means of travel. You

would never get past the guards on horseback, and you could not bring Sphinx up this goat track. He would break a leg for sure."

"You could help me." She didn't look at him as she said this.

"No," he stated. "I could not. I would not if I could."

"You could refuse to marry me."

"No," he repeated. "I could not. I would not if I could."

Ariadne made no response, but a small sigh escaped her, and a little shiver ran across her shoulders. It wasn't as if she had expected anything else. Ivor had much to gain from the marriage. If only her grandfather had not died so suddenly, just the day after the betrothal. With more time, she knew she could have persuaded him to release her from the engagement. She had always been able to win him over in the end, but it always took time and patience, and she'd agreed to the betrothal to buy herself that time. And then death had just crept in that night and taken him. His servant had found him dead in his bed, when the previous evening he had been hale and hearty, presiding over the Council meeting in his usual sharp and incisive fashion, celebrating his granddaughter's betrothal with some of the finest wines in his cellar. Wines destined for the cellars of West Country gentry, liberated in the dark of the moon by Daunt raiders from the smugglers' trains of pack mules going about their deliveries in the narrow Cornish lanes.

Ivor leaned across and took her hands from her lap, holding them in a tight grip. "Face it, Ari. Accept it. We will be married this day week. As soon as Lord Daunt is in his grave, we will be wed."

Her gray eyes held his deep blue ones in a fierce stare as she tried to free her hands. "You know that I love someone else, Ivor. I *cannot* marry you. It would be dishonest."

He dropped her hands with a laugh as mirthless as before. "That's rich, Ari, coming from one whose entire existence is based on deceit, on thievery, on piracy. Truth and morality mean nothing here in this valley. You were born into this life of dishonesty and trickery. We mock the laws of men and discount the imperatives of ownership. We take what we want, whether it's ours or not. I will take you to wife, Ariadne Daunt. Your grandfather has willed it; my family has agreed to it. It is for us to unite the two families. You belong to me, not to that *poet* of yours, scribbling his nonsensical verse in the houses of the gentry."

Ari's gray eyes burned with an anger all the more fierce for being impotent. She knew she could not win this argument or, indeed, run from the bitter truth behind it. "The Daunts are of lineage as ancient and proud as any in the counties of Somerset, Devon, or Cornwall," she retorted. "And my dower will be sufficient to overcome any minor moral scruples. Gabriel's family will welcome me as a daughter; he has assured me of that."

Ivor shook his head. "I wouldn't be so certain. For one, do you really think your family elders would pay your dowry to the Fawcetts? Just hand it over, meek and mild, with their blessings on their precious niece? I had never thought you naïve, Ari."

Tears stung her eyes, and she blinked them away. "Just leave me alone, Ivor. Go back down. I'm climbing to the top."

He hesitated, then decided that she was best left alone for the moment. Maybe she was going to meet her precious poet and maybe she wasn't. But she would not run away. Ari would never run when fighting was an option. She was a Daunt, born and bred.

He got up from his rock, dusting off his hands. "Very well. But you are expected at Council this evening before the feast for your grandfather's wake. Make sure you're there. We will both regret it if I have to come and find you."

There was something about his tone, an authority he had never used with her before, that shook her. Realization slowly dawned. "They have made you my guardian?" It was barely a question; she knew the answer.

"Yes," Ivor answered curtly. "Your grandfather is dead. Who better to watch over you than your future husband? I will see you at Council." He turned from her and began the long scramble back to the valley.

Ariadne exhaled slowly. She shouldn't have expected anything else. She knew the ways of the Daunt world—knew them but didn't have to accept them. She watched Ivor's retreating back. He was her friend, but she could never accept him as her governor. Her grandfather's death had released her from the family's control; she would not relinquish that independence now.

Rising, she turned her face to the cliff top, climbing steadily until she reached the tufted grass above, sprinkled with daisies and the occasional pink. Grazing sheep ignored her unorthodox arrival in their midst, and a few cows regarded her with lazy bovine stares as she shook down her homespun skirt and kicked dirt from her shoes before starting across the field to a small spinney at the far side.

✦ ✦ ✦

Gabriel Fawcett stood among the trees in the spinney, watching as Ariadne came across the field towards him. He held a small nosegay of late-summer roses from his mother's garden and felt the customary surge of blood, the swift pounding of his heart, as she drew closer. Sometimes he wondered how it was physically possible for one body to contain so much passion, so much lust and love, as he felt for this girl. Ariadne Daunt was out of his experience, almost magical in her difference from anyone he had ever met before. She was not of his world, and sometimes he thought she was not of *this* world at all. But he knew that she was very much of *this* world. The very name of Daunt brought dread to all who heard it.

It had not always been so. They were one of the oldest families in Somerset and one of the wealthiest in both estates and fortune, until Charles I had lost his head and Oliver Cromwell's Protestant Commonwealth had ruled the land with a dour fist. The Catholic Daunt family had raised their standard for King Charles and lost everything back on that cold January day in 1649 when the King had been beheaded. They had barely escaped with their lives, and they had been revenged ever since

upon all who they thought had betrayed them, on erstwhile friends and neighbors, indeed, on anyone who had
bowed their heads beneath Cromwell's yoke.

Outlaws, they had created their own land and their
own laws in a valley of the River Wye, a place easily forti-
fied and defended. And when it pleased them to create
mayhem across the usually peaceful countryside, they did
so. They terrorized the seaports of Devon and Cornwall,
piracy and even the vile business of wrecking were not
beneath them, and they amassed a fortune rumored to
rival that of any of the great landed families of the realm.

And Gabriel Fawcett had fallen in love and lust with
Lady Ariadne Daunt, the scion of one of the oldest and
now the most loathed family in the West Country. And
to his eternal astonishment, the lady loved him in return.
It was an impossible match, an impossible relationship,
and yet it *was*. An immutable, all-consuming fact, and
as he watched her now, her light step springing across
the mossy ground, her skirt hitched up to reveal slender
ankles, her lovely long feet clad only in a pair of light slippers, he knew he would die for her if he had to.

He took a step out of the trees, and Ari saw him at
once. She raised a hand in greeting and ran towards him,
burying herself in his embrace. She felt the swift beat of
his heart against her ear as she placed her head on his
chest and inhaled the fresh rosemary scent of his linen.

"Oh, how I have missed you," she murmured. "It has
been such a dreadful time, Gabriel. I don't know where
to turn."

He tilted her face and kissed her, his mouth hungry

for the taste of her. The nosegay was crushed between them, but he didn't even notice the thorn pricking his finger as he held her tightly against him. At last, his hold slackened, and she drew herself upright. Her body was tiny, seemingly fragile, but he could feel the strength and suppleness of her form as she stood so close to him. And he could see the deep shadows lurking in the usually clear gray eyes, the lines of strain around her wide, generous mouth.

"What has happened, my love?"

Ariadne took a step away from him. It was easier to keep her thoughts straight when she wasn't within the circle of his arms. "My grandfather, Lord Daunt, died three days ago."

He frowned, unsure how to respond. Ari had rarely spoken of her grandfather, her guardian since her father's death ten years ago. Indeed, she almost never spoke of her life in the valley.

"What does that mean for you?" he asked hesitantly.

She gave him a twisted smile. "It means, my dear, that I am to marry my second cousin, Ivor Chalfont, as a way of uniting the fortunes of the two families and finally ending the enmity between Chalfonts and Daunts . . . as if such a thing was ever a realistic possibility," she added bitterly. "The two branches of the family have loathed each other since before the Crusades."

An exaggeration, perhaps, she reflected, but it might just as well have been true given the depths of their hatred and rivalry.

"I . . . I don't understand." Gabriel's eyes had an almost

hunted look as he gazed at her in shocked bemusement. The crushed roses slipped from his hand, and without thinking, he sucked at the bead of blood on his forefinger where the thorn had pricked him.

Ari bent to pick up one of the roses, a small white bud that had somehow escaped the massacre. She said dully, "Ivor grew up in the valley. We played together as children. We were betrothed first as infants and then formally a few days ago, as part of this plan to unite our two families." She hesitated. Talking about her family never came easily to her, and she had tried instinctively to keep Gabriel untouched by her own history, as if in some way it would keep their love free of the taint of the valley.

But what did it matter now? After a moment, she continued, "Daunts are Catholic, Chalfonts are Protestant. My grandfather decided that if the two factions were joined as one tribe, then they would present a strong force to handle whichever political and religious faction finally ruled. The greater good of the united tribe would overcome individual family differences." Her laugh was short and bitter. "So someone has to be sacrificed to this greater good, and that seems to be me."

Gabriel shook his head as if to untangle his confusion. "But what of this . . . this cousin . . . Ivor? Is he not also to be sacrificed?"

She pushed the rosebud into a buttonhole on her shirt and said, "No, apparently, Ivor does not consider himself to be a sacrifice. He appears to find the idea a good one. It will benefit him, of course." By marrying the heiress to the ill-gotten Daunt fortune, Ivor would become rich.

But was that what motivated him? Somehow Ariadne didn't think it was as simple as that. Ivor had never been particularly predictable, and he rarely followed a simple path. It was one of the things she liked most about him. It had always made him a fun and exciting playmate in their childhood. She had never thought about what kind of husband he would make; the fact of that childhood betrothal hadn't impinged upon her thoughts until the last two weeks, when it had become a concrete reality. But by then, she had met Gabriel Fawcett, and she had looked at the world beyond the valley, and that concrete reality had become an impossible one.

"My family will gladly welcome you," Gabriel said with passion. "Ari, you must come with me now. We will protect you."

She smiled, somewhat mistily. "They will destroy your family and everything you hold dear if you dared to do such a thing. I couldn't let that happen."

"But I *cannot* lose you, Ari . . . my love, I will die without you."

She regarded him steadily. "No, you won't. But you may well die *with* me. We will find another way, Gabriel. I will not lose you, but for the moment, I must at least seem to be compliant. The marriage is not to take place for a week. I will think of something between now and then."

He looked at her in horror. "A week . . . just a week."

"Yes, but don't worry. A week is a long time to come up with an idea." She stood on tiptoe and kissed the corner of his mouth. "I should go. If I'm missed, they'll send out the dogs."

"Dogs?"

She laughed shortly. "Yes, they do have them, but I meant it metaphorically. I don't want to arouse suspicions." Except that Ivor knew the truth. He didn't need suspicions. But he wouldn't betray her, surely?

And with a sickening feeling, Ariadne realized she was no longer sure of that. He had discovered her liaison by accident when she had climbed the cliff one day a few weeks earlier to visit the secret place where she and Gabriel left messages for each other. It had been raining, and most of the valley's inhabitants were within doors, no one watching the track she habitually took up the cliff. The rain had made the path slippery, and she had been concentrating on watching her step on the treacherous shale, peering intently at the ground from beneath the thick hood of her cloak drawn low over her forehead. She hadn't been aware of anyone following her until she had reached the cliff top and was lifting the flat stone that revealed a small indentation in the earth.

"What are you doing up here in such wretched weather?"

Ivor's voice had startled her so much her heart had seemed to jump into her throat, and the folded sheet of parchment that she was taking out of the hole had fallen from her fingers. Ivor had bent swiftly and retrieved it before she could do so herself.

She could see again the intense, questioning blue eyes as he'd held the paper out to her, his voice unusually hard. "What is this?"

"Just a letter." She had made to thrust it into the inside pocket of her cloak, but he had stayed her hand, his long fingers curling around her wrist. Not painfully but firmly enough to mean business.

"Who from? Why would you be conducting a clandestine correspondence up here, Ari?"

She had shrugged with an assumption of carelessness. "I met someone on a walk a few weeks ago. We talked, enjoyed each other's company, and when we want to meet again, we leave messages, under the stone here."

"I see." He had frowned. "May I ask who this person is?"

"I'm not sure it's any of your business." Her voice had been tart. "What I do, whom I see, and where I go are of no consequence to you, Ivor."

"They are of consequence to your grandfather," he had reminded her, still holding her wrist. "I rather think he would disapprove, don't you?"

"Probably. Certainly, I would prefer it if you didn't mention anything about this, Ivor." She had heard the cajoling note in her voice and hoped she hadn't sounded too desperate.

Ivor had shaken his head. "Why would I? But who is it, Ari? Just satisfy my curiosity that far."

And because they were friends and she trusted him, thought of him as her closest friend and ally, she had told him all about Gabriel, about how they had met by chance in the spinney one afternoon, how they had seen each other regularly ever since . . . about the poetry he had written her. And Ivor had not shown any emotion at all. He had warned her to be careful and during the following weeks had inquired occasionally about her meetings with her poet, and she had confessed the deepening of their relationship, talked about what it felt like to be in love . . . and Ivor had merely listened.

But perhaps he had been concealing his feelings.

Ari wondered now whether she had seen in Ivor's reaction to her confession only the indifference she wanted to see. Perhaps she had allowed herself to be blind to his real response. Loyal friend though he had been throughout their growing, Ivor could well now feel that it was his duty, his right, even, to betray her to the Council. And they would see only one way to deal with the situation. They would simply remove the obstacle. Gabriel would be eliminated.

That was not a risk she could take, she realized, her thoughts suddenly clearing after the days of confused dismay. There was only one course of action that would protect Gabriel, whether Ivor betrayed her or not.

"What are you thinking?" Gabriel asked, alarmed by the bleak look on her face.

Her face was momentarily wiped clean of expression, and then she turned to him, holding out her hands in invitation. "That I don't have to go right away," she murmured. "And I want you so much, dearest. It feels an eternity since we were last together."

With a little shudder of a sigh, Gabriel took her in his arms, burying his face in the mass of black curls clustering around her small head. He ran his hands over her body, lifting her against him, before sliding with her to the springy moss beneath the beech tree.

TWO

"So where is she, Ivor?"

The sharp question came from the new head of the family, Rolf, now Lord Daunt. Ariadne's uncle was a man in his mid-fifties, a formidable figure, with shoulders that could bear the weight of a felled tree, a deep powerful chest, and muscular arms. His prowess with sword and cudgel was almost legendary in the countryside, even among the Daunt clan, where physical strength and fighting ability among the menfolk were taken for granted.

"Walking above," Ivor responded succinctly. "She'll be back soon." He crossed his fingers beneath the rough-hewn surface of the oak table. He had parted from Ariadne on the cliff path almost two hours earlier and had expected her to return much before this. He glanced around the gathering. The ten men all bore the traditional features of the Daunt family, the hawklike gray eyes, the thick curly black hair, aquiline noses, thin well-shaped lips, and square chins. Handsome in their way, but there was a hard, ruthless quality to all of them. They were not men one would wish to cross.

His present position among them was of recent standing. He had been appointed to the Council by old Lord Daunt the previous year in preparation for his eventual marriage to Lord Daunt's granddaughter. That marriage had been agreed upon when he was six years old. He could remember little of the time that had preceded his arrival in the Daunt valley as a lost and bewildered child, but he had known from earliest memory of the implacable enmity that existed between his own family, the Chalfonts, and their distant relatives, the Daunt clan. An enmity based on religion and politics that had threatened at one point to wipe out both families. Until his own father, Sir Gordon Chalfont, had agreed to send his son to be brought up among the Daunts in preparation for the wedding that would unite the two families and bring an end to the deadly enmity. Even now, fully grown as he was, Ivor still felt on occasion the bewildering sense of betrayal and abandonment that had overwhelmed him when he had been left among these ruthless strangers with their rough and ready ways.

Ariadne had been three when Ivor had arrived in the valley. Even then, she had been a fierce little girl, with a mass of curly black hair and intense and watchful gray eyes. She had been a tiny, doll-like figure, he had first thought, and even as a six-year-old, he was able to lift her easily. He remembered how he used to carry her around and how angry it had made her when he'd pick her up when she was in the middle of something and carry her off like a Viking's prize. She'd hammer at him with her tiny fists, claw at him with her nails, and hurl abuse at him in language that would have made a sailor blush. Her temper had made her father and the rest of the menfolk laugh; indeed, they seemed to take pride in her indomitable spirit, encouraging her rather than attempting to rein her in, and only her mother, a gentle soul ill suited to life in the rough-and-tumble of Daunt valley, had tried to tame her.

Ariadne had calmed down a little as she had grown, much of her surplus energy going into her lessons. She had a voracious thirst for knowledge and a quick mind that her grandfather in particular had nurtured. He had been a scholar, a philosopher, beneath the ruthless vengeance-driven life he led in exile, and he had taught his granddaughter himself, relishing her ever-expanding interests and encouraging her to read widely. Ivor had been included in the lessons, most particularly those that concerned politics and the art of debate, the intricacies of diplomacy and history, but he had gained more pleasure from the other side of his education, the activities that had focused on the warlike pursuits of sword and cudgel, the swift thrust of a dagger, the art of evasion and defensive maneuvers. Gaining competence in the skills of fighting and weaponry had somehow compensated for his sense of abandonment, the loss of his own family. It had enabled him to feel armored against the strangers who encircled him.

But he had never been included in a Daunt raid, in any act of theft or piracy. He was now twenty-three, and he had neither killed nor wounded. He had stolen nothing, burned not so much as a haystack, and until a few days ago, he had never understood his exclusion from the rites of passage that marked adulthood in the valley of the Daunts.

Even now, in the cool, shuttered dimness of the Council house, he could feel again the heat of the late-summer sun on the back of his neck in the armorer's yard as he'd bent over the sword he was sharpening that morning of the summons that had explained it all. Ariadne had been sitting on a saw horse, idly swinging her bare legs, watching him at work as she'd whittled a stick with her own dagger, a piece of perfectly chased silver that he'd never seen her without. As the voices around him droned on, his mind drifted to that morning . . .

"You two, you're both wanted in the Council house."

Ariadne regarded the newly arrived youth with an arrogantly raised eyebrow. "By whom, child?"

The young man blushed furiously at her tone. He was perhaps a year or so younger than Ari, but womenfolk did not speak with such derision to the men in Daunt valley. However, Lord Daunt's granddaughter was different, and he knew better than to challenge her. "His lordship has sent for you both," he responded sullenly.

"Ah, then, in that case, we'd better find out what he wants." Ari slipped her dagger into the leather sheath at the waistband of her skirt, hidden by the close-fitting woolen jerkin she wore over her shirt. Ivor set aside his sword in the rack where personal swords were kept when their owners were going about their daily business in the valley. Tempers

could run high in the valley, and less blood was drawn when men were unarmed. Ari and her little dagger were considered of no consequence, although privately, Ivor thought she could do a great deal of damage with her dainty little knife if provoked. He had seen her bring down a fleeing hare in one throw.

He held out his hand to her as they walked towards the large brick house where Lord Daunt lived and where the Council met. It was on the outskirts of the village, close to the water mill that ground the village's flour. Ari took his hand, and they walked companionably side by side. It was only a friendly contact. Ivor was under no illusions, although a watcher could have construed otherwise. But Ariadne's heart was a long way from her childhood companion, as Ivor knew only too well. As far as he was aware, he was the only person in on her secret, but that couldn't last if she persisted in pursuing her poet. At some point soon, Ari was going to have to face the reality. She was not destined to be the wife of an ordinary Somerset citizen, however wealthy and well-bred he might be.

The watchman at the door of the Council house nodded as they approached and opened the door for them. Lord Daunt was sitting in his carved chair at the head of the table, and Ivor felt Ariadne stiffen as she slipped her hand from his. This was a formal summons, not the casual visit her grandfather often initiated.

She curtsied and stepped up to the table. "Sir, you wanted to see us."

"Yes, Ariadne. It's time we settled a few matters." He regarded her closely, his gray eyes intent, as if he would read her *mind, before he turned the same scrutiny on her companion. "Ivor." He beckoned him closer. "The time has come for your betrothal to my granddaughter. The wedding will take place next month, or sooner should anything happen to me prematurely." A slightly cynical smile curved his thin mouth. "As we know, in this life of ours, such premature events are all too frequent. In such an instance, it will take place seven days after my death." He turned sharply to his granddaughter. "Did you say something, Ariadne?"*

Ari's face was white, her own gray eyes suddenly huge against the pallor. But her voice when she spoke was strong. "I . . . I do not wish for this betrothal, sir."

"And since when, my child, did you imagine your wishes were of the least importance to this family?" His voice was low, with all the hidden menace of a serpent's hiss. "You will do your duty, a duty that has been prepared for you from the moment of your birth. Ivor has understood that, why have you not?"

She stood straight, her small frame seeming somehow to dominate the dim chamber. "I have chosen not to think of the unthinkable, sir. I cannot marry Ivor."

Her grandfather looked at her almost with pity, but his voice was icy. "You will marry Ivor Chalfont, Ariadne. That is all there is to be said. And as of this moment, your betrothal contract is ratified." He pushed a parchment across the table to Ivor. "Sign."

Ivor looked at Ariadne, who steadfastly stared at the wall ahead, and then he took up the quill and signed. He held it out to Ari, who ignored it, still staring at the wall.

"Sign," her grandfather rasped.

And to Ivor's relieved astonishment, she took the quill and carefully wrote her name in the assigned place.

"Good. That is done." Lord Daunt took the parchment, wrote his own name below theirs, sanded the sheet, and folded it carefully, sealing it with candle wax and imprinting his own seal from his signet ring in the wax. He reached into his pocket and took out a silver box, which he slid across the table to Ivor. "Put this on her finger."

Ivor opened the box. The ring was one single emerald, large and square, in a diamond setting. It seemed far too large for Ari's small, delicate hand, but when he held out his hand for hers, half expecting her to refuse him, she put her hand in his without a tremor. Her face was expressionless, but there was something in her eyes that filled him with deep unease. He knew from experience that Ariadne picked the time of her fights and had on many occasions caught him off guard. He slipped the ring on her finger. It had been sized to fit, but the stone was far too large and extravagant a decoration for her delicacy.

"It doesn't suit you," Lord Daunt declared, "but it is the family betrothal ring, and therefore it is yours to wear."

"Just as it doesn't suit me to marry Ivor, but he is the family choice, therefore he is mine to wed," she stated almost distantly.

Her grandfather's eyes were lit with a momentary flash of anger, and then he said quite mildly, "I am glad you see the situation as it is, Ariadne. Your life will soon move outside this valley, yours and Ivor's. It is time for our families to resume their rightful places at court. The times are changing. King Charles maintains that he follows the Protestant

*religion, but it is said in secret that he practices Catholicism.
Be that as it may, he is old and failing, a life of debauchery
finally taking its toll." Contempt laced the old man's words,
and he moved a hand in a dismissive gesture of disgust, as if
consigning his King to oblivion.*

*He continued briskly, "His brother, the Duke of York,
who will inherit the crown, makes no secret of his Catholic faith. His wife is openly of our faith, and the time is
now right for us to return to the world. You, Ivor, have been
trained as a courtier. I have done what I can to educate you
in the ways of the court. You will stand accused of no crime,
no treason. You have led an unblemished life. This I have
ensured. After your marriage, you will go to London with all
pomp and ceremony, a wealthy young couple of noble estate,
and you will take your place at court."*

*He passed a hand across his eyes with sudden weariness.
A gesture Ivor had never seen before, and he thought the old
man looked worn out as his face was illuminated by a ray
of sun through the open window. His skin seemed paper-
thin, and the shadows beneath his eyes were black, the lines
around his mouth deeply etched. Was he dying? Had he had
a premonition? The thought for an instant terrified Ivor. It
was impossible to imagine the valley without the old man.*

*And then Lord Daunt waved a hand towards the door.
"That is all I have to say to you both. Prepare for your wedding, Ariadne. The women know what to do, and I'm sure
by now your bridal gown and trousseau are already well on
their way to completion."*

*Ariadne said nothing. She curtsied stiffly and walked out
of the house, ignoring Ivor hurrying behind her. Outside in*

the bright morning sunlight, she said only, "Go away, Ivor. I cannot bear to see you at the moment." And she walked away to her own house, where she lived with her own female attendant.

And the next morning, the old man had been found dead in his bed, eyes wide open, staring at the ceiling as if something had startled him.

✦ ✦ ✦

Ivor became aware of ten pairs of eyes looking at him with puzzled curiosity, and he pushed the memories of that day aside. Someone had been speaking to him, and he had failed to respond. He coughed. "I beg your pardon, gentlemen. My mind was elsewhere."

"Obviously," Rolf Daunt said drily. "And since the matter at hand concerns you most nearly, I would be grateful if we could have your undivided attention. I will ask again, is there any reason that you know of for Ariadne to be refusing this marriage?"

Ivor came fully to his senses, his mind snapping into focus. He shook his head. As far as he knew, only he, Ari, and her poet were aware of their attachment, so he could safely deny all knowledge of it. Since her grandfather's death, Ariadne had kept to herself, saying little to anyone, and he assumed her withdrawal had been considered a natural manifestation of her grief. No one had remarked upon it, at least . . . not until her bombshell that morning, when she had announced to her uncle that she refused to marry Ivor.

"Grief for her grandfather might account for it," Ivor

suggested. "It's possible she finds something distasteful about the idea of dancing at her wedding when her grandfather's body is barely in the grave." He looked around the table, feeling for the first time that he was taking his place in Council, that his opinion would now carry weight.

"That's nonsense . . . it was Lord Daunt's wish that in the event of his death, the wedding would take place seven days later. He made that clear in his final will. Honoring his wishes will be honoring him."

"Maybe so, sir, but I think Ariadne is so grief-stricken that she cannot accept that." Ivor wondered if he could use this newfound power to push for a postponement of the wedding and, if so, whether a delay would benefit Ari or himself. Would it give her time to accept the inevitable, or would it simply give her more time to agonize, to try to find a way out of it?

Short of turning her dagger upon herself, and that was not Ari's way, she would not succeed in avoiding this marriage, so better to get on with it, he decided. He continued with a confidence he was far from feeling, "However, I am sure, sir, that when the time comes, Ariadne will honor her grandfather's wishes."

"She will have no choice in the matter," Rolf declared. "And it is not right that she should be roaming the countryside at will and alone. You should have prevented her, Chalfont." He gestured to a young man standing guard at the door. "You, Wilfred, take three men and go above, find Lady Ariadne, and bring her back immediately."

Ivor said swiftly as the door closed behind Wilfred, "I will go myself, sir. There's no need for a search party."

"They will find her soon enough," Rolf stated with a dismissive gesture. "And we have not finished our discussion. Once the wedding is over, we will begin preparations for your journey to London. There, as my predecessor intended, you will advance the family's fortunes. With the right contacts, the right dispensations, we will leave this valley, and with the Daunt lands returned to us as the rightful owners, we will resume our place in the world."

It was spoken with firm confidence, but Ivor couldn't help wondering how easy it would be to get the world to forgive and forget the twenty-year reign of pillage and terror across the countryside. The Daunt lands had been broken up when the family had been driven into exile, and it was to be assumed their present owners would be reluctant to yield them up without a fight. But he merely murmured an assent, anxious to get out of the Council chamber and go in search of Ariadne. He could only pray that she was not with her poet if Wilfred and his friends found her before he did.

At last, Rolf signaled that the meeting was over, and Ivor hurried out into the afternoon. The steep cliff of the gorge threw the valley into shadow as the sun sank lower, and he cursed Ariadne. She should have known better than to have stayed away this long. He glanced up the cliff, just making out the narrow trail snaking to the top. There was no sign of the small figure picking her way down to the valley. Wilfred and his friends would have left on horseback by the main pass out of the gorge. They would have reached the cliff top five or ten minutes ago. It didn't bear thinking of what would happen if they found her with Fawcett.

Did Ariadne really love her poet? It was a novel idea and arrested Ivor mid-step. For a moment, he stood still, hands thrust deep into his britches' pockets. Somehow he had assumed Ari was merely in the grip of a fleeting romantic fantasy. Most girls her age had them, or so he believed, and having lived all her life in the shelter of the valley, there would be something almost exotic about a man from the outside world. She would come to her senses soon enough. Or so he had believed.

But Ariadne was not like any of the valley women. She had been treated differently, of course; she was special, and everyone knew it. No young man from the valley would have dared approach her for a dalliance or even something more serious. Ivor was accustomed to thinking of Ari as belonging to him. She was his friend, his companion, destined to be his wife, and until this moment, he realized, he had never once wondered if she could be considered attractive or desirable in the ordinary sense of the words. It had seemed an irrelevant consideration.

But clearly, her poet found her so. Abruptly, he felt a wash of intense jealousy, so surprising it almost took his breath away. The thought that they were up there on the cliff top somewhere, playing at lovers, or whatever it was they did together, was suddenly intolerable. She *belonged* to him. How *dared* she renege on such a binding pact? It was her destiny, and she knew it. It was one thing to dally with a romantic fantasy before that destiny had been presented to her as immutable, quite another now that it was fixed in stone. Now this romantic dalliance became a personal slight.

He started for the stables to fetch his horse. It was his business and his alone to find her and bring her home.

✦ ✦ ✦

Lord Daunt remained at the table in the Council house, drumming his fingers on the tabletop.

Three of his brothers had also stayed behind, and the youngest of them inquired rather tentatively, "Is something the matter, Rolf?"

"I don't trust Ariadne," Rolf declared after a moment. "She's always been impetuous and not inclined to obedience. Our father indulged her shamefully, and she thinks she can do what she likes. It's time she realized things have changed, and she'll do as I want, when I want."

He took a deep draught of the ale in his tankard. "My informants tell me that if the Duke of Monmouth lands along this coast, the West Country will almost certainly rise in his support. If his rebellion succeeds and he takes the throne, then the Protestant faction in this part of the world will become all-powerful, and our position in this valley will be even more precarious. Up to now, we haven't been troubled by London interference. My father believed it was because the King has Catholic leanings, whatever front he puts on for public show. But Monmouth is a fanatic, as bad as Cromwell in his heyday, and if he chooses to send the might of an army after us, we cannot withstand such a force, however protected we seem to be in this stronghold. But if the Daunt name is reinstated in court favor, through this marriage of Ariadne and Ivor Chalfont, our Protestant connections will ensure we don't invite persecution."

"The King is not ailing, is he?" Hector Daunt asked. "Monmouth surely will not make a move while his father is still alive."

Rolf shrugged. "True enough, but the King leads a life of dissipation, and it takes a toll. He could be struck down at any moment. It would take Monmouth several months at least to muster a decent invasion force, which is why we need to get Ariadne and Chalfont in position and established at court before the winter sets in. There is no time to indulge Ariadne's whims."

He reached for the jug to refill his tankard. "So I intend to force the issue. I need the three of you to go above and bring back this man." He pushed a piece of paper across the table.

Hector read what was written and nodded. "I know where this is." He pushed back his chair. "Come, gentlemen." He left the Council chamber, followed by his two younger brothers, leaving the eldest contemplating the contents of his ale tankard with a half smile on his thin lips.

THREE

riadne wriggled her shoulders into a more comfortable place between the spreading roots of the copper beech beneath which she lay, Gabriel still sprawled across her, his eyes half-closed. The springy moss was soft as any mattress, and she was tempted to sleep herself after the last passionate moments, but she could see through the dappling leaves above her that the sun was well past its zenith. The temptation to stay here in the spinney as night fell, never to return to the valley, was for a moment almost impossible to resist, but she knew it was only a dream possibility. She had made up her mind. Gabriel's safety must be ensured at all costs, even at the cost of her own happiness. She was responsible for his safety as she had been responsible for putting him in the danger in which he now stood. He knew the reputation of the Daunts, but he had no experience of the reality. Somehow his family had managed never to offend a Daunt and so had escaped the scourge of their vengeance . . . until now.

She stroked his back, murmured his name, and with a reluctant sigh, he moved himself sideways until he lay beside her, propped on his elbow.

"I love you, Ariadne." He stroked a dark curling lock from her cheek.

She caught his hand, pressing it to her lips. "And I love you, Gabriel." She moved his hand to her face, resting her cheek against his palm before slowly letting his hand fall.

Resolutely, she sat up, brushing her disheveled hair away from her face. "I must go, love. I must get back to the valley before sundown, before they set the guards for the night." She rose to her feet in one graceful movement, shaking bits of moss and grass from her skirt. "It will be all right in the end, dearest." She could hear the falseness in her voice even as she tried to smile, and her throat seemed to close with the rush of love and loss as she looked down at him, his long, lean frame stretched upon the moss, the hands that only a few minutes ago had touched her, held her, given her such joy. She could still feel his presence upon her, imprinted on her skin; her body still retained the memory of him, the hard length of him inside her.

Gabriel got to his feet and placed his hands on her shoulders, his eyes filled with shadows. "Don't try to pretend, Ari, there is nothing you can do to gainsay your family. No one has ever got the better of a Daunt."

"You forget, my love, *I* am a Daunt." And then the bravado left her. "No, what am I saying? We have to face the truth." She touched her fingers to his lips, tracing them lightly. "You need to leave here for a while, Gabriel.

Is there family you can visit in another county? Somewhere far from here, just for a few months until this is over?"

He looked blank for a moment. "Go away? Why should I go away, Ari?"

"Because if so much as a whisper of this reaches my uncles, you will die," she stated. "They will spit you on the end of a sword, my dear, and I could not bear that. At least if I know you are alive and well, I can face what I must. Ivor and I are to go to London, to the court, once we are wed, and there . . ."

She tried to smile, but somehow her mouth wouldn't move properly. She tried to sound strong for him, resolute, hopeful. "Maybe there we may meet again, and maybe, in all the bustle and whirl of such a large and busy place, we can find a place for ourselves. A secret place, just for us." She continued to caress his mouth with a fingertip. "What do you think, Gabriel? London, we could get lost in London. It just means we must be apart for a few months." This time, she managed a smile, but it was a tentative shadow of the genuine article.

His expression changed. "But you would be a married woman," he said, a deep frown corrugating his brow.

"Yes," she agreed. "But not in my heart. A forced marriage is not morally binding." Ari realized she was desperately reaching for something, anything that would give them hope, would take the bleakness from Gabriel's eyes. She took his hands in hers, holding them tightly. "In my heart, I will still belong to you, Gabriel. And no law of the land can set that aside."

He shook his head. "I want you for my wife, Ari, not my mistress. I could not bear some hole-in-the-corner grubby liaison. I *love* you."

Her voice faltered as she tried to explain. "I know, and I understand, but, my love, you do not understand what it means to be a Daunt. I am held, shackled by my family. I cannot escape them, at least not now, not without endangering both of us, but you first and foremost. Nothing is to be gained by that. This way, there is hope, hope for a future. Anything could happen in that future, but we have to be alive to have it." Her words gained strength, pouring forth with passionate intensity as she fought to convince him once and for all of the inevitability of this plan.

"We will see each other again, be together again. But not here." Suddenly, she could bear this inevitable leave-taking no longer. She stood on tiptoe to kiss his mouth, lingering for a moment, before stepping back. "Farewell, my love. For now. Go away from here as soon as you can, I beg you . . . promise me that."

Gabriel's head was spinning. One minute she had been in his arms, a passionate lover as hungry for his body as he had been for hers, and then she was saying goodbye, telling him it was over, that he must go away.

"Promise me," she repeated urgently. "Go as far from here as you can." And then she seemed to freeze, every muscle immobile, before she whispered, "Sweet heaven help us." She looked wildly around the spinney. "They are coming."

"Who?" He could hear nothing. And then the high-pitched, excited yap of a dog came through the still air.

"I knew if I stayed away too long, they'd come in search. They've brought the dogs, damn them, and they'll have my scent." Ariadne turned to him, her face white and set, her voice rushed and urgent. "Run, Gabriel. Back through the spinney. Walk through the stream. If they catch your scent in here, they will lose it in the water." She pushed at him. "Go . . . I'll head them off." And without another word, she was running away from him, out of the spinney in the direction of the barking dogs.

Gabriel didn't hesitate. Ari's panicked urgency infused him now, and he raced in the direction of the little stream that gurgled merrily through a clearing on the far side of the spinney. The sounds of the dogs faded as he ran, panting for breath. He had heard that foxes often ran through water to throw the hounds off the scent, and presumably, that was what Ariadne intended he should do. He stepped off the low bank into the stream, feeling the cold water encase his lightly shod feet almost instantly. He plunged across the stream, then walked through the water alongside the far bank, heart pounding as he strained to hear the sound of pursuit, but the countryside was quiet and serene, the green-brown water of the stream rippling over stones and weeds. It seemed he had lost them . . . for now.

But what of the future? Ariadne's fear was genuine; finally she had convinced him of that. Or the dogs had convinced him. He gave an involuntary shiver at the memory of the excited yapping. There was something inherently savage about being hunted by animals.

Fear prickled his skin, a deep, almost atavistic terror. Ariadne would not exaggerate the danger. If she felt he must go far from here, then she had good reason to fear for his safety. Nothing was to be gained for either of them by his staying. And maybe she was right to be hopeful for the future. If they could survive this dreadful time, anything could happen. There was always hope.

But where could he go? He couldn't tell his parents why he needed to leave the West Country; for all his bold talk, he knew that they would not willingly accept the Lady Ariadne Daunt as a daughter-in-law. She might as well be cursed by the devil as long as she belonged to that family. He had had vague hopes of presenting her as a refugee from the valley. His mother had a soft heart, and if Ariadne could persuade her of her own helplessness, her own lack of complicity in the Daunt family's ill-doings, then there was hope that Lady Fawcett would soften towards her. But that was a plan without a future now. Now he had to leave Somerset.

He splashed through the shallows, heading for a small gravel beach cut into the bank, where he could easily climb up to dry land. He seemed for the moment alone in the world, except for the cawing of rooks gathering to circle the trees, preparing to settle for the night.

If Ariadne was going to London, then what was to stop him going, too? His father would support such a move, Gabriel was sure of it. He had taken to muttering a lot recently about his son's idleness and head-in-the-clouds attitude. He would sanction a visit to court, where Gabriel could try to establish himself. Many young men pursued that course and found fame and fortune. King

Charles's court was known for the coterie of poets, paint-ers, philosophers, actors, and playwrights whose efforts received royal support. Why not Gabriel Fawcett?

He clambered up onto the bank and headed home, hope once more alive in his blood.

✦ ✦ ✦

Ariadne broke through the trees and saw the trio of horsemen and the dogs thundering across the meadow towards the spinney. She gathered up her skirts and walked forward, whistling to the dogs, patting her knees in invitation. They surrounded her quickly, jumping up at her, barking excitedly, tongues lolling, and she stroked them, calling each by name, calming them as the horse-men rode up.

"They found you soon enough, then." The man on the lead horse flourished a glove, which Ari recognized as one of her own.

"They would," she said coldly, not a hint of her racing pulse, the panic still surging in her brain. "They're hunt-ing dogs, and just why, pray, are you hunting me, Wilfred Daunt?"

"Orders from my lord," the young man said, looking somewhat abashed. "He sent us to fetch you back, and we thought we'd give the dogs some exercise at the same time. Didn't we?" He glanced at his two companions for confirmation. They nodded sheepishly. Ariadne, when she wished, for all her youth, could be almost as intimi-dating as old Lord Daunt. She had an air of superiority about her even now, when her hair was disheveled, her skirt hitched above her ankles, and her shirt untucked and twisted at the neck.

"Well, now you've found me, you may return," she said with the same icy calm. "I'll follow you down the cliff path. You may tell my uncle that I'll be in my cottage in half an hour."

Wilfred looked uncomfortable. "I'm supposed to bring you myself, Ari. You can ride pillion." He patted his mount's crupper.

She shook her head. "No, I left on my own, and I will return on my own. If that arouses my uncle's wrath, he may direct it at me, not at you, Wilf."

He glanced around as if looking for help and found it in the sight of a horseman galloping towards them across the meadow. He gave a little sigh of relief. "Ah, someone else has come for you. Chalfont will escort you back."

Ariadne followed his eyes and felt the last dregs of panic finally subside. Gabriel should be well clear by now, and the dogs were nosing around the meadow following any interesting scents they could find. She could return to the valley with Ivor as if nothing untoward had happened.

Ivor came up to the little group, his eyes on Ariadne. He took in her disheveled appearance, the residue of fear in her eyes, and fought down a wash of anger even as he felt relief that she had not been caught with her poet, however close an escape it had been.

"I trust you enjoyed your walk, Ari," he said pleasantly. "But the sun is low, and you've overstayed your absence."

It was a reproof, however mild a one, and she flushed with annoyance, but she swallowed a sarcastic response, saying only, "I didn't realize the time. It seems unnecessary, however, to send the dogs after me." She gestured to Wilfred and his party.

"That was not my doing," Ivor said. He nodded at Wilfred. "You had better return to the valley, Wilf. You will want to be in good time for the wake. I will escort Lady Ariadne."

Wilfred nodded and whistled up the dogs, and the trio set off towards the pass down to the valley.

"You are disgracefully untidy, Ari," Ivor said bluntly, swinging off his horse. He came up to her and swiftly adjusted the twisted collar of her shirt, doing up the top button. "If you had a mind to advertise the kind of sport you've clearly been indulging in this afternoon, you certainly succeeded." He looked around. "So where is he? Safely out of reach, I assume?"

She flushed and jerked angrily away from him. "My conduct is no business of yours, Ivor."

"Oh, but it is," he reminded her, his own anger coming to the fore. "Have you forgotten that you are betrothed to me, that we are to be wed in seven days? You will be my wife, Ariadne, and subject to my will in every way. Your business is my business, now and for the rest of our lives."

It was the truth, however unpalatable. She kept her head turned from him, looking across the meadow, gathering her composure. She had to remember that until she was certain Gabriel was safe, she must offer no resistance. Ivor knew everything, he held Gabriel's life in his hands, but she thought he would not betray them if she gave him no cause.

She turned back to him with a tiny shrug. "As you say. Shall we go down?"

The anger was still there, but she could read in his eyes his struggle to control it. He reached out a hand and lightly brushed her hair back behind her ears. "Put a good face on it, Ari. I am not such a bad prospect, you know. We understand each other. We have known each other since childhood. Surely we can make a life together, a life that will bring us both contentment. Can you not try to think kindly of me?"

"Oh, Ivor, I do think kindly of you," she said almost desperately. She couldn't bear it when he was kind and understanding. It was so much easier to hold him aloof when there was anger between them. And how could she possibly deny the years of friendship they shared? In many ways, they had been conspirators in the valley, united against the forces that governed their lives. But she didn't love him, and now that she knew what love meant, how could she happily settle for anything less?

"I value our friendship, Ivor, but I don't love you. I'm sorry . . . I can't change that." She tried to hold his gaze, to impart the strength of her feelings, but his own eyes were suddenly blank, wiped clean of all emotion.

When he spoke, his voice was cold and distant. "Well, love has never been an essential component of matrimony, my dear. You know that as well as I do. We must manage as countless others have managed before us." He moved so swiftly she was taken by surprise when he caught her around the waist and lifted her onto his horse. For a moment, he stood at his stirrup, a hand resting on her thigh. "I would settle for your friendship and respect, Ariadne. Whether I can give you the latter will be up to you."

Before she could respond, he had swung onto the horse behind her, his arm circling her waist. He nudged the horse into a walk and turned him towards the gap in the cliff where the pass led down into the valley. Another nudge, and the animal broke into a canter across the meadow.

Ariadne held herself upright, feeling his body at her back but keeping herself stiffly away from him. She had rarely met this cold and distant Ivor, who spoke with such bitterness. Oh, she had fought him, seen him angry, and met him angry word for angry word. She had even hit him once or twice when they were children, and he hadn't scrupled then to return the blow, but that had been child's play, and they had made up as quickly as they had fallen out. But this was very different, and she didn't know how to respond to him. Ivor was deeply hurt and bitterly angry, and she had caused that hurt. But she could not think how to put things right between them.

How could she forget Gabriel, dismiss him from her thoughts, pretend this overpowering love between them did not exist? But if she could not, then she and Ivor could not live together in anything approaching harmony.

If only she hadn't confided in Ivor in the first place. What had seemed such a natural confidence between

FOUR

vor drew rein outside Ariadne's stone cottage. It was in the middle of the village, close to the wooden bridge that spanned the river. She had been born in the cottage and lived there with her mother until Martha had died of typhoid fever when her daughter was eleven. Her father had lived there only nominally, most of his time being spent with the other men of the family and more often than not with one or other of the ladies of pleasure who were brought into the valley to serve its menfolk. It was the way of Daunt valley, simple and efficient.

Ari slipped to the ground before Ivor could offer a helping hand and without a word went into the house. She had nothing to say, and Ivor made no attempt to break the silence, turning his horse to the stables, his expression grim.

"Oh, where ever have you been, miss? Everyone's been a-lookin' for you. It's the wake feast tonight—"

"I know that, Tilly." Ari interrupted the girl before she

could get started. In Tilly's world, every little event was a cause for excitement and anticipation, unless it was fearful in some way. Once she wound herself up, there would be no unwinding her until she'd reached the end of the spool. "Is there any food?"

She realized she was ravenous, hardly surprising since she hadn't eaten since just after daybreak, and it was now dusk.

"There'll be the feast in an hour," Tilly pointed out, carefully pressing her flat iron into the intricate ruffles of a pair of lace-edged sleeves.

"Yes, I know, but I cannot wait an hour." Ariadne began opening cupboard doors in the one room that served as kitchen and living room. "We had some cheddar, Tilly. I know we did."

Tilly set her flat iron back on the hearth. She was a round, plump-cheeked girl, with small, merry blue eyes, a year or two younger than Ariadne. With a flourish, she lifted the lid on a cheese dome on the plain pine table, declaring, "Right afore your eyes, miss." Then she flushed and looked abashed. "Lady Ariadne, I should say."

"Why should you?" Ari looked askance as she cut a slice of cheese. *Lady Ariadne* was far too much of a ceremonial mouthful for daily use in the valley, and it was almost never used except on formal occasions in Council.

"Lord Daunt said as how we should all give you your correct title, miss. Now that you're to be wed, you being your grandfather's heiress."

Ariadne frowned at the connection but then gave an internal shrug. It was the bald truth, after all. The marriage and the fact of her inheritance were inextricably entwined, so why deny it? "Well, I'd rather you didn't when we're private, Tilly," she said through a mouthful of cheese. "Is there some of that pickle somewhere? The black one that goes so well with cheddar?"

Patiently, Tilly reached into a cupboard and set a jar of pickled vegetables on the table. "Where it always is, Miss Ari." She eased off the tight lid, and the aromatic spicy fragrance filled the air.

"Forgive me, I'm not thinking straight today." She cut another hunk of cheese and spread it with the thick, dark mixture.

Tilly nodded sagely. "No wonder, miss, so soon as it is after his lordship's death."

Ari agreed with a quick smile of thanks as she ate the cheese and pickle. Her makeshift meal cried out for a tankard of dark October ale, but the wine would flow too freely this evening, and she had no desire to put herself at a disadvantage she could avoid.

"You'll be getting dressed, then, miss?" Briskly, Tilly put away the cheese and sealed the jar of pickle, clearly indicating that Ari had dallied long enough. "I'll fetch some hot water for you." She looked at her mistress closely. "Looks like you could do with a wash."

Ariadne could have guessed how she looked even without Ivor's blunt assessment earlier, but she wasn't about to go into explanations with Tilly. She liked her, enjoyed her company, and appreciated her help, but she wouldn't burden her with a confidence she would find hard to keep. "I was walking above and lost track of the time," she said vaguely. "I had to run back."

Tilly seemed to find this perfectly acceptable and went to the range to fill a bowl with hot water from the steaming kettle on the hob. She set it on the table. "I'll fetch soap and towel. Your gown is all ready for you."

"My thanks, Tilly." Ariadne kicked off her slippers and sat on a stool to unroll her woolen stockings. They were torn at the heel, she noticed, and a moment came to her, vivid as if it were happening now, of digging her stockinged feet into the moss against a tree root as she moved her body in rhythm with Gabriel's, a swift rhythm building to a glorious crescendo.

She balled them up as Tilly set soap and towel on the table beside the bowl of water. "These need darning at the heel, Tilly. They must have worn thin." She tossed them into the wicker mending basket beside the range, then stood up to shrug off her jacket and unbutton her now less-than-pristine white shirt. Her skirt followed suit and then her chemise and petticoat. Naked, she dipped a washcloth into the basin and sponged her body, aware of how sweaty and grimy she was. She needed a full dip in the copper tub rather than this spit and polish of a wash, but there was no time for such luxury this evening.

She dried herself briskly on the rough towel before stepping into a crisply starched white cambric petticoat and then a low-necked cambric chemise edged with lace. "You'll need another two petticoats, Miss Ari, for the gown to fall properly." Tilly took the stiff garments from the large oak linen press in the far corner of the chamber.

Ari pulled a face. She disliked wearing so many undergarments, but she could not appear dressed without ceremony at her grandfather's wake. It would be considered outrageously disrespectful. She let Tilly drop the garments over her head and tie the ribbons at her waist. She peered down at herself as she adjusted the décolleté neckline of the chemise to show just the beginning swell of her breasts. Unfortunately, she was so ill favored in that area of her anatomy that there was very little to show for her efforts, she reflected disgustedly. Why couldn't she have taken after her mother instead of some obscure, tiny-boned, vertically challenged ancestor? Her mother had been robust, with an ample bosom and wide hips. Her father had been a typical Daunt. Tall, powerful, muscular, strong enough to pull an oxcart if it were required of him.

And between them, those two had produced this diminutive creature. Well, at least she could do without a corset, she reflected. It would do nothing for her at all. That was one small mercy. She stood still as Tilly draped the gold-embroidered cream silk underskirt over the petticoats and fastened it at her waist, then maneuvered a dark crimson silk gown over her head. The gown was looped at the sides to reveal the cream and gold underskirt, and the full sleeves ended at her elbows.

"I'll fetch the sleeve ruffs." Tilly brought over the lacy ruffles that she had been ironing with such care. "Here they are, and beautifully pressed, if I says so myself," she declared, buttoning them to the gown's sleeves so that they fell in soft, creamy folds down to Ari's wrists. "Beautiful you look, miss."

Ariadne fiddled with the lace-edged neckline of her gown. It was so wide it almost slipped off her shoulders, exposing what felt like a very chilly expanse of white skin. "If this is supposed to offer alluring hints of my bosom, it's not very successful," she remarked. "There's nothing really to hint at."

"Well, maybe so, miss." Tilly was ever realistic. "But the gown looks right pretty on you anyway, and you can always pretend there's summat underneath."

Ariadne couldn't help but laugh. It was all too absurd. The whole business was a farce. Why not imagine she had breasts like two bubbling puddings bursting from a low décolletage?

Her lack of curves hadn't troubled Gabriel, after all, and Ivor had never made any critical comments. Her laughter died on her lips. Just for a few moments, she had forgotten her present troubles.

"Summat the matter, miss?" Tilly asked with concern. "You look as if someone walked over your grave."

Ari shook her head. "Oh, maybe someone did, Tilly. It's passed now, anyway." She ran her fingers through her tousled hair. "So what are we to do about this tangle?"

"Oh, it'll brush out soon enough, miss. Then we'll put it up in a knot and tease a few ringlets out. Your hair's so thick and curly it always looks pretty. You sit down at the table, and I'll fetch the brush and combs." She disappeared up the narrow staircase at the corner of the room that led up to the small, simply furnished sleeping chamber. It was more of a sleeping loft than a real bedchamber, the sloping eaves making it hard for anyone much taller than Ariadne to stand upright.

Ariadne took a small hand mirror from the mantel

shelf. It was a precious possession, a piece of silver-backed glass, somewhat spotted with age but nevertheless highly prized. She stared at her reflection, seeing the gray eyes look back at her. What did other people see when they looked at her? she wondered. It was an interesting thought. She gave so little attention to her appearance in general, it had never occurred to her to wonder about other people's impressions.

"Here we are, then, and I've found some lovely velvet ribbon, too." Tilly's wooden-soled clogs clattered on the staircase as she hurried down into the living room, flourishing a length of crimson velvet ribbon. "Look perfect this will in your black hair, miss."

Ariadne sat at the table, holding the hand mirror so that she could watch Tilly's progress. The girl's fingers moved swiftly, teasing out the ringlets with one hand as she brushed with the other, until Ari's hair, black as a raven's wing, took on the almost purple sheen of a deep midnight sky. Tilly twisted the long strands into a thick knot that she piled high, securing it with silver-headed pins before tying the velvet ribbon around the knot, fastening an artful bow at the back. The glossy black ringlets curled around Ari's ears, trembled against her cheeks, and gathered at the nape of her neck.

"There, now." Tilly nodded her satisfaction. "Beautiful, Miss Ari. What about the emerald pendant to set off your betrothal ring?"

She had to wear the ring, of course, Ariadne remembered. Since her grandfather had watched Ivor put it on her finger, she had shut it away in the small box where she kept the very few pieces of jewelry her mother had given her, but tonight she must wear it. "Fetch the box, will you, Tilly?"

Tilly clattered back up the stairs and came back with the japanned box. Ariadne opened it and looked at the contents. The emerald pendant would go beautifully with the gown and, of course, the ring, as Tilly had pointed out. There were also matching ear drops. She took them out, holding them on the palm of her hand, and then, with a grim little smile, she screwed them into her earlobes. *In for a penny, in for a guinea.*

She fastened the pendant at her throat, watching the way the light caught it as it rested against the white skin above the cleft of her breasts, seeming to lead the eye down to what lay concealed beneath the lacy neckline. *And good luck to the voyeur,* she thought, before slipping the heavy ring on her finger.

"Well, I'm ready."

"Not until you put some shoes on," a voice said calmly from behind her. Ivor had opened the door without ceremony, just as if nothing were out of the ordinary. They had been running in and out of each other's house for years, and his sudden appearance now seemed to imply that nothing had changed. He stepped into the room, still holding the door latch. "Do you know you have bare feet, Ari?"

His voice sounded normal, none of the icy bitterness of earlier, and she felt a wash of relief at the lightly amused tone, even though she knew it was an act, one they had to put on for the evening. This was no time to show themselves publicly estranged. She turned on her stool, forcing herself to adopt the same tone, the easy familiarity of their usual discourse. "Actually, for the moment, I had forgotten. You look very splendid, Ivor."

It was true, he did. Instead of his usual leather britches, linen shirt, woolen jerkin, and riding boots, he wore black velvet britches, buttoned below the knee, plain black stockings, and a gold silk coat with flared skirts. His shoe buckles sparked silver, and his chestnut hair, usually tied at his nape, now curled in a shining fall on his collar.

"Lord, Miss Ari, you've got no stockings on, neither," Tilly exclaimed, flinging up her hands. "What can I have been thinking?"

"Don't blame yourself, Tilly. I was the one getting dressed," Ariadne replied with a shake of her head. "I'd better wear the silk pair, don't you think?"

"I'll wait outside." Ivor stepped back into the darkening evening, closing the door firmly. At least Ari had followed his cue. This evening was going to be difficult enough as it was without making their estrangement too obvious to the elders of the Council, or indeed to anyone in the village. Ari was about to have the ground cut from beneath her feet, and he dreaded to think how she was going to react, but he didn't dare to prepare her ahead of time. The whole object of the exercise, distasteful though he found it, was to ensure that she couldn't bolt.

Ari hitched her skirts and petticoats up to her knees to draw on the silk stockings. She tied the garters just above her knee and then slipped her feet into red silk slippers.

She stood up, shaking down her skirts. "How do I look, Tilly?"

"Perfect, miss. Sir Ivor is a lucky man." Tilly smoothed down a fold in the skirt and adjusted a ruff at Ari's wrist as she spoke, adding wistfully, "Just think, miss, next week you'll be a married lady. Aren't you excited?"

Ari contented herself with a vague smile and a muttered response that could have meant anything. She went to open the cottage door.

Ivor looked her over with a quizzical smile as she appeared. "You certainly brush up well, my dear."

"I could say the same of you," she responded, laying her hand on his proffered sleeve. "I can't remember when I last saw you dressed so elegantly."

He raised an eyebrow. "One must make an effort on occasion."

"Indeed."

He was referring to rather more than dress, she knew, and she accepted the truce. It was necessary for the moment. Nothing had changed since that acrimonious exchange a few hours ago, but since it seemed possible for them to slip into their old ways as if nothing had occurred to change them, she would be grateful for it.

The path to the Council house was lit with sconced torches at regular intervals along the riverbank, and as they approached the house, the sounds of laughter and music burst from the open doors. A wake was a party, after all. A celebration of a life well lived. Old Lord Daunt would have wanted nothing less.

It was clear as they stepped into the hubbub that

everyone was waiting for them. Slowly, the noise died down, and Rolf, Lord Daunt, came towards them, the crowd parting for him. "So, niece, and you, Ivor Chalfont, we meet over the body of my brother to fulfill his most treasured wish, that our two families unite in peace to retake our rightful place in the world. This was his will, and it is now mine." He gestured over his shoulder, and a man in the cassock of a priest stepped forwards, one of Rolf's brothers on either side of him. Whether they were holding him up or merely escorting him was hard to tell.

Ivor felt sorry for the poor man, who looked ashen with terror, as well he might. There were no resident men of God in the valley, so presumably, he'd been carried off in the middle of the afternoon from his peaceful vicarage by a pair of armed ruffians and ordered to perform a wedding ceremony in the devil's den.

"I see nothing to be gained by waiting for seven days, so we will celebrate the marriage now, a culmination of all that my brother worked towards during his life. Step forward."

Ariadne felt Ivor's hand tighten on hers, a hard, affirming grip, as he drew her forwards into the center of the room. She looked at him, her eyes filled with fury. Did he know? And she saw in his own dark gaze no surprise but just a flicker of something like apology. It was clear that he *had* known, that this outrage was with his full agreement. She pulled at her hand, but his grip was now a vise, and the crowd was forming a tight circle around them. They stood alone in the middle, the priest in front of them. Ari's eyes darted to the dais at the end of the room, where her grandfather's coffin sat, stark.

Rolf had a reason for this extraordinary haste . . . did he suspect anything? She thought of Gabriel, and her heart went cold. Had they discovered him? Could Ivor have betrayed her? Or was it simply because of what she had said that morning, when she had refused to comply with her grandfather's will? They wanted to make sure of her before she could do anything to prevent it. Her thoughts raced at frantic speed, but her eyes were blank, hiding her inner turmoil. If they suspected anything about Gabriel, then the best thing she could do was to get this wedding over with. Once she was married to Ivor, they would have no need to pursue their suspicions. If they had already found Gabriel and killed him, then what did it matter what happened now?

Ivor felt Ari's hand suddenly grow icy cold in his, the quick, panicked spasm as she tried to withdraw it from his grasp. Instinctively, he drew her close against his side, his fingers curling around hers, as he tried somehow to infuse her with his own bodily warmth. Slowly, he felt her rigidity soften with her gradual realization of the inevitability of this event. He glanced down at her. Her profile was hard and unmoving, the full curve of her mouth narrowed, her lips bloodless. But she gave no further sign of resistance.

Rolf had informed him of this new plan only an hour before, just after his return to the valley with Ari. As far as he was concerned, a marriage now or in seven days made no difference. It had to happen. Her hand was still cold and nerveless in his, but he didn't loosen his grip. He couldn't tell whether she was following as the priest rattled through the words of commitment, but she made the correct responses when required, her voice dead, her face expressionless. He spoke his own responses, firmly but also without emotion. There was an awkward moment when, at the appropriate juncture, Rolf handed him a plain silver band, and he realized he would have to remove the emerald betrothal ring from Ari's finger in order to slide the wedding ring into place. Ariadne gave him no help, merely stared straight ahead as he slipped the emerald from her finger, pushed on the silver band, and then replaced the betrothal ring.

A faint shudder ran through her, and her hand quivered for a second. She now belonged to Ivor Chalfont. The ring was a symbol of ownership; the Daunts did not entertain romantic notions about love pledges. Marriage was a business arrangement, an exchange of goods or benefits. And she had just been sold to advance the family's interests.

Rolf watched with a satisfied smile on his thin lips, and when the priest had muttered his final blessing, Rolf declared, rubbing his hands together, "So, niece, now you are safely wed. Just as my father wished and as your own father would have wished. So let us get down to the real business of the evening. Come, let us feast. Music, gentlemen." He gestured, and the musicians obliged, as servants moved among them with jugs of ale and wine, and the tables groaned with barons of beef, saddles of lamb, and whole suckling pigs.

Ari had no appetite, and her expression remained blank. When someone seized her and hurled her into the middle of the drunken throng, she went through the motions of the dance. She drank deeply from the silver chalice that Rolf had pressed into her hand after the vows and tried to pretend that none of this was real.

Ivor watched her. Her desperation was as obvious to him as his own angry unhappiness. He would have been happy with this wedding . . . more than happy, delighted to have Ariadne as his wife. The prospect of life in London, at the King's court, was full of possibilities. He had ambitions that lay outside this valley, and with Ariadne and her fortune behind him, he could see only advancement and a life of ever-expanding opportunities. But this was not the way it was supposed to be. He could not be secure in this union knowing that Ari loved someone else. And if he could not be secure with her, how was he supposed to conduct this marriage?

If they had been strangers to each other, it would have been easier. But he knew all there was to know about Ariadne, as she did about him. He knew when she was happy and when she was sad. He knew her faults and her many qualities. He knew the forces that had shaped her. He knew her secrets. And she knew his.

In ignorance, they could perhaps have found something new and fresh together that might eventually have helped Ariadne to forget Gabriel, but because Ivor knew all there was to know, *he* could not ignore him or forget about him.

There was no neutral ground on which to build anything new. And Ivor had no idea how to go on from this point.

FIVE

It was long past midnight before the toasts and speeches of the wake began in good earnest, man after man rising to his feet with brimming tankard to extol the virtues of old Lord Daunt, to tell stories about his campaigns and his successes, about the raids he had led and the hand-to-hand battles he had fought in his youth.

Ariadne sat on a stool in a quiet corner, cradling her goblet of Rhenish, her discarded shoes pushed beneath the stool as she listened to the speakers. This was what the evening was supposed to be about, not some hole-in-the-corner hastily performed marriage. The priest had been bundled off under escort, well rewarded for his fearful experience, and Ari had been grateful that the attention had been so quickly diverted from her and back to the real purpose of the evening. She steered clear of Ivor, and he made no attempt to press himself upon her, dancing with the young girls and the established matrons as merrily as if everything was perfectly normal.

Just what was to happen when the evening finally drew to a close? she wondered. Would she and Ivor simply go to their separate cottages? There had been no time, surely, to prepare a bridal chamber. But she knew the marriage would have to be consummated. Rolf hadn't gone to all the trouble of trapping her into the ceremony only to run the risk of annulment if she managed to get clear of the valley.

Someone was singing a melancholy ballad to the accompaniment of a solitary fiddle, and the room had fallen quiet, just the single voice and the single plaintive note of the instrument, and then other voices joined in, low and tuneful as they sang the old man to his last rest. And as the last notes died away, the mood changed again.

Rolf's voice rose above the crowd. "Come, it's time to put the bride to bed," and a cheer went up to the smoky rafters.

Ariadne gasped. Dear God, she hadn't expected this horror, not on top of everything else. But why on earth would she be spared it? she thought helplessly. She looked to Ivor, who had momentarily closed his eyes, his own expression filled with distaste. At least he hadn't been a party to this planned barbarism, then. But there was nothing she could do to stop it. They would ignore her protests and would carry her forth as easily as if she were a sparrow chick fallen from its nest. Best to turn in on herself, a trick her mother had taught her long ago when bad things happened in the valley: ignore what was happening, ignore the ribaldry, and protect what she could of her self.

They descended upon her, a drunken group of large Daunt men, scooping her up, seating her on her uncle's shoulder. He held her easily with a hand at her waist, and the entire party surged from the Council house into the torchlit night. Singing and chanting, a drum beating a barbaric rhythm that reminded her of some primitive blood sacrifice, which in many ways this was, the procession wound along the river path. Behind them came the young men surrounding Ivor, their bawdy sallies greeted with gales of drunken laughter. Lamps shone in the windows of Ivor's cottage, and a small party of young women stood waiting for them outside the door.

Tilly was among them, which gave Ari a little comfort. Tilly could be quite fierce at times, and she might be able to protect her from the worst of the excesses of indignity that lay ahead. Presumably, all the preparations for this bedding had been made during the wake. She would have laid any odds that Tilly had known nothing of the surprise wedding when she had helped her dress for the evening.

Rolf swung Ariadne off his shoulder and tucked her under his arm before ducking beneath the lintel of the cottage, which downstairs was in every detail a copy of Ariadne's own. He headed for the narrow wooden stairs at the rear, still carrying her, slung now over his shoulder like a sack of potatoes. He went up the stairs, the group of young women scampering behind him, the men crowding them as they struggled up to the loft bedchamber.

This was much more spacious than Ariadne's. The eaves were high enough for a man to stand upright, and there was room for a four-poster bed, a carved chest at its foot, a dresser, and the linen press. The bed was hung with white muslin and strewn with lavender and dried rose petals. A three-branched candlestick stood on the sill of the round window, and the candles emitted a delicate scent.

Someone had had the sensitivity to turn this rough-hewn room into a true bridal chamber. Who would have given the order? Ari wondered. Not her uncle Rolf, that was for sure. He had set her on her feet now, and she was aware of the men crowding the top of the stairs, drinking and laughing, as the young women moved to help her undress.

There was nothing she could do but endure. The women gathered around her in a tight circle, shielding her as best they could from prying eyes, but as each garment was removed, the raucous ribaldry grew ever coarser, and Ari felt her skin grow hot with anger and embarrassment.

"She's such a tiny little thing, Ivor, you'd best be careful you don't split her apart," some inebriated young colt slurred, and the next moment, a hard thrust to his chest unbalanced him, sending him tumbling backwards, knocking into the men on the stairs behind him so that they all fell in an ungainly heap.

Ivor took three steps down the stairs. "Take your vile tongue out of my house . . . and the same goes for the rest of you. You've had your fun, now get out and leave me to my own business. You, too, my lord Daunt." He had bounded up the stairs again and now confronted Rolf. "Enough is enough, sir. Leave Ariadne to her women now."

Rolf looked momentarily confused, but there was

something about Ivor's determination that penetrated his drunken haze. "Oh, if you must spoil sport, Ivor . . . I suppose you're overeager to get to your bride yourself. Come on, men, there's many a bottle left to broach before dawn." He stumbled to the stairs, and the rest of the elders followed him, casting darkling looks of disappointment at the groom, who held his place at the top of the stairs until he heard the front door close.

Ariadne stood in her chemise, looking at Ivor. "My thanks," she said softly.

He shook his head and said coolly, "It doesn't suit my pride to see my bride exposed to prying eyes. I'll leave you to the women." He went back downstairs. Ordinarily, the men would be waiting for him, to undress him and deliver him naked to the bridal bed, but his outburst seemed to have put an end to that little ritual, too. For which he could only be thankful.

He poured a goblet of brandy from the bottle he kept on the dresser and stood with his back to the range, waiting . . . waiting for the moment when he had to confront this travesty of a marriage head-on.

He heard low voices and footsteps above his head as the women moved around the bedchamber and then feet on the stairs. Tilly, her cheeks a little flushed, stopped on the bottom step and announced with portentous gravity, "Lady Ariadne is abed, sir. If you would be pleased to come up."

"In a few minutes, Tilly. You and the women leave now. I have no further need of you this evening. You may come to attend Ar . . . my wife in the morning."

"Yes, sir." Tilly managed an ungainly curtsy on the narrow stairs and turned to scamper back up to the bedchamber. In a moment, she and the other women came down together, all looking remarkably solemn.

"You're sure you won't be needing me again tonight, sir?"

"Quite certain, Tilly. And thank you for your efforts with the bedchamber. You had little enough time to work such a miracle." He took a small leather pouch from the mantel and handed it to her. "With my thanks, all of you."

Tilly beamed, the contents of the pouch clinking as she weighed it in her palm. "Our thanks to you, sir." She hustled her companions out of the cottage. As the door opened, the sounds of music and merriment drifted on the still night air. Presumably, the feasting would go on until dawn. Ivor shot the bolt across the door and dropped the heavy bar into place. He would have no further disturbance this night.

He refilled his goblet and then filled a second one before carrying both up the stairs. The chamber was softly lit with the candles on the sill and another one beside the bed. Ari sat up against the crisply laundered pillows, her rich black hair fanned around her face, which was almost as white as the cambric of the pillow. She was naked beneath the sheet, a nightgown lying across the end of the bed.

"You might find this welcome." Ivor handed her the goblet.

"My thanks." She took a sip and was heartened by the welcome burn of the spirit. She couldn't remember when she had last felt warm, but she knew the cold came from within her, a deep, icy block of it. She regarded Ivor over the goblet. "How could you agree to that . . . that travesty of a ceremony, Ivor?"

"I have no say in the decisions your uncle makes," he responded. "The marriage was to take place anyway. It seemed to me immaterial if it was this day rather than any other. It's not as if a delay would have brought you to a willing agreement." His eyes forced her to acknowledge the truth, and she turned her head away from the steady gaze.

"No, it wouldn't." She sipped her brandy. "At least you saved me from the worst of the bedding, and for that I thank you, even if it was only to salvage your pride."

He gave a short laugh. "Oh, my dear Ari, that is un-salvageable, believe me." He turned his back on the bed and went to the window, looking out into the still torch-bright night. The reflection of the flames flickered on the dark surface of the river. "How do you think it feels to be married to a woman who makes it clear she would rather be in her grave than in my bed?"

"That's not true," she exclaimed. "Of course I would not. But I can't make myself love you, Ivor, when I love someone else. How do you think *I* feel, forced into wed-lock with a man I cannot love? Oh, I care for you, I like you, you're my friend. But that is all, and now that I know what love between a man and a woman can be, I don't know how to settle for less." She plaited the edge of the sheet, the candle lighting emerald fires in the be-trothal ring, which quite dwarfed in size and splendor the plain silver wedding band behind it.

"Well, that brings us to an unpleasant but necessary discussion," he said, turning back from the window. "I take it you are no longer a virgin."

The harshness of his voice, the flatly definitive statement, shocked Ari. Her eyes widened, and then anger came to her aid. She had not betrayed him or deceived him. He had no right to sound so accusatory, almost as if she disgusted him in some way. "True," she responded. "I have never pretended otherwise."

He shrugged. "Maybe not. Nevertheless, it poses certain problems. When do you expect to bleed?"

Ari stared at him. "What has that to do with anything? A week, maybe ten days hence . . . I don't keep an exact record of these things."

"Well, you should," he said bluntly. "Did your mother tell you nothing?"

Comprehension dawned finally. "Of course she did," she snapped. "But I fail to see what business it is of yours."

"Well, then, I suggest you think a little. We cannot consummate this marriage until after your next bleeding—"

"What are you saying?" she interrupted.

"I am saying that until I am certain you are not carrying another man's child, I will not consummate this marriage." He drained his goblet. "Do you understand, Ari?"

"Oh, yes," she said slowly. "I understand. But you should know that Gabriel did not . . . did not . . ." She stopped in frustration, wondering why she was so embarrassed to say the words. How could she be embarrassed any further in this dreadful farce? "You need not fear that," she muttered lamely.

"You mean he did not release his seed inside you," Ivor said brutally. "Is that what you're trying to say, Ari?"

She nodded and said with difficulty, "He was very careful."

"Maybe so, but accidents happen anyway, and I'm taking no risks." He went downstairs without another word, returning after a few minutes with the brandy bottle and a knife. He refilled both their glasses before saying, "Your uncles will wish to see proof of the consummation in the morning."

Ari looked at the knife. She needed no further explanation, merely asked quietly, "Where will it be best to cut me?"

"Not you," he said with a touch of impatience. "Me." He dropped the knife on the bed beside her. "You will cut my inner arm, here, just inside the elbow. It will produce sufficient blood without having to cut too deeply, and the wound can be easily hidden."

Ari wished she were inhabiting an unpleasant dream, but hard-edged reality was a living force in the chamber. She reached beneath the pillow behind her and drew out her own intricately carved silver knife. "If I must do this, I will use my own knife."

"You carried your knife to your own wedding?" For once, Ariadne had surprised him. Ivor shook his head in amazement. "Where did you conceal it?"

"A sheath in my petticoat. Tilly sews them into all

my underclothes," she informed him, running her finger along the blade. "We will need a scarf or a handkerchief to act as a tourniquet, in case I make a mistake and cut the vein too deeply."

"I trust you won't do that," he commented wryly, opening a drawer in the dresser and bringing out a thick red kerchief.

Ariadne looked at him, looked at the red kerchief and the knife in her hand, and felt a sudden insane urge to laugh. Her lower lip quivered, and Ivor said sharply, "Something about this wretched business amuses you?"

"It's a farce, Ivor. One is supposed to laugh at farces," she responded. "Why should we take any aspect of this travesty seriously?"

"Because in essence, our lives lie in the balance," he responded, rolling up his ruffled sleeve. "Or yours does," he added. "If I exposed you as a whore, dear girl, your uncles would kill you on the spot to avenge family honor, and then they would hunt down your Gabriel and send him to a lingering death. I doubt you want that." He extended his arm. "Now, get on with it."

She bit her lip. "I didn't mean to make light of what you're doing for me, Ivor. But you must see a little of the absurdity."

"You'll have to forgive my lack of humor, but at the moment, I don't," he responded curtly. "Right now, I am holding out my vein for you to cut so that we can produce a bloodstained sheet that will satisfy your uncles that family honor has been preserved. Now, will you please get on with it?"

Ariadne nodded. He was right. There was no ghoulish humor to be milked from this situation. With a sinuous movement, she slid from the bed, wrapping her nakedness in the coverlet as she did so. She knotted the coverlet between her breasts and picked up the knife from the bed. "Tilly told me that one of the village women will never cut flesh without putting the knife through a candle flame." She took the weapon to the candles on the sill and passed the blade through the flames several times. "It can do no harm, even if it does no good."

She came back to the bed where Ivor stood. "Perhaps you should hold your arm over the sheet so that the blood falls where it should." She gestured to a spot on the immaculate sheet. She was totally in possession of herself, even though she felt as if she were moving through a dream world. This had to be done, and she would do it competently.

Ivor held his arm over the sheet and Ariadne perched on the edge of the bed, taking a firm grip of his forearm with one hand. The red kerchief lay on the bed beside them. She lifted her knife, put her free hand against the blue vein in Ivor's arm, and, without a tremor, placed the tip of her knife against it and cut. Just once, just below the surface, but the blood bubbled up, dark red.

Ivor turned his arm instantly, and blood dripped onto the white sheet. They both watched it for a moment, transfixed, and then Ariadne moved swiftly, bending his elbow, pushing his forearm up, his hand onto his shoulder. "Hold still." She got off the bed and fetched the brandy bottle.

"Another one of Tilly's words of wisdom." She took his hand and opened his arm. The blood welled from the cut. "Forgive me. This will hurt, but I believe it will do no other harm and maybe some good." She poured brandy over the wound, and Ivor gave a gasp at the sharp sting. Ari closed his arm again, pressing his hand into his shoulder. "A minute or two, and then I will bind it."

"Tilly has something of the physician about her, clearly," Ivor observed, flexing his hand against his shoulder.

"There are women in the valley, the midwives and others, who have such knowledge." Ari twisted the kerchief into a band. She took his hand and opened his arm. The blood still welled but more sluggishly. She bound the red band around it, tying it tightly. "I believe that will do."

Ivor nodded and stood up. He regarded the blood-stained sheet. "Tilly will vouch for your purity in the morning."

Ari tried to ignore the sardonic edge to his voice. She felt an overwhelming need to sleep and suddenly sat on the edge of the bed, her legs seeming unwilling to hold her another minute. The coverlet was still wrapped around her, but with a twist and a turn, she could be in bed, the cover over her and her head on the pillow. She felt herself sway.

"You can't keep your head off the pillow, and I have no intention of sleeping on the floor. Neither will I sleep downstairs," Ivor declared briskly. He leaned over the bed and jerked the heavy bolster from behind the pillows. "Unwind yourself and lie down. The bloody spot is yours, if you remember." He thrust the bolster down the middle of the feather mattress and turned away to take off his clothes.

It was a small enough price to pay, Ari thought. This entire pantomime had been for her benefit. She untwisted herself from the coverlet and lifted it in a shake that dropped it securely over the entire mattress. Gingerly, she maneuvered herself a space around the small bloodstain on her side of the bolster and lay down, her head sinking into the pillow. Her eyes, however, would not close.

Ivor was kicking off his shoes, throwing off his clothes, unrolling his stockings. If he was aware that she was watching him, he gave no indication. He snuffed the candles on the sill between finger and thumb and then walked around the bed to the other side of the bolster. Ari watched him through half-closed eyes in the light of the single bedside candle. He was the first fully naked man she had ever seen. There had been no opportunity in her lovemaking with Gabriel for either of them to undress properly. She had no idea how Gabriel would look naked. But Ivor was a revelation.

There seemed so much of him. So much length and rippling muscle, so much ease of movement, such smoothness, and such a luxuriant trail of chestnut hair down his belly, forming a thick forest at the apex of his thighs. She caught a glimpse of his penis as he lifted a knee onto the bed before inserting himself beneath the coverlet. She had glimpsed Gabriel's penis just once, after they had made love, a small, flaccid piece of flesh curled damply into his pubic hair. Ivor's penis was by no means erect, but it seemed, to her drowsily sensual examination, to be a full and powerful organ merely at rest against his thigh. And then he tucked himself into his side of the bolster, blew out the night candle, and the chamber was lit only by the dying flicker of torchlight through the window.

SIX

The liveried manservant moved efficiently around the antechamber to the King's privy chambers at the Palace of Whitehall. He adjusted cushions and straightened the rug before the fireplace in which, despite the warmth of the September morning, a massive log blazed. The Duchess of Portsmouth was always complaining of the cold, and when she was in residence with the King, every fireplace in the royal residence was kept alight.

The man paused to mop his brow before sticking the poker into the fire to adjust the log. The mullioned casements were open onto the river, and the sounds of river traffic drifted from below, the shouts of oarsmen in their skiffs touting for customers to row across the mighty Thames, which was thronged with the barges of the rich and noble dwarfing the bobbing watercraft of humble tradesfolk and the even humbler river rats who plied their trade in the flotsam they hauled up from the riverbed and scavenged from its slimy banks at low tide. The strains of music rose above the cacophony as an elegant barge sailed past, the musicians in the bow playing for their noble employer sprawled at his ease in the richly upholstered cabin.

The footman went to the window to take a deep, cooling breath of fresh air, except that it wasn't fresh. The air was putrid with the river stench. The carcass of a cow bobbed gently downstream as the tide took it towards Greenwich, a rat scurried through the thick mud at the river's edge, and the royal barge, pennants flying, rode high on the water at the Whitehall Palace landing, having just disembarked its royal passenger and his friends after a morning's hunt in the park at Hampton Court.

Voices, booted feet, the bark of a dog, a woman's laugh came from the corridor outside, and the footman jumped back into the antechamber, casting one last glance around before diving for a small door behind an ornate screen in the far corner. Only the loftiest of servants were permitted in his majesty's presence, and he didn't qualify. The door took him down long, narrow stone corridors winding through the vast backstage of the massive palace, the biggest in Europe, it was said. These were the corridors inhabited by the faceless multitude who kept the palace working, its royal inhabitants warm, fed, secure, and in total ignorance of the mechanics that ensured their comfort and safety.

The double doors that opened into the antechamber from the richly decorated corridor beyond were flung wide by two flunkies, and the King, booted and spurred and in great good humor, swept into the chamber. A plump lady in riding dress clung to his arm, a pack of deer hounds surged around the couple, and in their wake came a chattering pack of courtiers, all booted and spurred.

"By God, that was a goodly chase," his majesty declared, flinging his plumed hat onto a low chair, following it with his whip and heavy gauntlets. His wig fell in luxuriant dark curls to his silk-clad shoulders. He bent to kiss the plump lady's cheek as she smiled up at him. "You rode like an angel, my little Fubbs." He seized her around her waist, lifting her for another kiss. "Ah, isn't she magnificent, gentlemen?"

A chorus of agreement met this statement, and the lady, Louise de Kéroualle, Duchess of Portsmouth, acknowledged it with a light laugh. "Gentlemen, gentlemen, you flatter me. And you know what they say about flatterers?" Her eyebrows rose as she graced the company with an arch smile. "Just because his majesty is pleased to compliment me is no reason for the rest of you to fawn."

"Louise, Louise, so harsh, my darling. Of course they find you perfection. And you must not blame them for finding perfection where their king finds it." Charles laughed and drew her to the fire. "We must have wine . . . and I dare swear, my love, that you are frozen to the bone. Sunderland, dear fellow, ring for wine." He gestured with a beringed hand to one of the courtiers. "And a bumper or two of sack . . . indeed, I've a mind for a bumper or two of sack."

He deposited himself in a gilt armchair and drew his mistress onto his knee. "And what of you, Fubbs, what will tempt you?"

"Just these, sire." Louise pressed her full red lips against his. "That is all I desire." She stroked his cheek with a fingertip, nothing in the adoring sensuality of her expression revealing how she hated the nickname. It was an ugly sound, for all that it celebrated her plump and luscious figure, and not even the knowledge that the King had named one of his yachts HMS *Fubbs* in her honor could resign her to it. Irrationally, she always felt as if he were poking fun. But she leaned against him, moved her hips in an infinitesimal and invisible rhythm, and felt him grow hard beneath her.

Servants came in with jugs of wine and sack, trays of pasties and sweetmeats and tiny songbirds in aspic. The dogs howled at the smell of food, and Charles, with a languid wave of his hand, instructed, "Bring them bones, and make sure there's much meat on them. They've been running hard since dawn."

The servants came back with thick, meaty, marrow-filled bones and, without expression, tossed them into the pack of circling dogs. The hounds fell on them, snapping and snarling in competition. The King smiled with benign satisfaction and patted Fubbs's rounded bottom as he eased her off his knee. He bit deep into a meat pasty and followed it with a draught of sack.

"His grace the Duke of York," a footman announced from the double doors, bowing as the heir to the throne stepped into the room.

James looked around the noisy room, at the greasy-mouthed courtiers, now hastily bowing, the rapidly emptying tankards, the pieces of flesh and bone scattered on the rich Turkey carpets, the snapping dogs. Louise was perched on the arm of the King's chair, delicately gnawing the flesh of a tiny thrush, but she rose instantly to curtsy. A flicker of disdain touched the corners of the Duke's mouth.

Charles saw his brother's expression and felt a familiar surge of irritation. His brother's pious asceticism annoyed him. "Greetings, brother." He spoke through a mouthful of pasty and took a deep gulp from his tankard. "We missed you at the hunt this morning."

"I was attending early mass in the chapel with my wife," James responded with a dour smile. "I trust you enjoyed the chase, sir."

"Immensely . . . immensely." Charles flung out a hand in an exuberant gesture and rose to his feet. "You wish private speech with me, brother?"

The Duke of York merely bowed his assent, glancing pointedly once again at the crowd of sweat-rank huntsmen, the pack of slavering dogs. His gaze flicked across the King's mistress, a woman he wouldn't trust any farther than he could throw her. It was well-known that Louise had her own political purposes, not necessarily in her royal lover's best interest.

"Come to my privy chamber, James." The King strode to a far door. "I bid you good day, gentlemen. Portsmouth, come to me in two hours."

The Duchess of Portsmouth curtsied and flicked the tiny bones onto a footman's passing tray. With the King retired to his bedchamber, she had no reason to stay in the antechamber, and with a stately rustle of her rich

damask skirts, she moved to the double doors. The courtiers bowed as she passed, and she inclined her head in
acknowledgment. She was the King's favorite, at present
even surpassing her rival, Nell Gwyn, in his favors, although she was far too clever to imagine that Nell would
ever fade from the picture. The actor's hold over the King
was far too strong. But Louise knew that she herself had
much more power over the King than his Queen Consort, Catherine of Braganza, and she possessed a fortune
to match. Her coffers were enriched not only by her
lover's generosity but also by gifts from her own king to
whom she owed fealty. Louis XIV bought her loyalty, and
she repaid him in kind, her spies and her own ears sup-
plying vital pieces of information to the French court.

It pleased her to know that her sharp intelligence and
skillful manipulations were concealed from prying eyes
by her outward appearance, the almost childlike innocence of her doll-like features and guileless blue eyes.
Men did not watch their tongues around her; they had
eyes only for her fashionably lush beauty.

Charles stood with his back to the fire in his bedchamber, still gnawing on a mutton chop. "That's good," he
informed his brother. "Can't be doing with these mincing
little birds Louise likes so much. Nelly loves 'em, too," he
added with a small smile. He enjoyed keeping his rival
mistresses on their toes, and truth to tell, he had no idea
which one he favored more. He loved Nelly's ribald wit,
her vulgar tongue, her lack of awe when in his presence,
but Louise, now, there was a woman whose advice he
could rely on. Louise had a brain, a very sharp one. She

always had an opinion, and while he did not always agree with it, there was always merit in it.

He licked his fingers, tossed the bone onto a table, and surveyed his brother. "So, what is it?"

James clasped his hands behind his back. "I understand that you have celebrated mass in private several times, brother."

Charles frowned. "And just what little bird whispered that in your ear, James?"

The Duke shook his head. "I cannot say, but Charles, if you celebrate in private, surely it is time to profess the true faith to your people?"

"Don't be a fool, James. The country's up in arms about the issue as it is. They don't trust you, they won't stand for a return of Catholicism, and it's difficult enough for me to insist on naming you, an affirmed Catholic with a Catholic wife, as my heir. That Protestant bastard of mine is a constant thorn in my side, demanding I acknowledge some nonexistent marriage contract with his mother. I would never have married Lucy Waters if my head had been on the block. I acknowledged him as my bastard, made him Duke of Monmouth, favored him in every way, and how does he thank me? By trying to assassinate me. And now there's talk of his invading and inciting a rebellion in the West Country. If I publicly renounced the Protestant faith, Monmouth would be landing in the west and raising an army before I had time to confess my sins."

"Then you will die unshriven," James stated. "Your immortal soul lost to the pits of hell."

"I'll take my chance," the King returned sharply. "I have one duty in this life, and that is to preserve the peace in this country. There's been enough bloodshed. When the throne is yours, then stir up the devils if you wish, but it'll not be laid to my hand."

The Duke bowed and took his leave without another word.

Charles turned to stare down into the crackling logs, seeing fires of rebellion in their flames. He would keep those fires from the land for as long as he was able, but he feared that once he was laid to rest and his Catholic brother came to the throne, there would be no holding back the fierce Protestant revolt that would result. Nothing, unless James kept his faith secret and in public practiced Protestant worship. But James was a fanatic. Nevertheless, he was the one true heir to the throne on his brother's death, and when all was said and done, in essence, it was not for the people of this country to choose their sovereign. That choice was God's, and his brother of York was the rightful successor.

The country was deeply divided now, the rich and influential families maneuvering for a position of safety when the schism happened. Sensible families were mingling Catholic and Protestant branches so that they could ally themselves with whichever faction came out on top of the bloodshed. Charles, for all his debauched and extravagant lifestyle, had spent too many years of his growing in poverty-stricken exile not to sympathize with those maneuverings, however cynically motivated.

SEVEN

*A*riadne awoke to a strange silence and the bright sun of midday. She lay for a moment, warm and relaxed in the deep feather bed, gathering her bearings as the memory of the previous evening and night came back with full force. She propped herself up on her elbows and looked around the chamber. She was alone, as she'd guessed. The bolster that Ivor had put down on the bed was no longer in place, and she realized he had put it back against the headboard.

It was the silence that she found unnerving. On any ordinary morning, the village would be alive with sounds as people went about their daily business, but there was now just an eerie silence. She listened for sounds from below, footsteps, a chair scraping along the floor, a poker riddling the coals in the range, but there was nothing. It felt alarmingly as if she were the only person left in the village.

Which was, of course, ridiculous. She kicked aside the

covers and got out of bed. Her eye was drawn instantly to the dried red stain on the sheet, and she grimaced at the memory of what she'd had to do. She'd seen enough knife cuts turn bad. Where was Ivor? The wound should be cleaned. She looked out of the window. The river flowed as peacefully as ever, but the street below was deserted, as was the bridge. The mill wheel still turned, however, and she could see a group of children on the opposite riverbank, so she wasn't inhabiting a ghost village after all.

As she looked out, she saw a man come out of a cottage farther along the lane. He buried his head in the water butt and came up shaking off the cold water like a dog after a swim. The night's drunken revelry had presumably taken its toll on the inhabitants of Daunt valley, Ari realized, stepping away from the window in case he should look up and see her standing there naked.

Her nightgown still lay across the bottom of the bed, and she pulled it over her head, hearing the sound of the door open and close downstairs. Footsteps clattered on the stairs to the loft, and Tilly's head preceded her arrival in the chamber.

"Oh, you're up and about, then, Miss Ari . . . Lady Chalfont, as I should say." She gave a knowing little nod of her head.

"There's no need for that, Tilly," Ari said brusquely. The idea that she now bore a different name was unsettling; it seemed to set in stone the fact of this marriage. She watched Tilly go to the bed, where the bloodstain seemed suddenly huge against the white sheet.

The girl said nothing, however, merely stripped the

sheet from the mattress and bundled it up. Then she looked at Ariadne with the same knowing smile. "Should I heat hot water for a bath, Miss Ari? It will ease any soreness."

Ariadne felt like the fraud she was, but the prospect was a very appealing one, and she said with enthusiasm, "If you would, Tilly. It would be most welcome."

"I'll set it up below in front of the fire, miss." She hastened to the stairs.

"What are you doing with the sheet, Tilly?"

Tilly said matter-of-factly, "I'm to show it to Lord Daunt, Miss Ari."

Ariadne merely nodded. Much good would it do him, she thought with a secret pleasure. He deserved to be deceived. "Do you know where Sir Ivor is, Tilly?"

"No, miss, I thought to find him here with you."

"He's an early riser," Ari said carelessly. "I expect he's riding out somewhere."

"Yes, that'll be it, I'm sure. Help to clear his head, I expect." Tilly disappeared down the stairs. "I'll fetch the water," she called. "And then I daresay you'll be glad of a bite of breakfast. It's past noon." The door opened and closed behind her.

Ariadne looked around the bedchamber. In all the chaos and emotional upheaval of the previous night, she hadn't really taken in what was to be her new home. She opened the linen press and saw that her own clothes had found their way there. The small casket of her few pieces of jewelry was on the dresser, together with her brush and combs. She could see nothing belonging to Ivor in the chamber.

Barefoot, she went downstairs. Ivor's living room was as familiar to her as her own; she had been in it often enough. She saw now, though, that it contained another linen press, presumably for Ivor's clothes. A pair of boots stood against the boot jack by the door, and his cloak hung on a peg on the wall. There was a faint, musky, masculine smell to the room, mingling with wood smoke and leather.

Tilly struggled in with two heavy pails of water. She filled the copper cauldron hanging over the fire in the range. "I'll go along home and fetch the bath, Miss Ari. I don't reckon Sir Ivor has one. Can't find it, at any rate."

"Oh, why don't I go home and have my bath there?" Ari said, suddenly longing for the privacy of her own cottage.

"You can't do that, Miss Ari. It wouldn't be right." Tilly was aghast. "You live here now. What would people say?"

"I can't imagine," Ari said drily. "What *would* they say?"

"Well, they'd say summat was wrong, that's for sure," Tilly declared on her way out of the door, closing it with a decisive bang that signaled an end to the subject.

Ariadne couldn't help a small smile. There was a loaf of wheaten bread on the table and a crock of golden butter. She cut herself a slice, buttered it liberally, and ate it at the window, watching the village slowly waking up from its night of carousal. But where was Ivor?

Tilly came back, lugging the copper hip bath. She set it in front of the fire and filled it with the now-steaming water from the cauldron. "I've brought soap. Not sure if Sir Ivor had any." She took a piece of rough lye soap from her apron pocket. "I'm sure there'll be towels in the dresser above."

Ariadne set the fire screen between the bath and the rest of the room. It would give her some privacy, at least. She pulled her nightgown over her head and stepped into the bath, sliding down until her head was resting against the curved back and her knees were drawn up to her chin. She scoured herself with the harsh soap, washing it off with the piece of flannel that Tilly passed her. The door opened just as she was dipping her shoulders beneath the water.

"Good day to you, sir," Tilly said, greeting Ivor with a bobbed curtsy. "Miss Ari is taking a bath, sir."

"So I see."

Ariadne tried to make herself disappear into the water, but, small though she was, the hip bath wouldn't take all of her under the water. She heard Ivor's booted feet on the wooden floor crossing the room to the screen. She couldn't make a fuss, not in front of Tilly, who would assume nothing untoward about a man finding his wife bathing before the fire. And besides, she told herself, she had seen *him* naked last night. The memory of his long, lean, and powerful nakedness rose unbidden in her mind's eye, and she was aware of a strange sensation in the pit of her stomach, as her hips shifted involuntarily beneath the water.

His russet head appeared over the top of the screen, his black eyes suddenly sparkling with the mischief of the old Ivor. "Good day, mistress mine," he murmured, his gaze running over her bare shoulders, the line of her arms covering her breasts, the curves of her up-drawn knees. "I trust you find the water refreshing?"

"Very," she returned, not looking at him. She would not let him put her out of countenance, any more than she already was. At least he couldn't read her mind.

"Would you like me to wash your back?" he inquired kindly.

She ignored the question, keeping her eyes steadfastly fixed on some point in the middle distance. "Tilly, would you bring me some towels?"

Ivor laughed and backed away from the screen as Tilly came around it with an armful of towels. Furious, Ari stood up, gathering towels against her dripping body in case he decided to pop his head over again. She was used to his teasing, but this was too much. Given everything that lay between them at the moment, he had no right to behave with the humorous camaraderie of their usual encounters . . . not that he'd ever invaded her modesty before, she amended. Not even in jest, so this was some kind of revenge, she supposed. Hastily, she pulled her nightgown back over her still-damp skin and stepped out from behind the screen.

Ivor was leaning back in a chair at the table, his legs crossed at the ankle, grinning with a deviltry that she knew too well. In other circumstances, she would have fallen upon him in mock combat, but not now.

"There's bacon and fresh eggs in the pantry, Tilly," Ivor said. "Would you be good enough to make us some breakfast?"

"Aye, sir. And I'll fry up a few potatoes in the bacon

fat." Tilly moved the fire screen away. "I'll just see to the tub first."

"No, I'll do that. It's too heavy for you. You cook." Ivor unfolded himself from his chair, hoisted the heavy, water-filled copper tub, and carried it outside, pouring the contents on the grass. He left the tub outside to dry in the sunshine. "So, did you sleep well, wife of mine?" He took a jug of mead from a cupboard and set it on the table. "You were out like a light when I left this morning."

The mischief seemed to have disappeared from his mood now, and there was an edge to his voice. "Where did you go?" she asked in neutral tones.

"Hunting for pheasant. There's a brace hanging in the shed. They'll make a good stew when they've hung for a day or two." He poured mead into two tankards and pushed one towards Ari.

She took it with a nod of thanks, noticing that his arm was a little stiff, the bulge of the makeshift bandage pushing against his shirt sleeve. She glanced at Tilly, who was working at the range, her back to them. "Would you come up to the bedchamber for a moment?" she asked softly.

He looked at his arm. "It's fine."

"I'd like to see," she insisted, soft but determined.

He shrugged, rose from the table, and went ahead of her up to the bedchamber. He glanced at the sheetless bed. "Tilly's done her work, I see."

Ari ignored this. "Roll up your sleeve."

He obliged, holding out his arm for her inspection. She unwrapped the red kerchief and lightly touched the small wound. She gave a sigh of relief. "It's not red or hot; there's no infection. We won't need to consult Tilly. How does it feel?"

"A bit stiff. Tie it up again, Ari."

"Have you a clean kerchief?"

"In the bottom drawer of the dresser. Your belongings are in the top two."

She took out one of her own linen handkerchiefs. "This will be less bulky." She tied it around the wound and examined her handiwork. "There, that'll hold until tomorrow."

"Somehow I hadn't realized you were a competent healer," Ivor remarked, rolling down his shirt sleeve.

"I'm not . . . I listen to Tilly, that's all. I've never had to do anything myself before." She stuffed the stained kerchief into the pocket of her nightgown. "I'll wash this out later."

"Well, I remain impressed nevertheless." He gestured to the stairs. "Will you go down, ma'am?"

"You go. I think I'll dress before we eat."

He raised an eyebrow, and a flicker of amusement crossed his countenance. "Don't worry, I won't insist on any aspect of my conjugal rights as yet, my dear. You may dress in private."

His tone was sardonic, and her temper, as so often, rose to meet his challenge. "You are too kind, sir," she snapped.

His mocking laughter came up to her as he went down the stairs. Ariadne stood frowning for a moment, before going to the linen press for her clothes. Ivor's pride was hurt, she understood that. It seemed he felt cuckolded even before the marriage was consummated. It didn't make much rational sense, given that neither of them had engineered the situation, but then emotions were rarely rational. She must try to rise above her own, she decided, if they were to muddle through this tangle with some pride and dignity intact.

She tied the ribbons on her chemise and petticoat and dropped a simple muslin gown over her head, tying a plain white apron at her waist. She thrust her bare feet into a pair of slippers, and feeling at much less of a disadvantage, went down to the living room, where Tilly was setting laden plates of fragrant fried potatoes, eggs, and crisp bacon on the table. She was starving, she realized, as she sat opposite Ivor, who was hungrily spearing fried potatoes.

"So I presume this transfer of my belongings occurred during the wake last night?" Ari said, folding bacon into a piece of bread as Tilly disappeared into the scullery with the greasy pans.

Ivor swallowed his mouthful. "Lord Daunt gave the order, yes." He speared another forkful of potato on the tip of his knife and dipped it in egg.

"And did he also give order for the decoration of the bridal chamber?"

Ivor's laugh was caustic. "What do you think?"

"My uncle lacks the sensibility for such a sensitive act." She sipped her mead, regarding him thoughtfully. "So I have to assume it was you."

"It seemed necessary to me to go through the proper motions," he responded.

"Even for such a travesty of a wedding?" She could hear the challenge in her voice, despite her earlier resolution.

He set down his knife and said evenly, "Yes, even for that. Sometimes, my dear, observing the courtesies is all we have to combat frequently brutal situations. I have learned that in my time among your family."

She could not deny the truth of his observation. "Are Chalfonts so different? They're a branch of the same trunk, after all."

He shrugged. "You're right, of course. The tree itself was always rotten. We must face it, Ari, we're descendants of a tribe of rogues and vagabonds who still haven't learned the manners of civilized folk." He tried for a light tone as Tilly returned from the scullery. He leaned back to give her room to fill his plate with more bacon and potatoes.

"It's no laughing matter," Ari stated. "It's all too true . . . No, thank you, Tilly, no more for me. That was delicious."

"Right, then, I'll be away to fetch some water for the washing." Tilly picked up the two wooden pails and left the cottage.

Ariadne leaned her elbows on the table as the door closed behind the girl. "But if my grandfather's plan is to work, at least you and I will have to learn the manners of civilization." She shook her head with a disbelieving laugh. "Can you see us at court, Ivor? All dressed up, bowing and simpering, and flattering and pretending all the time? I won't be any good at it, I can tell you that now."

"Oh, we'll learn," he said, but he sounded a little doubtful. In truth, it was difficult to imagine Ariadne's free spirit confined in a cage of courtly pretense.

"It might be easier for you," she said thoughtfully. "You've already had to adapt to a different life." They had talked in the past about what it had been like for Ivor, as a small boy, to be separated from his family and everything that was familiar to him, having to learn the ways of another life altogether. "I've never had to be anyone but myself."

"I was only six," he pointed out. "Hardly formed. Once I had learned to forget my mother, I learned to become a part of the valley very quickly. It will be as hard for me as for you to dissemble in London."

They were talking now with all the old ease and familiarity, sharing their deepest thoughts, revealing their weaknesses, always in the utter certainty that their confidences would be kept. Abruptly, Ari reached her hand across the table, catching Ivor's, twining her small, delicate fingers with his. He had long fingers but the rough nails and callused palms of a working man, one who sawed and chopped wood, wielded a sword, thatched roofs, and hammered nails.

"I could not bear to lose our friendship, Ivor," she said softly. "We cannot let this marriage come between us."

For a moment, he looked at her in disbelief, then threw back his head with a shout of laughter. "Oh, Ariadne, only you could say something like that. Marriages are supposed to be unions, they symbolize a joining of minds and bodies, and you see ours as an instrument of division." He clasped her hand tightly for a moment and leaned towards her. "*I* will not let this marriage divide us, Ari. Whether you do is entirely up to you."

He released his grip and pushed back his chair. "I have work to do. And the women are waiting for you in your old cottage, which has been set up as a workshop. They are to furnish you with a wardrobe for the journey." He unhooked his hunting knife from the wall and left the cottage.

Ariadne sat at the table, looking absently at her hand, which lay across the table, her fingers stretched as if still reaching for Ivor's. Her hand felt cold. Slowly, she withdrew it, tucking it into her lap. Presumably, Rolf had told him of the daily plans for herself; her husband should have the ordering of her day, after all.

She pushed back her chair and stood up. She felt as if she were suffocating. Everything had happened too quickly, as if they feared that if she were given time, she would somehow escape her destiny. And they were right. If she could, she would. But for as long as she and Ivor remained in the valley, there would be no opportunity for more than the trivial acts of defiance she had always relied upon to give her a spurious sense of freedom. Well, she would indulge in one more such act today. The women with their measuring tapes and pins and bolts of material would wait in vain.

She went up to the bedchamber and changed her thin muslin gown for a homespun skirt and jacket, woolen stockings, and heavier shoes. She was going to climb the cliff, and flimsy sandals wouldn't give her traction.

She let herself out of the cottage just as Tilly came back with her wooden pails. "Eh, Miss Ari? Where are you going? They're waiting for you in the cottage yonder. I'll be along myself as soon as I've washed the dishes and put fresh sheets on the bed."

"I have other things to do, Tilly." Ari brushed past her and walked swiftly behind the cottage. She crossed the small vegetable plot that formed every cottage's back garden and threaded her way through the buildings to the steep cliff towering above the valley. The path was a thin white line, which began after a jumble of rocks at the base of the cliff.

She climbed over the rocks and onto the path, glancing once behind her. The village was still somnolent, only a few people appearing on the lanes, women mostly, filling water pails, collecting flour from the mill. The men were presumably treating the aching heads of dissolution, she thought, and then wondered why Ivor was not suffering similarly. He was as bright-eyed and energetic as ever. And he certainly hadn't appeared the worse for anything last night, planning for the bridal chamber, knowing all the while that there was to be no bridal night. Planning for the public proof of her lost virginity, all as cold and clear-headed as if he had never taken a drink in his life.

She thought with a sense of shock that Ivor Chalfont, this husband of hers, was a man to be reckoned with. Not just her friend and confident childhood playmate but a man who made plans and executed them to the last detail.

It wasn't that she hadn't known that about him, she

thought as she climbed, swiping perspiration from her brow with the back of a hand. It was just that she hadn't seen the fact of it as it affected her own life and hadn't really taken it seriously.

She looked up. For some reason, the cliff top seemed a lot farther away than usual, and the path steeper and more treacherous.

EIGHT

*B*elow, Ivor stood on the wooden bridge, his hand shading his eyes, looking up at the cliff. Damn the woman. She was almost at the top. Why did Ari have to make things so much more difficult than they needed to be? Rolf would be furious that she hadn't spent the morning with the dressmakers, and he himself would look like an inept husband who couldn't control his wife.

And then that wave of jealous anger flooded him once again. She was going to her lover? There could be no other explanation.

Well, not this time.

He set off at a run through the village to the base of the path. He stepped around the rocks at the beginning of the path and started upwards. And after a few minutes, he stopped. What was to be gained by a confrontation with the poet? Ari wasn't going to run off with him; she was too practical to do something so foolhardy. His quarrel was with Ari, not Gabriel Fawcett. He turned back and found a comfortable spot on the pile of rock. She would have to come back this way eventually. He would be waiting.

✦ ✦ ✦

Ari reached the top and hauled herself up the last few steps to the grassy summit. She stood up, regaining her breath. Maybe, just maybe, Gabriel had left something for her under the stone. Some indication of where he was going, what he was going to do. He hadn't had much time to make plans since their parting just yesterday afternoon, but it was possible he'd left her some communication.

Without a backwards glance down the path, she raced across the grassy meadow to the gray rock that seemed to jut out of the grass like a beacon. Kneeling, she lifted the stone. A folded piece of paper was tucked deep into the indentation. He *had* left her something.

Her fingers shook a little as she lifted it out and unfolded it. *My dearest, I will follow you to the ends of the earth. Oh, my dearest Ari, I will hold your heart in my breast every second we are apart, and pray God we will be united once more. Look for me in London. Dear one, think kindly of me always.*

Ariadne folded the sheet again and tucked it into her shirt to nestle in the cleft of her breast. *Look for me in London.*

He was going to follow her to the capital. Her heart lifted, but only for a moment. By leaving here, Gabriel would escape one danger, but in London, there would be many others. How could she possibly make sense of this marriage to Ivor when she was constantly afraid for Gabriel and constantly looking out for him to appear around every corner? What would Ivor do if he came face-to-face with the man he felt had cuckolded him? The man his wife still loved? It didn't bear thinking of. Ivor was a warrior, Gabriel a misty-eyed poet. He would not stand a chance against Ivor's strengths and skills. And *she* would be ultimately responsible.

She turned away, leaving the stone upturned in the grass. There was no need for a hiding place now. She hesitated, reluctant to return to the valley but knowing that she must. There was nothing for her up here and a world of trouble below if her absence became too obvious. She set foot on the path and made her way slowly down towards the gleaming strip of river, the afternoon sun hanging low in the sky.

✦ ✦ ✦

Ivor inadvertently closed his eyes against the afternoon sun, enjoying the gentle warmth on his eyelids, the soft red glow beneath. He was tired; the previous night had taken its toll, even though he had not drunk as deeply as his fellows. But it had been a dance of wit and wisdom to bring both him and Ari out of it without suspicion, and he was aware of a deep fatigue, the rock at his back smooth and warm.

A shower of stones brought him to his senses as gravel, dislodged by Ari's descent, slipped down the dry path to clatter against the rocks. He pushed himself upright and turned to look up at the path. Ari was a few feet away, slipping and sliding down the last few feet of the path.

He had been concealed by the rock, but when he stood up, she saw him at once and stopped, planting her feet firmly on the slippery path. "Ivor?"

"Ari?" He surveyed her calmly. "You have been above?"

She nodded. "Yes, but what's it to you?"

"Rather a lot, as it happens." He stepped around the rock and reached up to take her hand, giving her a gentle pull, which obliged her to jump the last few steps to the flat.

She landed squarely and removed her hand from his, brushing down her skirt in a gesture more nervous than purposeful. "Why are you waiting for me?"

Ivor weighed his words and then decided that the brutal truth was the only pointful route. "The rules have changed, my dear. You may not leave the valley without my permission. Lord Daunt gave order that you should spend the day on your travel wardrobe, and you chose to disobey him. That leaves me, as your husband, in an awkward position . . . one I prefer not to be in."

This was not the Ivor Ariadne was accustomed to. That Ivor didn't give her orders or issue veiled threats. In an instinctive effort to restore the balance between them, Ariadne shrugged. "For heaven's sake, Ivor. Pomposity doesn't suit you. I'll go to the women now." She made to push past him, but he took her arm. There was nothing painful about the hold, but Ari knew she could not shake it off.

"What were you doing?"

She turned her head away from him, although her arm remained held fast. "Nothing that should alarm you, Ivor. I promise you that. I was doing nothing that would cause you harm."

"I don't know whether you understand what could cause me harm, Ari, how many things could cause me harm. Not just me but you, too." His fingers tightened around her wrist. "Now, what were you doing above? Did you see your poet?"

She turned her head aside with a mute headshake.

Ivor looked at her closely, and his gaze caught the small piece of white poking up from the neck of her gown. "What is that? A love letter?" His fingers twitched the paper out of its nest before she could stop him. "A love poem from your poet, Ari?" The sarcastic derision in his tone masked a hurt he would not acknowledge.

"Don't." She made to take it from him, but he held it away from her.

"Let us see what flights of eloquence your lover can reach in extremis." He unfolded the sheet one-handed, while she watched, helpless. Ivor mustn't know of Gabriel's plans to follow them to London.

But then, without reading it, he folded the paper again and gave it back to her. "Put it away, Ari, and if you've any sense, you'll burn it before anyone else sees it." His voice was his own again.

Ariadne crumpled the paper in her fist, relief flooding her. She should have known Ivor would never read someone else's personal correspondence. But then, in the last day, she had been seeing a side of him she had not come across before, and she couldn't be sure how that Ivor would react. She said stiffly, "If you would be so good as to release me, sir, I have my business to attend to."

Ivor did not immediately release his hold on her wrist. He took her chin with his free hand and forced her to look at him, his gaze grave and intense. "There are watchers everywhere, Ari. While you were under your grandfather's direct protection, you were safe enough from prying eyes, but no longer." He shook his head in frustration. "You have to understand that you are no longer a free spirit in this valley, indulged and protected. You are a tool now, a means to an end."

His hands moved to take her shoulders, bringing her body around to face him. "If you will survive here, Ariadne, you will accept the position you are in now. I am in the same position, and together we must weave a path through this quagmire. Do you understand what I'm saying?" He gave her a little shake in emphasis and felt the tension slide from her shoulders beneath his fingers as she accepted his words.

Ari moved out of his hold. She turned to look at the valley and said quietly, "Yes, of course I understand, Ivor. Sometimes acceptance is hard."

"I know that."

"Perhaps when we are out of here . . ." She waved an encompassing hand around the village. "Perhaps then we can make a path for ourselves. We do understand each other, after all." She wasn't looking at him as she spoke, her eyes on the slow-flowing river.

"We understand each other to some extent," Ivor corrected. "How we conduct a marriage in these circumstances is a different matter. Do we have purely a business arrangement, Ari? Or can we hope for anything more?"

He hadn't intended to bring this up so directly, but it was so close to the surface he didn't know how to keep it in check. He knew what he wanted, a full, loving partnership with Ariadne, as his lover and his friend. But could she give him that?

"My friendship, my loving support, those I can give you," she said slowly and with difficulty. "But true love must have passion. I feel no passion for you, Ivor. I cannot love you with passion, only with friendship."

"I see." He let his hands fall from her. "I thank you for your honesty, Ari."

"It does not mean we cannot have a contented life together," she said, hearing how hollow it sounded even as she spoke the words.

"Contentment?" He gave a short laugh. "Well, I suppose for some people that would be sufficient. Unfortunately, Ariadne, it is not sufficient for me."

She turned to him. "But we did not make this betrothal, Ivor, this wedding. You have never felt passion for me any more than I have felt it for you. It's not just of you to make me feel at fault because I cannot feel that kind of love for you. You cannot feel it for me, either."

"Ah, but there's a difference, my dear Ari. I can imagine feeling it for you." His mouth curved in the travesty of a smile, and then he turned away and walked off into the village.

Ariadne watched him go. What did he mean? That

somehow he believed he could find love and passion for her in this enforced marriage? But how, unless he felt some of that already . . . No, that was impossible. She would have felt it, guessed at it, before now.

But she felt helpless and unhappy as she walked to her own cottage, flinging open the door to a chorus of female consternation at her absence. She said nothing but walked to the range and dropped the balled-up paper containing Gabriel's message into the flames. Then she turned back to the room. Bolts of material, velvets, damasks, silks, taffetas, lay spread out on trestle tables with filmy piles of lace and sheets of supple leather.

"So, ladies, what do we have here?"

"Come to the fire, Miss Ari, you need to strip to your chemise." Tilly took charge. Whatever Miss Ari had been up to, she was here now, and they could brush through anything as long as the end result satisfied the new Lord Daunt.

The materials were all of the finest, French silks and damasks, Brussels lace, luxuriant furs of ermine and sable, and the softest dyed cordovan leathers. All, Ariadne assumed, acquired during the various raids and smuggling excursions by the Daunt bloods and their elders. They never brought anything inferior into the valley, although no one in the valley wore any of these luxuries. They were stored for trade in the storehouse in the midst of the village. But carefully stored. Those who were responsible knew how to care for such fine goods.

"So what am I supposed to need, Tilly?"

Tilly beamed. "Oh, his lordship has decreed a complete wardrobe, Miss Ari, everything from petticoats and nightgowns to full court dress."

"And how are we, in this backwater, supposed to know what's fashionable at court?" Ari inquired, unbuttoning her jerkin.

"We have pattern books, miss," one of the girls piped up. "See . . ." Eagerly, she opened a bound sheaf of illustrations on one of the tables. "The petticoats are very stiff, and the stomachers are so tight."

Ariadne examined the picture and grimaced. "How could anyone breathe in that? Well, I, for one, will not wear anything like it."

"Fortunately, Miss Ari, the gown will sit well enough on you without such tight lacing," Tilly declared, divesting her mistress of her jerkin and busily unfastening the waistband of her skirt. "Now, stand still while we take measurements. We have little enough time."

"What do you mean, Tilly, little enough time?" Ariadne held still with difficulty as women wielding tape measures moved over her.

"Lord Daunt has given us but three weeks to complete your wardrobe, Miss Ari. You must start for London before the bad weather sets in, otherwise the roads will be impassable and you'll have to wait until the spring. His lordship does not want that delay."

"Oh, really." Ariadne wondered why her uncle was in such a hurry. Her grandfather had never indicated any urgency about his plan to rehabilitate the family. Was there something significant happening at court that meant Lord Daunt had to have his players in place by a certain time?

The question occupied her throughout the tedious business of measurements and consultations. Did she like this design . . . or this one? Did she prefer an ermine lining to her cloak, or sable, or even a rich red fox? Her muffs must match her cloaks, and her gloves and muffs must be dyed to match the outer garments.

It was hot in the cottage, and the smell of wool and velvet and fur was suddenly overpowering. She felt stifled again, trapped in the valley, trapped in a hollow marriage. Three whole weeks before they were to leave for London. It was too long; she couldn't bear it. If she and Ivor could be alone, without the pressure of incessant eyes upon them, maybe they could come to some truth about their future, some plan to make it work despite everything.

She had a sudden idea. Maybe there was a way to get them out of the valley sooner. "How on earth do we know what is necessary in fashionable dress in London?" she demanded, pushing aside a bolt of watered silk. "We live here, in this valley. We don't even know what goes on above, what's fashionable at the balls in Taunton or Exeter. I could arrive in London with a wardrobe that was fashionable ten years ago."

A stricken silence fell among her attendants, and then Tilly said, "Lord Daunt said these were the latest designs, Miss Ari."

"And I wonder how he knows that," Ari said grimly. "Let me look at those patterns again." She examined the illustrations more closely, then exclaimed, "Lord help us! These are almost twenty years old. Look at the date." She jabbed at the faint scribble at the top of one sheet, but the scratchings made no sense to her wide-eyed audience, none of whom could read.

"How long has he had these, and where did he get them from?" She could guess the answer easily enough. The men of the valley were always robbing travelers on the road to the city. Presumably, these illustrations had been in some unfortunate lady's portmanteau together with the rest of her possessions and kept for years in the great storehouse in the village.

"Let me dress, Tilly. I am going to see Lord Daunt before we waste much more time on this exercise." She scrambled into her own clothes, pulled on her boots, and left the cottage, walking briskly to the Council house, planning her speech.

Rolf was in the Council chamber when Ariadne marched in without ceremony. He looked at her, his displeasure as clear as his bloodshot eyes, heavy eyelids, and air of postdissipation suffering. "I did not send for you, Ariadne."

"No, sir," she responded. "But I need to talk to you. Five minutes of your time, if you can spare it." She moved briskly into the center of the room. "I understand I am to have a new wardrobe for this expedition to London?"

"Of course. You can hardly enter the royal court looking like a milkmaid," he returned with an irritable gesture that encompassed her rustic clothing.

"I agree," she responded. "But if I might remind you, my lord, London is some two hundred miles from here, and the patterns you have provided for this extensive wardrobe are twenty years out of date. Why are we wasting beautiful materials, dressing me up like a doll from a twenty-year-old fashion plate? I am not prepared to be embarrassed by my clothes, sir. Classified a country bumpkin from the moment I walk into Society. I hardly think that would enhance our cause, Lord Daunt."

Rolf regarded his niece with disfavor. "You are impertinent, Ariadne."

She inclined her head in acknowledgment. "Yes, sir, I probably am. Nevertheless, my point is valid. May I suggest a simple traveling wardrobe prepared for me here, and we carry the materials with us to London and find fashionable milliners to do the best they can with them?"

Rolf poured himself a goblet of wine. He hated to acknowledge that his niece was right, but at the same time, her objections seemed to indicate her acceptance of her upcoming task. After a moment, he said, "If we curtail the preparations for your journey, you and your husband should be able to leave sooner than I had hoped. Within ten days . . . that is good."

He drank deeply. "You may instruct your women to prepare a simple wardrobe that will take you to the city. I will be discussing with your husband where you will be lodged when you arrive. The materials will travel with you under separate escort, and seamstresses who understand prevailing fashion will be employed on your court wardrobe." He nodded dismissal. "That will be all. In future, you will communicate with the Council only through your husband, and he will convey our wishes to you."

Ariadne curtsied, every line of the movement a mockery, but Rolf did not see it. He turned aside to refill his goblet, and Ari left the Council house, closing the door with exaggerated care behind her.

Now, finally, she was going to be free of the valley. Ten days was nothing. And then she and Ivor would be on their own, *free*. The word seemed to take concrete shape in her mind, and her step increased as she went in search of Ivor.

She saw him standing on the bridge, watching her as she walked away from the Council house. He inclined his head in question, and she walked towards him. He stepped off the bridge as she reached it. "What's amiss, Ari?"

She smiled. "Nothing's amiss. It's good news. Uncle Rolf was trying to dress me as if I lived twenty years ago. I suggested an alternative. I daresay he was about to do the same for you?"

He laughed. "Yes, but I did not have the wit to complain. Damask doublets and chin-high ruffs were on order. I confess I was unsure."

"Well, it is arranged now. Our wardrobes will be made up in London by seamstresses who know what they're doing, and we leave in ten days . . . just ten days." She touched his arm. "Once we are free of the valley, Ivor, maybe we can make things better between us."

He looked at her for a moment. "Maybe." But she could hear no conviction in his voice. She bit her lip, then turned to walk back into the village.

Ivor looked across the bridge. A house stood close to the bridge, one he had frequented on many occasions, as had every young man in the valley and many of the older ones, too. Ariadne belonged to him, and his need for her grew more painful the longer he was deprived. She was so sure of her invincible love for her poet. And Ivor was so sure of his right to take her in the conjugal bed and make this marriage complete. He had to wait until he was certain she did not carry another man's child, but was he supposed to contain himself until then?

He needed release, and it was Ari's fault that he could not take it in the manner ordained by the Bible.

He walked back across the bridge.

Ariadne stopped on the opposite bank and turned. She saw Ivor striding across to the other bank and with disbelief watched him stop at the whorehouse.

What could he be thinking? They were in the morass of emotional turmoil, married yet not married. He refused to consummate the marriage unless he was certain her relationship with Gabriel had produced no consequences, and yet he was prepared to take his body into a whore's bed while his wife lay stiffly on one side of a bolster waiting to prove to him that she did not carry another man's child.

Angry tears blinded her for a moment. And then she realized what fueled her anger. She was jealous . . . jealous and hurt that he could so easily find solace for his own hurt pride. He was *her* husband, *God damn it.* He didn't belong in some other woman's bed.

Ariadne stalked back to her own cottage and stopped on the threshold. Of course, this was no longer hers. She lived in the marital home, with a whoring husband who didn't give a damn how many children he might father on a harlot's body. Her breath caught on a sob, and she leaned against the wall for a moment, struggling for composure. Her world was falling apart around her ears, and she seemed helpless to stick it back together again. What was happening between herself and Ivor? They had been so close, such dear friends. And now they were like angry strangers. She was overwhelmed with a wretched mix of angry and hurt feelings, all spiced with her own guilt that it was her impulse that had brought them to this pass.

NINE

*A*riadne turned from what had once been her own front door and made her way back to Ivor's cottage. Tilly was busy at the range, clattering pots. The living room had been swept and dusted, and the aroma from the bubbling cauldrons made her mouth water despite her unhappiness.

"What are you cooking, Tilly?" She hoped her voice sounded normal to Tilly, although it sounded thick in her own ears, filtered through a knot of tears in her throat.

"Venison stew. Sir Ivor had a haunch hanging in the shed, just ripe for eating," the girl responded cheerfully. "Did you see Lord Daunt, then?"

"Yes, and he's changed his mind. We're to leave in ten days. You're to prepare a simple traveling wardrobe for me, and the materials will travel with us to London, where we can get proper advice on fashions." She moved to the stairs. "I'll just change my shoes, and then I'll come and help with the supper."

"So we're not good enough for the likes of London folk," Tilly muttered, throwing a carrot onto the board and attacking it with a sharp knife.

"I don't think that," Ari said, pausing on the stair, struck by another thought. "And you will be coming with me, Tilly. Has Lord Daunt said anything to you?"

"No, Miss Ari." Tilly scraped the carrots into the steaming cauldron and began to chop an onion.

"Well, you may rest assured that you will be," Ari declared. "I cannot go without female assistance, and who better than you to provide it. If you wish it, of course," she added.

"Go to London, Miss Ari?" Tilly turned from the stove, her round cheeks flushed from the heat. "I'll be afeard in that city, full of thieves and murderers, it is. But I'll not let you go alone, miss."

Ariadne smiled. "And I can promise you will not fall afoul of a thief or a murderer, Tilly. And, indeed, my dear, I don't know how I should go on without you."

She made her way up to the bedchamber. Here, too, everything was in order, the bed freshly made, a fire laid in the small hearth. She kicked off her shoes and slipped her feet into a pair of soft woolen slippers. Ordinarily, she would be looking forward to an evening by her own hearth. She often relished her own company and the quiet privacy of her own house, but tonight would be different. It would be a quiet evening by the conjugal hearth, with the husband who was husband only in name.

If he returned from the whorehouse, that is. Tears pricked her eyes again, and she blinked furiously.

She went to look out of the small window. It gave her a direct view across the bridge to the stone cottage where Ivor had gone, like any one of the village men in search of male pleasures while their women stayed by the hearth, stirring their suppers on the range. He had entered that cottage knowing she was watching him; that seemed the final insult. Although rationally, Ari didn't know why it should make a difference. Why would it be better for him to sneak around behind her back?

Oh, it was insupportable, she thought on a fresh wave of miserable anger. She was supposed to sit here by the fire waiting for him to leave a whore's bed and come home for his supper. She marched downstairs. "I'm going for a walk, Tilly."

"Supper'll be ready in an hour." Tilly glanced over her shoulder. "Why're you going out in your slippers?"

"The ground's dry enough," Ari responded, opening the front door. It was almost dusk, and a watchman was already moving around the village, lighting the pitch torches that filled the valley with light during the deepest recesses of the night. The inhabitants of Daunt valley didn't like darkness and shadows. They sought the night's invisibility up above, when they went about their dark work, but in their own valley, they didn't trust the murky obscurity of shadowy corners.

She walked along the river, aware that the temperature had dropped and she was cold, a sharp breeze gusting across the water, sending little wavelets rippling against the bank. She folded her arms, hugging her chest, wishing she had thought to bring a shawl, but she wasn't ready to go back to the cottage yet, although the prospect of its lantern-lit, fragrant warmth was enticing.

She heard a footstep behind her, and then, before she could turn, a woolen jacket encased her shoulders, redolent of Ivor's familiar scent. He stepped up beside her. "It's cold. Why aren't you wearing a cloak or at least a shawl?"

She shrugged. "I didn't think it was so windy when I left."

"It seems logical, in that case, to turn back," he pointed out. "Instead of walking farther away from home."

"Home?" She increased her pace a little. "I don't have my home anymore."

He sighed. "It cannot be otherwise, Ari. And in my eyes, it is more your home now than mine. You are its mistress. Can you not accept that?"

"Oh, I can accept it perforce," she said coldly. "And I suppose if you choose to spend most of your time over there . . ." She gestured across the bridge. "I suppose I will accept it even more readily."

He stopped abruptly, putting a hand on her elbow. "What are you saying, Ari?"

She turned on him, her eyes glistening under the light of the torch overhead. "What am I saying? You know perfectly well what I am saying, Ivor. We part company, and immediately you go to the whorehouse. Did you enjoy your harlot? Did she satisfy your needs?"

He was suddenly very pale beneath the weather-beaten tan, his own eyes narrowed. "You have no right to question what I do, Ariadne."

"Oh, really?" She lifted an incredulous eyebrow. "I must suffer because I did not come a virgin, pure as the driven snow, to your bed, and yet you have been with countless women, I am sure, and, judging by this afternoon, have every intention of being with countless more. Does that strike you as fair, Ivor? I fall in love with one man; you have no feelings whatsoever for the woman whose bed you share. An exchange of favors, money for her body. Don't you think there is something just faintly hypocritical about that?" She heard the words pouring from her in an angry, fluent torrent and couldn't seem to stop them.

"It is the way of the world, Ariadne," he said coldly, her bitter words inciting his own. "There is nothing hypocritical about it. I have needs, and my wife cannot satisfy them at present; therefore, I use the outlet available to me. A man is entitled to expect his bride to be a virgin. You, however, lost your virginity through an act of fornication, and as a result could be carrying another man's child. I am prepared to forgive your fornication, and once you are certain you are not with child, then we will begin married life as if none of this had ever happened."

Ariadne stared at him under the light of the torch. How could Ivor, the person she had grown up with, loved as her friend, shared her troubles with, listened to his confidences, soothed his hurts, how could he prate such pious, sanctimonious claptrap? Her rational mind told her he was only responding to her attack, but her rational mind was not in control at this moment.

"Can you hear yourself?" she demanded. "Can you

hear what hypocritical nonsense is coming out of your mouth? You and I have never subscribed to such societal nonsense. My so-called fornication was no betrayal of you or of any promises I had made to anyone. I neither need nor want your *forgiveness*. I suggest you keep it for yourself." She swung his jacket from her shoulders and thrust it at him. "And I don't need this, either."

She stalked away, leaving Ivor clutching his jacket, watching her retreating back, and cursing his insensitivity. He had thought he should assert himself. It was what was expected of him, and yet all he'd done was make a pompous fool of himself. Anger and frustration had driven him to the whorehouse, and he had wanted Ariadne to know it. But now, looking through Ari's eyes, he saw it as an act of childish spite.

They knew each other too damn well. He would never have behaved in such a way with someone he hadn't grown up with, didn't feel was almost a part of himself, another limb in some ways. A stranger or a mere acquaintance could not possibly hurt him the way Ariadne could. And, he realized belatedly, the same applied to her. No one could hurt her as he could. Not even her poet. The love affair between Gabriel and Ariadne wasn't founded upon the depths of the years that formed the base of his own relationship with Ari. Her love affair with her poet could only be superficially threatening to him.

Ivor turned his steps to his cottage. Ari had been going in the opposite direction, but the cold would bring her in soon enough. And he would set a very different tone for this evening.

Tilly was putting knives and spoons on the table when he entered the cottage. "Oh, there you are, sir. Miss Ari didn't find you, then?"

"I'm not sure she was looking for me, Tilly," he said pleasantly, hanging his jacket on the wooden hook by the door. "Something smells wonderful." He went to the stove and poked at the contents of the cauldron with a wooden spoon. "You found the venison?"

"Aye, sir. It was just ready for the pot." Tilly put a loaf of fresh-baked bread on the table.

"Yes, I thought it would be. I'll catch trout tomorrow. They were rising well this evening. I should hook enough for a decent supper." He licked the spoon before returning it to the cauldron. "I'll wash at the pump."

"There's hot water there, sir, if you prefer." Tilly gestured to a copper kettle. "I'll fetch a basin if you'd like."

"I can fetch it myself, Tilly." Married life had something to recommend it, Ivor reflected, filling a basin with hot water and carrying it into the tiny scullery off the main room. As a bachelor, he had fended for himself domestically, when he didn't join in the communal meals with the other single men in the refectory, and he'd generally washed at the end of the day, when he'd troubled to do so, with the other men at the village pump. He stripped off his sweaty shirt and splashed water on his chest, face, and neck.

"Here's a clean shirt." The soft voice behind him was Ari's. She laid a fresh homespun shirt over the rough wooden rail on the scullery wall. Her expression was calm, her eyes containing none of the hostility of their last meeting, a mere half hour before. "Would you like mead, cider, or wine with your supper?" She opened a cupboard by the door that led to the outhouse in the small vegetable garden beyond.

"Which would you prefer?" He toweled himself dry roughly and pulled the shirt over his head.

"Tilly's cooking generally warrants wine," Ari said, taking a leather flagon from a shelf. "And with well-hung venison, a good, rich burgundy." She uncorked the flask and inhaled deeply, then tilted it to her lips, tasting it. "This will do nicely. It was one of my grandfather's favorites. He liked the fruits of the Burgundian routes when the smugglers came in."

"I share his enthusiasm," Ivor responded, combing his hair with his fingers. He wondered whether to refer to their quarrel or simply follow Ari's lead. She seemed prepared to put acrimony aside, and an evening of harmony was appealing. In truth, he felt too exhausted to step onto the tournament ground again today. If she was willing to put up her lance, then he was equally so.

He followed her back to the living room. Tilly was filling bowls from the cauldron, and the rich, gamey aroma filled the room. Ivor took down two pewter goblets from the dresser and put them on the table, then used his knife to cut the bread while Ari filled the goblets.

"Tilly, you will join us?" he inquired pleasantly as he took his place at the table. He knew that Tilly frequently joined Ariadne at her evening meal.

"No . . . no, thank you, sir. I'll eat with the other women." Tilly unhooked her shawl from the peg by the door. "There's a damson pie in the bread oven, and I'll be back later to clear up the dishes."

"There's no need for that, Tilly," Ari said swiftly. "I will see to it. There will be no need for you to return until the morning."

Tilly hesitated, then gave a small smile and nodded. "Aye, I expect you'll be glad of your privacy, Miss Ari. Just leave them dishes for the morning. I'll see to 'em then." The door closed behind her.

It was obvious what the girl was thinking, Ari thought. She was discreetly leaving the newly married couple to a night of unbridled passion. Her eyes caught Ivor's across the table. He looked pensive and then speared a piece of bread on the point of his knife and passed it across to Ari.

She took it with a murmur of thanks, and for a while they ate in a silence that was almost awkward. After a moment, Ari said, "Do you know how long this journey to London will take?"

"Hard to say, exactly." Ivor rose to refill his bowl from the cauldron on the range. "It should be a journey of some four or five weeks by coach, and we must complete it by the beginning of November, before the weather makes the roads impassable. Did Lord Daunt say anything when you saw him this afternoon?"

"Very little," she responded tartly. "My uncle was good enough to inform me that from now on, anything I wish to communicate to him has to go through you, and any information I want I have to seek from you." She planted her elbows on the table, propped her chin in her cupped hands and regarded him quizzically. "You are to be post-man, apparently."

He grimaced. "A role I little relish." He held out his hand. "May I give you some more stew?"

"My thanks." She passed him her bowl. "Four or five weeks by coach will be insupportable. Surely on horse-back we can do it much faster. Sphinx can easily manage twenty miles a day."

"Maybe so." He set her refilled bowl in front of her. "But not every day. The horses will need to rest every few days. And we will need a coach for all the luggage. You cannot travel such a distance with nothing but a side pan-nier or a pillion bag. The coach will slow us up." He sat down again and took a draught of wine. "The one thing we cannot afford, Ari, is to look like vagrants. We must travel in a degree of style."

She nodded. "The fact that we come from a line of bandits and brigands, outlaws in every respect, must be forgotten. I understand that." Her smile was caustic. "Maybe we should change our names."

"That would defeat the whole object," Ivor pointed out. "Our task, as I understand it, is to rehabilitate the names of Daunt and Chalfont, to return them to the noble status they once held."

"No easy task," she responded, crumbling bread into her stew. "Are we to court the Duke of York or the King, do you know?"

"Both. Play up the Catholic allegiances of your fam-ily while hinting delicately at the Protestant loyalties of mine. We are to straddle two stools, my dear."

"Well, since I have no feelings one way or the other, that shouldn't be too difficult to manage convincingly." Ari scraped her bowl and pushed back her chair. "I'll fetch the pie."

Ivor watched her as she slid the pie out of the bread oven on the flat paddle. She was such a little bit of a thing; she could so easily get lost, diminished, by the grandeur of the King's court. The clothes themselves could overwhelm her physical presence. He smiled inadvertently at the thought. No amount of grandeur and ceremony could diminish Lady Ariadne Daunt . . . Chalfont, he corrected. She punched way above her weight, as anyone attempting to discount her or put her in her place would soon discover.

"What are you smiling at?" She slid the pie onto the table and reached for a jug of rich golden cream from the dresser.

"Oh, just a random thought," he responded.

She contented herself with a raised eyebrow and cut the pie.

A knock at the door interrupted them. "Who the hell could that be?" Ivor pushed back his chair. He went to open the door, and a blast of cold air set the candles flickering. He peered down at the small boy standing on the threshold.

"You're wanted in Council, sir. Right away, sir."

"All right. Off you go." He shooed the lad away, closed the door, and came back to the table.

"Shouldn't you be answering the summons?" Ari inquired casually. "A royal command, surely?"

"I'll go when I'm good and ready," Ivor returned. "More wine?" He lifted the flagon in invitation.

"Thank you." She pushed her goblet across, taking pleasure in Ivor's assertiveness. Things had changed in the valley since her grandfather's death, and the only positive change she could see was that Ivor was no longer one of the youths, the young men whose opinions held no sway. The new position seemed to suit him; he seemed broader and more powerful in some ways, which was, of course, ridiculous. Physically, he hadn't changed in the least. But his bearing had changed, and the look in his eye. He was a match for Rolf now, she thought, and the knowledge pleased her. It compensated in some way for her own lack of influence. She had been able to sway her grandfather when she wanted to, and everyone in the village had known it. It had given her a certain status. But that status had gone with her grandfather, so she would now have to execute her influence through Ivor, who had never previously proved resistant to her plans and opinions. That surely hadn't changed?

It was an interesting question, but she kept it to herself. When he had finished his pie in leisurely fashion, he said casually, "My compliments to Tilly on her pastry. I'll go to Council now." He slung his cloak around him and went out into the night, leaving her to clear away the dishes. When he hadn't returned after more than an hour, she tamped down the fire for the night, extinguished all but one candle, and went up to the bedchamber.

It was less awkward this way, she reflected, undressing swiftly and climbing into the cold bed in her shift. If she was abed and asleep by the time he came back, there would be no need for difficult conversations.

She blew out the candle and lay shivering in the bed, wishing she'd had the sense to put a warming pan through the sheets, wishing she'd set a flame to the fire laid in the small grate, wishing she had something warm in the bed beside her.

She was still wide awake when she heard the door below open and close. She curled more tightly under the covers, where she was at last creating her own warm trough in the feather bed. Ivor's footfall was soft on the stairs; obviously, he had taken his shoes off below. The glow of his candle shone behind her tightly closed lids.

She could feel him standing beside the bed, holding up the candle so that it threw a pool of light on her curled figure beneath the coverlet. Then he turned aside, taking the light with him. She tried to regulate her breathing, to keep it smooth and even, as if she were deeply asleep. The candlelight was extinguished, and the bed dipped as he put a knee on the edge, before sliding gingerly beneath the cover. For a moment, she could feel his breathing as if it were her own, so close beside her, the warmth of his body filling the space between them. Then he moved his arm, and his hand rested for an instant on the turn of her hip. She barely breathed, and then he muttered an imprecation, reached up behind his head for the bolster, and shoved it roughly under the covers between them.

Ivor turned on his side, facing away from her, and soon his deep breathing filled the chamber.

TEN

*A*riadne had been aware of the nagging pain in her belly since she had woken that morning. She felt cross and out of sorts and found herself snapping at the seamstresses, whose hands were constantly upon her as they pinned and tucked. The traveling wardrobe was almost complete, and Tilly was fussing with the set of the shoulders on one of the two riding jackets deemed necessary for the journey.

"Oh, Tilly, I have had enough," Ari said impatiently. "Leave it now. It feels perfectly comfortable."

Tilly set another pin and cast her mistress a knowing glance. "The flowers, I suppose," she said confidently. " 'Tis about your time. You go on home now, Miss Ari, and I'll bring you some chamomile tea and a hot bottle for your belly."

Ari could think of nothing she wanted more than her own bed and Tilly's ministrations. She offered a wan smile to the women with their pincushions and scissors, needles and thread, and went out into the brisk chill of the morning. Autumn was definitely in the air, the leaves beginning to turn on the trees along the river-bank, the nights drawing in. She crossed her arms over her breasts beneath her shawl, feeling chilled to the bone, as she hurried back home, hunched a little over her aching belly.

Ivor would know soon enough, of course, and then, when she was no longer bleeding, he would expect to consummate the marriage. And the thought of that filled her with sick panic. These last days, she had been able to push the prospect of that act of consummation to the back of her mind. But now she must finally face it. How could she give herself to Ivor with wholehearted desire when she felt such passion for another man and when she knew that Ivor was blisteringly aware of those feelings and would not be able to forget them? How could it be anything but a cold, practical union that would destroy their friendship while putting nothing in its place?

She let herself into the cottage and huddled in the warmth of the range, stroking her aching belly, waiting for Tilly. Only Tilly knew how to ease the pain of this monthly inconvenience. She had a collection of herbs and vials of remedies for most everyday ills, her knowl-edge gleaned from her own mother, who had been the nearest to an apothecary the valley could produce.

Tilly hurried in, the door banging shut behind her. She regarded Ari's hunched figure sympathetically as she hung her cloak on a hook. "Now, you get on upstairs and sort yourself out, Miss Ari, and I'll just put the warming pan through the bed. Then I'll fill a bottle with hot water for your belly and make you some tea."

Ari nodded and dragged herself up the stairs. She found the thick cloths she needed in the dresser and her warmest night shift. Tilly came in with the copper warming pan and energetically ran it beneath the covers to create a nest of soothing heat.

"In you get, now." She turned back the coverlet. "I'll fetch up the hot water bottle and the tea directly."

Ariadne inserted herself into the warmth and felt her limbs instantly begin to relax. Tilly was back in a few moments with an earthenware cylindrical container, its neck stuffed tightly with an oil-soaked rag. Ari took the container, which was filled with hot water, and rested it on her belly. The warmth was instantly soothing.

"Now, here's your tea. Got a few bits and pieces in it to help you sleep." Tilly held out a steaming mug. "There's chamomile and valerian and just a tincture of poppy juice with a touch of honey."

Ari took a sip. Valerian had an unpleasant smell, but she knew its good properties well, and the honey masked the taste. "You are wonderful, Tilly. I don't know how I'd go on without you," she said with a grateful smile.

"You want me to tell Sir Ivor the flowers have come, when he comes in for his supper?" Tilly sounded a little tentative now.

Ariadne sipped her tea. Tilly, of course, would be assuming that Ivor would not be pleased at the news that his wife was not pregnant. The girl would assume that he had hoped to sire a child quickly, as, in normal circumstances, perhaps he would.

She shrugged. "It matters not, Tilly. He'll know soon enough." She handed Tilly the empty mug and slipped down into the welcoming warmth of the feather bed, and soon enough, her eyelids felt heavy, and the strange trancelike sleep of valerian and poppy juice enveloped her.

✦ ✦ ✦

Ivor was in the stables inspecting the horses. Ariadne's Sphinx was a beautiful strawberry roan gelding, her sixteenth-birthday present from her grandfather. He was strong and fast and would carry Ari's light weight for many miles without tiring.

"He's in right good condition, sir," the stableman said, watching Ivor checking the animal's hocks for strains. "Nothin' wrong with 'im at all."

"No, I'm sure not. But we've an arduous journey ahead of us, and I want to be sure there are no signs of possible trouble." He patted the animal's withers as he walked around his rear, stroking the muscular neck as he lifted the velvety lips to check for sores or canker.

"I take care of the horse meself, sir." The stableman sounded a little put out. "You'll find nothing wrong with 'im."

Ivor nodded. "I know, Judd, but I need to satisfy myself. Let's take a look at Turk."

Judd whistled to a boy who came running. "Put Sphinx in his stall, and bring out Turk."

Ivor performed the same inspection on his own gigantic black. Turk blew through his nostrils and bared his teeth, stamping a hoof impatiently on the hard-packed earth. "He needs a gallop," Ivor commented.

"Aye, sir, but he'll take no one but you on his back," Judd pointed out. "Any of the others I could exercise meself. But not this one."

"No. And I've no time today. Let him loose in the paddock. He can kick his heels up there for an hour or so." He blew gently into the horse's nostrils, which seemed an incongruously intimate gesture with this stomping beast, but the animal merely whickered and pressed his nose into Ivor's shoulder.

"What about the carriage horses? We'll need two pairs so that we can run them on alternate days."

"Aye, Sir Ivor. I've selected the four I think'll do the job best."

Ivor followed him into the stable building. The coach that would carry their luggage stood in one corner. It was a cumbersome vehicle with huge iron wheels, and it would be hell on earth to ride inside it over the deeply rutted cart tracks that formed most of the roadways between Somerset and London. They could expect the way to get a little smoother as they drew close to the city, but they had more than two hundred miles to do across rough and desolate country before that.

Fortunately, Ari was a fine horsewoman, he reflected. And she had considerable powers of endurance. She would need them in the weeks ahead.

Once he'd satisfied himself that the carriage horses

were up to the journey and that the wheelwright had attached a spare coach wheel to the rear of the vehicle for when the inevitable happened and they lost a wheel somewhere along the way, he left the stable yard.

It was mid-afternoon, and his mind turned to supper. It was his responsibility to provide the food for the table in his little household, and he mentally ran through the supplies of game hanging in the shed. Tilly always found something succulent there, but the image of fresh-caught brown trout sizzling in butter sharpened his appetite.

He made his way back to his cottage for his fishing tackle. Ari would still be enduring the ministrations of seamstresses, he assumed. She found it tiresome, and it tended to make her poor company for the first half hour after her release. On impulse, he turned his step towards Ari's old cottage. If the women were still at their work, he would give her a welcome early release. She loved to fish, and it was time they recaptured some of their old friendly ease, doing the things they had always enjoyed together.

There had been too much stress since their marriage on preparations for the upcoming journey. It had been much harder for Ari than for him. He at least could escape with his gun into the fields or with his rod along the riverbank. They would fish for brown trout together.

His step quickened as he imagined her ready smile, the shine in her eyes at the prospect, and just the thought of having her beside him, quietly casting into the smooth brown waters of the Wye, a companionable silence between them, filled him with a deep sense of pleasure.

He opened the door to her cottage and found it deserted.

He poked his head around the door of his own cottage, expecting to see Ari at the table or helping Tilly with supper. Instead, he saw only Tilly, sitting by the range plying her needle. The fire burned brightly, and a bubbling cauldron sent aromatic steam to the rafters.

"Where's Ariadne?" Ivor inquired, stepping into the room. "I thought she'd still be busy with the dressmaking."

"Not feeling too well, sir. She's abed and asleep." Tilly set aside her sewing and stood up. "Can I fetch you something?"

Ivor shook his head. "No, thank you. I had it in mind to fish for some trout for supper. I thought Ari might care to join me. What's the matter with her?"

"Oh, 'tis nothing serious, sir. Just the flowers." Tilly turned to stir the cauldron on the range. "It takes her bad some months. I'm just making her some soup."

Ivor said nothing. Tilly would have no idea of the significance this month of that regular event. With a distracted frown, he went to the dresser for the flagon of ale. He filled a tankard and took a thoughtful draught. Now their marriage could start in earnest.

Abruptly, he set aside his tankard and started up the stairs to the bedchamber. He stood at the top of the stairs. Ari was a small, hunched ball under the covers. He watched for a moment to see if she gave any indication of being awake and then climbed back down. "I'll eat in the refectory tonight, Tilly. No need to disturb Ari."

"Right, sir. If you're sure you don't want supper. I've soup for Miss Ari here, but I can whip up a meat pasty for you easy."

Ivor shook his head. "No need. Look after Ari. I won't be back until late." He went out into the early dusk and walked along the riverbank until the village was behind him. He sat on a rocky outcrop and considered his next step. It would be a few days before the bleeding stopped and they could finally consummate their marriage. But he couldn't imagine a silent, hasty coupling. There had to be some ceremony, some acknowledgment of what it meant. And yet why should he think so? His wife loved another man and would not welcome any physical union with her husband, however willing she was to accept its necessity.

He jumped to his feet. He was in the mood to drink and eat in congenial and uncomplicated company, and he would find that in the refectory with the young men of the village. The pitch torches were already alight, and light spilled from the building with the sounds of merriment as the kegs of beer were broached and the flagons of wine opened. Legs of lamb and shoulders of pork turned on spits over the open fire of the kitchen attached to the rear of the refectory, and the succulent smells of roasting meat and hot bread filled the air as he went into the building.

Men sat on benches running along the tables, sprawled at ease, tankards at hand, laughing over ribald jokes. Ivor was greeted with a chorus of unquestioning welcome and took a place on one of the benches, accepting a brimming tankard and a few minutes later a loaded platter of roasted meat and potatoes. For now, he let his personal puzzles lie dormant and returned to bachelorhood with remembered ease.

✦ ✦ ✦

It was long past the midnight hour when Ivor made his way back to his cottage. He didn't think he was drunk, but he was happy to admit that he wasn't as steady and as sober as he preferred to be. He let himself into the cottage. The fire was tamped down for the night, and a single candle burned for him on the mantel. He took up the candle and climbed upstairs as softly as he could in his slightly unsteady state.

He could hear Ari's deep breathing as he entered the chamber and shielded the candlelight with his cupped hand to keep it from shining on the bed. She was still a tiny curled mound on her side of the bed, leaving a large expanse on the far side. He hesitated, wondering if he would risk waking her if he slipped into that inviting space. He'd intended to sleep downstairs tonight, unsure what degree of privacy she would need in present circumstances, but now he wondered if it was necessary.

He set the candle on the mantel and perched on the windowsill to remove his boots. His movements were clumsy, and the boot slipped from his hand with a thump on the floorboards. The mound in the bed stirred.

Cursing under his breath, Ivor tackled his other boot and managed to set it down with exaggerated caution beside its mate and turned his attention to rolling down his stockings. He stood up gingerly to remove his belt and britches and yank his shirt over his head, all the while keeping an eye on the sleeping form in the bed. He couldn't see his nightshirt anywhere and debated opening the linen press, but the hinges needed oiling, and it sometimes squeaked like a mouse in a cat's jaws.

He gave up the idea and blew out the candle before creeping naked into bed. He was asleep almost instantly, and within minutes, the stertorous snores of a man sleeping off a night's drinking filled the chamber.

Ari lay listening. She had been awake from the moment Ivor had set foot in the chamber and had waited, keeping silent, hoping he would assume she was asleep and not start a conversation she didn't want tonight. It didn't take her long to realize that he was rather the worse for wear, and the thought brought an unconscious affectionate smile to her lips, one that if Ivor had been awake would have presaged one of her teasing comments. Ivor almost never let himself go. He had a horror of losing control, a feeling they both shared. It was with some relief that she felt him slide into bed beside her. At least horizontal, he couldn't come to any harm.

She had expected the bolster at her back as usual, but tonight she could feel his body warmth even though he wasn't touching her. What would his skin feel like? Not the weather-beaten skin on his arms, legs, hands, face— she knew what that felt like—but the secret skin, kept concealed beneath his shirt and britches. His *private* skin. The urge became irresistible. Tentatively, as his snores deepened, she slipped a hand across the space separating them, and her fingertips encountered warm, bare flesh. She snatched them back hastily but his breathing didn't change, and she let her fingers creep back to rest lightly against his side, feeling his ribs lift and fall with each sleeping breath.

What would it be like to feel all of him, the whole length of his skin against her own nakedness? To feel him inside her, possessing her? To hold him against her?

Ari shivered, and she didn't know why. It was a strange shudder of *what*? Fear? Anticipation? She withdrew her fingers and rolled over onto her side, away from her sleeping husband, and finally drifted off into sleep herself.

✦ ✦ ✦

Ari awoke to the first faint streaks of dawn in the small window and the first chirrup of the dawn chorus. And then to a heavy warmth against her hip, which turned out to be a hand on her flank. She lay rigid for a moment as she understood that Ivor's body was touching hers, his belly against her back, his long legs following the line of her own. And her mind was filled with the memory of her secret exploration a few hours ago. She had wondered then what it would feel like to have his whole length pressed against her. But she hadn't imagined being swathed in her thickest shift when that happened, she reflected with an ironic smile.

Even so, the knowledge of the naked man at her back sent that little shudder rippling across her skin again.

Gingerly, she edged a foot outside the coverlet and slowly inched herself after it until she was standing beside the bed. Ivor grunted and flopped onto his back, then rolled onto his other side.

Ari breathed a sigh of relief. She crept to the dresser, took out what she needed, and tiptoed down to the living room. The embers glowed in the range, but it was still too early for Tilly to come and rekindle the flame. Ari took up the poker, riddled the embers until a little flame appeared, then tossed in kindling followed by carefully placed logs. She filled a kettle with water and set it on the range as the fire took.

She let herself out to the privy. The grass was rimed with frost for the first time since the beginning of last spring, and she shivered in the dawn chill. The privy was as inhospitable as ever, and she hurried back across the crisped grass into the warmth of the house.

She washed, threw out the dirty water onto the vegetable plot, and went to release the chickens from the coop Ivor had built for them, on stilts to protect them from the overnight predation of foxes. The rooster emerged first, strutting and crowing loudly as his hens came squawking down the ramp, chattering away at Ari and to one another in their oddly conversational fashion.

They always made Ari laugh, and she went inside for the pail of scraps Tilly would have set by the scullery door for their breakfast. She threw the scraps, and they began pecking and picking and chattering busily, and Ari hurried back into the warmth. The range was burning brightly now, and the sun coming up above the cliff top was slowly banishing the long shadows the cliff cast across the valley.

She was stirring a pot of oats on the range when Ivor came down the stairs. She glanced over her shoulder. He was dressed once more in shirt and britches, but she couldn't banish the remembered feel of his nakedness against her, the warmth of his hand on her turned hip, and to her embarrassment, she felt her cheeks warm. She concentrated on stirring the pot, praying that he had no recollection of the night, of his naked body in such intimate contact with her own.

"You're up early," he said in his normal voice. "Are you feeling better?"

His casual tone reassured her, and she responded in kind. "Yes, much, thank you. Would you like some porridge?" She gave him a quizzical look. "It's very good for settling the belly in the morning after a night's drinking, I'm told."

"Is it, indeed?" he answered drily. "Well, my mouth tastes like a cesspit, and my head's thick as a blanket, so if porridge does anything for that, I'll take some gladly." He sat down at the table, stretching his legs. His feet were bare, and he wriggled his toes, staring at them with the curiosity of one who had never seen his own feet before.

They were very long feet, high arched, with long toes and squared-off nails. Ari wondered why she'd never noticed Ivor's feet properly before; she'd seen him shoeless often enough.

Gabriel had small, neat feet that matched his thin, compact frame. The thought came unbidden, and confusion swamped her anew. She *must* not think of Gabriel.

Not if she was going to survive this emotional maelstrom that threatened to drown her. She had to accept that he was gone from her now. She had to learn to forget him, to think of him as dead to her in every practical aspect. Only thus could she manage to live the life she had been given. She would never see him in London. And even if she did see him? What on earth could she do about it?

A faint whiff of burning came from the pot, and she whisked it off the fire, setting it on the side.

"They look normal enough to me," she observed, pouring a tankard of mead and putting it on the table beside Ivor.

"What do?"

"Your feet. You seem rather struck by them this morning."

Ivor shook his head as if to dispel cobwebs. "Sweet heaven, no wonder I don't drink deeply very often."

"You're in the minority," Ari observed, ladling creamy porridge into a bowl. She put the bowl on the table, made a hole in the center with the back of a spoon, and poured golden honey into the middle. Then she stirred the whole and gave him the bowl. "My grandfather taught me to do that. It makes ordinary porridge taste quite extraordinary. Try it."

Ivor took a spoonful of the rich, sweet oats and inclined his head in acknowledgment. "A revelation. Where's yours?"

"Coming," she responded, bringing her own bowl to the table. "I thought you'd sleep till noon."

"I'm never able to sleep much beyond dawn." He took

a draught of mead, feeling the honeyed brew begin to clear his head. "What are your plans for the day?"

Ari grimaced. "More time with the seamstresses. Just a few bits and bobs to finish up."

"You'll be ready soon, then?"

"By hook or by crook." She finished her porridge and set down her spoon. "I can't wait to get out of here, Ivor."

"We will, and if there are still things that need to be done for your wardrobe, then surely Tilly can take care of them while we're traveling. She'll have idle time enough."

"I'll have idle time enough for what, sir?" Tilly stood in the door. Neither of them had heard it open.

"Oh, to finish any buttons and bows on my traveling wardrobe, my dear," Ari said.

"Sooner I shake the dust of this place from my feet, the happier I'll be, even if it has to be London and them murdering thieves on every corner," Tilly muttered. "Everyone's out o' sorts around here these days, since old Lord Daunt died." She took the empty porridge pot off the stove and bore it into the scullery for scrubbing.

"Well, at least we'll have one enthusiastic companion on the journey," Ivor remarked, getting up from the table. "I have to see Lord Daunt." He headed for the stairs to get his boots.

Ari stayed at the table for a moment, considering. Nothing had been said of the matter that concerned them most nearly, but perhaps Ivor was waiting until they could actually do something about it. She gathered up the porridge bowls and took them into the scullery. How would it be when it was all over? When they'd consummated this marriage of someone else's convenience? Would Ivor insist on his conjugal rights every night? Or would he be as happy as she that the deed was done and they could manage to live again simply as friends, when they could resume their old ease and companionship, the friendly teasing, slip back into the old ways as they had done during the last hour at the breakfast table?

He could take a mistress or simply visit bawdy houses when the need arose . . . but *no*. She knew herself well enough to know that she would not be able to endure that. Her pride would not let her.

ELEVEN

$\mathcal{R}$olf stood with his back to the fire in the Council house, his morning tankard of ale in one hand, the other resting on his hip as he regarded Ivor Chalfont. "I have documents for you to carry to court. They were drawn up by my father." He summoned a servant with a flick of his hand. "Bring me the casket."

The man bowed and disappeared into a back room, returning bearing an oak casket, iron-bound with a heavy padlock. He set it solemnly on the table and stepped back.

Rolf took a key from his inner pocket and unlocked the padlock, lifting the lid. He took out a scroll of parchment. "This you are to present to his majesty, King Charles." He handed it to Ivor.

Ivor unrolled it, and as he began to read, his brow creased. "I don't understand. Lord Daunt seems to be abjuring the Catholic faith, offering himself to King Charles as a loyal subject. His granddaughter, now married to a staunch Protestant and therefore obliged to embrace her husband's loyalties, is his representative . . . a loyal Protestant." He looked up at Rolf. "Why?"

Rolf's smile was thin as, without answering, he took another scroll from the casket. "In the event of his majesty's death and the ascension of the Duke of York to the throne, you will present this to King James."

Ivor read and shook his head. "This is so duplicitous. I, as the son-in-law of an ancient Catholic family, am to swear fealty to a Catholic king on behalf of my wife."

"Duplicitous, maybe, but Lord Daunt's greatest wish was to reestablish our family's position. And that is now mine and therefore yours. You will go to the court at Whitehall, you will present your credentials to King Charles, and you will also encourage Ariadne to make friends in the Duke of York's court."

"I understand." Ivor tucked the scrolls into the pocket inside his jerkin. "Why now? Why not last year or the year before?"

Rolf shook his head. "Had I had my way, it would have happened as soon as Ariadne passed her twelfth birthday and was of marriageable age, but my father would not consider it until he felt she was old enough to understand the complexities." He took a draught from his tankard. "I doubt she has the wit to understand properly now. However, this has been long in the planning, starting, of course, with your adoption. My father planned a perfect couple, with appropriate credentials, to play the cards dealt them. It is your time now."

"I see. And what of this talk of the King's bastard, the

Duke of Monmouth? If he succeeds in his bid for the succession, then we have no credentials here"—Ivor patted his jerkin—"to give us credit in a successful rebellion."

"Should Monmouth mount an armed rebellion in the event of the Duke of York's succession, and should he succeed in defeating the King's armies, then you, as a Chalfont, will declare yourself for the new Protestant monarch and carry your wife and her family's loyalties with you. Do you see?"

"I see I must perfect the art of the turncoat," Ivor said grimly.

"Indeed, you must." Rolf nodded a curt dismissal, and Ivor took himself off into the refreshingly clean air.

It wasn't that he had any particularly strong affinity with either side in this battle of religions, but he disliked intensely the expectation that he would play both ends against the middle. And he disliked even more the knowledge that as far as the Daunts were concerned, he was merely a pawn in their game, to be moved around the board as they saw fit.

He knew that Daunt valley lived only by its own rules, but he had never been concerned by the knowledge during his growing. Now he had to take a position. Did he play their game without a conscience, or did he decide where his loyalties and inclinations lay without reference to the position Lord Daunt expected him to take?

And Ari? Did she have an opinion? They had both been groomed for this play, and only now did it occur to Ivor that they did not have to allow themselves to be manipulated on Lord Daunt's chessboard. Once they were free of the valley, they could actually play the game any way it suited them. Lord Daunt's reach was a long one but surely not long enough to extend into the royal court at Whitehall. News traveled slowly; if his pawns decided to play by their own rules, it would be a long time before Rolf realized it. And by that time, who knew what the power play would be?

Old Lord Daunt, Ari's grandfather, had left out of his calculations the consideration that maybe his chosen players might decide to act according to the dictates of their consciences rather than the dictates of pragmatism. Ivor was by no means sure what his conscience would dictate once he was immersed in the tangled manipulations and deceptions of political life, but he intended to discover and make his own choices accordingly. And from what he knew of Ariadne, she would feel the same way.

✦ ✦ ✦

Ariadne stood patiently as the final pinning and tucking took place. She had no mirror long enough to see how she looked in her new finery but could imagine from the way her carefully fitted garments felt. She was aware of a sense of elegance, a very new feeling for one who was accustomed to tumbling about the countryside, concerned only that her clothes should not hinder her movements.

"Very handsome."

Surprised, Ari looked towards the door. Ivor stood there with an appreciative gleam in his deep blue eyes. "Oh, do you think so?" She turned with a swish of her skirts, a little movement indicative of feminine vanity that brought a smile to his lips.

"Most certainly." He came into the room, letting the door close behind him. She looked enchanting, he thought, in a deep red velvet riding habit, her tiny waist accentuated by the long braided jacket. The high collar of a ruffled white shirt seemed to lift her small and very determined chin, and the rich folds of her velvet skirts shaped the soft curve of her hips.

Ivor was startled by a sudden surge of desire. He had shared a bed with Ari but he had kept himself scrupulously separate, in both mind and body. Now there was no reason he should not anticipate losing that division. Now he could look at his wife with the eyes of a desiring husband, not just those of a disappointed friend.

Ariadne felt the change in his eyes, the sudden jolt of awareness. And it set up an answering awareness in herself. Her skin tingled, and she straightened her knees as if they were buckling beneath her. Something seemed to be shifting; the safe ground on which she had always trodden with Ivor had grown untrustworthy. It threatened to move beneath her at any moment. He had looked at her countless times over the years, made teasing comments on her appearance, and she had never responded in this strange nervous fashion. She swallowed and said with a little laugh that sounded false to her ears, "You should see the hat. It is a positive confection. Pass it to me, Tilly."

Tilly lifted the wide-brimmed black felt hat, resplendent with gold braid and three white plumes, and arranged it carefully on Ari's dark head. She tilted her head for Ivor's inspection. "What do you think? Will it not make me the talk of London?"

"I rather suspect you won't need a hat to do that," he commented. "Just be yourself, and you'll set the town on its ears."

"I am not sure that's a compliment," she said.

He laughed. "Well, it was not intended as an insult, let's put it that way." He crossed the room to the table, where the dressmakers' work was piled in an overflowing cascade of rich velvets, embroidered silks, and figured damasks. "Dear God, this lot is considered merely a traveling wardrobe?" He lifted a gown of bronze silk, the bodice embroidered with seed pearls. "I can't see you wearing this in a country hostelry . . . assuming we're lucky enough to find one and don't have to bed down in a hedgerow ditch," he added.

"Lord, Sir Ivor, what do you know about what a rich lady needs?" Tilly demanded. "There's nothing here that Miss Ari won't be needin' on such a long journey. Lord Daunt said no expense to be spared. Miss Ari's to hold her own with any other rich lady traveling the same road."

"I stand corrected," Ivor murmured, laying the gown back on the table.

His eye was caught by a flimsy mound of cambric, silk, and lace. Petticoats, shifts, chemises, stockings. Rolf was generally known as something of a skinflint, but he clearly did not deserve the sobriquet on this occasion.

"Well, I've a mind to go fishing, so if you've a mind to join me when you can escape, Ari, I'll be trying the deep water beyond the bridge. There's a big pike in that water, and he's defeated me time and time again, but I'm in the mood for battle."

✦ ✦ ✦

"Oh, help me out of these clothes," Ari said impatiently as the door closed behind Ivor. "If I have to stand still another minute, I shall scream." She tugged at the braided fastenings on the jacket of the habit.

"Oh, let me do it, miss." One of the dressmakers pushed her hands aside. "If you tear the braid, it'll take hours to repair."

"Forgive me, Daisy." Ari was instantly contrite and stood still as a post while the woman delicately divested her of the riding habit and the white ruffled shirt. Stripped to her chemise, she rolled her shoulders with a sigh of relief and grabbed up the woolen homespun gown she'd been wearing before. She slipped it on, fastening the laces of the bodice with quick fingers, and gave another sigh of relief.

"That's better. Now, where are my shoes?"

"By the door," Tilly informed her, heating a flat iron on the range. "I'll finish pressing this linen now, and then I'll be along to make your supper."

Ari left the women to their work and went out with a jaunty wave, picking up her skirts to run along the riverbank towards the bridge. No one paid her any attention. They were accustomed to her headlong progress through the village, and she didn't notice her uncle standing in the doorway of the Council house, tankard in hand, watching her with a disagreeable frown on his brow.

She found Ivor where he'd said he'd be, in the water, just up from the bridge, his britches rolled up to his knees, casting his rod into a deep pool formed by a curve in the bank. Ari didn't speak, afraid a sound would scare off the pike. She sat down and took off her shoes, hitching her skirts up above her knees with an expert twist of material at her waist, securing the folds with her hair ribbon. The dark curly locks tumbled around her face, and she tucked them behind her ears with impatient fingers.

"You do look a regular urchin," Ivor remarked softly as she slid down the bank into the water, barely disturbing the surface.

"May as well make the most of the freedom while I have it," she responded in a whisper. "Where is he?" She peered at the dark, weedy water of the pool.

"Under a stone about five feet away." Ivor withdrew his rod, checked the bait, and cast again, letting the weighted hook sink below the surface. "He's a crafty bugger. I can't count the number of times he's led me on, sometimes just takes the bait right off the hook and then vanishes somewhere into the bank. This is my last shot at him."

"Will you miss the valley?" Despite her earlier pro-testations, Ari had wondered herself if she would miss the only life she'd known. She wouldn't miss Rolf and the elders in the least, but there was no denying that the freedom from social constraints would be hard to give up.

"Some of it," Ivor said. His line jerked suddenly. He leaned back, his rod bowing as he began to reel it in.

"You've got him," Ari said excitedly. "Ivor, you've got him."

"Perhaps. Sweet heaven, he's a fighter. Get the net, Ari." His line was jerking madly, the rod deeply bowed. The fish was trying to drag him into the pool as it fought to escape, and he set his feet more firmly into the mud of the riverbed, leaning his weight back against the fish, his arms straight as he played the line.

Ariadne scrambled up the bank and grabbed the net. She slid back into the water, took a step towards Ivor, and her foot disappeared into an unexpectedly deep drop in the riverbed. She lost her balance and slipped, the water closing over her head. She fought her way up and then realized her foot was caught in the weeds at the bottom, and she couldn't get her head out of the water.

Ivor swore and dropped the rod, splashing to where Ari had disappeared. He could see her hair floating just below the surface and realized what had happened. The weeds were treacherous in this part of the river, which was what made it such a treasure trove for the secretive pike. He took a breath and ducked beneath the surface, grabbing Ari around the waist. He pulled hard, and they both came up, breaking the surface in a fountain of spray.

Ari gasped for breath, blinking water out of her eyes. "That was scary. I couldn't free my foot."

"No, I realized."

"You dropped your rod?" She wrung water out of her hair between her hands.

"Yes," he agreed, watching its rapid disappearance up the river as the pike took off with it. "I hope he gets rid of the hook. He deserves better than that."

"I'm sorry." She looked regretfully at the vanishing rod.

"Hardly your fault." Ivor looked at her closely. She was rather pale, and her eyes were still frightened. He could only imagine the panic one would feel trapped beneath the water like that, even for such a short time. "Let's get you onto dry land." He lifted her easily out of the water and set her on the bank, jumping up beside her.

"I was so frightened," Ari said, almost in wonder. She didn't think she'd ever been really scared before. "What would have happened if you hadn't been here?"

"You wouldn't have been in the water in the first place," he pointed out in a rallying tone. "You're shivering." He took her hands, chafing them, and then he wrapped his arms around her. He was as wet as Ari was, but he thought only of imparting some of his body warmth to her. She clung to him, and without thought he tilted her chin with one finger, and as she turned her dark, wide-eyed gaze up to him, he kissed her. It took him by surprise, and yet as soon as their lips met, he realized how much he had been longing to do just this.

Ariadne couldn't think. She was too numb to think. She felt his mouth on hers, soft, pliant, yet firm and warm. She didn't move, just stood still against him, her arms clinging around his waist as if to a lifeline, and when his tongue demanded entrance, she parted her lips for him, tasting the sweet essence of his mouth, feeling a rush of warmth pulse through her blood, making her heart beat faster, bringing a flush to her cheeks.

Ivor raised his head finally and looked down at her from his greater height, a slightly surprised look in his eyes. "Well, now," he murmured. "I've been wanting to do that for a very long time, but somehow I didn't think my first marital kiss would be like embracing a half-drowned kitten."

Ari just shook her head. Why hadn't she pushed him away? She had told herself she was resigned to the fact of their marriage, to acceptance of its consummation, but her heart was not involved in this arrangement. And yet, instead of pushing him away, she had clung to him, parted her lips for him, invited him to deepen the kiss. Had she yielded simply through surprise and the shock of her immersion in the river?

Of course, that was all it had been. It was best forgotten, considered nothing more than an aberration. She declared, "I am not remotely like a kitten, half-drowned or not."

"No," he agreed. "There's a lot more of the lioness about you, my dear." He could read the near panic-stricken confusion in her eyes and understood that she had not expected to find herself responding to his kiss. It gave him a tiny smidgen of reassurance. Maybe there was hope that they could make more of this than a passionless and compulsory contract.

She shivered again suddenly as the sinking sun disappeared behind a cloud.

"Come . . . you'll catch your death of cold." Ivor took her hand. "*Run*, Ari." He broke into a run himself, pulling her along with him, and she picked up her pace, racing along the bank, her wet hair streaming in the wind. They reached the cottage, and Ivor flung open the door, pushing her ahead of him into the warmth.

Tilly was rolling pastry at the table when the door flew open. "Lord love us," she declared, her floury hands lifting in astonishment. "What've you been doin', the pair of you?"

"Swimming," Ivor said shortly. Tilly was treating him now with the same familiarity she used with Ariadne, and sometimes he wasn't sure he cared for it. "Fetch dry clothes for Ari, and help her get dry and changed in front of the fire. I'll see to myself above." He issued orders briskly as he propelled Ari closer to the fire. "Come on, get out of those clothes."

Tilly heard the note of authority and responded at once. "Aye, sir. I'll just fetch Miss Ari's things from above. Should I light the fire for you up there? 'Tis all laid."

"No, I won't need it," he said, pushing aside Ari's hands as she tried to unlace her bodice. Her fingers were numb with cold. "Just keep still, Ariadne, and let me help you."

She obeyed, her teeth beginning to chatter. Why was she so cold when Ivor didn't even seem to be aware of the fact that he was as wet as she was? It didn't seem fair.

Tilly came down just as Ivor was pushing the opened gown off Ari's shoulders. "I'll take over now, sir." Tilly set down a pile of clothes and towels on a stool by the fire. "You go on up and dry yourself."

Ivor nodded and climbed up to the bedchamber. He was feeling the chill himself now and was grateful that Tilly had set a towel out for him on the chest at the foot of the bed and he didn't have to rummage for one himself.

Ari tried to help as Tilly pulled away her wet clothes before swathing her in towels. Tilly just tutted and got on with the business at hand with matter-of-fact efficiency that Ari finally accepted. In a very few minutes, she was dry and warmly wrapped in a thick night-robe. Tilly took away the pile of wet clothes, dumping them in the wash tub in the scullery.

"I'll wash 'em tomorrow," she said, coming back into the room as Ivor came downstairs, dressed in dry shirt and britches. "I'll fetch down your wet things, sir, and I'll do 'em at the same time as Miss Ari's."

"My thanks." Ivor was accustomed to his washing, such as it was, being taken care of in the communal laundry. Once again, he reflected that there were material benefits to married life.

Ariadne watched him as he took a flagon of brandy from the dresser and filled two cups. Something had happened after that moment on the riverbank. She was noticing him in a different way from before. He raised his head from the flagon and cast a glance over her as she sat ensconced in the rocking chair, and she was startlingly aware of the depth of his eyes, the line of his mouth, the sense of his physical presence in the small chamber.

He brought a cup over to her. Her hand was still shaking a little, and he placed his over it, steadying her grip as she took the cup. The firm feel of his hand, the scent of his skin, the tang of leather and sweat, of wind and sun burned into the tanned complexion as he leaned so casually over her sent a jolt deep into her belly. She noticed how the lamplight caught the chestnut glints in his dark hair. Of course, she'd noticed all these things before but not with such clarity.

"Drink this. It'll warm you," he said in his customary tones.

Was he oblivious to these strange new eyes of hers? Ari wondered, dazed.

She took the cup and responded in what she hoped was her own normal voice. "I'm a lot warmer already. I am so sorry about your rod and losing the pike. I don't know how I could have been so clumsy."

"You weren't clumsy. Neither of us knew of that drop-off in the riverbed." He stood with his back to the range and sipped his brandy. An imperative bang at the door startled them both. The door opened before the sound of the knock had truly faded, and Lord Daunt came in, his bulk seeming to diminish the room.

"My lord uncle," Ari said in surprise, half rising from her chair. "Is something the matter?" Rolf wasn't in the habit of performing his own errands. He always summoned those he wanted to attend him in the Council house.

"Yes, Ariadne. It is time you stopped running wild around the village like a gypsy girl, and you, Chalfont, you should have a firmer hold on your wife. I won't have it." His face was red with annoyance.

"I ask your pardon, my lord," Ivor said smoothly. "May I offer you brandy?" He filled a cup and invited the irritable head of the Daunt family to come to the fire. "You must forgive our informality, but we had an incident at the river."

"Incident?" Rolf took the cup, his small eyes sharpening. "Invaders from above?"

"No, uncle," Ari said, heartened by the brandy and her spirit rising to the challenge of her irate relative. "Just a recalcitrant pike."

"A *what*?" Rolf blinked suspiciously.

"Ivor . . . my husband," she added with delicate emphasis. "My husband was trying to catch an old and wily pike, who has eluded every fisherman in the valley for years. He caught him this afternoon."

Rolf's expression changed. "You caught the old emperor?" Suddenly, he was a young man himself again, ready to try his hand with the legendary pike of the Wye. "Where is he? Must be at least fifteen pounds."

"Alas, my lord, he got away," Ivor said with a half smile. "And he took my rod with him."

Rolf's expression reverted to its customary disagreeable arrogance. "Indeed?" The single word implied that he didn't believe a word of it. It was just another fisherman's tall tale of the one that got away.

"Indeed, sir, it was my fault," Ari said. "Ivor sent me to get the net. He was so close to bringing him in, and somehow I slipped into a drop-off, and my foot became caught in the weeds, and to save me, my husband was obliged to lose both the pike and his rod."

"And that, niece, brings me back to why I'm here," Rolf declared, dismissing fish from the conversation. "I will not tolerate your scrambling around riverbanks, let alone falling in. You are Lady Ariadne Chalfont, and you, Sir Ivor, need to take better control of your wife. You are no longer children, free to play as you please. From now on, Ariadne, until you leave for London, you will appear in the village properly dressed, and you, Sir Ivor, will ensure that she does." He drained his brandy, regarding his empty cup thoughtfully, then said, "Which batch did this come from? 'Tis uncommonly good."

"I believe it was in the latest Cornish package," Ivor answered. "Ned Jarret can usually be relied upon for the best. He's the canniest smuggler on the Cornish coast." He took up the flagon in invitation.

Rolf seemed to hesitate, then stood up. "No, I've no time to drink brandy by your fireside, Chalfont. Just mind my words, and make sure your wife behaves herself. She'll never pass muster in London if she keeps running around like a street urchin." With that, he strode out of the cottage, the door slamming in his wake, setting the crockery in the dresser rattling.

It was only after the crockery had settled down again that Tilly, looking rather alarmed, showed herself on the bottom stair, her arms full of Ivor's discarded garments. "Lord Daunt is not best pleased." She scurried across the room to the scullery. "So there's no pike, then? I was expecting to cook that for your supper. You've been promising fish, sir, for the last three nights."

Ivor raised an expressive eyebrow, and Ari stifled a rueful chuckle. "We seem to be putting everyone out at present." She leaned back in the rocker and called to Tilly in the scullery, "Coddled eggs would be lovely, Tilly. You make them so well, and I'm sure there are a few mushrooms left from the other morning. And some bacon, perhaps."

Tilly reappeared. "Aye, I can do that if you fancy it. And I was making an apple pie when you came in all wet. Will that suit you?"

Ivor stood up. "Tilly, you are a wonder. The most accomplished cook I've ever been lucky enough to meet. I ask your pardon for the lack of fish. Tomorrow, I promise."

"Don't make promises you can't keep, sir," Tilly declared. "If we're to leave soon, there'll be no time for fishin'." She took a basket of eggs from the dresser.

"How right you are," Ivor murmured under his breath. He glanced at Ariadne, who was rocking quietly, her eyes on the fire, her hands cradling her brandy. It was, indeed, time to put off childish things.

TWELVE

"Well, that's all set, then, everything packed up an' ready." Tilly regarded the assembly of trunks and band-boxes in Ariadne's old cottage.

"Yes," Ari agreed almost absently. She glanced around. The cottage was deserted except for herself and Tilly. She shut the door and turned the key. "Tilly, there's something I need to talk to you about, but it must be just between ourselves."

"Aye, Miss Ari." Tilly looked askance. "If 'tis a secret, I can keep it as well as the next."

"Yes, I know." Ariadne twisted her hands against the folds of her skirt. It was a delicate subject, and she wasn't sure how Tilly would react. Then she took a breath and said firmly, "You once told me that there were things you could take to prevent conception, herbs you could make into a potion of some kind. Is it true?"

Tilly stared at her. "Well, yes, miss, 'tis true enough. My mother taught me about that and the other medicines she showed me. But . . . but why would you be wanting such a potion, Miss Ari? You're a married woman."

"This journey to London is so long, Tilly, and I cannot be pregnant," she explained directly. "It will make everything so much more difficult. If there is something I could take to stop that . . ." She opened her hands in a self-explanatory gesture. "Can you make something up for me?"

"But what would Sir Ivor say?" Tilly was wide-eyed in shocked astonishment.

"He won't know," Ari responded. "I shall not tell him, and neither will you. I know that I am not pregnant now, the bleeding has only just stopped, so if I start to take precautions at once, then there will be no danger of conceiving on this journey."

"I suppose so." Tilly still looked shocked. "But is it right, Miss Ari, to deceive your husband about something like that? He'll expect a son and heir. All men do. 'Tis a matter of pride."

"Men's pride and women's inconvenience," Ariadne said shortly. "This is just during the journey, Tilly. When we're settled in London, it will be different. I intend to ride all the way, and if I'm pregnant and vomiting every five minutes, I won't be able to ride, and I won't be able to tolerate the coach. It'll hold everybody up, and the weather will get worse and make it harder to travel, and apart from anything else, I could easily lose the child in such circumstances." She threw out the last like a gambler throwing down his last ace.

"Well, I suppose so, Miss Ari. When you put it like

that, it'd probably be for the best," Tilly said, still sounding doubtful. "I'll make some up for you. You have to take it every night before you go to bed."

"Thank you." Ari gave her a radiant smile, her relief evident. "You are a good friend, Tilly."

Tilly blushed a little. "Well, I should hope so, miss. I'll tell the lads now that they can take this lot to the coach if we're to leave at dawn tomorrow." She unlocked the door and hurried out of the cottage.

Ari sat down on a trunk and looked around what had been her home until her wedding night. It didn't feel like home anymore. The valley, since her grandfather's death, didn't feel like home, either, and she was ready to leave it, to start a new life. And to start her marriage to Ivor.

He would presumably guess on his own that the bleeding had stopped and they could finally consummate their union. How was he feeling about that? she wondered. Did he see it as something that had to be got through, put behind them as a necessary fact of this marriage? Or did he feel any excitement at the prospect? A sense of anticipation, perhaps? Vividly now, she remembered the kiss on the riverbank. His eyes had held much more than a simple sense of inevitability, an acceptance of a task that must be completed. He had kissed her with passion. And she had responded. Involuntarily and with desire. For that moment, the old familiar ease of friendship had become subsumed by a surge of pure lust. And then afterwards, she had had that peculiar revelation that she was seeing him with new eyes.

Gabriel's image rose in her mind's eye. He was so very

different in every way from Ivor. Slight where Ivor was powerful, fair where Ivor was dark, his voice light where Ivor's was deep and smooth. Gabriel was a pale poet flitting lightly across the surface of the earth. Ivor was a dark warrior whose feet made solid contact with the ground. How could she possibly be drawn so powerfully to both of them?

She loved Gabriel. Her first love, her only love, filled with sunshine and birdsong. What she felt for Ivor was something darker than love; it didn't need sunshine and birdsong, it responded to gale-force winds that bent the trees and whipped up the surface of the river in full flood.

And she was becoming ridiculously fanciful, Ariadne decided, getting up from the trunk. Perhaps it was just her mind's way of reconciling her to the inevitable. Gabriel was lost to her, and she had to accept what had been allotted her. She lay in Ivor Chalfont's bed now, and somehow she had to make the best of it.

The door opened, and three burly lads came in. "Beggin' your pardon, Miss Ari, but Tilly said as how the luggage was ready to go," the leader said.

"Yes, that's right, Terry. I was just checking to make sure it's all here." She gestured vaguely at the trunks. "Everything's here."

"Right y'are. Come on, lads, let's shift this lot."

Ari went outside and walked towards the bridge, a gentle stroll, as she was careful since Rolf's castigation to moderate her usual madcap pace around the village. She walked to the middle of the bridge and leaned on the single railing, looking up the river to the main pass out of the valley. At dawn tomorrow, their entire procession of coach, horses, and armed outriders would pass through the narrow, rocky defile and out into the wide world. The road, such as it was, would take them across the sparsely populated Somerset Levels and through the Polden Hills. Only after there would the way become less rough in parts.

She turned to look down the river to the cliff that rose at the end of the gorge. The river shrank to a thin stream, flowing beneath the cliff to widen once it emerged into the countryside beyond. There were caves beneath the cliff, and some years ago, she and Ivor had tried to explore them, an adventure that had not gone down well with the Daunt elders, she remembered with a grimace.

She was saying goodbye, Ari realized as she turned back to the village. Once she had left the valley, she would never return to it, and yet it seemed to be a part of her, to flow in her veins with her blood. She returned to Ivor's cottage, wondering whether he would have returned home yet. He'd been in conference with the Council most of the day.

Ivor was not in the cottage, but Tilly was doing something in the scullery when Ari came in. The girl emerged with a small green glass vial in her hand. "Here you are, Miss Ari. You take a spoon of this each night."

Ari took the vial and held it up to the light. She took out the oiled stopper and sniffed the contents. "It doesn't smell very nice."

"Don't taste nice, neither, I reckon," Tilly commented. "Ma only gave it to women who'd had too many babies

already or if they were sick and couldn't carry safely and
their menfolk wouldn't leave them alone. I never heard
tell of using it just because . . ." She shook her head in
patent disapproval and went back to the scullery.

Ari decided it was simpler not to discuss the morality
of the precaution. "How does it work?"

"I don't know, don't think Ma knew, neither, but if you
take it regular, you'll not fall for a baby." Tilly reappeared
holding a plucked chicken. She threw it on the table and
took up a heavy knife, beginning to eviscerate and joint
the bird with deft efficiency. "I'll cook this for supper, and
what's over will make a good pasty for the journey tomorrow," she declared. "There's already meat pies an' a flitch
of bacon to go with us. Enough provisions for a couple of
days, at least." She wiped her brow with the back of her
hand. "What we'll do after, the Lord only knows."

"No need to sound so gloomy, Tilly." Ivor stamped
his feet in the doorway to get rid of the dried mud on his
boots. "There'll be food aplenty, don't you worry. We've
enough money to buy the royal storehouse."

"Really?" Surreptitiously, Ari slipped the vial into her
apron pocket as she turned to the door with a ready smile.
"Has Rolf disgorged some of the Daunt wealth?"

"Yes, and a chest full of jewelry. Most of it belonging
to the family, but I suspect we don't want to inquire too
closely into the provenance of some of the other pieces."
He filled a tankard from the ale flagon. "The coach is almost loaded. The roof is so packed it'll be a miracle if we
can get through the pass."

He went through to the scullery, and Ari heard him

pouring water from the bucket into a bowl. She hurried up to the bedchamber and buried the green vial under her shifts in the dresser. She would take the spoonful when Ivor went to the privy before bed.

She felt rather melancholy during supper, and Ivor seemed distracted. Tilly disappeared to supper with the women as soon as she'd set the chicken and a pan of potatoes and carrots on the table. "I'll be back here afore dawn, Miss Ari."

"We'll be up and about by then, Tilly," Ivor responded, carving the bird. He served them both, filled a wine cup for Ari, and sat down. They ate for the most part in silence, but once or twice Ari felt Ivor's eyes resting on her, a slight questioning look in his eye.

As soon as they had finished, Ari took the plates into the scullery. "I think I'll get ready for bed," she called. "As we have to be up so early tomorrow."

Ivor came into the scullery, carrying their empty cups. "A wise move. I think I'll go for a drink in the village . . . say my farewells. I won't be above an hour."

She nodded, scraping the plates vigorously into the chicken scraps. "Seems a bit cannibalistic to feed them chicken bits."

"They're scavengers; they eat anything." He bent, and for a second she felt the brush of his lips against her neck. It was so fleeting she could almost have imagined it, except that she hadn't. "I'll be back in an hour," he repeated, and she thought there was a touch of emphasis to the statement. The door closed behind him.

She touched her nape reflectively, almost expecting to

feel some manifestation of the warm tingle that his fleeting lips had left behind—nothing, of course. She finished cleaning the dishes and went to the outhouse before taking a spoon up to the bedchamber, where she took out the vial and carefully measured a dose, swallowing it down in one gulp. Tilly was right; it tasted foul and smelled sulfurous, like rotting grass. She pushed the stopper back in and buried the vial under her shifts again. The contents of the dresser would go in the cloak bag that would contain her personal possessions for the journey.

She rinsed her mouth with salt to freshen it and get rid of the foul taste, undressed, and shook out her night shift. She was about to drop it over her head when she stopped. If she went to bed without her shift, Ivor would know the monthly bleeding had stopped and would act accordingly.

She could keep him from knowing for a couple of days yet, but that would mean this long-awaited consummation would have to take place in some probably filthy roadside hostelry. Surely better here, where the sheets were clean, the chamber familiar, their privacy assured. Once this first time was over, it would not be so awkward and difficult the next time.

The act had assumed monumental proportions in her mind. The long wait for the inevitable had created expectations of embarrassment and discomfort. Did Ivor feel the same way? Somehow she doubted it. Very little threw Ivor off stride. He would consummate his marriage in the same calm, efficient manner in which he did everything. It was impossible to imagine him fumbling and embarrassing them both. Which was somewhat reassuring. And at least she wasn't a complete novice herself, which, in the circumstances, was a mixed blessing, she thought without humor.

She glanced out of the window towards the refectory from where the sounds of laughter and music drifted on the cool evening air. Of course, if he was getting drunk with his friends for one last time, he wouldn't be able to manage the act anyway. But as she looked out, she saw his unmistakable figure emerge from the building. He stood for a moment on the threshold, looking around him, as if he was saying goodbye, just as she had done on the bridge that afternoon. Then he swung around and strode towards home, not a hint of instability in his step.

Ari discarded the shift, tossing it onto the end of the bed, blew out the candle, and climbed hastily into bed. She pulled the coverlet up to her chin and lay in the shadowy darkness, the flickering light from the village torches beyond the window making strange shapes on the sloping walls. She heard the door open and then close, the thud of the bar as Ivor dropped it across. She heard his footsteps recede and guessed he was going to the outhouse.

She waited.

✦ ✦ ✦

Ivor made sure the chickens were safely shut away and returned to the scullery. He locked the back door and took off his boots and stockings so as not to wake Ari as he climbed upstairs. He entered the bedchamber, his eyes growing quickly accustomed to the dim, shadowy light.

The white garment on the end of the bed told him all he needed to know. He stepped to Ari's side of the bed and looked down at her. Her eyes were open, and she turned her head slightly on the pillow to look at him.

He smiled a little, but his eyes were grave, deep blue pools in the flickering darkness. "Are you ready, Ariadne?"

She nodded. "If that is what you wish."

"For God's sake, Ari," he exclaimed softly. "Of course it is what I wish. I am not made of ice, dear girl. The last weeks have been almost unendurable." He began to unbutton his shirt as he stood there, before saying painfully, "I realize, of course, that for you they have been a respite before something you dreaded."

"Not exactly," she said, hating to hear the hurt in his voice. "Not dreaded, Ivor." She was about to say that as she and her body knew what to expect, there would be no conventional pain or discomfort, and she had no reason for dread, but she stopped herself in time.

"You cannot wish to make love to a man who is not the one you love," he stated, unbuckling his belt. "I understand that, and I will be as considerate as I am able."

He tossed his shirt, belt, and britches onto the chest at the foot of the bed. "I am going to light the candle. I do not care to make love in the dark. It is not something to be hidden and ashamed of." Flint and tinder scraped, and the candle bloomed into light. He stepped closer to the bed.

Ari looked at him in his nakedness and was flooded with pure sexual desire. He was such a magnificent figure, his belly flat, his hips slim, his legs long and powerful, his

chest broad and muscular. You didn't have to love someone body and soul to desire him in this way, she thought.
What she felt now, looking at this husband of hers, was
quite simply an astonished wanting.

Ivor leaned over and took the edge of the coverlet
from her hand, where she still held it under her chin.
"Sauce for the goose," he said with a half smile. "I have
not looked upon you yet." He drew down the coverlet,
very slowly, revealing her body inch by inch. Ari lay still,
her hands beside her hips, as her nakedness was revealed
to his hungry gaze.

Ivor folded the covers neatly at the end of the bed and
stood looking down at her. She was every bit as he'd imagined, her skin opalescent against the sheet, her breasts
small and perfectly round against the narrow ribcage, her
belly smooth and white, the hip bones prominent. He
leaned over and put his hands on either side of her body,
against her hips, feeling her slightness. Then he kissed
the groove between her breasts, his tongue flicking lightly
across the swell of flesh, touching the rosy nipples that
lifted and hardened beneath the caress.

Ari stirred on the bed, her hips lifting a little in an
involuntary movement as the cleft of her body moist-
ened beneath the flicking tip of his tongue. Somehow
she hadn't expected these slow, expert caresses, this sense
that time was of no importance, the feel of the air on her
naked body, the touch of his hands and tongue, a slow
unfurling of desire.

She moved her hands to his body, to press into the
lean muscularity of his backside as he knelt above her.

He smiled, running his own hands down her body as she lay beneath him, enclosing her ribcage between his palms for a moment before bringing his mouth to her navel, his tongue dipping into the soft indentation, then painting a slow path over her belly, pausing to flick her hip bones in turn, before gliding between her thighs. She stiffened in shocked surprise at this intimate invasion, something she'd never even imagined before, and then his tongue parting the folds of her sex in a warm liquid caress drew a soft involuntary moan of bewildered pleasure from her lips.

She ran her fingers through his hair and stroked the curve of his ears, as her hips moved beneath the moist strokes of his tongue. As the climax built, her fingers twisted in his hair, tugging at the roots, and her body leapt upwards to meet the swirling wash of delight.

As it left her, receding slowly, her body sinking back into the deep feather mattress, Ivor slipped his hands beneath her bottom and lifted her to meet his slow penetration of her warm, moist, and welcoming core. Ari took a breath, absorbing the sensation, reveling in its newness. She had never before felt this all-consuming possession, this sense of being filled to her essence, and her hands bit deep into his buttocks as he moved with ever-increasing speed above her, and her hips lifted and moved with him, matching thrust for thrust, and when it was over, when Ivor fell heavily upon her, his head on the pillow beside hers, his loins still joined with hers, his penis pulsing damply within her, she was aware of a glorious, satisfied exuberance coursing through her body as she lay spread-eagled, one hand resting on Ivor's sweat-slick back, her other arm flung wide along the mattress. A low chuckle escaped her lips.

Slowly, Ivor heaved himself sideways, his penis slithering out of her, resting damply against her inner thigh. "What's funny?" His voice was muffled against her shoulder.

"Nothing at all," Ari said, stroking down his back.

"Ah." He rolled sideways onto his back, one hand resting on her belly. "Well, I won't press the matter. Is there anything you want?"

She laughed again. "Oh, no, Sir Ivor. Not at present. I can't imagine what else you could give me for the moment."

He turned his head on the pillow, his eyes hooded, languid with the aftermath of pleasure. "Good. I'm glad. Now, sleep. We have to be up before cock crow." With an effort, he hauled himself up to reach for the coverlet, pulling it up over them. He leaned sideways and kissed the corner of her mouth. "So much for that."

"So much for that," Ariadne echoed, turning on her side as sleep claimed her.

THIRTEEN

*A*riadne awoke the next morning with a hand on her shoulder. It was still dark, and she lay for a moment disoriented, feeling as if she had slept only a few minutes.

"Wake up, Ari. It will be dawn in half an hour, and we have to be out of the valley at sunup."

She blinked into the flickering light of the candle Ivor held high above her. "I don't want to get up." Her body felt hammered into the deep feathers, filled with a wonderful lethargy that was quite unfamiliar.

"No, neither did I," he responded briskly. "Nevertheless, Ariadne, you must get up. There is hot water on the dresser to refresh yourself, and Tilly is preparing breakfast. Be quick, now."

He was dressed, she saw, right down to his sword belt and boots. He must have left her to sleep until the last possible moment. She kicked aside the covers, and when the cool air struck her body, the memories of the night came back in full force. She felt almost embarrassed to show her nakedness to the man who had done such wonderful things to and for her, but Ivor hadn't waited. The moment she had shown a sign of getting out of bed, he had left the loft, his booted feet sounding on the stairs.

It rather seemed, as far as Ivor was concerned, that what happened in the night stayed in the night, Ari reflected wryly. With the day that lay ahead of them, that was probably for the best, her rational mind told her. But she couldn't manage to banish that glorious feeling of exuberance on which she had fallen asleep. Only in the cold light of day, something niggled, detracting from the purity of the memory.

Surely she had had no right to feel like that with Ivor when she was so deeply in love with another man? But it had been so different. With Gabriel, there had only ever been a hasty scramble of clothes and a flash of heated passion, edged with the fear of discovery. Last night had been a long and leisurely climb to an ecstatic peak. And she had felt not one flicker of guilt. Was she so fickle? Were her feelings so shallow? So basically worthless that not one thought of Gabriel had disturbed that sensual dream? It was an uncomfortable thought, but there was no time to dwell upon it now.

She dressed in her old riding clothes—time enough for the elegant outfits when they were out of familiar land and on the proper road to London—packed her cloak bag, tucking the vial under her shifts, and went downstairs.

Tilly was dressed for the journey in what seemed like

several layers of petticoats beneath her red woolen gown, a matching woolen jerkin, and a sheepskin jacket. She looked as round as a baby robin. She turned from the range and set a pan of eggs on the table. "Best eat up quick, Miss Ari. Everyone's ready to go."

Ariadne wondered if she could stomach eggs when she still felt half-drugged with sleep. But Ivor came in, bringing a blast of cold, predawn air with him. "Eat, Ari. We won't stop until noon . . . Tilly, give her a tankard of small beer. We've a long way to travel before we can rest."

Ari, still standing at the table, picked up the platter. She regarded Ivor surreptitiously as he took up a tankard of small beer. He really was quite different this morning; indeed, it was difficult to imagine the lover of the night in this hard-lined figure, his expression calm yet determined, his movements purposeful. Everything about him spoke of a man in charge, and even his eyes had lost the soft warmth of the night.

She ate as much of the eggs as she could manage, drank half of the small beer, and said, "I'll fetch my bag from above."

"I'll get it. Make use of the outhouse. It'll be a while before you have anything but a bush for privacy." Ivor set down his tankard and took the stairs two at a time.

Ariadne said nothing, going out of the door into the dawn chill. When she emerged from the privy she stood for a moment in the garden to cast one last glance around the cottage before going around to the front. Ivor stood there, holding Sphinx, who greeted her with a welcoming whinny. She stroked his neck and blew softly into his nostrils. He responded with a nuzzle and a little whicker of pleasure.

"Ah, so you're on your way."

Ari turned at the sound of her uncle's harsh voice. He came up the lane, warmly wrapped in his cloak, his eyes a little bloodshot. "So it would seem, sir," she replied. "I'm sorry we dragged you from your bed betimes."

"I'm always up before cock crow," he responded. "Just wanted to make sure everything's in order. You have everything ready, Chalfont?"

He seemed to be ignoring her, Ariadne thought. She was merely a necessary adjunct to this family business, rather like the jewelry in the iron-bound casket, set firmly under a seat of the coach, her usefulness defined only by her husband.

If Ivor noticed Ari's deliberate exclusion, he gave no sign. "I believe so, Lord Daunt."

"Good. Then I will expect to hear from you by courier when you reach London. I wish you God's speed." Rolf turned away and walked back to the Council house without a backwards glance or a personal farewell for his niece.

"Well, that puts me in my place," Ari observed, turning Sphinx towards the pass out of the valley.

Ivor grimaced. If he could have prevented that encounter, he would have done so. As it was, he had no power to change Rolf's attitude towards his niece. But since Ari couldn't stand the man, it didn't really matter. He shrugged and nudged his horse to follow Sphinx. Soon the valley and its personal politics would be far behind them.

What lay ahead was another matter altogether.

✦ ✦ ✦

The narrow cliffs of the defile seemed to close over them as the little procession passed through it, the top-heavy coach swaying, the extra team of horses tied behind. Four armed outriders, two ahead of the coach and one on each side, kept their eyes on the road ahead. Tilly was perched up on the box with the coachman, huddled in a thick woolen cloak. She had never been out of the valley before, and everything about her posture indicated her anxiety as everything she had ever known disappeared behind her. As they reached the end of the pass, the sun came up, a few streaks on the eastern sky, and by the time they had reached the flat land of the Levels, it was high in the sky, although offering little warmth on the autumn day.

Ariadne and Ivor were riding just ahead of the coach but behind the two outriders acting as scouts. Sphinx was restless, prancing a little, lifting his head impatiently, pulling at the reins. He could smell freedom, and he was clearly anxious to shake the fidgets from his long legs. Turk, Ivor's huge black, was behaving similarly, and after a mile or so, Ari said, "Could we just give them their heads for a few miles? Let them run . . . I would dearly love a gallop."

Ivor glanced sideways at her. He was holding Turk back with a firm hand, but he could feel the animal's impatience in every sinew of the powerful muscled body beneath him. "Very well. But don't tire Sphinx. He has a long way to go before sundown." He put two fingers to his lips and whistled, and the outriders ahead drew rein on the narrow track.

Ivor rode up to them, Ari close behind. "We're going to ride ahead for a while. The horses need to run," he informed the outriders. "Keep close behind us. It should be safe enough here. There's nowhere for an ambush to hide."

Indeed, the flat swamp and marshland of the Levels stretched on either side, and the faint glimmer of the sea shone on the far horizon. There was barely a bush or a crop of saplings to break up the flatness.

"As you wish, Sir Ivor." The men drew their horses to one side of the track so that Ari and Ivor could move ahead.

Ari nudged Sphinx's flanks with her heels, and the horse leapt forward with a joyous toss of his head and set off down the track. Ari could hear Turk's hooves pounding behind her and then beside her. His chest was more powerful than the smaller gelding's, and soon he pulled ahead, galloping hell for leather down the track. Sphinx lengthened his stride, goaded by the race, and for a few miles they rode in a glorious gallop, the air whistling past their ears. Ari's hood flew back as the wind whipped past, and her hair knotted on her nape came loose from its pins, to fall into two heavy braids down her back. An involuntary exultant cry broke from her lips at the sheer joy of the speed and the rushing wind, and she leaned lower on her horse's neck, encouraging him to greater speed.

Ivor was ahead of her, but slowly he began to draw rein, easing Turk back into a canter, and reluctantly Ari did the same, so that when Sphinx came up with Ivor's black, both horses were slowing to a trot and then gradually to a walk.

"That was glorious." Ari tossed her plaits back over her shoulders. "I really didn't want to stop."

"Neither did I, but it was enough for the horses. They've a long way to go."

Ari made no demur. Glancing over her shoulder, she saw that they had left the coach far behind, and the two advance riders, their horses built for endurance rather than speed, were a long way back on the track. "There's a stream over there." She gestured with her whip. "Shall we water the horses while we wait for them to catch up?"

Ivor nodded and turned Turk aside to cross the green plain to where the stream bubbled, crystal clear, through the water meadow. Ari dismounted and led Sphinx to the low bank. Ivor let Turk drink his fill as he looked around. There was no sign of habitation. The risk of flooding on the Levels prevented it, although in the summer, the flat green plain was used for grazing, and crops grew strong in the well-irrigated soil. Now, though, by the beginning of autumn, once the harvest was in, the farmers retreated to the higher ground of the Polden Hills, and there was something rather bleak about the flat, deserted landscape.

"There's a bush over there," Ari said. "Would you hold Sphinx?"

He took the reins, commenting with a smile, "You have about five minutes of privacy, I would say, before the rest come up with us."

Ari hurried for the bush, and when she returned a few minutes later, she could see no sign of Ivor, and the horses were loosely tethered to a low branch of a scrappy weeping willow tree. She looked around for him, suddenly alarmed. "Ivor . . . Ivor, where are you?" Her voice rose a little, even as she told herself he couldn't have gone far.

"I'm here. What's the matter?" Ivor scrambled up the bank a few yards away, where the stream took a slight turn. "What is it?" His voice was sharp, his hand on his sword, half out of its sheath.

"Nothing . . . I didn't know where you were," Ari said, feeling foolish.

He shook his head and strode over to her side. "That's not like you, Ari. To panic for no reason." He tilted her chin on his forefinger, looking down at her upturned face. "I was just taking advantage of the moment of privacy myself."

"Yes . . . of course," she said, feeling even more foolish. "This place just feels so vast and empty. Silly of me, I know." She twitched her chin from his light grasp and turned away. "The coach has almost reached us on the track. Shouldn't we go back?"

"By all means." Ivor untethered the horses. "Give me your foot." She put her foot in his palm, and he tossed her up onto the saddle before mounting Turk. He gave her a puzzled look as they rode back to the track where the coach had stopped to wait for them. What had alarmed her? he wondered. Ariadne was generally fearless. Perhaps it *was* this strangely open space stretching all around them. When you grew up in an enclosed valley, surrounded by protective walls and armed guards, perhaps there was something intrinsically alarming about this sense of vastness, the ground meeting the sky in a seemingly unbroken horizon.

Ariadne was too confused about her reaction to Ivor's momentary disappearance to think too clearly. It had been a stupid response to his absence. Perhaps she was coming to rely on him too much? The thought stunned her. She had never been dependent on anyone. It wasn't practical. And yet, since she had moved into Ivor's cottage, slept in his bed, eaten supper with him every night, somehow she had begun to think of them as joined, partnered. And after last night . . .

Why hadn't he mentioned last night? The question hadn't been far from her thoughts all morning. Had it not been as wonderfully satisfying for him as it had been for her? Or had it just been another experience, no different from the many he had had in the whorehouse across the bridge, not worth thinking about the next morning?

But Ivor did not dissemble; it was not in his nature. He had been as much her partner in that lovemaking as she had been his. The dominant partner, certainly, but his pleasure had been as real as hers. There simply hadn't been an opportune moment to refer to it this morning, let alone talk about it, she told herself. There was no point in suffering wounded feminine pride in these circumstances.

Feeling much more like her pragmatic self, Ariadne drew rein at the coach. "How are you bearing up, Tilly?" she called up to the huddled figure.

"It's so big out here, Miss Ari," Tilly said, seeming to draw even further into her cloak. "There's no one, nothing anywhere. 'Tis all sky and marsh."

"It is a bit overwhelming," Ariadne agreed, glad to forget her own earlier confused alarm with the need to reassure Tilly. "If you need to stretch your legs or find some privacy," she added delicately, "I will come with you just over there." She gestured with her whip to the convenient bush.

"I don't know, miss. I'm afeard to get down." Tilly looked around again. "But I own I'll be glad of a privy."

"Come on, then." Ari dismounted and reached up her hand. Tilly scrambled down from the box. "We'll be back shortly," Ari informed Ivor. "I expect everyone will be glad of a short respite."

Ivor cursed silently, but he couldn't deny the little party what he'd taken for himself, however anxious he was to get across the Levels before nightfall. They'd find shelter of some kind in a farming village in the Polden Hills, where the ground was higher and not flood-prone, but they had to find it before dark. He looked across the plain to the faint dark outline of the hills that bisected the Levels. A good five hours' ride still, and they would have to stop again around noon.

Impatiently, he waited for the scattered members of his party to rejoin the track. Ari was chatting cheerfully with Tilly as they came back, and the girl was looking more cheerful as she scrambled back onto the coach with a helping hand from the coachman. She was still not prepared to discard any of her many layers, despite the mid-morning sun, but she sat upright instead of huddled and looked around her with eyes that were not so wide and frightened.

Ivor was about to dismount to help Ari onto her horse, but if she saw him make the move, she ignored it, mounting without his help. Ivor wondered wryly why he'd even thought to help her. It was not his usual practice. Ari had been climbing on and off horseback without assistance since she'd first learned to ride. But he supposed she was going to have to learn to accept help ordinarily offered a lady in polite society, so it was probably as well to get some practice in before they reached London.

He took his place in the procession ahead of the coach and behind the armed outriders, expecting Ari to come up beside him. Instead, she chose to ride beside the coach, talking cheerfully to Tilly. He supposed it was right that she should be making an effort to distract the girl from her fears, but nevertheless, he missed her company.

As the morning wore on, it became clear that something was occupying her mind. Even when she abandoned the slow-moving coach and moved up beside him, she seemed preoccupied, responding absently to any conversational sally, so that after a while he gave up.

When the sun was at its zenith, he called a halt. "We'll stop here for a half hour to take some refreshment and rest the horses. There's a mere just over there." He dismounted. "Release the horses from their traces, Willum, and water them." He glanced at Ariadne, who had dismounted, but she moved past him with that same air of distraction, leading Sphinx to the small pond a few yards distant.

"Is something troubling you, Ari?" he asked directly, as they stood side by side, their horses drinking at the mere, where tall marsh willows swayed at the edge, throwing the shapes of their elegant wavery strands onto the still surface.

"Why should anything be troubling me?" She stroked Sphinx's bent neck, gazing absently across the pond, noticing that as her eyes grew accustomed to the vast loneliness of the plain, she was less alarmed by the sense of space.

He gave an involuntary chuckle. "Oh, come now, Ari, you sound just like a woman."

"Why shouldn't I? I am a woman, aren't I?" She was genuinely surprised at his comment.

"Your great appeal, my dear girl, is that you have never put on any of the airs or affectations of your sex," he informed her crisply. "Prevarication doesn't suit you. I know something's troubling you, so what is it? How can I put it right if I don't know?"

This surprised her, too. Did Ivor really think it was his responsibility to put right whatever was disturbing her? He hadn't felt that sense of responsibility in all the years of their growing together. Did he now think he had to be her protector, her guardian in every respect? It was a novel thought, and Ariadne wasn't at all sure that she liked it. She was responsible for herself and always had been.

"It's not your place to put things right, Ivor, not when they don't really have anything to do with you."

He frowned. "I can't help feeling that it is my place, Ari. You are my wife. Husbands protect their wives."

"I'm not your usual kind of wife," she declared.

He laughed with rich enjoyment. "Indeed, you're not, dear girl. And thank the good Lord for that."

Ari grinned reluctantly. "I am just feeling a little out of sorts," she said, before adding deliberately, "And perhaps I'm tired after last night."

At that, he smiled, a long, slow, and utterly sensual smile. He caught her plaits in one hand, bunching them at the nape of her neck so that her face lifted towards him, and he bent and kissed her mouth, a hard, swift kiss of possession. "That is a reason for being out of sorts, my sweet, that I find eminently acceptable," he murmured as he lifted his mouth from hers, releasing his hold on her plaits. "Later I will do what I can to help you recover your usual good humor. But for now, let us go and eat before there's no food left." He gave her braids a playful tug and slung an arm around her shoulders, urging her back to their companions.

FOURTEEN

They rode mostly in silence for the rest of the day. Ivor was watchful, his eyes everywhere, scanning the countryside. They presented an inviting target for brigands and highwaymen, although such groups were less likely to be roaming the open spaces of the Levels. Once they reached the Polden Hills, there would be more possibilities of ambush. There were lawless folk everywhere, and the counties of the West Country were fiercely independent. Smuggling was rife along the extensive coastline, piracy and wrecking common pursuits, and bands of highwaymen lurked in the dark shadows of the hills and across the moors of Devon and Cornwall.

But they reached the lower slopes of the Polden Hills without seeing another soul on the track. "Now we look for a hostelry of some kind." Ivor glanced with some anxiety up at the long shadows thrown by the hills. The horses were tiring now, and the team pulling the heavy coach was breathing heavily as they hauled their burden up the sloping track.

"There should be a farming village close to the base of the hills," Ari suggested. "They farm the Levels in summer, and it would make sense to be relatively close to their fields."

Ivor nodded, wishing he knew more about this landscape. They were out of Daunt territory now, and he had never ventured farther afield than Taunton, which they had left far behind them. He called to the outriders a short way ahead of them, "One of you ride on and see where the next village is."

One of the two raised a hand in acknowledgment and galloped up the narrowing track. "Why don't we go ahead?" Ari asked. "Our horses are faster."

"We don't want to find ourselves attacked without support," Ivor responded shortly. "With the men we have, we can hold off an ambush, but I don't give us much chance with just the two of us . . . however handy you are with that knife," he added with a half smile. He turned to look at her. "Are you tired?"

"A little," she admitted. "But more hungry than anything else. A chicken pasty at noon doesn't last very long."

"Well, I wouldn't hold out too much hope for a decent supper around here," he advised. "There's not enough traffic on this track to encourage lavish hospitality in any hostelry, assuming we find one."

"And if we don't?"

"We'll get permission to bed down in a barn. We've

provisions enough for the horses and for ourselves. Hard rations, certainly, but it will have to do."

Ariadne grimaced. It wasn't an inviting prospect. They pressed on, the path growing steeper as they entered the hills. "Oh, he's coming back," she said suddenly, pointing with her whip at the horseman coming down the track towards them. "What did you find, Jake?"

"An inn of a kind, under the sign of the Fallow Deer," he said as he reached them. "About a mile up. They've a loft for you and Miss Ari, Sir Ivor, and a good barn for the rest of us. They'll sell us hay for the horses, straw to bed down in. Plenty of ale and scrumpy, from their own orchards, and they'll sell us eggs and bread, and if we want to kill a couple of chickens, they're happy enough for us to make a fire in the forge."

"Could be worse," Ivor muttered.

"It's an adventure," Ari said. "Don't sound so gloomy."

He laughed. "Then let's go adventuring, my dear." He turned in his saddle, calling back to the coachman. "About a mile farther, and we'll stop for the night. We'll go on ahead and see you at the sign of the Fallow Deer. Stay with the coach, Jake. Miss Ari and I will go on ahead."

Ari gave a little whoop of pleasure, nudged her weary horse into a canter, and pulled away from the procession.

"Ari, wait for me." Ivor's voice was sharp as he came up to her. "You are *never* to ride ahead of me. Do you understand?"

She frowned at him. "It's only a mile."

"That's as may be, but this is a rule you must always obey. Is that clear?"

She wasn't accustomed to being spoken to in such a tone. Until the world had changed after her grandfather's death, it had been generally assumed that she was her own mistress and able to look after herself. That was certainly the attitude the old Earl had taken, and Ivor had never presumed to question her actions. But there was something in the deep blue eyes that told her she would be wise to accept the injunction. Besides, they were away from familiar territory where she was well-known, so maybe he had a point. She swallowed her moment of irritation and responded with mock humility. "Very well, sir. Anything you say, sir."

He wondered whether to press his point further in the face of her lighthearted response and then decided to leave well enough alone. If she left him behind again, it would be a different matter. But for all her easygoing mischief, Ariadne was no fool. She knew the dangers of this journey as well as anyone.

The inn was little more than a slate-roofed cottage set a little way back from the track. A low stone wall separated it from the path, and the patch of ground before the front door was just scraggly grass and bare earth. The sign of the Fallow Deer swung rather forlornly and somewhat crookedly above the front door. A few outbuildings were clustered close by, and beyond them, a few fields, now shorn of the wheat harvest, showed only turned brown earth. The inn stood on the outskirts of a small hamlet, a mere scattering of cottages with small vegetable plots. Chickens wandered the track among the cottages, scratching in the earth, and one or two dogs roamed at will.

The sun was now very low in the sky, and the shadows were creeping across the ground. A brisk wind had got up, and there was the promise of rain in the heavy gray overhang of cloud. Ivor dismounted and went to the door, which opened just as he reached it. An angular man, a corncob pipe in his mouth, surveyed the riders with an air neither welcoming nor otherwise.

"You the lot wantin' a bed for the night?"

"Beds and supper," Ivor stated, drawing a leather purse from inside his coat. He was not about to waste time with the landlord. "I understand you can provide both."

The man regarded Ivor, eyes suddenly narrowed. "T'other fellow said there was a coach an' horses, an' men."

"They're coming up behind," Ivor said briskly. "I came ahead to make the necessary arrangements." He opened the drawstring neck of the purse and took out a guinea. The gold flashed in the dimness. "You've a loft where my wife and myself can have a bed. We will need supper for the two of us. My men will take care of the horses and their own needs in the barn. I believe you can supply them with whatever's necessary for their comfort and that of the horses, for the right price." He rolled the guinea between his fingers.

The innkeeper's eyes were riveted on the glittering coin. "For another one o' them, sir, they can 'ave whatever they want."

Ivor nodded. "And you can provide a decent meal for my wife and myself?"

"Aye. The wife's a dab hand with a Cornish pasty,

there's a flitch of bacon an' a couple of partridges ready hung. If that'll do you."

"Amply, I thank you." Ivor placed the coin into the man's outstretched hand. "I'll pay the rest of the reckoning when we leave in the morning." He glanced over his shoulder at sounds on the track. "And here, I believe, are the rest of our party." He dismounted, turning to give a hand to Ariadne, but she was already on the ground, loosening Sphinx's girth strap, looping the stirrups up onto the saddle.

At some point, that was another conversation they were going to have to have, Ivor reflected. But while they rode through the wilderness, it was probably best to leave Ari to be self-sufficient, as she knew so well how to be.

A woman appeared in the open doorway, her none-too-clean apron dusted with flour. She nodded at the new arrivals before saying, "Well, if you're comin' inside, best get on wi' it. The rain'll start soon enough." It was a typical country welcome, not much of one at all. Folks in these hinterlands tended to keep themselves to themselves and look with suspicion at strangers.

"Thank you, mistress." Ari took charge, moving past Ivor to greet the woman with a smile. "I'll own we're all very weary after a long day in the saddle." She stepped past the landlady into a taproom, from which a rickety staircase rose in the far corner. It was not unlike her own cottage, except that the taproom floor was matted with clotted sawdust, and the air, reeking of ale and tobacco, was thick enough to coat a spoon. A long, stained slab of pine served as a bar counter, a wooden settle stood to one side of the fireplace, where a fire smoldered rather than blazed, and a few scattered stools provided the rest of the seating. *Cheerless* was the word, Ari thought, but at least it was shelter, and there was a strong sense of a storm brewing. The wind banged the open shutters against the outside walls.

"Tilly needs to be in here with us," she said softly to Ivor, who had stepped in after her.

"Of course," he agreed instantly. "Forgive me for not thinking of it earlier." He turned to the woman, who stood now at the bar counter, wiping ineffectually at the stains with her apron. "My wife's maid will need accommodation within, mistress. And she will sup with us."

"Lor', Miss Ari, 'tis beginning to rain." Tilly's voice came opportunely from the door to the taproom. She stood swathed in her many garments, looking around the room with some disfavor. "Looks like a proper storm is brewing." She spied the landlady at her dusting and stepped in. "If you've the makings for a punch bowl, mistress, Sir Ivor and Miss Ari would be glad of it, I'm sure. Show me where to find it, and I'll have it ready in no time. An' if you'd like a bit of help with supper, I'd be glad to give a hand. 'Tis hard, I know, to have folk drop by when you're not prepared for 'em."

The landlady looked at Tilly closely and instantly recognized her for what she was, a West Country lass with the same broad Somerset dialect of her own speech. "I'll not say no to a bit of help," she said. "Kitchen's this way."

Tilly discarded her cloak over a stool and unfastened the sheepskin jacket. "Keep an eye on these, Miss Ari," she instructed, dropping the jacket over the cloak. "Rob you blind soon as look at you, I wouldn't be surprised."

"She may have a point," Ivor said with a chuckle. "But at least in Tilly's hands, we'll have an edible supper."

"Yes, let's go and look at this loft." Ari started for the stairs. She climbed up into a sleeping loft similar to her own. It was very sparsely furnished. A straw mattress on a rough bedstead and little else. "Where's Tilly to sleep?"

Ivor came up behind her and looked around. "You and she take the bed. I'll get some straw and bed down on the floor."

Ari stared at him. "I don't think that will be in the least satisfactory, *husband*."

He shook his head, half laughing. "My dear, a night of unbridled passion in a wayside loft is hardly practicable."

"Maybe not. But I intend to have it, nevertheless," she said with the stubborn lift of her chin that he knew so well. "We will make a bed for Tilly downstairs on the settle in the taproom, near the fire. She will be perfectly content."

"We'll talk about that later." Ivor unfastened his cloak and turned his attention to the fireplace, where a few bits of kindling lay on a bed of old embers. "Wonder when they last lit a fire in here." He picked up the poker and stuck it up the chimney, rattling it against the sides. "Well, that's something . . . no birds' nests, at least." He disappeared down the stairs, and Ari heard him giving brisk instructions.

She unfastened her own cloak and went to the small round window under the eaves. The sky was a purple-black color, and the trees were beginning to sway as the wind blew strong, gathering speed as it came from the distant sea across the flat plain of the Levels. There was no sign of moonrise and not a glimpse of the evening star.

She *did* want a night of lovemaking with her husband. The memories of the previous night were fading, and she needed to repaint them. Somehow she had to work through this confusing tangle of feelings. Why was it possible to feel such needful lust for one man when the memories of what she believed to be an eternal love and passion for another were still so bright? Perhaps last night had not been as wonderful as she remembered. Maybe her relief that the obstacle of consummation was overcome without any of the discomfort or downright repulsion that she had expected had colored the experience. But Ariadne didn't think it was that . . . not in her heart of hearts.

Footsteps clattered on the stairs, and a young boy of about ten came in bearing a basket of wood on his back. "The gennelman says I'm to light the fire, mistress."

"Thank you." Ari pulled back the covers on the bed. The straw mattress was lumpy and probably jumping with fleas. She went to the staircase and called down for Tilly, who came to the bottom of the stairs.

"Yes, Miss Ari . . . punch is almost ready."

"We brought some of that extra-thick coarse sheeting, didn't we?"

"Oh, aye." Tilly came up the stairs and examined the straw with a wrinkled nose. "Fleas and lice, too, I'll be bound. The sheeting's in one of the bags in the coach. I told 'em to pack it on top of the rest so we could get at it easily." She retreated downstairs again.

"What on earth are you doing?" Ivor reappeared on the stairs. "The punch is ready."

"But the bed isn't," she said succinctly. "Not unless you want to wake up covered in flea bites."

"It's a hazard of travel," he observed. "What are you doing about it?"

"Tilly's gone to fetch the sheeting. It's thick and coarse enough to stop them getting through." Smoke billowed into the chamber from the newly lit fire, and she coughed. "We could always smoke 'em out, I suppose."

"Well, leave that to Tilly, and come down and drink your punch."

Ariadne complied, eager to escape the still-billowing smoke. The outside door opened on a violent gust of wind as Tilly struggled in, her arms so full she could barely see over the top of her burden. Ivor leapt forward, yanking the door open as the girl fought her way into the taproom. "Lor', that's some storm a-brewin'. The horses are mighty restless."

She set her burden on a stool and felt in her apron pocket, taking out a small muslin bag. "I'll sprinkle this first, then we'll put down the sheets, an' then we'll sprinkle some more. Should do the trick." She was still talking as she went back upstairs.

Ivor was stirring a punch bowl over a trivet in the hearth. "What is she talking about?"

"Oh, a mixture, garlic, cloves, mint, basil, I think, and some other things no one else knows about that keep fleas away." Ari came to sit on a stool by the fire. "Tilly has remedies for everything. Her mother was a renowned herbalist and taught Tilly all she knew."

"Useful," Ivor said, ladling the pungent, steaming liquid from the bowl into a tarnished pewter cup. "Try that."

Ari took a sip, and the heady mixture of rum, brandy, hot water, and butter, with a liberal dash of nutmeg and cloves, seemed to invigorate her tired limbs. "Oh, that is good." She listened to the rushing sound of the wind, the rattling of the shutters now closed against the battering. "Will they be all right in that barn?"

"It's sturdy enough. Besides, they've all known worse weather," Ivor responded, sipping from his own tankard.

Tilly came back downstairs for the sheets, and Ari rose to help her. "No need, Miss Ari." Tilly waved her away.

"Nonsense. It'll be quicker with the two of us." Ari grabbed the pile and headed up to the loft. "I'm sure Tilly would be glad of a cup of that punch, Ivor, when we're finished."

Ignoring Tilly's objections, she helped her sprinkle some of the herb mixture onto the straw and then smother the whole with the thick, coarse linen. More of the herb mixture went over the sheets, and then Tilly shook out the blankets and covers and threw them back onto the bed. Ari wondered whether she and Ivor would be sprouting sprigs of basil and mint in the morning, but at least they wouldn't be covered in itchy lumps.

"You'll sleep on the settle below, Tilly," she said.

"Lord, Miss Ari, there'll be men drinkin' at the bar, like as not."

"No, you'll be quite undisturbed." Ari laughed. "Sir Ivor has paid for the inn for the night, just for us. It won't be open for anyone else . . . not," she added, "that there'll be many out in this storm looking for a pint of ale. Let's see what we can do about supper." She went down to the taproom and found it empty. Ivor's cloak was no longer on the stool, so he must have gone out.

The punch bowl still sat on the trivet, and she refilled her own tankard and filled another for Tilly, who took it and drank it down in one long gulp. "Thank you, miss. I'll go an' help out with supper now. Her pastry looks light enough, but there's no knowing what she'll be doin' with those pheasants."

Ariadne sat down by the fire, stretching her booted feet to the andirons, listening to the roaring wind. However primitive their accommodations, they were a lot pleasanter than a night outdoors in the storm.

The door opened and slammed as Ivor came in, shaking water from his hat and cloak. "The horses are bedded down snug enough. Sphinx isn't too happy, but he's safe. The men have a keg of scrumpy, so they have no complaints." He draped his wet cloak over a stool close to the fire, where it steamed gently. "By the way, the outhouse is foul, way at the back of the kitchen garden. If you've any sense you'll use a chamber pot tonight."

Ari grimaced but made no objection. Privacy was a lost cause on a journey such as this.

Their host came in from the back and set two crusted bottles on the bar counter. "These do ye? You said wine with your supper."

Ivor took up one of the bottles and examined the color in the lamplight. "Let's try it." He poured a small quantity into a cup and sipped. "Good . . . very good," he pronounced. "You've obviously got a good supplier, Master Danton."

The landlord looked as pleased as he was capable of doing. "Aye, our band look after us well enough."

The landlady, her cheeks flushed from the range, emerged from the kitchen with a tureen. "Cabbage soup," she declared, setting it down on the counter. "That girl of yours is takin' some out to the barn. I told her the wind'd knock her off her feet . . . took no notice." Muttering, she fetched two bowls from a dresser beside the fireplace, thumped them onto the table with a pair of spoons, and returned to her domain.

"Tilly's carrying a tureen of soup to the men?" Ivor asked in astonishment. "In this weather . . . what the hell's the girl thinking of?"

"Other people who've been on the road as long as we have and are probably chilled to the bone," Ari retorted, her tone a little tart. She took her bowl back to her stool by the fire. "She'll probably eat with them herself."

Ivor frowned but accepted the reproof. "The lad could have taken it, if she'd said."

"You don't know Tilly very well, do you?" Ari observed, sipping her soup hungrily. "This is very good, but of course, it has Tilly's magic touch."

"Indeed," he agreed with a dry smile. "I shall go in search of bread." He ventured into the kitchen regions and came back triumphant with a loaf of oat bread. He set it down on a stool between them.

It was Tilly who brought in a pheasant stew and a Cornish pasty. "Here you are, then. All's well in the barn. Sphinx has settled now, Miss Ari, thought you'd like to know. The men are snug, but Jake wants to know if you want one of 'em to stand guard, Sir Ivor."

Ivor considered. The wind howled, the rain beat against the shutters. No one in their right mind would stage an attack on a night like this. And in truth, he didn't have the heart to instruct one of his exhausted retinue to stand watch throughout the night. Not in the light of Ari's sharpness on the subject of Tilly and the welfare of his men.

"I'll go out and see them when I've finished supper, Tilly. You eat yours now. Come to the fire."

"No, sir, I'll be havin' mine in the kitchen with Mistress Danton and her man."

"If you're sure," Ari said. "But you'll make up a bed in here on the settle."

"Aye, that'll be fine, miss. When you're ready to go to bed, just call me, and I'll bring some water up." Tilly bustled off, her numerous petticoats rustling around her.

Ari yawned deeply as she dipped a crust into the last mouthful of pheasant stew. Punch followed by several glasses of a very fine burgundy, combined with a bellyful of cabbage soup and rich, gamey stew, was sending her to sleep on her stool.

"Go on up to bed," Ivor said. "I'm just going to talk to

Jake." He paused by her stool and lightly passed a hand over her black curls. "I'll be up shortly to chase away the fleas."

"Don't be long." She gathered up the plates and carried them into the kitchen as Ivor went out into the storm.

"I would have fetched 'em, Miss Ari," Tilly protested as she came into the kitchen. Tilly was sitting comfortably by the fire with the landlord and his wife. Both Master and Mistress Danton were contentedly smoking corncob pipes.

"No trouble, Tilly. I'm going to bed now."

"I'll bring some hot water up for you. Kettle's just boiled. You'll be glad to wash the dirt of the road off you, I reckon."

"Thank you. I bid you good night, Mistress Danton . . . Master Danton."

They nodded in return, and Ari took an oil lamp and went up to the loft. The fire still burned, and she put more wood on it before taking her night shift from the cloak bag. The green glass vial was tucked in the folds, and she swallowed what she assumed was a spoonful and put it away again. Tilly came up with a jug of hot water and a warming pan as she was taking off her clothes.

"Anything else, Miss Ari?" Tilly set the jug on the rickety dresser and went to insert the pan of hot coals beneath the covers.

Ari shook her head. "No, I can manage, thank you, Tilly. Sir Ivor has gone to the barn. He'll be back shortly." She stepped out of her petticoats and unlaced her chemise. "You don't think the warming pan will encourage the fleas?"

"Lord, no, miss. They'd never chew their way through those sheets, even if they had a liking for basil and cloves and such," Tilly responded comfortably. "I'll say good night, then." She went away, bearing the warming pan.

"Good night, Tilly." Ari dropped her night shift over her head and hitched the chamber pot out from beneath the bed. She used it quickly, thrust it back into the accumulation of dust, and slipped into bed. It was warm, and despite the coarseness of the sheets and the lumpiness of the mattress, it felt like heaven to her weary body.

She was asleep before Ivor came up to the loft. He stood for a moment looking down at her curled figure, her head cradled on her palm, her long black lashes fanned against her pale cheeks. So much for a night of riotous passion, he thought with a smile, stripping off his clothes, draping them over a stool in front of the fire in the hope that they would dry before sunup. Assuming the sun would show itself after this storm.

He climbed into bed, sliding an arm beneath Ari's sleeping form and rolling her against him, before his own eyes closed.

FIFTEEN

A door from the kitchen below opened and closed with a bang as the wind snatched it from the hand that opened it. Ivor stirred, his eyes fluttering. Someone visiting the outhouse? Silence fell again. He slipped back into sleep.

The innkeeper moved down the path through the vegetable garden, a dark shadow among the darker shadows. The rain came down in sheets, and he shielded his flickering lantern light within the fold of his cloak. Behind him the cottage was in darkness. Tilly slept soundly on the settle wrapped in her sheepskin jacket and thick cloak. The innkeeper's lad dozed by the fire in the range, and his wife lay wide awake under the greasy coverlet of the bed in the alcove beside the bread oven. Waiting.

Ari didn't know what had awoken her, but she lay in the darkness for a few minutes listening to the silence of the house around her and Ivor's deep regular breathing, feeling the warmth of his naked body through the thin muslin of her night shift. Tentatively, she reached out a hand and let it rest on his belly. His breathing continued undisturbed. She let her hand slide farther down, her fingers slipping through the wiry tangle of hair at the base of his belly. She felt the soft flesh of his penis nestled between his thighs. Her fingertips moved over it, and it twitched a little. Ari smiled, an idea occurring to her as she remembered the previous night. If he could give her so much pleasure with his mouth, then maybe she could return the favor.

She slid down the bed, pulling the covers over her head, inhaling the warm, humid scent of his skin as she moved down his body. The even rhythm of his breathing continued undisturbed. She lifted his penis, and it twitched again. Then, as she enclosed it in her palm, she felt it thicken and harden. With a deft wriggle, she moved far enough down so that she could take the corded shaft of flesh into her mouth.

She could taste salt on her tongue, like seaweed, and instinctively, she grazed her teeth along the length of his penis, delicately touching the tip with her tongue, tasting the drop of moisture there. She could feel now that his whole body was awake, even as his sex quivered against her lips. She felt his hands curling into her hair, his fingers tracing the whorls of her ears under the covers. He seemed to grow even harder and thicker in her mouth, and she slid her hands beneath him to cup the hard round sacs.

Ivor groaned as the pleasure awakened his body, set his skin singing. Ariadne emerged laughing, pink-cheeked, from the covers. "Am I doing it right?"

"You know damn well you are," he said, pulling her up roughly with his hands under her armpits until she was lying on top of him. He hauled the hem of her shift up to her waist and ran his hands over her bottom and the tops of her thighs. "Where did you learn to do that?"

"You taught me." She laughed, lying along his length, propping herself on her elbows on either side of his body. "I think I'm an apt pupil."

"More than apt," he said, smiling, his hands still resting on her backside. "Lift your hips a little, and draw your knees up."

She obeyed with alacrity and then bit her lip with sudden surprise as he twisted his hips and entered her from below in one smooth movement. "It feels different," she said.

"There are many different ways to enjoy this particular activity," he said, watching her face in the faint light from the fire's embers as he moved his hips upwards. "Use your body to find the position that pleases you most. You're in control of your own movements now. I'll follow your lead."

It was a heady thought, but as she experimented, circling the hardness within her, first one way, then the other, feeling how the sensation changed, grew more intense, she closed her eyes, letting the feeling grow until she sensed the chasm opening beneath her, and her body tightened in anticipation, and when she fell, it was as if she'd broken apart in a million pieces.

She fell heavily onto his chest, and Ivor stroked her back, his hand pushing up beneath her shift, his other hand twisting in the unruly tumble of black curls falling onto his shoulder. He had no idea what time it was, but the fire in the grate still smoldered, and the wind still howled and rattled the ill-fitting window shutter.

And then there was the first shout of alarm, and he caught a flicker of flame through the cracks in the shutter, the faint smell of smoke growing stronger.

He swore a barnyard oath and pushed Ari off him as he leapt to his feet. She lay shocked out of her afterglow, wondering what on earth had happened, and then she smelled the smoke, heard the shouts. "What's going on?" She struggled up.

Ivor already had his shirt on and was tugging on his britches and his boots. "Attack," he said curtly, buckling his belt. He grabbed his sword and took up the two flintlock pistols he had placed beside by the bed earlier, thrusting them into his belt. "Stay here. If you value your hide, Ariadne, *don't move*." And he was gone, his boots clattering on the stairs.

Ari tugged on the leather britches she wore beneath her riding skirt and tucked her chemise into the waist, then thrust her feet into her boots. She pulled on her riding jacket; the skirt was surplus to present requirements. Her knife went into the waistband of her britches, and she half tumbled down the stairs in her haste.

Tilly was standing wide-eyed in the middle of the room. "What's happening, Miss Ari? Is it an ambush?"

"Something of the sort." Ari yanked open the door.

"Stay here, put water on to boil, and see if you can find anything to serve as bandages, in case anyone gets hurt." Judging by the noise that greeted her, the latter was inevitable, she reflected grimly. The mayhem was in the yard in front of the barn. She could hear the high-pitched whinnying and stamping hooves of the terrified horses as the smoke filled the air.

She ran around the cottage and paused at the entrance to the barnyard, taking stock. It was hard in the smoky, flickering light of the fire to distinguish one man from another, but as far as she could see, the six Daunt men were hard pressed, fighting back a group of about ten. She saw Ivor, his sword slashing as two men attacked him from either side. Other shadowy figures were hauling trunks out of the burning barn, the trunks that contained all the wealth that was to set them up at court. The jewel casket was safely under the bed; Ivor had stowed it away as soon as they'd arrived. But the rest of it, the rich materials, the provisions, the silver chalices and gold-rimmed platters that were to furnish a home fit for a wealthy noble couple in London, were all stacked in the barn.

Someone had betrayed them. Ari hesitated, then made up her mind. The screaming horses were defenseless, Ivor was not, and possessions were not irreplaceable. She raced for the barn, hauling on the double doors as smoke billowed out at her. Coughing, covering her mouth and nose with her arm, she ran bent double into the smoke, flinging back stall doors, leaping to one side as panicked horses stampeded for the outdoors. They would scatter far and wide in their terror, but they could be rounded up later.

She ran for the pump in the middle of the yard and filled a bucket. Darting around the battleground, she hurled the bucket of water at the nearest brigand, who was hauling one of the trunks to a wagon waiting at the entrance to the yard. The man yelped as the icy water hit him. Dripping, he spun around, but Ari had ducked out of sight beneath the belly of the horse in the traces. Deftly, she released the cart horse from the traces and gave him a sharp slap on the flank. The smoke and noise had spooked him sufficiently to kick up his heels and make his own escape.

Ari grinned. Without a horse, they couldn't get away with their treasure. She looked around to see where else she could usefully enter the fray. Her breath stopped in her throat as she saw that Ivor had been driven against the fence, his two attackers pressing him hard, swords in hand. The sound of a shot from a flintlock pistol spun her around on her toes. Jake had fired, and one of the enemy was on one knee, clutching his chest, before he slowly crumpled to the hard-packed earth. She looked back at Ivor. The loud report had had no effect on his assailants. His sword flashed from side to side, but she could see he couldn't get at his own pistol with both men pressing him against the fence.

She took her knife from her waistband, her breath very still now, forcing her mind to focus, to close off the sounds around her, the sights, the smells, concentrating only on the target she had chosen. She held the knife lightly between forefinger and thumb, drawing back her arm, her eyes fixed on the point between her quarry's shoulder blades. Then she threw. The blade left her fingers, flew through the smoke, and buried itself deep into the man's back.

He gave a cry of surprise and pitched forward. His companion, startled, took a step back, and in the same instant, Ivor's sword took him under the arm, and he fell to the ground.

Ivor looked across the chaotic scene. He saw Ari standing still a few feet away, her knife hand held loosely at her shoulder. And then she ran forward, bending to retrieve her weapon. Where next? Her eyes raked the yard, but Ivor had already plunged back into the fray, his bloodied sword slashing.

Ari looked down at the bodies at her feet. They were not dead, she decided, but they were certainly *hors de combat*, and as her eyes made sense of the chaos against the background of the dancing flames, she could see that the Daunt men were prevailing. It was their business, after all, robbing and ambushing, setting fire to barns, creating bloody mayhem in their wake. They were the best in the business, she thought with a sardonic twist of her lips. Only fool amateurs would attempt to take them on.

It was all over in the next few minutes, the would-be brigands on the ground, clutching their wounds. "Secure them, and leave them against the fence," Ivor instructed as he assessed the damage. "Who else is hurt?"

"Just a scratch, sir," the coachman said, tearing off

a piece of his shirt with his teeth to fashion a bandage around his bleeding arm. "And Jake there got his shoulder out of joint."

"Tilly's inside waiting," Ariadne said. "She'll put your shoulder back, Jake, and she'll have bandages and poultices and whatever."

"Where are the horses?" Ivor looked around, frowning.

"I let them loose. We'll have to round them up when it's light," Ari told him.

He looked at her as if he were seeing her for the first time. Anger glowed in his deep blue eyes. "Get inside," he instructed sharply.

It was an odd tone to use to someone who'd just saved his life, she thought, but she was going inside anyway, so she wiped her knife blade on a piece of straw and made her way back to the cottage.

Tilly was in the taproom tearing an old sheet into strips. Her little bag of herbs was on the counter together with a jug of steaming hot water. "How bad?" she asked, glancing up as Ari came in.

"Our own men? Nothing too much. Jake's put his shoulder out, and Abe has a cut on his arm. There may be other minor wounds, but everyone's on their feet . . . at least, our men." She went to the fire and piled on more logs. "It'll be dawn soon. Where's our genial host and his lady?"

Tilly shook her head. "Haven't seen 'em. Once the shouting started and the fire, the lad went off running like the devil was on his heels. There's not a soul in the kitchen."

"Wise of them to beat a retreat," Ari observed. "I wouldn't give much for their chances if our lot got hold of them. At least the rain stopped the fire from taking too quickly."

The door opened on a wet gust, and the Daunt men came in in a group, wet, muddy, and bleeding. "Jake, you first," Ari called, seeing the man's ashen face as he cradled his limp arm against his chest. "Tilly, can you put it back for him?"

"Sit you down there, now," Tilly instructed, pointing to a stool. She moved behind him, her hands feeling his shoulder socket. He bit his lip hard to stifle a cry of pain at the probing. "Hold still." There was something about Tilly's calm manner that instilled confidence. She gave a pull and a push, and Jake yelled and then breathed a deep sigh of relief.

"Eh, lass, I reckon you've done it." He put his hand tentatively up to his shoulder, moving it slightly in the joint. "Aye. Feels good."

"Let me strap it." Tilly fashioned a sling from some of the old sheeting she'd been tearing for bandages. "Reckon a tot of brandy'll set you up fine now." She looked around. "Who's next?"

Ivor was filling cups liberally from the innkeeper's brandy cask, handing them around to his men as they waited for Tilly's ministrations. He said nothing to Ariadne, although he passed her a cup with the rest.

"Are you hurt?" she asked as she took it.

He shook his head. "Nothing that won't heal in the

fullness of time." He looked at her, that same anger glowing in the blue depths of his eyes.

"What's the matter?" Ari asked directly.

"Are you hurt under all that soot and filth?" he asked instead of answering her.

"No. And what's a little soot? It'll wash off." Soot didn't seem an adequate explanation for his anger. She left him and went to the counter, dipping a cloth into the hot water to wash her face. The cloth came away black as pitch. She must look like a chimney sweep. She poured water into a bowl and carried it up to the loft. There seemed nothing further for her to do in the taproom, and Ivor was issuing orders for guarding the trunks and rounding up the horses as soon as dawn broke.

She was weary, Ari realized, now that the excitement was over. It seemed an age since she had woken and started that blissful interlude between the sheets. An interlude so brutally shattered. She shrugged out of her jacket and slowly eased off her boots and britches, shaking down her night shift.

Ivor's steps sounded on the stairs as the shift fell to her ankles. She turned to greet him with a tired smile, which died as she saw his expression in the light of the candle he held.

"I told you to stay here," he declared, setting the candle on the mantel. "Just what in *hell* did you think you were doing?"

Ari felt her own temper rise as the events of the night took their toll. "Setting the horses free of a burning barn, saving our possessions, saving your life, as I recall. Did I do something wrong?" Her voice was as sharp as an ice pick as she faced him, a sparrow to his falcon.

Ivor pressed finger and thumb into his eyes in a gesture of utter weariness. "I told you to stay here," he repeated.

"Did you? I didn't hear," she responded. "And on the whole, I'm glad I didn't. You might not be here if I had."

His expression lightened slowly. He shook his head, and there was now a glint of amusement to replace the earlier anger in his eyes. "You really won't ever be an obedient wife, will you, Ariadne?"

She gave him a look of astonishment. "No, of course not. Whatever made you think I might be?"

"Oh, I don't know," he returned, shaking his head. "A moment of lunacy, probably . . . or perhaps a little wishful thinking."

"Not something to be indulged too often," Ariadne stated. "Do we have time to go back to bed before dawn?"

He looked at her a little warily. "If you've sleep in mind, then, yes."

"What else?" she asked with an innocent smile. "I'm exhausted." She fell back on the straw mattress, opening the top sheet in invitation. "Sleep, Ivor."

He pulled off his boots, blew out the candle, and climbed fully dressed into bed beside her.

"Where are the innkeeper and his wife, do you think?" Ari asked, turning into the curve of his arm.

"I have no idea and not the slightest interest," he responded. "Any more than I care two farthings for those brigands outside in the rain."

"But we'll have to do something with them," Ari murmured. "We can't leave them tied up in the rain forever."

"Go to sleep . . . unless you want to go and join them." His arm tightened around her, and she could feel his smile as she slipped into an exhausted sleep.

SIXTEEN

Ariadne awoke in broad daylight. The storm had passed, leaving a clean-washed pale sky and sodden ground. Ivor was gone from the bed, and she could hear raised voices through the ill-fitting window. Pushing aside the covers, she staggered to her feet, aware of every muscle in her body. She went to the window, throwing open the shutters. Below was a scene of ordered busyness. A miserable-looking group of would-be brigands was huddled on the wet grass while Tilly moved among them tending brusquely to their wounds. Two Daunt men stood guard with an air of indifference.

She could see no sign of Ivor and none at all of the owners of the Fallow Deer. She dressed rapidly and went downstairs. The taproom was deserted, although the fire burned brightly enough. She stuck her head into the kitchen. No one there, either, but again, the fire in the range was hot and bright, and a kettle of water steamed. She realized she was ravenous, but there was a conspicuous absence of breakfast, not even a loaf of bread.

Ari went back through the taproom and outside. "Can I help, Tilly?"

Tilly, in the process of attaching a poultice of what looked like rotting moss to the bleeding thigh of one of their assailants, shook her head. "No, thanks, Miss Ari. But they're having trouble with the horses, and Jake's shoulder's too sore to do much. Sphinx is still spooked."

"I'll go and see what I can do." Ari vaulted the low wall that separated the patch of front yard from the rear. Ivor was leading Turk into the yard. The big black reared at the lingering smell of smoke from the barn.

"What can I do?" Ari asked, laying a soothing hand on the horse's withers. "Have you seen Sphinx?"

"He's about a hundred yards distant, and keeping his distance," Ivor responded. "I don't think anyone will be able to do anything with him except you. There's a rope halter on the water butt over there. Oh, and there are some bruised windfalls in a basket behind the barn."

Ari fetched the halter and found the apples. She took two, dropping them into the pocket of her jacket. "Where are the rest of the horses?"

"Coming in slowly. We managed to salvage enough bran for a decent mash, and Jake's mixing it with his one good arm. Abe's cut is deep, but he can hammer a nail, so he's helping to make a corral out back for them. It'll hold 'em overnight."

"So we're to stay here all day?"

"Licking our wounds," Ivor agreed. "We've lost our

212 ← JANE FEATHER

host and hostess, but there are sufficient provisions for us to have a decent meal, and after a night's rest, we'll start off at daybreak tomorrow."

"You don't expect another ambush?"

His laugh was sardonic. "Unlikely, dear girl. I think the lesson's been learned."

Ari nodded and left him, going in search of Sphinx. She saw him, as Ivor had said, standing warily a few hundred feet from the inn. The village felt completely empty, as if all its inhabitants had been driven off by a long ship of Viking raiders. Either that, or they were cowering behind locked doors.

Ari approached the horse slowly, talking softly to him, the halter concealed behind her back. He could lead her a merry dance through the hills if he chose to be difficult, but she knew he was hungry and scared and in need of familiarity.

"Here, boy." She held out an apple on her flat palm. "It's quite safe now." He let her approach within a few feet, and then he tossed his head and retreated a few yards, still watching her warily, his eyes rolling.

Ari sighed. It could be a long morning, and she was very hungry. She took a bite out of the bruised windfall and watched her horse, who watched her back. "It's good," she said, holding it out on her palm again. This time, Sphinx approached with a dancing step, head high on his arched neck. He came close enough to snatch the apple from her hand and then retreated, but this time not so far.

Ari took a bite out of the second apple, watching him

now out of the corner of her eye. Then she turned and walked casually back towards the yard, whistling softly to herself. She could sense Sphinx move behind her, tentative steps in her wake, and she nodded in silent satisfaction. He was following her home to safety, and soon she would be able to slip the halter over his head.

✦ ✦ ✦

Ivor had Turk secured in the corral by the time Ari and her horse came into the yard. "What are you intending to do with those vermin from last night?" Ari inquired, releasing Sphinx into the enclosure.

"Send them on their way, once Tilly has patched them up. They're no use to us, and I don't think we need to involve what passes for the law in these parts, do you?" He bit into a windfall, leaning back against the rough railing of the corral.

"No," she agreed. "Can I have a bite? Sphinx ate all mine."

Amiably, Ivor held out the apple, and she took a bite, spitting a pip to the ground at her feet. "Are we safe here for the day?"

"Why not? We didn't break the law . . . we didn't attack innocent travelers in their beds. No one knows who we are."

"I doubt that's true," Ari said, leaning in for another bite. "When the Daunts leave the valley, the whole countryside knows. Although," she added thoughtfully, "maybe the news didn't reach this far across the Levels."

"Probably not." Ivor tossed the apple core into the

enclosure. "Otherwise, I doubt we'd have been attacked. We're finished here for the moment, and I'm famished. Let's see if anyone's getting breakfast."

"Tilly's still busy with the wounded."

"Well, you're not unversed in kitchen arts, are you, ma'am?" he asked with a mockingly raised eyebrow.

"No," Ari conceded. "But Tilly is better at feeding the five thousand."

"We are hardly that." He ushered her ahead of him back to the cottage. Tilly was still bandaging and applying poultices, and Ariadne accepted that cooking breakfast for their small band had fallen to her hand.

It was a strange day. It felt for the most part as if they were the only people on earth; not another soul appeared in the village, and the innkeeper and his wife had vanished into the ether. There were provisions aplenty, ample supplies of wine, beer, and brandy, and an impromptu holiday atmosphere invaded the group. Their enemies dispersed as well as they could, carrying off those who could not walk under their own steam. The village remained deserted, and the Fallow Deer became a campsite for a party of travelers taking respite from their journey.

Ivor was prepared to let them rest, the horses in particular. They would perform better if they'd been given time to recover from the shocks of the precious night. But he was still anxious to be on the road again. They had many miles to cover before the bad weather set in.

It was early evening when the sounds of a scuffle came from the backyard. Ivor was on his feet immediately, a half-eaten chicken drumstick in his hand. Abe came in, hauling the inn's lad by his shirt collar. "Found this one lurking behind the barn." He pushed the boy into room.

Ariadne looked closely at the pale, shivering child. "He's hungry and scared, Ivor." She pulled a thigh from the roast chicken and held it out to him. "It's all right, no one's going to hurt you."

The boy took it tentatively, his gaze never leaving Ivor, who stood looking down at him, frowning. "Where are your master and mistress?" Ivor demanded.

The lad shook his head, biting into the flesh of the chicken. "Don't know, sir. I swear, sir, I didn't know they was goin' to tell 'em you was here. They never told me nothin', sir. I swear it."

Ivor set down his drumstick. "Who are *them*?"

"Baxter's folk, sir. When rich folks stay at the inn, master lets 'em know." The boy wiped his greasy mouth with the back of his hand and looked hungrily at the carcass on the table.

"I see." Ivor picked up his drumstick and took another bite. "And who did your master say was here?"

The lad shook his head vigorously. "Don't rightly know, sir. Don't think master or missus knows, neither. Just as how there's trunks and packages and good horses and whatnot . . . so bound to be some good pickin's, like."

"And do *you* know who we are?" Ariadne asked, slicing into a loaf of bread, offering the boy a piece on the point of the knife.

He shook his head, eyes wide, before hesitantly taking the bread from the knife. But there was something in his look that alerted Ari. She moved quickly, the bread knife touching the boy's throat. "Come now," she said persuasively. "You do know, don't you?"

The lad looked terrified once again. He swallowed against the tip of the knife and said, "Reckon you be Daunt, ma'am."

Ari nodded and withdrew the knife, using it to slice another piece from the loaf. "Are you sure your master and mistress didn't know that?"

He gave a vigorous nod. "Oh, aye, ma'am. If they'd 'ave known, they'd never 'ave tried to take you."

Ari nodded and glanced at Ivor, who merely shrugged and said to Abe, "We'll keep him here until we leave in the morning. Feed him and keep a watch over him." He drained his ale tankard. "I'm for my bed. We leave at daybreak. Ariadne . . ." He put an arm around her shoulders and directed her to the stairs.

Ari offered no resistance. The bed was still a tumbled mass of covers from the morning's emergency departure. She started to straighten them, but Ivor, pulling off his boots against the boot jack, said, "Just get into it, Ari. We're both exhausted, and this God damned journey has only just begun. We must be up before daybreak."

Ari looked at him with a ruefully raised eyebrow. "May we not play a little?"

"*No, we may not*," he declared, half laughing despite his preoccupation with the day's events. "Take your clothes off and get under the covers."

"Whatever you say, sir." Ariadne removed her clothes, garment by garment, watching him from beneath heavy-lidded eyes. He was trying to ignore her but not very successfully, she noted with satisfaction as she tossed her shift onto the chest with the rest of her clothes and stood for a moment naked in the candlelight beside the bed.

His body was aroused, and he turned abruptly from the bed. "Get in, Ariadne, *now.*"

She twitched aside the covers and put one knee on the bed, looking at him over her shoulder, her gray eyes sparkling with mischief. "Are you sure we couldn't help each other to go to sleep? We don't have to be too energetic."

Ivor was aware of confusion. Ariadne, who had told him that she could only love Gabriel Fawcett, was the hungriest, most inventive of lovers a man could wish for. What was it about her that enabled her to separate that *in love* feeling for simple sexual satisfaction with another man?

"No, we don't," he agreed, feeling his erection gently dying. "But tell me, Ari, do you still love Gabriel Fawcett?"

It was a bath of icy water. Ari had been trying so hard to steer a path through the tangle, and it had seemed to her that the only way to do that was to try to put the past behind her. Now Ivor was forcing the issue. She climbed into bed, pulling the covers up to her chin. She said slowly, "Yes, I do love Gabriel but not in the same way I love you, Ivor. You're my dearest friend, and I love you with friendship, but I also love to make love with you." Her voice quivered a little, and she stared fixedly at the ceiling. "It seems like I'm betraying both of you, and yet I don't know what else to do. Gabriel is gone from my life, and you are in it. What am I supposed to do, Ivor?" The question came out as an almost desperate plea, and she turned her head slightly on the pillow, her gray eyes huge and shadowed against her pale countenance.

"I don't know." He blew out the candle and climbed into bed beside her. "I only know that sometimes I feel that I'm playing second fiddle. I don't know which of your responses I can trust anymore."

"You didn't feel that this morning," she said, lying still, feeling cold and adrift.

"No, but I wasn't thinking this morning. My body wants you, Ari, but my mind tells me to be careful. If you love this man as deeply as you say, then whatever we do in the ways of love cannot *mean* anything . . . anything that really matters. You are my wife. I want my wife's loyalty and love. And when I'm reminded that I don't have it, then I feel that the act of love is merely going through the motions."

"As if you were in the whorehouse, you mean?" It was a bitter question, an attempt to protect herself from the hurt he was inflicting.

Ivor said nothing for a long moment, in which Ari regretted she had ever let her tongue speak those words. Finally, he said, "Shall we agree that you didn't say that, Ariadne?"

"Yes, please," she said softly, rolling onto her side facing away from him. But was it still the truth? Did she simply enjoy lovemaking with Ivor for the sake of it, for the pleasure it brought her? Did Ivor enjoy the act simply for the ephemeral pleasure it brought him? Were they just so good together in the ways of love that she could forget Gabriel?

No. It couldn't be possible. The pleasure she took with Gabriel was so different. It was poetic. They talked all the time, and in his company she saw the world differently. She saw colors differently; they were brighter, more vivid. The world even smelled different.

With Ivor, it was a hard, defined world, the lines clear, black, white, gray. There were truths and realities in her world with Ivor, dreams and promises in Gabriel's landscapes. And truth and reality were the cards she had been dealt.

And somewhere in the back of her mind glimmered the thought that Ivor's world was and always had been hers. The pastel, fuzzy-edged world of loving Gabriel was such a new experience it had entranced her, offered her a glimpse of a fairy tale.

SEVENTEEN

Gabriel Fawcett was exhausted, swaying in his saddle, as he rode through New Gate into the raucous hurly-burly of England's capital city. Fear had spurred him on the road from Somerset, and it had been almost a week before he had stopped looking over his shoulder at every crossroads and had slept without waking at every creak of a floorboard in the various noisome hostelries that had given him a bed. But he had detected no sign of a Daunt pursuit and was beginning to allow himself to believe that he was in no more danger than any other traveler alone on the unruly roadways.

The city overwhelmed him. His father had given him directions and an introduction to a merchant acquaintance of his from many years past. He had to find his way to Lincoln's Inn Fields where the lawyers congregated. There he would be able to find his father's lawyer and exchange his letter of credit for guineas to furnish him with lodgings and a new coat and britches before he presented himself to Master Ledbetter, the merchant, on Threadneedle Street. His father had assured him that Master Ledbetter would furnish him with an introduction to King Charles's court. After that, it was up to Gabriel to make the best use of the opportunies that arose.

For a young man, country born and bred, the prospect was terrifying. But it was at court that he would find Ariadne. She had told him that she and her new husband were to establish themselves at Whitehall, and he had told her in his note to look for him there.

He intended to keep that promise. Once they were together again, then he would know what to do. But what of her husband? What of Sir Ivor Chalfont? What kind of man was he?

And more to the point, would he be willing to let his wife go?

Gabriel shuddered. It wasn't the first time he'd asked himself these questions. Chalfont came out of Daunt valley. It was a fair assumption that he would not simply stand aside when another man claimed his wife. But that was a problem for another day. For now, he needed supper and a bed for the night. When he was fed and rested, his next steps would be clearer. Besides, Ari would probably have a plan. She usually did.

A tavern at the sign of the Black Cock caught his attention as it swung creakily in a gust of wind issuing from a narrow lane just ahead. It would do as well as any other, he thought, instinctively checking his deep pocket for the reassuring bulk of his pistol. His sword was sheathed at his waist, a short dagger buckled to his belt. He could look after himself even in such a dingy hole as the Black Cock, and he desperately needed to sleep.

He reined in his drooping horse and, with a courage he was far from feeling, stuck his head around the inn door and bellowed for the innkeeper.

♦ ♦ ♦

Ariadne sat on a boulder beside the rutted track, rain dripping down the neck of her cloak, waiting for the men to change the broken wheel on the coach. They seemed to have been journeying in increasing misery for months, although it had only been three weeks. They had left the great Druid stones of Salisbury Plain behind them days ago, the last sunny day she could recall. It seemed to have been raining ever since.

Tilly perched beside her, huddled in her various layers, shivering and silent. The horses waited patiently, heads bowed against the rain, while the men labored with the heavy coach. The luggage was piled on the side of the road to make the job easier, but it was an enormous task nevertheless.

Ivor finally made an appearance through the rain, Turk seeming to emerge from a gray curtain, a ghostly black mammoth of a creature. Ari stood up and waited for them to get closer.

"There's not much up ahead," Ivor said, drawing rein beside her. "But there's a barn of sorts and a couple of tumbledown sheds. It'll shelter us from the rain, at least, and we can build a fire while we wait for the coach to be ready."

TRAPPED AT THE ALTAR ✦ 223

Ariadne glanced up at the rain-sodden sky. "It'll be dark soon."

"Then we'll have to stay there 'till daybreak," he said briskly. "Come now, Ari, it's not like you to lose heart."

"I'm not," she denied, "but I'm cold and wet to the bone, as are we all."

"Then mount up and follow me. I'll have a fire lit soon enough." He rode over to the coach to talk to the laboring men.

"Can you get on Sphinx, Tilly?" Ari led the horse over to the boulder. "Stand on the rock and climb up behind me." She mounted, holding the horse steady as Tilly scrambled onto his back behind her. Ivor nodded and took the lead, heading along the track the way he'd come.

The barn was little more than a rough shack, which, judging by the smell, had once housed goats. It had a loft, though, reached through a rickety ladder. "We can sleep up there," Ari said instantly. "And the men can stay down here. The horses can bed down in the sheds over there."

"There should be enough dry bedding inside the coach." Ivor was relieved to see Ariadne return to her usual assertive self. She'd looked such a miserable, half-drowned waif when he'd seen her on her rock a few minutes earlier that he'd felt a stab of anxiety. She was such a diminutive creature, she'd looked as if a puff of wind would blow her away, huddled and shivering in her soaked cloak.

"Tilly and I will light a fire, if you get some of the men to bring in the bags that have bedding and provisions." She unclasped her sodden cloak, holding it away from her with an air of distaste. "If we can get a really good fire going, maybe we can dry some of this stuff."

"Can't light a fire without wood," Tilly stated, looking around. "Where are we goin' to find dry timber around here?"

"I'll check the sheds," Ivor said swiftly. It wouldn't do for Tilly to lose heart, either. "Stay here. I'll be back in a minute."

Ariadne climbed the rickety ladder to the loft. The roof seemed intact, and it was dry, at least, and the floor, although dusty, seemed clean enough. "We're in luck, Tilly," she called down. "There's a pile of straw here, and it doesn't seem too moldy. Come on up and help me fashion a mattress."

Tilly climbed the ladder, her head poking through the hole in the floor as she surveyed the loft. "Certainly seems dry enough," she conceded, bringing the rest of her body into the low space. She tackled the straw, and Ari left her to it, going back down just as Ivor returned with an armful of wood.

"It's damp, but I think it'll take eventually." He dropped the wood in the center of the shed. "We need something to get it to light."

"If we break that up . . ." Ari pointed to a wooden feeding trough. "It would act as kindling. It seems dry enough."

Within an hour, the fire was lit, and the men came in, divesting themselves of their dripping cloaks. The coach, newly mended, was outside, the horses tethered in the sheds with nose bags.

Tilly was stirring the aromatic contents of a large copper kettle set on a trivet over the fire. She looked up as the men entered and said sharply, "Before you all get too comfortable, someone fetch me the sack of potatoes from the coach and that bag o' flour. These rabbits had little enough on 'em to feed us all, but a few potatoes and some nice 'erb dumplings will bulk it up. Oh," she added, as one of the men turned to go outside again. "And I think I spotted some carrot tops over by the side of that shed. Overgrown, most like, left over from someone's garden, but better than nothing, I reckon. And," she added as an afterthought over her shoulder, "more water, if I'm to make dumplings."

Tilly's word was law on this journey. She was the source of all domestic comfort, dispensing food, medicine, and advice freely, and she seemed to relish her role. It was vastly different from her subservient position in Daunt valley, where, like most of the women, her job was to keep her mouth shut and do as she was told while attending to the men's needs.

Two of the men set up a beer keg in one corner of the shack, and the men gathered around with pitch-coated leather tankards. Ivor opened a flagon of wine and poured two cups. "Ari?" He held out one cup.

"Thank you." She took it, drawing closer to the fire.

"Are you warmer now?" he asked, standing beside her.

"Yes, much. And if we can keep the fire in all night, we should have dry clothes by morning." Cloaks were spread out around the fire, steaming gently. She would have liked to change out of her damp riding habit, but their quarters were too crowded and confined to make that practical.

"We'll keep it in," Ivor assured her. "The men will sleep around it, and someone will have sufficient interest in keeping it fed." He drank from his cup, staring sightlessly into the fire.

Ariadne hugged her arms around her, taking occasional sips from her cup, wondering how this strange awkwardness had come upon them. They were uncomfortable with each other, their conversations stilted at best but mostly just simple exchanges of information or instruction. Ivor was no longer the careless, happy-go-lucky companion of her childhood or the comfortable confidant of later years. And the memory of those few nights of lovemaking was so distant and indistinct they might not have happened at all. Ever since that night when he'd said that without her feeling love, making love meant nothing to him, he had made no move to touch her, even when their sleeping arrangements afforded them the privacy. Every night, she dutifully took a spoonful of Tilly's potion, but she was beginning to wonder if there was any point to it anymore. She was certainly in no danger of conceiving at the moment.

She moved away from him as the men came back with Tilly's shopping list, and taking out her knife, began to peel potatoes. At least while she was doing something useful, she felt less bereft. She could feel Ivor's eyes on her as she bent to her task, but after a moment, he turned away from the fire and went to join the men at the beer keg.

Tilly glanced once at Ariadne, a sharp, shrewd assessment, before she returned to chopping ancient, wrinkled carrots and their green tops into the stew. Most nights, she slept in the same space as the married couple. When they were lucky enough to find an inn with a separate bedchamber, she slept on a mattress outside the door. But she was fairly certain that for the last several weeks, there had been little activity in the marriage bed. Miss Ari was looking peaky and unhappy, Sir Ivor sometimes black as a thunder sky.

The rain began to let up as night fell. Ivor lit the lanterns, and the little shack took on qualities of warmth and comfort and safety that in the daylight would have seemed impossible. Tilly dished up rabbit stew and dumplings, the beer and wine flowed, and the Daunt men ate and drank, sang and joked, leaning back on piles of baggage, as easy and comfortable as if at their own fireside.

These men had spent many a worse night, Ariadne reflected, watching them from her own corner of the fire. They had sat out on frozen beaches with their lanterns, drawing ships onto the rocks; they had raided farms at black of night, they had robbed horsemen and carriages on the wilds of Bodmin Moor and returned to the valley at dawn, as merry as Robin Hood's men. Although none of their spoils went from the rich to the poor.

She stole a glance at Ivor. He, too, seemed at his ease, as if he'd shared in those dubious adventures, but he never had. He had never been included in anything outside the law, and now, of course, they knew why. They were to be respectable, their respectability based on a midden of ill-gotten gains. Her mouth twisted at the cynical reflection. But it could be argued that without the repression and persecution of Cromwell's Protectorate, the Daunt family would have continued on the path of righteousness.

It could be argued.

She drained her wine cup and stood up. "Tilly, we should go to bed."

Tilly, who was dozing happily in the warmth, soothed by a tankard of beer, blinked and nodded, hauling herself to her feet. "Right, Miss Ari."

Ivor stood up. "Are you going to bed?"

"It's time," Ariadne said. "And we should make an early start."

He nodded. "I'll sleep down here with the men tonight. We should be safe enough, but we'll set a guard anyway." He moved to the ladder, holding it steady for her as she stepped onto the bottom rung. "I'll call you at dawn."

She nodded. "Good night, then." Her tone was bleak, but she turned her face away from him and climbed up into the loft, Tilly following behind.

Ivor stood for a moment, his hand on the ladder. He ached to go up to her, ached to hold her again, just to feel her warm against him as she slept. But there was a coldness in his breast that wouldn't melt. He knew he was punishing them both with this restraint—or rejection, he wasn't sure what to call it—but he couldn't seem to help himself.

He couldn't let down his guard and simply enjoy what she would give him. It wasn't enough. Long ago, he had believed that the people who cared for him, who told him they loved him, had meant it. He had believed their caresses were true expressions of love and protection. At the age of six, he had discovered the lie, abandoned with no warning among hostile strangers by the people he had trusted. He wasn't prepared to make the same mistake twice. He could not trust Ariadne to be true to him; she had told him as much. He needed to know that she was bound to him not by duty or the need to make the best of the situation but because she wanted to be, *needed* to be. Because she loved him truly and not just in the ways of friendship.

He would not love alone. He could not afford to be so vulnerable again.

EIGHTEEN

They approached the city just before dusk on a mild November day by the road to New Gate. The road was wide enough for two-way traffic, and the Daunt party met a stream of carts, carriages, and horsemen leaving the city for the evening before the gates were closed at curfew.

Tilly sat wide-eyed on her seat on the box by the coachman as the procession of folk of every class and creed flowed past them. Merchants in fine linen jostled with barrow boys in filthy jerkins, farmers drove empty carts, their day's produce sold, and milkmaids drove cows and goats back from the city, where they had been selling fresh milk to the city's inhabitants.

The stone edifice of New Gate reared up before them, their entrance through the city walls into the strange and unknown life within its warren of lanes and alleyways, busy markets, and quieter green spaces through which the mighty River Thames flowed, as bustling a thoroughfare as any of the main London streets.

Ariadne was too busy for a few moments calming Sphinx, who was objecting vigorously to the crowds around him, to take much stock of her surroundings as they passed through the double roadway of the gate. She was aware of the foul stink, however, emanating from the grim buildings of the prison piled atop the gate and stretching to either side. And she could hear the mournful wails of the prisoners drifting from barred windows onto the fetid air of the late afternoon.

Ivor rode just ahead of her. His back was ramrod straight, his eyes everywhere. He spoke to the watchmen in the gatehouse, showing the safe conduct pass that Lord Daunt had given him, one of a package of letters of introduction intended to smooth their path in this alien land. The watchmen waved them through, the last travelers to enter the city before they closed the gates in the wall until daybreak.

The street that took them within the walls was teeming with activity, even though the gates were now closed. Sphinx bridled and pranced as an iron-wheeled carriage pulled by a team of great cart horses emerged from an alleyway. The coachman cursed as he saw that the gates were closed, a fluent stream of violent language pouring from his lips. Tilly cowered, pulling the hood of her cloak tighter over her head.

"I suppose you know where we're going?" Ari asked, bringing Sphinx up beside Turk.

Ivor shot her a look that in a previous life would have made her chuckle. But they didn't do much laughing these days. "Holborn," he said shortly. "Close to Lincoln's

Inn Fields. An inn, which your uncle says is commodious and will make a decent base until your wardrobe is completed and we can find suitable lodgings closer to Whitehall."

They threaded their way through the streets, through men spilling from taverns on either side, past two men brawling in a fetid courtyard surrounded by a crowd of cheering boys. Both Turk and Sphinx reared as a dancing bear was led past them on the end of a chain, and Ari turned her head aside. There were cruelties aplenty in the countryside, but somehow in these stinking, mean lanes they seemed worse.

After what seemed endless twists and turns, a green space opened up in front of them, a white-plastered building at its corner. A cluster of gray stone buildings ranged along two sides of the space, and men in the somber black gowns of the legal profession crossed the green between the buildings. The sign of the King's Head hung from the plastered building, and it seemed to be doing a vigorous trade with both the black-clad lawyers and the well-dressed ladies and gentlemen gathering on the forecourt. Ivor gestured to the coachman to drive through the archway to the stable yard beyond, and he drew rein at the front door. He turned to give his hand to Ariadne to help her dismount.

She was about to slide to the ground unaided but saw his warning look. She dismounted decorously, her hand in his, and shook down the skirts of her red velvet riding habit, conscious with some satisfaction that she was every bit as richly dressed as the inn's other customers.

Up-to-the-minute fashion was perhaps not as important as the luxury of the materials, she reflected. She ignored the curious looks directed at the newcomers, handed her reins to a groom, who had appeared instantly, and placed her hand on Ivor's arm as they went into the inn.

The landlord stood bowing in the square hall. "My lord, my lady, welcome to the King's Head. I trust I may be of service."

Ivor smiled, guessing that the innkeeper was aware of the carriage, the outriders, the mountains of baggage that had accompanied these potential customers. "I require a bedchamber for Lady Chalfont and myself and a private parlor, accommodation for her maid and for our men. Stabling for the horses, of the best kind, you understand." This was accompanied with a fierce frown that despite everything brought an involuntary smile to Ari's lips. She turned her attention hastily to a dim oil painting on the wall beside her.

The innkeeper bowed and squeezed his hands together and promised that all would be provided exactly as his lordship required. If his lordship would be pleased to follow him, he would show his lordship and her ladyship the accommodation he had available.

"You may show Lady Chalfont. She will decide whether it will suit our needs. We shall be staying for several weeks," Ivor declared. "I shall see to the disposition of our baggage."

Ari followed the innkeeper up the stairs. The place was by no means immaculate, but she hadn't expected it to be. Inns in general didn't pride themselves on cleanliness, but there was a faint smell of beeswax and a hint of lavender in the air, despite the dust on the stairs. She would set Tilly to work directing the inn's maids to scour their accommodation. Tilly would be in her element.

The landlord, with a flourish, threw open a door into a corner parlor on the second floor. "Best in the house, my lady."

"Is it, indeed?" Ariadne said with an air of disdain. She looked around, deciding privately that it would do very well once Tilly had had her way with it. There was a fireplace, at present unlit, a table in the bow window with two chairs, which would do well enough for dining, and a pair of chairs by the fire, together with a settle against the wall. The floor was of bare wooden boards, but with a touch of wax, they would shine. A rag rug in front of the fireplace needed beating, but Tilly would see to that.

"And the bedchamber?" she inquired.

The landlord was looking a little hesitant now at his prospective guest's apparent lack of enthusiasm. He opened a door in the far wall into a bedchamber looking out at the back of the inn over the green. It was a pleasant vista, Ari decided, a quiet and almost peaceful oasis in the midst of this hideously noisy city. The four-poster bed, dresser, linen press, armoire, and foot chest were all adequate. They had their own sheets, fortunately, and Tilly would deal with the inevitable livestock in the mattress, if a new mattress could not be procured.

"If my lady would like, there's a truckle bed for your maid." The landlord indicated the extra mattress beneath the bed.

Tilly would sleep in the parlor, Ari decided, not that it would matter if she slept in here . . . She pushed that thought aside. Now that they had found a resting place, however temporary, it was time to deal with the situation of her marriage . . . *somehow.*

"So, madam, will it do for us, do you think?"

She turned to the door at Ivor's voice. He stood in the doorway to the parlor, tapping his whip lightly against his boot, looking around.

"Yes, I believe it will. Once Tilly has had free rein, of course," she added, turning to the landlord. "My maid, Mistress Tilly, will take charge of cleaning these rooms. You will put your servants at her disposal, if you please."

"Of course, your ladyship. Anything your ladyship requires." The man bowed so low his forehead almost touched his knees, and it was Ivor's turn to look away to hide his quivering lip. Ariadne was playing the haughty noblewoman to perfection. It was almost impossible to imagine the raggle-taggle hoyden of Daunt valley in this present incarnation.

"Supper, then?" Ivor said. "We did not stop on the road to dine, so we are all sharp-set. We shall need a substantial meal. What can you offer us, mine host?"

The man beamed. "A chine of beef, my lord, a barrel of oysters, some new-drawn pullets, and if you've a fancy for a fine carp, then my lady wife has a friend in the fishmonger."

"Oysters and the chine of beef," Ari said swiftly. The fish would have been fresh that morning, but it was now almost dark, and Daunt folk were accustomed to only the freshest-caught fish. They'd also eaten enough chicken, she decided. Chicken and rabbit were the easiest to acquire on their journeying. "And you will please ensure that our men have their fill of both."

The landlord looked surprised, but if these noble folk were prepared to pay to feed their servants as they fed themselves, then who was he to complain? "Of course, my lady."

Ariadne smiled at him for the first time. "Then I think we shall deal very well together, Master . . . ?"

"Master Rareton, my lady. Master of the King's Head. I'll order that dinner at once. What of wine, my lord? I've a good claret for the chine and a fine Rhenish for the oysters, if that'll do you."

"Why don't you show me?" Ivor said easily. "We'll leave Lady Chalfont to organize the domestic arrangements."

"Yes," Ari said. "Send up the maids, if you please, Master Rareton."

The host bowed himself out, and Ivor prepared to follow him. He offered a smile as he met Ari's eyes. "*Will* this do, Ari?"

She felt the lingering warmth behind the smile and with it a little tingle of hope. Maybe Ivor was as tired of this estrangement as she was. Maybe, if she made the first move, the *right* move, they could put things right. "Yes," she said firmly. "But I need Tilly."

"I'll send her up straightway." He followed the landlord down to the cellar to inspect the wine.

Ari pulled back the coverlets on the bed and looked

with disfavor at the grubby sheeting pulled over the straw mattress.

"Lord, you'll be eaten alive on that thing." Tilly's welcome voice came from behind her.

"What should we do? Use the heavy sheeting again?"

Tilly shook her head vigorously. "If we're to be 'ere for a while, then we'll have to burn this an' stuff it with fresh straw. "Look at 'em." Even in the dim light of dusk, the bugs were jumping in the straw.

Ari shuddered. "Do what has to be done, Tilly. The landlord's sending up his maids. Tell them what you want. We'll sort out the parlor in the morning."

She went into the parlor as Tilly directed a small army of maidservants. Ivor came in carrying two bottles. "Rhenish or claret?" He set them on the table and took two pewter goblets out of his coat's deep pockets. A manservant had followed him with an armload of firewood.

"Rhenish," Ari decided. "Can we light the candles?"

The manservant set a taper to the fire and then lit the candles on the mantel and the table. The room flickered into life. Sounds of merriment rose from the taproom and the ordinary below as the inn began its evening.

Ivor poured the golden wine. He looked at Ari over his glass, a speculative look that made her skin prickle. "So, in the morning we must find milliners," he said, and she felt a wash of disappointment. She had expected something else, words that went with the look.

"Yes, I suppose so," she agreed without expression. "How do we do that?"

"Mine host, probably. This is a fashionable inn." He

drank deeply. "His cellar, at least, is not to be complained about."

"No," she agreed dully, sipping from her own goblet. "Is all well, Tilly?" She greeted Tilly's head around the bedchamber door with relief.

"Oh, aye, Miss Ari. They're changing the straw in the mattress now, an' the maids are finishing up with the cleaning and lighting the fire. I'll be going for my dinner now."

"Yes, of course. You'll be eating with the men?"

"Oh, aye, there's a special table set for us all in the back kitchen," Tilly announced, clearly pleased with the arrangement. Daunt folk preferred to stay together. "Beef, they're saying." She grinned, her freckled cheeks shining. "Been a long time since we tasted beef, miss."

Ariadne was about to agree when Ivor said, "Tilly, you must remember to call Miss Ari Lady Chalfont from now on. Such informality won't do in the city."

Tilly looked a little crestfallen, as if taken to task for some error. "Oh, beg pardon, sir, I wasn't thinking."

"No, it's all right, Tilly," Ari said swiftly. "There are so many new things we have to remember. I have to remember to be helped from my horse, for instance." Here she cast a somewhat irritated look at Ivor. "Try to remember. But don't worry if you forget. It won't matter."

Tilly, looking much happier, went off for her dinner, and Ivor said sharply, "Actually, Ariadne, it *will* matter. People will notice such slips, and we cannot afford to draw attention to ourselves just yet."

"You don't think we already have done?" she exclaimed. "We arrive in this great cavalcade, march around, giving orders left, right, and center, and no one's going to wonder who we are?"

"Of course they will," he said impatiently. "We are Sir Ivor and Lady Chalfont from Somerset. But they won't know anything else, and we're at present lodged far enough from Whitehall not to draw attention from that quarter. When we're ready for that, then we make a grand entrance. But in the meantime, we practice these new ways. You, me, Tilly. Is that clear, Ari?"

"As day," she responded. She bent to warm her hands at the fire, only it wasn't her hands that were cold, it was that piece of ice that seemed lodged beneath her breastbone. How could she approach him as she wished when he closed off every avenue? A lifetime in this atmosphere was not to be contemplated.

NINETEEN

*A*riadne awoke on their first morning at the King's Head to the sounds of the hostelry beginning its day below. A keg rolling over the uneven paving of the hallway, voices shouting orders, a dog barking. It was still barely light, only a gray glimmer through the window that looked onto the peaceful green field of Lincoln's Inn. She knew Ivor was not beside her, even without the tentative hand she stretched across the mattress. But he had been there all night, although he had come to bed after her. She could still feel the residual warmth of his body, although he had not touched her in the hours of darkness.

But that was going to change. If he would do nothing positive to change things, then *she* must.

She had never been able to tolerate just standing by while bad things happened, either to herself or to others. It had been impossible on the journey to take any definitive, independent action, but here it was different.

Infused now with a renewed sense of purpose, a plan of action, Ari pushed aside the covers and stood up, stretching. Ivor must have rekindled the fire before he'd left the chamber, because it glowed brightly in the hearth, and the room was quite warm. Barefoot, she padded to the window, peering out into the early light. Black-clad figures, arms filled with heavy volumes, crossed the green field, moving between the gray stone buildings of the Inns of Court.

Ari turned from the window and went to the door to the parlor. She opened it, expecting to see Ivor taking an early breakfast, but there was only Tilly, just stirring on the truckle bed. The fire had gone out, and the room was dark and cold.

"Good morning, Tilly."

Tilly sat up, blinking, as she remembered where she was. "Lord, Miss Ari, I slept like the dead," she declared, pushing aside the blanket and getting to her feet. She scrambled into her discarded gown and thrust her feet into her clogs. "Best sleep I've had in weeks."

"I know the feeling," Ari said with a smile. "Sir Ivor lit the fire in the bedchamber before he left, but we need to relight this one. It's freezing in here." She retreated to the bedchamber for her woolen dressing gown.

Tilly, yawning, bent to throw kindling on the fire. "Where's Sir Ivor gone, then, Miss Ari?"

"I wish I knew." Ari came back into the parlor, carrying a lighted taper from the bedchamber fire, and lit the candles. The fire came to life, and the room felt instantly more homely. She went to the window, which looked down on the inn's forecourt, wondering if she would see Ivor. There were folk aplenty abroad already but no sign of her husband's tall, broad-shouldered figure.

She turned swiftly as the door to the corridor opened.

"Ah, good, you're up. I've ordered breakfast, and hot water will come up afterwards." Ivor sounded cheerful as he came in, his cheeks glowing with the fresh cold air of morning, his hair disheveled by the wind. "I have the names of two milliners who mine host says know everything there is to be known about court fashions. They will present themselves at nine this morning. Abe is sending up the trunks with the materials, and I suggest you and Tilly turn this parlor into a workroom." He drew off his leather gauntlets and cast them onto the settle.

"And where will you be?" she inquired.

"Oh, I'll find a nook in the taproom," he said carelessly, tossing his cloak to follow his gloves. "But I have my own work to do."

She nodded. "Finding lodgings, I suppose?"

"That and presenting our credentials to Rolf's contacts. I'll do that first. One of them may have suggestions for suitable lodgings. Ah, here's breakfast."

Two menservants carrying laden trays came in and set out kidneys, bacon, hot bread, and a dish of veal scallops on the table in the window embrasure. A jug of small beer accompanied the meal. "That be all, sir?"

"That'll be all, thank you." Ivor sat at the table. "Come, Ari, eat." He helped himself liberally and filled two tankards from the ale jug. "You'll break your fast with the men in the back kitchen, Tilly."

"Aye, sir." Tilly went off, closing the door behind them.

Silence fell in the parlor. "So, whom do you visit first?" Ari said finally. Comfortable silences were one thing, but these days, the silences between them were like black chasms where something unspeakable lurked at the bottom.

Ivor buttered his bread. "A distant Chalfont relative, Lord Lindsey. He lives close to Whitehall, and Rolf assures me he will receive me readily enough. He's a loyal King's man, a staunch Protestant, as the Chalfont family has always been."

"And me? Will he receive me kindly?" Ari sliced into a veal scallop, spearing a piece on the tip of her knife.

"That remains to be seen. But I suspect your fortune will be sufficiently persuasive," Ivor responded with a dry smile. "Besides, you are merely a wife; you have no status of your own." He watched her reaction and ducked just in time as a hunk of bread flew across the table at him.

"I don't find that amusing," she declared.

"I didn't expect you to, but it is the truth nevertheless, my dear." He speared a kidney, and the mischievous glimmer in his blue eyes made her heart beat faster. For a moment, she had the old Ivor back with her.

"And do you think that, too?" she demanded, her own eyes glittering with challenge.

Ivor laughed and pushed back his chair, draining his tankard as he got to his feet. "What do you think, madam wife?"

She looked at him directly, all amusement gone from her expression. "I don't know what to think anymore, Ivor. You're a stranger to me."

He looked at her, somber now. "I wish it didn't have to be so, Ari, but I do not know how else it can be." He picked up his cloak and gloves. "I will not return for dinner. Have a profitable day, and I'll see you for supper this evening."

The door closed behind him, and Ari leaned her elbows on the table, resting her forehead in her palms. For a moment, she felt utterly defeated, but she had a plan, she reminded herself. What if it failed?

She shook her head. If it failed, it would be the most devastating embarrassment she could begin to imagine, but it wasn't going to. It was unthinkable, and she would not allow it to happen. Tonight Ivor would have the surprise of his life. She stood up with renewed energy and went into the bedchamber, where she stood for a moment looking at the bed. Could she make it work?

She heard sounds from the parlor and tore herself away from her imaginings. Abe and two of the other men were bringing up the trunks of materials.

"Where d'you want 'em, my lady?" Abe inquired, shouldering a leather, iron-bound chest.

"Anywhere you think, Abe." He nodded, and she went back into the bedchamber. Tilly was there with a jug of hot water.

"No point getting dressed, Miss Ari, not if the seamstresses are coming," she said, pouring water into the basin. "But there's plenty of hot water for a wash."

"Later I should like a proper bath, Tilly. D'you think it could be arranged?" She wrung out the cloth, spreading it over her face, luxuriating in the warm, moist cleanliness.

"Reckon so, miss. I'll warn 'em below ahead of time, they'll have to heat the coppers, but it ought to be possible." Tilly was remaking the bed.

"I shall need your help," Ari said, sponging between her breasts. "Before supper."

"Oh, aye?" Tilly looked at her curiously as she plumped up the pillows. "To do what?"

"I'll tell you later." Ari took up her hairbrush and brushed her tangled black curls. She grimaced. "My hair's so dirty, it feels full of grit from the road. I shall wash it when I have my bath. Do we have any rosewater or lavender?"

"There's lavender aplenty in the garden here, and rosemary." Tilly smoothed out creases in the coverlet. "And I've some rosewater I brought along when we left the valley. And a bit o' soap, I reckon."

"Good." Ari nodded briskly, and a little smile played in the corners of her mouth. Ivor would not be able to resist her plan. No red-blooded male could possibly resist what she had in mind.

✦ ✦ ✦

The two seamstresses arrived punctually. They were mother and daughter, Mistress Tabitha and Mistress Mary, fashionably dressed and coiffed, and they regarded Lady Chalfont with narrowed, assessing eyes as she stood before them in her shift. "Have to do something about the bosom, Mary," Mistress Tabitha pronounced.

"Indeed, Mama. Something sewn into the gowns to push them above the décolletage." The daughter nodded, her side ringlets shivering against her powdered cheeks.

Her mother was going through the piles of rich materials spread out over the table and the settle. "Well, we can do something with these. Nice bit of taffeta, this. Make a good jacket, it will, over a skirt in that gold damask."

Ariadne began to feel like a dressmaker's mannequin for all the notice they took of her. And they took even less of Tilly. After a while, she went into a trance, obeying instructions to move this way and that, to hold her arms like this or like that, as the two women went about their business. They didn't ask for her opinion, and she didn't think she'd have one, anyway. Tilly sat on a stool by the fire in a huff, darning stockings with sharp jabs of her needle as the hours passed, broken only by a short interval when dinner was brought up.

"A cloak in that sky-blue silk with an ermine lining, I think, Mary," Mistress Tabitha declared, setting a pin into what would be the sleeve of an emerald-green damask gown. "And that will do for today."

Ari jerked her head around. "No, I don't want you to take any of the furs," she said, speaking, it seemed, for the first time. Her voice sounded almost unfamiliar.

Mistress Tabitha looked astounded. "Not take any of them, madam? But they are to be part of the wardrobe. You must have muffs and fur lining to your cloaks."

"Indeed, and you may do that another day," Ariadne said firmly. "It seems to me you have quite enough to be going on with, with all these gowns and jackets and skirts. When you return, we will discuss the furs."

Tilly had ceased her needle stabbing and looked at Ari

in surprise. Mistress Tabitha frowned, sniffed her disapproval, then said, "As you wish, my lady."

"That is my wish," Ari reiterated calmly. "When will you come back for a fitting?"

The seamstress looked at the pile of pinned silks and satins, damasks and brocades. "In two days, madam, these will be ready for a first fitting."

"Then you may take the furs at that time."

"Very well, madam. Mary, send down for John Coachman to carry these down to the carriage. You will be needing shoes, my lady. Should I bring the shoemaker with a selection when we return for the fitting?"

"Indeed, if you would be so kind." Ari gave the woman her most dazzling smile, hoping to make up for the offense she had so clearly committed.

Mistress Tabitha's haughty disapproval seemed to abate a fraction. "I think my lady would look very well with a heeled shoe. It would provide height. Jeweled heels are most particularly fashionable at court."

For one more accustomed to going barefoot inside and booted outside, the idea of shoes with jeweled heels seemed utterly ridiculous, but Ari merely smiled and murmured that she was sure Mistress Tabitha must be correct, as knowledgeable as she was. And the lady, her daughter, and the vast quantities of materials disappeared on the broad shoulders of John Coachman and his youthful assistant.

Ariadne sighed with relief as the door finally closed on the seamstresses. The afternoon was already drawing in.

Ivor had said he would return for supper, so she had close to two hours for her preparations.

"Would you see about that bath, Tilly? Set it up in here."

"Right away, Miss Ari. They should have enough water by now. I told 'em to be ready by sundown."

Ari went into the bedchamber and stood assessing the room, tapping her teeth with her forefinger. Then she gave a short nod of decision and returned to the parlor, where a copper hip bath was already in place on spread sheets before the fire and two burly menservants were filling it from copper kettles.

Steam curled from the bath, and Tilly was adding drops of rosewater. The delicate scent filled the warm chamber. Two more kettles were added, and Tilly sprinkled rosemary and lavender on the surface before setting a screen between the tub and the door.

Ari stepped out of her night-robe and shift and into the hot water with a small exhalation of pleasure.

TWENTY

*A*t was close to eight o'clock when Ivor returned to the King's Head. He had had a productive but tiring day and was hungry for his supper. The inn was lively at that hour, but he ignored the taproom and went upstairs. The parlor was empty, although the fire burned, and the candles were lit. There was no sign of supper anywhere, but the air was perfumed with a faint, elusive, flowery scent.

"Ariadne," he called with a degree of irritation.

"In here."

He frowned. What was she doing in the bedchamber at this time in the evening? It was suppertime, and he was sharp-set. He opened the bedchamber door. "Is something the matter? Are you ill?" And then he stood, gazing dumbstruck at the bed.

Ariadne's naked body lay in a nest of sable and ermine, her pale skin glowing softly in the light of two candles on either side of the bed. The only other light came from the fire, and that same delicate scent infused the air.

Ivor swallowed involuntarily, his senses swirling as he gazed at her, her glossy black curls tumbled around her head on the white pillow, the daintiness of her body against the rich furs, the rosy crowns of her small breasts, the smooth lines of her form, the concave belly and luxuriant black tangle of hair at its base, the creamy length of her thighs, the perfect dimpled knees, the slender ankles and long, narrow feet.

She was perfection in miniature, he thought, taking a step to the bed. "What is this?" His voice sounded thick, but he couldn't take his eyes off her.

"Me," she said softly, smiling up at him. "Just me, husband."

"Dear God," he muttered, putting a knee on the bed. A necklace of emeralds circled her pale white throat, and the great Daunt emerald ring glowed on her finger as she moved her hand seductively over her breasts in a gesture of offering. It was not an offer Ivor could refuse. No man on God's green earth could refuse it.

He bent to kiss her breasts, his tongue flicking at the pink nipples that lifted to the moist caress. He drew his tongue between the small mounds and then painted a trail down her belly, dipping into her navel, down between her thighs. Her skin carried the scent that had so struck him earlier, delicate, flowery, fresh, and so seductive.

He lifted his head. "No, I cannot."

Shock filled the gray eyes as they gazed up at him, and he shook his head. "No . . . no, I cannot touch you until

I have the washed the day's dirt from me. You are as fresh as morning dew on a snowdrop, and I cannot bear to sully that." He stepped back from the bed, his eyes never leaving her body. "Do not move an inch."

She lay still, watching him as he threw off his clothes. He poured water into the basin. It was warm water, all part of the elaborate preparations she had made for this little scene, he thought with wonder. There was even a piece of soap. He washed the sweat from his skin, aware of her hungry gaze.

"Hurry," she murmured, shifting slightly on her fur bed, feeling the soft silkiness of sable and ermine caress her already tingling skin.

He smiled at her, his old mischievous smile, except that it was now filled with a deep sensuality. "Has no one told you of the pleasures of anticipation, my sweet?"

The endearment sent waves of delight through her, and her eyes fixed on the pulsing erection that gave ample evidence of his own pleasure in anticipation. He came to kneel at the foot of the bed, taking her feet in his hands, lifting them in turn to kiss the toes, taking each one in his mouth before stroking his tongue down the soles of her feet, making her wriggle against the furs, which did even more to stimulate her sensitized skin. His hands grasped her ankles lightly as he lifted her legs onto his shoulders, running his hands down the backs of her thighs, his fingers creeping ever closer to her moist and opened core.

She heard her own gasp of wanting escape from her lips as the tantalizing touch came close but never quite close enough. He held her legs apart and dropped his head, his mouth finding her sex, his tongue licking, stroking, his teeth lightly grazing the little nub of flesh as it rose hard with longing. His tongue entered her, and she gave another gasp of surprise and delight, feeling his breath cool on her heated flesh, the wicked, tantalizing twist of his tongue inside her. When he lifted his head and moved up her body, his mouth taking hers, she could taste the essence of herself. Her hands grasped his buttocks, kneading the hard muscle, trying to drive him into her, but he held himself back as his tongue danced with hers, stroked the insides of her cheeks.

Finally, he took her legs again onto his shoulders and knelt back between her thighs. He lifted her bottom on his palms and drove hard inside her in one swift thrust that made her cry out in surprise. He moved hard and fast within her, his eyes never leaving hers, watching as she rose up and up with him. Suddenly, he slapped her flank, and she bucked like an unschooled pony as her climax rushed over her, her fingers knotted into the taut flesh of his buttocks. His head fell back, the corded muscles in his throat standing out as he was swept with his own wave. And then only the most delicious release as, still joined, they fell together into the furs.

Ari lay beneath him, one hand still resting on his backside, her other thrown to the pillow behind her. Ivor released his hold on her ankles and let her legs fall to either side of him. After a moment, he raised his head and looked down into her face.

"You are a very wicked woman, wife of mine."

"Merely fulfilling my conjugal duties," she returned with a weak smile.

"Indeed." He moved sideways, disengaging from her body, and lay with his hands flung above his head, gazing up at the tester as his breathing returned to normal.

Ari rolled onto her side, placing a hand on his still fast-beating heart. "Ivor, we must make this a beginning. I love you in the only way I can, the only way I know. It is as it is. Can we not build on what we have?"

Ivor said nothing for a moment. He had in truth been unhappier these last weeks than he could ever have imagined being. And she had done this for him . . . for them. This elaborate play was meant to give them a springboard. From this platform of sublime joy, they could move up, beyond the sour taste of the past weeks to an acceptance of what they had.

Gabriel Fawcett was in the past, in Ariadne's past. So she held some lingering feelings for him, but this was now, and there was no denying that in this now he and Ari had a bond that transcended most others. It wasn't possible to make love like that without there being some real feeling beneath. He knew it in his blood.

"Love," he mused, placing a hand over hers as it rested on his heart. "Such a complicated feeling." He smiled, stroking with his free hand through the glossy, fragrant curls scattered across his chest. "I think I have loved you, Ariadne, in some way or another, since I first knew you . . . a small child with a determined chin, a vocabulary to make a stable hand blush, and the most accurate eye for a knife throw of any grown man."

"I was only three," she protested, kissing the hollow of his shoulder.

"Well, maybe it took a couple of years," he conceded, drawing black curls through his fingers. "But you are somehow a part of me, of my life, and I cannot bear to be at odds with you. These last weeks have been worse than any I could have imagined."

"For me, too," she murmured, nestling her head into his shoulder. "Can we put them behind us now?"

He twisted a curl around his finger. "We must," he said, hitching himself onto an elbow to look into her eyes. His gaze was deep and penetrating, yet still a shadow lingered. He touched her lips with a forefinger.

And Ari felt Gabriel in the room with them. She could see in his eyes that Ivor could not forget the man she had sworn she loved, the man who held her heart, and Ariadne knew that she could not forswear Gabriel. It was not in her nature.

They were silent for a moment, and then Ivor seemed to shake himself out of the shadows. He kissed her lips and declared, "I was hungry when I came home, and now I am as ravenous as a wolf." He reached down and patted her bottom. "Don't tell me you have not organized supper, wife of mine."

"Oh, it's organized," Ari responded, thankfully accepting that the moment of darkness had passed without comment. "You'll find everything in the parlor by now." Tilly would have played her part, and supper would be set by the fire next door. Smoked oysters, a roast chicken, a dish of sweetbreads and salsify, and buttered parsnips. There would be macaroons and Canary wine, and afterwards, well . . . that would take care of itself. Gabriel's shadow had to fade eventually.

She rolled off the bed, drawing a thick sable around her, and went barefoot into the parlor. Ivor followed, shrugging into a dressing robe. "Smells good," he said, pouring wine into the goblets on the table. He gave her a glass and raised his own. "What shall we drink to?"

Her eyes met his over the rim of her goblet. "To the next step."

He nodded slowly. "Yes, to the next step, and every one after that."

It was a promise. The ground was cleared, and each step they took upon it from now on would only make them stronger.

And when supper was done, Ivor pushed back his chair and came to Ariadne, drawing her to her feet. He cupped her chin in one hand, tilting her face upwards. His eyes glowed. "I want you now to put yourself in my hands, Ariadne. I know it won't be easy for you, but so far, this night has been of your making, and it's my turn now. Give yourself to me." He laid a finger over her lips. "You will not speak; this will not be a time for words." A smile touched his lips. "I'll not insist on silence, though. You may find that hard with what I have in mind."

Ari felt a deep quiver of excitement at the base of her belly, a quickening, a moistening in her loins. Lust, pure and simple, engulfed her, her nipples hardening already beneath the sable robe.

"Do you understand?" he asked softly, and she nodded, feeling herself melting into a liquid puddle of desire.

✦ ✦ ✦

It was a long, languorous night. Ari wasn't sure whether she slept in between the lovemaking or merely floated in a trance of delight. Ivor seemed tireless, moving over her, around her, within her, turning her this way and that, positioning her as he chose, and she gave herself to him completely, discovering the pleasure of passivity. He drew little murmurs of delight from her, and sometimes she heard herself moan with longing when he paused in his pleasuring, and more than once, she cried out, and he stifled her cries with his kisses.

Dawn was breaking when at last she fell asleep, curled against his body, and it was full morning when she awoke again, once more to find herself alone in the feather bed.

"Lord, Miss Ari, you've been abed half the morning," Tilly exclaimed as she bustled in with hot water. "I had your breakfast taken away; it had gone cold."

Ari struggled effortfully up against the pillows and blinked in the sudden sunlight. "Where's Sir Ivor?"

"Oh, bless you, miss, he's been up and about these two hours past. Told me not to disturb you but that he'd be back later when he's seen to our new lodgings."

Ari pushed aside the coverlet and swung her legs out of bed. Her body felt sore and used up in the most glorious way. She wanted to lie in bed all day, savoring the feeling, reliving the memories of those wonderful hours, but it wasn't possible. She wasn't ill, and there could be no other reason for lying abed all day.

"I'd like some small beer and bread and butter, Tilly." She went to the washstand to splash water on her face. Her eyes wouldn't seem to open properly.

"Why? Are you ill, Miss Ari?" Tilly looked at her with concern. "That's no breakfast at all."

"Maybe not, but 'tis all I feel like this morning." Ari toweled her face dry vigorously. "I shall go for a walk and get some fresh air."

She went to the window of the bedchamber as Tilly departed and looked out on the green below. It was alive this morning, black-clad lawyers hurrying by with their heavy tomes under their arms, clusters of them paused in earnest conversation across the green, their black gowns flapping in the brisk wind. Messenger lads raced in various directions, entering and leaving the tall houses lining the outer rim of the square. A trio of scruffy urchins kicked a bundle of something between them, and two washerwomen emerged from one of the houses, laundry baskets held effortlessly on their heads as they walked, skirts swinging with each step.

A figure came out onto the top step of a house just to the right of the inn. The man paused, looking around him, then hastily tucked something into the deep pocket of his long-skirted coat before coming down the steps and heading off across the green. Ari stared at him. There was something startlingly familiar about him.

Look for me in London.

Surely it wasn't . . . it couldn't be Gabriel? But it was. She knew his walk, the way he held his shoulders, the slender, reedlike frame, the fair head glinting in the sun. He kept looking nervously from side to side with swift, jerky movements, and his hand was on the hilt of his sword. Everything about his demeanor indicated a frightened man. But what could he be scared of? The scene on the green was peaceful enough.

The trio of urchins saw him and stopped their play. One of them yelled something at him, and they all laughed. Gabriel drew his sword, and Ari took a swift breath. There was no reason for that. He was making himself prey with his fearful attitude, his nervous walk. It was obvious that in this city, if you looked vulnerable, you would be. Surely Gabriel knew that. But then she thought of who he was, a gently bred country lad who had never faced anything more dangerous than a bull in a field. He knew how to use his sword, every young man did, but he seemed somehow stripped of any natural defenses. She ached to run down to him, to protect him, get him off the green, away from the threat of the urchins, tuck him away somewhere safe. But she wasn't dressed, and besides, she was a married woman, trying to begin afresh in her marriage. Gabriel could have no part in her life now.

But she couldn't bear him to be hurt, and no one was taking any notice of the little drama being played out amongst them. But then it was just part of the everyday scene in this unruly city. Passersby looked to their own business, not that of their fellows.

The urchins were taunting him now, unafraid of the drawn sword that he waved at them as they drew closer, encircling him. She noticed Gabriel's free hand was clutching the pocket of his coat, where he had put something as he stepped out of the house. The boys had noticed, and their eyes were fixed upon his hand as they made little running darts at him.

Ari flung open the door to the corridor outside the bedchamber and shouted for someone. A servant in a green baize apron appeared instantly, looking startled. "Get out onto the green," she instructed sharply. "There's a man under attack by a group of ruffians. Chase them off."

The man hesitated, looking even more startled, and Ari stamped a foot and shouted. "*Now*, I tell you." He turned and raced down the stairs, and she went back to the window. The scene hadn't changed, although the boys were getting closer, dodging Gabriel's swinging blade, laughing and jeering, but there was deadly purpose now in their movements.

"For God's sake, Gabriel, do something," she muttered under her breath. "Don't just wave the blade, *use* it. Frighten them. It won't take much."

The footman appeared and yelled at the urchins, marching across the green towards them, his fists bunched. They took one look at him and fled, racing away across the green. Gabriel bent double, catching his breath before slowly sheathing his sword. He looked anxiously around once more, then hurried across the green towards the inn.

Ariadne stepped away from the window. She was

shaken by what she had seen, not just by the sight of Gabriel, not even by the thought that he was probably in the taproom below finding some Dutch courage, but by the revelation that he was so totally unable to take care of himself. It was all very well to live in that rose-tinted world of soft colors and pretty poems, of lovemaking under the dappled shade beneath the wide-spreading leaves of a beech tree. But that wasn't the world they had to live in.

She thought of the attack at the inn in the Polden Hills. What would Gabriel have thought if he could have seen her fighting like any one of the men? Filthy, sooty, bloody. It would have horrified him.

She pushed the thought aside. It was of no importance. What mattered was what she was to do now. Gabriel would be looking for her . . . or perhaps just waiting for her to find him. She had to speak to him, if just to persuade him to go back home, where he would be safe on familiar ground. He would be in no danger now from the Daunt clan. He posed no threat to them anymore. Ariadne was safely beyond his reach.

Whatever could have possessed her, a Daunt through and through, to imagine she could live in Gabriel's world? It had seemed to offer so much promise, a whole landscape of peaceful loving. Clear-eyed now, Ariadne looked at herself, at who she was. She was not cut out for peaceful loving. She thrived on something else altogether.

But that did not alter the present situation. Gabriel had to be taken care of before he was hurt and before his presence in the city could disturb the promise that she and Ivor had found in the glorious rough-and-tumble of last evening and the long night that had followed.

And she had to do that without Ivor being aware of any of it. Ivor, the all-seeing Ivor. It would not be easy, but since when had she expected her life to be easy?

A sardonic smile touched her mouth.

✦ ✦ ✦

In the taproom below, Gabriel tossed a pewter cup of brandy down his throat and thumped the cup down emphatically on the counter. "Another."

The landlord, expressionless, refilled the cup and turned back to the conversation he was having with a couple of regulars at the end of the bar counter, reflecting that the young man looked in need of a stiffener. He was green as grass.

Gabriel began to feel better as the strong spirit burned in his throat and belly. He felt the heavy weight of the purse of guineas in his pocket. He'd been to see his father's lawyer that morning to give him his letter of credit, and the man had been gratifyingly obliging. Squire Fawcett was an old and valued client. Gabriel was now in possession of sufficient funds to purchase a new coat and britches and make a respectable presentation of himself to his father's friend in Threadneedle Street, who would give him the necessary introductions to make an appearance at court.

He had managed to fight off those ruffians, who had been after his purse. Gabriel called for another brandy, feeling rather pleased with himself. They had been after his purse, and he still had it. A small victory but a good one.

TWENTY-ONE

*A*riadne looked around the suite of furnished rooms in the lodging house on Dacre Street, just a short walk to the park of St. James's and the sprawling edifice of Whitehall Palace. They were quite handsome rooms, a decent-sized entryway, a salon, a dining room, a bedchamber with a small parlor adjoining, kitchen and servants' quarters on the floor below.

"Well, what do you think?" Ivor inquired, pulling back the heavy brocade curtains at the long windows of the salon.

"Rather grand," Ari said. "And very drafty. There's too much window."

"True enough," he agreed. "But it's a price you have to pay for the appearance of luxury."

"How expensive is it?" She ran a finger over the carved molding of a rosewood table.

"Hideously, but we can afford it." He turned back to the room. The tapestries on the walls banged idly in the drafts from the windows, and the Turkey carpets lifted under the whistling wind blowing beneath the handsome double doors. "We'll have to block the drafts somehow and keep fires going in all the hearths. We'll also need a cook."

"I doubt Tilly will take kindly to that." Ari folded her arms with a shiver.

"She can't take care of you and do the cooking," Ivor pointed out.

"Tilly wouldn't agree. We could hire a maid, though, maybe two, to help her out. She'd like that."

Ivor nodded. "I own I'd prefer to keep the household as much to our own people as we can. Abe and the others will manage the stables and the heavy work. We'll hire a couple of youngsters to help Tilly."

"When do I meet this relative? You said he was quite congenial."

Ivor had insisted that Ari remain in the King's Head while he made the necessary contacts and the arrangements for the next stage of their business, and she had rather resented being kept out of the action, but now it was surely time for her to step upon the stage.

"Lord Lindsey and his lady will pay a courtesy visit to you as soon as we are properly settled," Ivor told her. "This house is owned by a friend of his. He rents out the various apartments to courtiers who are not housed in the palace."

"And makes a tidy profit, I daresay," Ari observed drily.

"I daresay," Ivor agreed as aridly. "However, we cannot expect to move in the top echelon of royal circles if we do not have an address to go with the position. The palace is a short stroll across the park, not one, however, to be taken by you alone at any time, and not even with Tilly close to dark," he added.

"Why not? Is it dangerous?"

"It's renowned as a playground for libertines and debauchery in general," Ivor told her. "Perfectly respectable in daylight and in the open, for a lady accompanied by her maid, but what goes on after sundown and in the shrubberies is another matter altogether."

Ari laughed. "You forget, my dear Ivor, that I am a Daunt, the child of brigands, robbers, kidnappers, and the like. I doubt your St. James's Park can hold any terrors for me. Besides, I have my knife."

He shook his head. "Oh, trust me, I am not afraid for *you*, Ari, I know better than that, but your reputation is another matter. We are here, if you recall, to rehabilitate the reputation of the Daunt family. You won't do that by getting the name of a reckless debauchee up for a tumble under the bushes in St. James's Park."

"Point taken." Her smile was rueful. "I don't think I'm going to enjoy respectability."

"Oh, you'd be surprised. I'll show you how much there is to enjoy this evening."

Her eyes sparkled. "Now, that sounds promising. But why must we wait until this evening? There's a perfectly good bedchamber . . ."

He silenced her with a finger on her lips. "However gratifying I find your enthusiasm for bed sport, madam wife, I regret to say that that was not what I had in mind."

"Oh." She sucked his finger into her mouth. "Are you quite certain?"

He laughed, gently reclaiming his finger. "Quite certain . . . at least for right now. How would you like to go to the theatre?"

"To see a play?" Her gray eyes widened.

"That is what one usually does at the theatre."

"When do we leave? I must dress . . . there's a gown in lavender damask over a black underskirt, with black lace. It's most dramatic." She pranced away from him, the words tumbling from her mouth. "Come and see if you approve."

"Not now. I have to go out again. I'll be back in two hours, and then I can see the complete picture."

She paused, giving him a shrewd look. "Go out to do what?"

"Acquire a sedan chair for you. And liveries for the men. Lady Chalfont cannot be carried through the streets of London in a hired chair with scruffy chairmen at the poles. We must begin as we mean to go on, my lady."

"Daunt men in livery?" She went into a peal of laughter. "Oh, I wish you the very best of luck, Sir Ivor."

He merely smiled. "Our men, little Daunt, have known all along what this mission would entail. They are perfectly amenable."

"You mean Rolf put the fear of God in 'em," she said.

He shrugged. "Maybe, but they are loyal to you, Ari. As is the entire valley. You should know that by now."

She did, of course; she just hadn't thought of the men accompanying them in quite that way. She had grown up with them and simply accepted them more as friends than as servants. She had, of course, always known they would protect her as Lord Daunt's granddaughter, but she'd spent much of the time in the valley trying to evade that protection. Now she saw them in another light. She inclined her head in rueful acknowledgment and left the salon.

Tilly was in the bedchamber, hanging Ari's new wardrobe in the armoire, filling the linen press and the dresser drawers with snowy, frothy lace and muslin shifts, silk fichus, and shawls. The new shoes were arrayed in a line against the wall.

Ari had grown accustomed over the last two weeks to the thought of all this finery and footwear, but she had never seen it amassed in this way before. "Lord, Tilly, when am I ever going to wear everything?"

"All in good time, I reckon, Miss Ari," Tilly responded phlegmatically. "Once you're at court, you'll change your gown twice a day, or so I'm told."

"By whom?" Ari perched on the corner of the bed, idly fingering a shawl of delicate Indian muslin. Such a prospect sounded quite outlandish. Like everyone else in the valley, she was accustomed to changing her linen weekly, but she wore her outer garments until they were sufficiently soiled to make laundering absolutely necessary.

"One of the maids who works with the lord and lady on the next floor. There's three suites in the house, she tells me. She works for Lord Mallet and his lady, and along from them in the west wing is Sir Joshua and Lady Shipton. But we 'ave the biggest apartments, she tells me." A note of proprietorial pride entered Tilly's voice as she shook out the folds of a turquoise velvet cloak.

"Do you think you can manage the cooking, Tilly, as well as look after all this?" Ari gestured largely to the bedchamber and the mass of garments.

"I can manage for you and Sir Ivor, miss, and take care of you, but the men . . ." Her voice trailed off.

"If we hired two girls to help you, would that make it easier? Or should we hire a cook, just to take care of the kitchen?" Ari played idly with the fringe of the bed coverlet, as Tilly considered.

"I don't want no cook but myself in my kitchen," Tilly announced. "And neither is anyone goin' to touch your clothes, Miss Ari, but me."

"Then we'll get you some help." Ari looked up. "You shall make up your mind about who will suit you, Tilly. There are girls aplenty desperate for work out in the streets."

"Oh, aye," Tilly muttered. "I've seen 'em, too. Poor mites for the most part, don't look strong enough to carry a scuttle of coals."

"You'll fatten them up," Ari stated, getting off the bed. "Now, help me choose something to dazzle London with. Sir Ivor and I are going to the theatre."

✦ ✦ ✦

Ivor returned just before winter's early dusk. It was a fair night but cold, with a hint of frost already in the air. The apartment, however, was well lit. He looked in the salon, but there was no sign of Ari there, although a fire burned brightly, creating pockets of warmth against the needling drafts. He turned to the bedchamber. That, too, was deserted.

"Ari? Where are you?"

"In here. I think it's called my boudoir." Her voice, filled with amusement, came from beyond the small door that led through the paneled wall of the bedchamber into the small parlor. He went through.

"So, what d'you think, husband?" Ariadne turned slowly for him, her turquoise skirts flowing around her, the black silk underskirt making a dramatic counterpoint. Black lace edged the low neckline. The seamstresses had done their work well, and her breasts rose in a seductive swell, creamy against the froth of black lace. Her dark curls threaded with pearls clustered around her face, gathered in an artless-looking knot on her nape.

"A veritable fashion plate," Ivor said appreciatively. "How did Tilly learn to do your hair like that?"

"Lady Mallet's maid. She and Tilly seem to have become friends since we arrived, and Lucy is very good with hair, so she did this and showed Tilly how to do it. It is elegant, isn't it?" Ari looked with a degree of complacency at her image in the mirror of beaten silver above the mantel.

"Very." Ivor hid a smile at Ari's pleasure in her appearance, such a feminine sentiment, one that he was sure she had never really experienced before. "I must change my coat and cravat to be worthy of you."

Ari followed him back to the bedchamber. "Did you have dinner somewhere?"

"A chop in a chophouse," he responded, examining the contents of the armoire. "What of you?"

"A mutton pie from a pieman who came down the street. Tilly and I shared it. There wasn't time to cook with all the unpacking."

"Well, we'll sup after the theatre." Ivor tied a white lawn cravat at his throat before shrugging into his coat of midnight-blue velvet. The color accentuated the penetrating blue depths of his eyes, and Ari wondered why that amazing blue had seemed just a simple, integral part of Ivor over the years in the valley. The sensual power in their depths had not struck her at all.

"Is something wrong?" Ivor asked, disconcerted by her fixed gaze. "Is there a smudge on my cravat?"

"No . . . no, of course not." She laughed, shaking her head in easy dismissal. "I was lost in thought for a moment. What is the play we're going to see?"

"*The Man of Mode*, by George Etherege. It's very popular, I understand, and very witty." He inserted a diamond pin into his cravat and picked up Ari's ermine-lined evening cloak, draping it over her shoulders. "Shall we go, madam wife?"

Ari had never ridden in a sedan chair before and stepped somewhat warily into the one waiting in the street. She recognized the pole men, despite their smart dark green liveries. Tom and Bill were brothers, both burly wrestlers in their free time, and they grinned at her as she acknowledged them cheerfully.

"Something a bit different, eh, Miss Ari?" Tom said as she settled on the narrow bench.

"Lady Chalfont," Ivor hissed. "For God's sake, man, try to remember."

"Oh, aye, Sir Ivor, beggin' your pardon, sir." Somewhat abashed, Tom touched his forelock. "'Tis hard, though, seein' as how we've known her from a little lass."

"I know, but *try* to remember. It could be a matter of life and death, Tom." Ivor looked at Ari. "Are you settled?"

She twitched at her skirts. "As much as I'll ever be."

"Then let's go." Ivor nodded at the two men, who bent and hoisted the poles onto their shoulders. Ari suppressed a little yelp of surprise as she rose in the air in the swaying chair. She sat rigidly still, clinging to the edge of the cushioned seat as the men started off. Ivor walked beside the chair, his cloak blowing open in the wind, his hand resting on the silver hilt of his dress sword.

The sounds of music, voices raised in laughter and anger, and the raucous cries of barrow boys reached them as they drew close to Covent Garden. Forgetting the instability of her position for a moment, Ari leaned forward to see more clearly as they turned into the grand piazza. Crowds gathered in the long colonnades, and light blazed from the open doors of Drury Lane Theatre. She didn't think she'd seen so many people in one place before, spilling from taverns, intimately entwined behind pillars, brawling on the cobbles, and her eyes grew larger with every new sight.

The sedan stopped at the broad, shallow flight of steps leading up to the theatre. Ivor gave Ari his hand as she stepped daintily out of the chair, managing her wide skirts with one hand, her delicate chicken-skin fan with its beautifully painted ivory sticks dangling from her other wrist. She looked up the stairs into the brightly lit maw of the theatre. Lavishly dressed ladies and gentlemen moved up and down the steps, fluttering fans, talking excitedly, nodding at acquaintances. To her astonishment, she noticed that some of the ladies carried tiny dogs under their arms or peeping out from fur muffs. Dogs in Ari's experience worked for a living; they weren't carried around like pieces of jewelry.

"So this is London," she murmured. And indeed, this was the London she had imagined, this glittering stage set, rather than the inns and dirty alleyways, the crowded, noisy cobbled streets, the pathetic urchins and deformed beggars. The air in Covent Garden was heavy with perfume and the rich aromas of roasting meats, overlaid with the heady fumes of wine and brandy, mingled with smoke from the charcoal braziers where chestnuts were roasting under the colonnade. Beneath it all, somewhere, would be the fetid reeks of the city as she knew it, but here in this glittering piazza, they were not apparent.

"Come." Ivor offered his arm, smiling at her obvious fascination with the scene. "It's even more magnificent within."

Once inside the pillared foyer, he spoke to a liveried footman, who with a bow and a murmured "This way, sir, my lady," preceded them across the foyer and into a side passage, lit by sconced lamps and lined on one side by doors. Some of them were ajar, and Ari glimpsed slivers of the theatre itself as they went past. Their escort opened a door and stood aside. "Sir, my lady. Your box."

Ari stepped past him into a small, narrow box that hung out over the main body of the theatre. The stage was almost directly in front of her. The pit beneath the box was packed and noisy, mostly young men standing in groups, talking, laughing, drinking. Orange girls plied the aisles, their baskets of fruit hanging from their necks, calling their wares.

She looked up along the boxes. Some were empty, but many were filled with fashionable ladies and their escorts, a vivid array of color, of sparkling jewels, amid the rise and fall of voices.

"What d'you think of it, Ari?" Ivor was enjoying her astounded reaction. The scene was as new to him as to Ariadne, but he was not as enthralled by it. In many ways, he missed the simple life of the valley. There was something sugary and unreal about all this glitter covering a heaving cesspit of poverty-stricken misery.

"It's hard to believe there are so many people in this city," she said with a half laugh, adding, "So many rich people, I mean. There's plenty of the other kind."

"Indeed," he agreed, pulling out a small gilt chair for her. Ari was not as blind to the realities of this city as he'd thought. "Pray be seated, my lady."

Ari sat down, raising her fan in a gesture that enabled her to look at the boxes around her without making it too obvious. "How much does a box like this cost?"

"A lot, I expect, but this is a loan from Lord Lindsey, for our use while we are in town. He and his lady don't use it anymore. Lady Lindsey is in somewhat fragile health, I gather. He's happy for it to be used."

"Mmm." Ari nodded thoughtfully. "He seems a most congenial relative, Ivor."

"There are ways in which I . . . or, rather, we can be of service to him. He is very aware of that." Ivor turned as the door opened. "A bottle of Rhenish and some savory tartlets, if you please."

"How delightful." Ari leaned forward, resting her arms on the edge of the box. "Oh, look, something's happening." A trumpet had sounded, and the crowd had risen as one body to its feet, all looking towards a central box, elaborately gilded and swagged with velvet.

"Ah, it seems we are to be honored with the King's presence," Ivor said. "Try not to stare, Ari."

"Well, I've never seen the King," she said stoutly, her eyes still fixed upon the royal box.

"As it happens, neither have I." Ivor stood just behind her, looking over her head from the shadows.

The royal procession entered the box with another trumpet fanfare. The King wore a full periwig, falling in luxuriant black curls to his shoulders. He was accompanied by two women, both a-sparkle with precious gems, both magnificently gowned, their bosoms almost bare beneath the smattering of lace at the necklines. Their coiffures were dressed with yet more gems, and they waved fans languidly as they cast their eyes over the boxes.

"Who are they?" Ari asked in a whisper.

"The King's favorites, I believe. Nell Gwyn and the Duchess of Portsmouth, Louise de Kéroualle. Of course,

Nell is rather familiar with the stage," Ivor added with a chuckle. "She's made a remarkable ascension from orange girl to the King's bed. 'Tis said he adores her."

Ariadne had heard tales even in the valley of the King's favorites, and particularly of the erstwhile orange girl. "She's a good actor, too, though, isn't she?"

"Was," he corrected. "I don't think she treads the boards anymore. The King has made her far too wealthy and has enobled their bastards. A mother on the stage would hardly be appropriate."

"And the Duchess? What of her? She's not particularly beautiful, is she?"

"No, but 'tis said she's very clever, and his majesty values that. I suspect she's also rather an accomplished bedfellow," he added drily. "She also happens to be Catholic, which makes her unpopular in certain quarters." He paused, then said, "If you receive an introduction, you should mention the Daunts' Catholic affiliation."

"And what of Nell Gwyn? What is she?"

Ivor laughed. "Ah, now, I heard a story. Apparently, one day, the lady Nell was traveling in her coach through a crowd, who turned nasty. The King's debauched lifestyle is not hugely popular among his people. They surrounded the coach, shouting abuse, and Nell leaned out and said something along the lines of, 'Good people, you are mistaken. *I* am the Protestant whore.'"

Ariadne laughed. "I should like to meet her. I'm not so sure of the Duchess, but Mistress Gwyn sounds amusing."

"With luck, you will meet them both," Ivor said. "The

King is looking this way. Lean forward a little, flick a curl from your cheek . . . yes, that's perfect."

"You sound like my pimp," Ari said, only half laughing. "Am I supposed to seduce the King? That was never mentioned before."

"Don't be absurd, Ariadne," Ivor protested, his mouth thinning with annoyance. "You're insulting. I wish you only to draw his attention. There is a reason we are here, if you remember. This is your grandfather's wish, but you cannot hope to reestablish the reputation of your family by treating it as an insulting joke."

"I didn't mean to insult you, Ivor," Ari said swiftly. "I spoke without thought."

"You do that too often," he stated. "Try to moderate your tongue . . . ah." His tone changed. "I do believe you have attracted his majesty's attention."

Ari watched from behind her fan as the King beckoned a footman from the back of the royal box. His majesty didn't take his eyes from Ari's box as he spoke to the man. The footman backed away, and the King leaned a little forward and smiled at Ariadne. There was no mistaking it. King Charles had smiled directly at her.

Instinctively, she flicked her fan, smiled at him, then flicked it back to cover all but her eyes. His majesty laughed and turned his attention to the stage, where the actors were beginning to assemble.

TWENTY-TWO

The actors on the stage began to speak, but to Ariadne's astonished indignation, the hubbub in the audience didn't diminish. She leaned forward in an attempt to hear what was happening on the stage below her. In the pit, the mostly male audience continued to chatter, to move around, to hail acquaintances and orange girls as if the stage were empty.

"Why won't they be quiet?" Ari demanded. "Some of us want to hear. Why doesn't the King tell them to be quiet?"

"He's not exactly riveted by the play himself," Ivor observed, turning his head as a knock sounded at the door to the box. "That'll be the wine . . . Enter."

Instead of the usher with the wine and tartlets, however, it was a flunky in the King's livery. He bowed. "His majesty requests madam's presence in the royal box in the interval," he stated in a monotone. "And that of her escort." The last was a perfunctory addition, and he departed as suddenly as he'd come. Clearly, an answer was not expected.

"So, let the games begin," Ivor murmured, and Ari felt a shiver of apprehension not unmixed with excitement. She glanced towards the King's box. Ivor was right. His majesty was chatting with his companions, taking scant notice of the action on the stage.

The noise in the pit was subsiding now, and the actors could at last be heard, but Ari's pleasure in the stage was diminished by the prospect of the upcoming royal audience. It seemed almost fanciful to imagine that she, of all people, the unruly daughter of an outlawed earl, ill schooled in the finer things of life, let alone the conduct and expectations of a royal audience, was about to be presented to King Charles himself. At least, she thought, she looked the part, which was some comfort, and after a while, the novelty of the play itself took over, and she lost herself in the witty dialogue and absurdity of the situation being played out before her.

When the intermission began, the audience instantly started its conversational rounds once more, and the noise of voices rose from the pit. "So what do we do?" she asked Ivor in a whisper as she saw the King turn towards their box. His majesty raised a beringed hand and beckoned. As he did so, the door to their own box opened, and the flunky from before stood expectantly in the opening.

"Sir, madam." He bowed. "How are you to be introduced to his majesty?"

"Sir Ivor and Lady Chalfont," Ivor said smoothly, offering Ari his arm. He laid a hand lightly over hers in a

gesture of encouraging reassurance as they followed the
flunky along the corridor to the royal box. Doors to the
other boxes stood open now, and gentlemen were moving
between them, paying social calls. Ari noticed that the
women were not on the move. Only the gentlemen, it
seemed, paid calls at the theatre. Except, of course, for a
summons to the royal box.

The royal box had double doors, and these stood open,
flunkies on either side. King Charles was standing with
his back to the theatre, a chased silver goblet in his hand,
the other resting on the head of a spaniel sitting in the
royal chair. He was laughing at something one of the ladies had said, but as soon as Ari and her escort appeared,
he turned the full force of his attention upon them.

"Sir Ivor and Lady Chalfont, your majesty." The flunky
announced them without expression.

"So, a beautiful newcomer to our theatre," Charles
declared, extending a hand. "Lady Chalfont, where have
you sprung from?"

Ariadne curtsied as low as she dared without falling
over, her lips brushing the royal hand in homage. "From
Somerset, sire. My husband and I are but newly arrived
in London."

"Indeed . . . indeed." He made a gesture to her to rise
and turned to Ivor. "Sir, I bid you welcome to our fair
city."

Ivor bowed over the royal hand. "Your majesty is most
gracious."

Charles indicated his companions. "Her grace of Portsmouth and Mistress Gwyn are pleased to receive you. We enjoy the company of newcomers, is that not so, ladies?" He smiled benignly at his companions.

Ariadne curtsied low to both ladies, who responded with sketched curtsies of their own. Ivor bowed and received smiles in his turn.

"So, what brings you all the way from Somerset, Sir Ivor?" Mistress Gwyn inquired from behind her fan. "Is it not a wilderness of a place?"

"Some parts, perhaps, madam."

The King frowned. "'Tis damned lawless in parts. I hear little good about the people of the West Country."

"I trust, sire, that you hear only good of my husband's family," Ariadne murmured, mentally crossing her fingers. She could only hope that his majesty didn't inquire too closely into her own lawless antecedents. She took her example from Mistress Gwyn and peeped at him over her fan. "They are loyal subjects of your Protestant majesty."

"Glad to hear it," Charles said with a vague dismissive gesture. "And we are always delighted to see new faces at our court. I trust you will attend my lady wife, madam, when she holds audience. I will ensure you receive a particular summons."

"You do me too much honor, sire." Ari curtsied again. The spaniel on the King's chair lifted its head and jumped down, coming to Ariadne, sniffing at her skirts. Ari automatically bent to stroke the animal's head, lifting the heavy, silken ears with a practiced touch. The dog pushed her nose into Ari's palm, and the King chuckled.

"By God, she likes you, my lady. Miss Sarah here is very particular in whom she takes to. You have a liking for dogs?"

"Indeed, sir. I grew up with them. Hunting dogs for the most part, but I have hand-reared several puppies."

"Have you, now?" The king beamed. He bent to pick up the spaniel, handing her to Ariadne. The dog instantly licked her face, and the King's beam grew wider. "Tell me more of yourself, my lady."

✦ ✦ ✦

Gabriel sat dazed amid the hurly-burly raucous crowd in the pit, his eyes riveted on the King's box above him. The disturbance in the royal box in the interval had drawn many curious eyes, and he was not the only one assessing the newcomer. But he was the only member of the audience in the pit who knew who she was. She was here. Ariadne, *his* Ariadne, was here, and she was talking to the King.

He had known he would see her eventually. Their paths had to cross in the few square miles of the city inhabited by fashionable London, and yet, despite telling himself this, he had sometimes despaired of ever finding her. He hadn't known how to begin to search for her, except to visit the places where she might be found. And tonight he had found her.

But she didn't look like his Ariadne. She was a radiant lady of the court, alight with jewels, the lithe, slender body he could still sometimes in his dreams feel between his hands now encased in turquoise and black, a dramatic counterpoint to the dusky pearl-threaded curls framing her face. But the face was the same. He couldn't see her eyes clearly at this distance—the brilliance of the many candles in the royal box blurred her image—but he knew their gray clarity as if it were embossed on his mind's eye.

And the man beside her, the man whose hand rested lightly but without undoubted possession on her arm? Her husband. And Gabriel felt strangely diminished by the man's sheer physical presence. He was dressed richly but without ostentation, and Gabriel felt instantly that the heavy, gold-embossed fob he wore in the lacy fall of his own cravat was almost vulgar.

And he could never hope to stand where they stood now, in the King's intimate presence. Ari was talking so easily to his majesty, a dog cradled naturally in her arms, one hand—oh, how he remembered her hands, so strong, so sensitive, so quick to arouse him—pulling at the animal's ears as she talked to the King with as much ease as if she were talking to a close friend.

Gabriel burned with longing and with resentment. This was not how it was supposed to be. He was here to rescue her from a forced marriage, to take her away to live the life they had promised each other. And for the first time since their parting, he wondered if she had forgotten about him.

He pushed his way out of the pit, out of the theatre, into the brisk, cold night air. He would wait for them to come out.

✦ ✦ ✦

Ari's head was beginning to ache with the heat in the box from the many candles and the heavy perfumes worn by both men and women, which barely disguised the musky smell of overheated flesh in the richly elaborate damasks and velvets. Her gown seemed suddenly too heavy and constricting, but she managed to keep a smile on her face as she set Miss Sarah back on her chair.

"Madam, I will ensure that the Queen sends you an invitation to attend her," Charles said again, in a tone that contained dismissal as he held out his hand. "And I shall much look forward to renewing our acquaintance."

Ari curtsied deeply over the royal hand and rose slowly as he turned his attention to her husband. "We shall see you at court, Sir Ivor. Attend one of my morning receptions."

Ivor bowed his appreciation of the order and backed out of the box. Ari followed suit, desperate to escape the suffocating atmosphere.

"Your direction, Sir Ivor?" The flunky intercepted them as they moved away.

"Dacre Street," Ivor responded, aware suddenly that Ari was leaning heavily on his arm. He looked sharply at her. She was very pale. "You don't look well, Ari. Do you want to stay for the rest of the play?"

She shook her head. "I don't think I can take any more of this noise and crowd and heat. I need air."

He said nothing, merely steered her down the corridor and back into the foyer. It was as noisy and crowded as it had been before the play, but outside on the steps, the cold winter air was instantly reviving.

"I think I'm hungry," Ari decided as she took a deep, cold breath. "The meat pie was a long time ago, and the tartlets weren't substantial enough for a kitten."

He laughed, relieved to hear her sound like herself again. "Come, then, there's a good hostelry in the piazza where we can sup."

Ari revived with scalloped oysters and veal cutlets in a small back room of the Queen's Head on Charlotte Street. "So I'm to attend Queen Catherine's audience," she said after a moment, playing with the stem of her wine cup. "Alone, I assume."

"We'll see when you receive a summons. In any case, you will take Tilly. You cannot go out unattended. But I must attend the King's reception tomorrow." He helped himself to another cutlet. "I suspect, however, that his majesty's interest really lies with you."

"Well, I'm not about to join the ranks of royal mistresses," Ari declared. "I'll go back to Somerset sooner than do that."

"I trust that won't be necessary," Ivor responded drily. He was wondering whether Ari would be able to steer her way through the maze of court diplomacy, keeping the King amused while also keeping him at bay. Apart from the fact that she had no experience to prepare her, her nature was so open and straightforward that playing the royal game while keeping her true feelings hidden would not be easy for her.

After a moment, he said, "I think it would make sense for you to cultivate the Duchess and Mistress Gwyn. I doubt they'll welcome another rival. It's said they have enough trouble with their own competition, and I'm sure they'd do anything possible to protect you from the King's favors, for their own sakes as much as yours."

"Mmm." Ari considered this. "So, if I appear to be a country-bred innocent, eager for their advice and guidance, they would be only too happy to offer it?"

Ivor laughed. "I'm sure they would. If you think you can play such a part."

"But of course I can. 'Tis but the truth, after all," she said with an innocent smile. "I am as country-bred as any milkmaid."

✦ ✦ ✦

Gabriel stood in the doorway of a tavern in the piazza, a tankard of porter in his hand, his eyes on the door to the Queen's Head. It had been easy enough to follow Ariadne and her husband from the theatre, as they'd left early, before the full audience had poured through the doors into the piazza. He assumed they were having supper and had taken up his position opposite, with porter and a venison pasty to sustain him. He wasn't sure what he was to do when they emerged, whether he should try to attract Ariadne's attention. If she knew he was there, she would find a way to speak with him.

But he could not risk drawing the attention of her husband. Sir Ivor couldn't know anything about himself and Ariadne, about their shared past. He wouldn't be suspicious, looking for anything untoward. And Gabriel was certain that Ari would not betray herself or him, even if surprised. She was far too quick a thinker.

But they seemed to be spending a damnably long time over their supper.

He was almost ready to give up when they emerged from the Queen's Head. Ari was laughing, her hand resting on her husband's forearm, and he was smiling down at her in a proprietorial manner that made Gabriel feel slightly sick. He moved out of the doorway and approached them.

As he did so, a sedan chair came between himself and his quarry, the chairmen setting it down in front of the inn. Gabriel ducked around the poles and moved into Ari's view just as she was stepping up into the sedan chair, her hand resting on Ivor's forearm as he handed her in. For a second, her eyes widened, shocked recognition flashing across the gray surface of her gaze, and she became motionless, her foot suspended a few inches from the ground. And then her expression was wiped clean, her foot continued its progression, and she climbed into the sedan chair, settling her skirts around her.

Ivor frowned at her. "You look as if you've seen a ghost," he remarked, looking around him. But he could see nothing unusual amid the general throng. A man was walking away, pushing through the crowd, and a group of whores called out a bawdy invitation when they saw him looking in their direction. He turned back to Ari, but she was calmly sitting back in the chair, her hands clasped over the folded fan in her lap.

"Is everything all right?" he asked, looking at her closely.

"Yes, of course." She smiled. "Why shouldn't it be? That was a lovely evening."

He inclined his head in acknowledgment. "I'm glad you found it so." He gestured to the chairmen that they should move on, and they hoisted the poles.

Ivor kept pace beside them. Now what was the matter? He could feel Ari's discomposure as if it were a physical manifestation. Smile as she would, nod and reassure him that nothing could possibly have disturbed her peace of mind as much as she wished, she could not fool him. He'd known her far too long.

Gabriel doubled back through the crowd and walked behind the sedan chair, just one of any number of strolling revelers in the piazza where all London came to play. He kept himself in the crowd, indistinguishable from any other young buck on the lookout for a little amusement. And he followed them to Dacre Street. He watched from the shadows as Ariadne descended from the chair and entered the house, escorted by her husband, and then he slipped away, satisfied that he had done all he could for one evening.

TWENTY-THREE

A message come for you, Miss Ari. Very grand the messenger was, all covered in gold braid." Tilly came into the salon the following morning bearing a folded parchment. "He said I was to give it directly to you." She held out the letter. "He said there was no reply . . . look at that fancy seal."

Ari turned from the window, where she'd been standing for the last hour staring down at the street. She glanced at the seal and was momentarily shaken out of her preoccupation. "It's the royal seal, Tilly. From the Queen. Look, see her initials, C.R., in the wax. Catherine Regina."

"Lord." Tilly's eyes widened, and she looked at her hand that had so recently held the royal seal in its palm. "'Tis from Queen Catherine?"

"From the Queen Consort herself." Ari slit the seal with her fingernail and opened the sheet of vellum. The missive was written in a bold and unfeminine hand, presumably by an equerry or secretary. *Her Majesty requires the company of Lady Chalfont at an audience at four o'clock on the afternoon of the 24th day of December, in the year of our Lord 1684.*

"That's today," Ari said, glancing at the clock. "'Tis almost one o'clock now."

"You're to dine with Sir Ivor at two o'clock, miss." Tilly was staring at the Queen's missive, which Ari had tossed onto the pier table. She couldn't read what it said, not being lettered, but just the very idea of its provenance was enough to render her awestruck.

"He's not back from the palace as yet," Ari said. Ivor had decided to waste no time in attending the King's audience, reckoning that he needed to make an appearance while the memory of their meeting was still fresh in his majesty's mind. She went to the door, forcing her mind to concentrate on the coming afternoon. This was no time to be thinking of Gabriel, and what she was to do about him. "Come, Tilly, let us find something suitably elegant for me to wear to the Queen's salon." She swept into the bedchamber and flung open the doors of the armoire.

When Ivor returned an hour later, he was met by his wife in the foyer, standing like a fashion plate in the double doors to the salon. He raised his eyebrows. "You are magnificent, madam wife. Is this in my honor?"

"No, in the Queen's," she said, sweeping him a perfect court curtsy. "I am bidden to an audience at the palace at four o'clock." Complacently, she flicked the emerald-green silk skirt of her gown, looped over a pink taffeta underskirt, and did a little twirl. "Is it not pretty?"

"Very," he agreed, taking her hands, pulling her to him. "At the risk of disturbing perfection, I am going to have to kiss you."

A few minutes later, she came up for air. "I hope you haven't creased my collar, Ivor." She smoothed the wide white lace collar of her gown and patted her carefully coiffed hair.

"Hardly a flattering reaction to a husband's embrace," he observed with a wry smile. "Are you not going to ask me about my own morning?"

"Yes, of course, over dinner." She took his hand and pulled him into the dining room. "We have no time to waste if I'm to be at the palace at four."

Ivor made no demur and took his place at the table, while one of the two maidservants who had joined their household set down a tureen of soup. He served Ari and then himself, observing, "Turtle soup . . . what a luxury."

"So tell me what happened at court." It was easier than she'd expected to push her present problem to the back of her mind with so much happening in their daily life, and for as long as it stayed at the back of her mind, she could keep Ivor from detecting her anxious preoccupation.

"Ah, well, it was bedlam, to be quite honest. The ante-chamber to the King's bedchamber was thronged with courtiers, and the corridors leading to the antechamber were packed with supplicants, not just for the King but for his ministers, all of whom were in attendance upon him in his bedchamber. When he finally made his ap-pearance, after his toilette, the crowd pressed forward. It was astonishing that no one was trampled underfoot." Ivor dipped bread into his soup. "It was a great waste of time and energy, in my opinion."

"So you did not speak with the King?" Ari did not conceal her disappointment. After their reception at the theatre, she had expected some kind of special treatment.

"He was good enough to acknowledge me with a nod in passing," Ivor told her with a sardonic smile. He took a sip from his wine cup. "I should be grateful . . . it was more than many folk received."

Ariadne could tell how annoyed he was. Ivor was not accustomed to being treated in such cavalier fashion. "I imagine it will be same for me this afternoon," she said, wrinkling her nose. "Is it worth it, Ivor?"

"Sometimes it's worth swallowing one's pride." He dug into a dish of sweetbreads and mushrooms. "May I serve you?"

She passed her plate before saying, "But is it worth it in this instance?"

"We have been sent here on a mission, having agreed to it. I feel an obligation to complete it as far as we can." He looked across the table at her. "Besides, my dear, once our family fortunes are established, the world will be our oyster. We will establish our own residence, here or in the country, if you wish. It is even possible that the King will return the confiscated Daunt estates to you. Our own children will have a solid inheritance, no adverse family history to battle." His eyes narrowed as he spoke, watching her closely. He had been wondering, particularly since Ari's faintness the previous night at the theatre, whether perhaps she had conceived. It wouldn't be for want of trying in the weeks since their reconciliation.

Ari kept her eyes on her plate, aware of his close look. She guessed what he was thinking, but she wasn't ready to give up her nightly potion yet. She wasn't ready for a child, not until the uncertainty of this life was over. How could she possibly keep her wits about her as she would need to when she was nauseated, fatigued, and swollen like a stuffed pillow? And she needed her wits about her even more now, until she could find a solution to Gabriel's reappearance.

There would be time enough to think of children when this turmoil was smoothed out. It was imperative that Ivor remain in ignorance of Gabriel's presence. Their present harmony was too recent and too fragile to risk. He could well see Gabriel's arrival as a betrayal of their new-declared trust in each other. This was her mess, and she would put it right somehow.

"Will you accompany me this afternoon?" she inquired, forking a sweetbread.

"As far as the palace but not to the Queen's apartments. I was not included on the invitation, was I?"

"No," she confessed. "Just me."

"Tilly will await you in the antechamber to the Queen's chambers. There will be other maids accompanying their mistresses."

"How do you know all this?" She was genuinely curious. To her knowledge, there had never been any discussion in the valley about the customs and obligations of the court.

"Your grandfather told me in some detail before his death."

"Of course. Until his persecution after the King's murder, he was an established courtier, a confidant of the King's. I was forgetting." She had been born after her grandfather's self-imposed seclusion in the valley and had never given much thought to what the family's life must have been like when her grandfather was a rich, established, landed nobleman at the court of King Charles I, with all the power and influence of the King's close friend. Until just before her grandfather's death, the possibility of living her own life outside the valley had never occurred to her.

And when it had, it had been predicated on a life with Gabriel Fawcett.

Ivor had been watching her closely throughout dinner. She was off center, had been since the previous evening, and he couldn't think why. When he asked her if anything was wrong, she denied it immediately, offering a bright smile that somehow didn't ring true. He saw now the sudden darkening of her eyes, as if a cloud had crossed them. But it was only momentary, and then she seemed to visibly shake it off, giving a tiny, almost unconscious shrug before smiling at him across the table, saying with that same slightly false brightness, "Well, it's another adventure."

"Yes," he agreed coolly. "Another adventure."

✦ ✦ ✦

They walked across the park of St. James's in an icy wind, the bare branches of the trees ice-tipped. The clouds were gravid with the promise of snow. Tilly, wrapped in her cloak, looked around warily, her eyes returning always to the sprawling edifice of the palace across the canal. She couldn't quite grasp the fact that she was going to go into the Palace of Whitehall, maybe even see the Queen . . . maybe the King. It was more than a girl from Daunt valley could comprehend, and she imagined the disbelief of her old companions in the valley. The thought brought a wave of homesickness, but it passed quickly under her fascination with her new surroundings.

Despite the cold, there were plenty of people in the park and almost as many in the grounds of the palace itself. Courtiers, merchants, servants all swarmed the courtyards and the outer corridors of the buildings. Everyone seemed in a hurry, and no one took the slightest bit of notice of the three people hesitating for a moment in the first great palace quadrangle.

"Where are the Queen's apartments?" Ari asked, trying not to sound as cowed as she felt by the sense that everyone else knew where they were going and what business they were on, while the three of them stood like country bumpkins in a city marketplace, being brushed aside by all and sundry.

Ivor peremptorily hailed a passing flunky. "Lady Chalfont is bidden to her majesty's apartments. Which direction do we take?"

The man looked at them, took in Sir Ivor's commanding countenance and the finery of their garments, and bowed. "If you will follow me, my lord, I will escort you."

Ari hid a smile as she tucked her hand securely into

Ivor's satin-clad arm, and they followed their escort as he threaded through the crowds, down seemingly interminable drafty corridors, all equally crowded, and finally into a galleried hall.

"Her majesty's antechamber is that door, my lord." He pointed to double doors across the hall. "Her own attendants will escort you from there." He bowed and hurried away.

"Tilly and I will go alone from here," Ari said with decision. "Will you wait here, Ivor? I don't know how long an audience with the Queen takes."

"Once you've made your curtsy, you will be free to leave." Ivor looked around the paneled space. Deep window embrasures lined the wall that looked out onto a small courtyard. Tapestries lined the remaining three walls. They flapped forlornly in the drafts needling through the long windows. The floor was like a giant checkerboard, tiled in black and white marble squares. It was an inhospitable space despite the presence of small groups of chattering courtiers.

"I'll be here. Go in now," he said, adding softly. "There won't be another woman to hold a candle to you, I promise."

Ariadne gave him a brave smile, gathered up her emerald silk skirts, and glided to the doors to the Queen's apartments. Tilly scurried along behind her, casting fearful but awed glances from lowered eyes.

Two armed men stood on either side of the double doors. Ariadne handed one of them her invitation, or, rather, royal command, and looked haughtily ahead of her. "My lady." The men threw open the double doors into a smaller apartment, where maidservants stood in silence along the walls, hands folded against their aprons, eyes lowered.

An equerry came towards the newcomers. He took the document from the guard and bowed to Ariadne. "If you will follow me, my lady. Your maid will wait here."

Tilly scuttled to a vacant place against the wall, and Ari gathered her skirts again and followed the equerry through another set of double doors into the Queen's presence chamber. She was met by a gust of female voices, a waft of heavy perfume, and the thick scent of wax candles.

The equerry led her across a rich Turkey carpet towards a rather plump lady seated on a gilt chair raised on a small dais, her ladies of the bedchamber gathered about her. One of those ladies Ari recognized instantly from the previous evening as the Duchess of Portsmouth. The King's mistress served his queen consort. It spoke volumes for life in this royal court, she thought. But then she was making her curtsy, and the Queen was speaking to her in a heavily accented voice.

"Lady Chalfont, we bid you welcome. His majesty most particularly recommended you to our notice."

Ariadne curtsied deeply, her head bowed. She kissed the Queen's extended hand and rose as the hand indicated she should, her skirts settling gracefully around her. "Your majesty is most gracious."

"Not at all, Lady Chalfont." The lady's black eyes twinkled with something akin to malice. "We must all obey our husbands, must we not, ladies?"

Titters from behind strategically wafted fans greeted this sally, and Ari smiled and curtsied again. "Indeed, madam. As you so rightly say, husbands are to be obeyed in all things."

"And your husband, my lady? Does he make obedience easy for you?"

"So far, madam. However, we are but recently married . . . so it is perhaps premature to make such an assumption."

Queen Catherine laughed. "You are wise for your years, Lady Chalfont. You shall take a dish of tea with me. Are you acquainted with the drink?"

"No, madam." Ari took the shallow china cup handed to her by a footman and peered at the pale liquid.

"It is a very popular drink among the nobility of my country," the Queen said, taking a sip from her own cup. "We Portuguese find it very refreshing, very good for the blood."

Ariadne took a sip. It struck her a savorless brew, but as everyone around her was drinking with apparent enjoyment, she followed suit.

"Oh, ladies . . . ladies . . . are you drinking that insipid stuff again?" A boom of a voice heralded the arrival of the King and several of his gentlemen. Charles came forward, resplendent in gold and crimson silk and Brussels lace. His cheeks were flushed, his eyelids drooping heavily, and his forehead was rather shiny, as if he were hot. He carried his little dog underneath one arm as he came up to the Queen. "Madam." He kissed his wife's hand before turning to survey the curtsying group around her.

"My lady Portsmouth." He smiled at his mistress, who

rose from her curtsy with her own discreet smile. "And who have we here . . . why, my lady Chalfont." He took her hand, drawing her upright. "Charming . . . quite charming. Don't you think so, my dear madam?" The question could have been directed at either his wife or his mistress as he cast his eye somewhat possessively from one to the other.

"Indeed, sir," the Queen said with a small smile. "We are most pleased to welcome Lady Chalfont."

"Good . . . good. I shall be a frequent visitor to your presence in that case, madam." He spoke without question this time to the Queen and then turned his lascivious gaze upon Ariadne. "We are well met, as it happens, my lady. I have a present for you."

"A present, sire?" Ari couldn't disguise her astonishment or her discomfort. She could feel jealous eyes on her from every corner.

Charles dug into the deep pocket of his coat and pulled out a spaniel puppy. He held it by the scruff of its neck, and the little creature squirmed. "I noticed how fond you are of dogs, madam, and my bitch whelped last month. This little lady is the pick of the litter," he announced, holding the dog out towards Ariadne.

She put out her hand in time to catch her as the King released his hold, and the small liver and white bundle dropped onto her palm. She was so small, cowering into her hand, huge brown eyes looking fearfully around. "Oh, you poor little thing," Ari said involuntarily, holding her up against her shoulder, cradled by her hand. "She's terrified."

The King shrugged. "I thought her safe enough in my pocket. So do you like your royal present, my lady?"

Ari curtsied somewhat belatedly, the puppy still held to her shoulder. "Your majesty overwhelms me with his generosity. She is delightful, and I cannot find adequate words to thank you, sire."

"Prettily said," he declared with a nod. "I exchanged a few words with your husband as I came in. He appears to be awaiting your pleasure without. A most uxorious husband, it would seem." He laughed heartily at this, and the company joined in, except for Ari, who felt her all-too-ready temper rise.

"Sire, my husband's consideration deserves its own reward," she said sweetly. "I'd venture to suggest that 'tis a reward worth earning."

Charles looked affronted for a moment. Ari noticed with alarm that his color was even higher, almost choleric, and his eyes were rather bloodshot, his breathing quite heavy. Then, to her relief, he threw back his head and roared with laughter. "And a saucy minx he has for a wife, I declare. Well, madam, we can only envy him his due reward." He bowed to his wife, kissing her hand, then offered a nod to the Duchess of Portsmouth and left, still chuckling, his gentlemen following in his wake.

Ariadne remained in a deep curtsy until his majesty had departed and then rose slowly, the puppy still held against her shoulder. What was she to do now? She was rescued by the Queen, who laughed and said lightly, "You are indeed honored, Lady Chalfont. My husband does not part lightly with his bitch's litters. What shall you call her?"

Ari lifted the tiny creature from her shoulder and held her on her palm. "I would deem it an honor, madam, if you would name her. She is such a pretty creature."

Catherine looked gratified. "So she is. Let us see . . . ladies, do you have any suggestions?"

A chorus of suggestions, all totally inapt in Ari's opinion, greeted the invitation. She smiled, acknowledging each one with a little nod of appreciation, waiting for her majesty, who finally said, "Juno, I think. Does that not seem a goodly name for such a pretty little thing. Lady Chalfont?"

"Juno is a perfect name, madam." Ari curtsied once more, the puppy tucked into her crooked elbow. "A proud name for a dog to be proudly christened by a queen." She was rather good at this courtier business, Ari reflected with a degree of surprise, seeing the Queen's approbation in her pleased smile. "If your majesty will give me leave, I believe Juno is in need of her freedom." The puppy helpfully was wriggling and emitting little yelps of anxiety.

"Of course, Lady Chalfont." Catherine waved a hand in dismissal. "But you and your husband must attend our Christmas revels. I insist upon it. We celebrate the Christmas mass in the chapel at noon. I will send an equerry to your lodgings to acquaint you with the day's festivities."

"You do us too much honor, madam." Ari curtsied once more and gratefully took her leave, backing out from the Queen's presence, Juno still tucked into the crook of her elbow. In the antechamber, Tilly, still standing like a statue against the wall, started forward as Ari appeared, accompanied by an equerry.

Tilly's eyes widened as she saw what Ari was holding, but a warning glance made her bite her lip. She offered a demure curtsy, and Ari thanked the equerry with a smile and a nod and walked to the door leading to the antechamber and freedom, Tilly on her heels.

Ivor was standing in one of the window embrasures, arms folded, waiting as he had been throughout. After the King had acknowledged him, pausing to exchange a few convivial words, he had been subject to curious glances and whispered speculation among those gathered in the Queen's antechamber, but he had maintained an air of cool indifference. The more mysterious he seemed, the more power he would have to influence their reception in the court. At this point, no one knew anything about Lord Chalfont and his lady, except that they seemed to have found the King's favor. That was sufficient to ensure that they would be regarded attentively from now on.

He let his gaze sweep casually around the antechamber, ignoring the occasional smiles, the half gestures of invitation that his vague scrutiny drew from those his eyes fell upon before moving on. He saw a lot more than his air of casual indifference would imply, however. He had done his homework well and knew the identities of most of the courtiers, and he mentally made note of who would be worth cultivating on his next visit. His gaze fell upon a fair-haired young man standing alone in a far corner of the antechamber. He seemed to be staring at

Ivor with a fixed intensity that puzzled him. The young man looked out of place, ill at ease, although his dress was appropriate enough. But he was young and no doubt intimidated by finding himself in the middle of the court, Ivor reflected. One could hardly blame him.

His gaze sharpened as Ariadne appeared through the double doors. She looked calm, composed, as she walked towards him, ignoring the rising tide of murmured speculation as she moved through the throng.

"My lord." She curtsied to her husband, who bowed and was about to offer his arm when he noticed what she carried in the crook of her elbow.

"What is that?" he murmured, barely mouthing the question.

"A present from the King," she replied, loudly enough to be heard by all around her. "Is she not pretty, sir?" She held the puppy out. "Her majesty was gracious enough to name her for me. She is called Juno."

"Exquisite," Ivor said smoothly. "How gracious of their majesties, madam." He stroked the puppy's wrinkled forehead between her long ears and then said, "Tilly, will you carry his majesty's gift, please?"

Tilly, completely nonplussed, received the puppy in her arms. Ornamental dogs were not in her purview, and she had no idea what to do with this shivering, clearly terrified little creature.

"Keep her warm and close, Tilly," Ari instructed softly. "Tuck her into your sleeve. When we get home, we'll settle her down." For now, she could not be hampered by an untrained puppy as she made her way out of the antechamber, looking straight ahead, responding only occasionally with a somewhat lofty nod to the bows and curtsies of the less fortunate who now recognized her as an established member of the court.

Ivor couldn't conceal his amusement at this show. Ariadne had taken to her new role like the proverbial duck to water, he thought. The contrast between the Ari of Daunt valley and this radiant young woman was almost impossible to believe.

Outside in the winter cold, however, Ari dropped her performance and drew her cloak more tightly around her. "We are bidden to the Christmas revels at the palace, Ivor."

"I know. His majesty issued the same command." Ivor steered her around a splash of vomit on the gravel pathway. "The Duke of York will be there. There will be a Catholic mass in the Chapel Royal, which both the Queen and the Duke and his wife will attend, and a Protestant service in the abbey. You will go to the chapel; I will attend the other."

"I am to make myself known to the Duke of York, then?"

"With the Queen's blessing already bestowed, it will be simple enough. Then we see which way the wind blows."

Ari didn't respond, walking quickly beside him, her hands buried in her muff, her head lowered as if she were watching her step. Ivor took her hand and tucked it into his elbow. He could feel the tension in her body as she continued to walk hurriedly beside him.

"Are you finding this more difficult than you expected,

Ari?" he asked abruptly, wondering if he had been mistaken earlier and she had fooled him, too, with her performance.

"No . . . no, of course not. Whatever makes you think that?" She didn't look up as she spoke.

"Perhaps because I can feel you jangling like an out-of-tune harpsichord," he said bluntly. "If something is troubling you, I want to know it. We are married, committed to this enterprise and to each other. Now, suddenly, you seem uncertain, and I want to know what has disturbed you."

It had come back to her. The moment they had left the palace and the excitement of playing her part no longer buoyed her, the dreadful anxiety about Gabriel flooded back. She felt as she had as a child waiting for some misdeed to be discovered. The apprehension was almost intolerable.

Resolutely, she raised her head and looked directly at Ivor. She was ultimately responsible for her present trouble, and she would put it right herself. Somehow her feelings for Gabriel had changed. Oh, she felt a deep fondness for him, held close the smiling memory of the time they had shared together, but she was not that person anymore, no longer the dewy-eyed girl who had fallen in love with a man who embodied everything that her life had lacked: the gentleness, the softness, the finer edges.

But she knew now that she had been tempered in the life of Daunt valley. She was tough and strong and had a great many more rough edges than fine ones. Ivor was her partner, her true mate. It was for her to tell Gabriel the truth, to let him down gently but definitely. There could be no misunderstanding. She would not hurt him any more than she could help, but her loyalty was to Ivor. And the thought of how he would feel if he ever found out that she had had any contact with Gabriel after their new beginning terrified her. His trust was too new, too recently earned, to be tried.

She had to have one last meeting with Gabriel. And then it would be done.

And so she met Ivor's gaze directly and smiled a little ruefully. "I am out of sorts, you're right. And it *is* because I am a little scared of what we're doing, of making a mistake, of saying one wrong word that will bring the house of cards down around our ears. I just didn't want to admit it to myself." It was so close to the truth that it sounded convincing even to her ears.

"You're not alone, my sweet. I am always here. I have absolute faith in you." He bent and brushed the corner of her mouth with his lips. "It's a strain, I understand that. It is for me, too, sometimes. But we will get through it together, I promise."

"Yes," she murmured. "Together."

TWENTY-FOUR

$\mathcal{G}$abriel left the palace a few minutes after Ariadne emerged from the Queen's apartments, and no one so much as turned a head as he passed, threading his way through the throngs as if he were invisible. Outside, he headed for the green expanse of St. James's Park. He could walk there, just one more anonymous figure in the cold gray light of a late Christmas Eve afternoon. Despite the wind and the thick gray clouds, the park was far from deserted, folk hurrying along the narrow gravel paths, walking around the canal, all within sight of the mass of Whitehall Palace, where the royal flags whipped back and forth in the wind. There were rustlings and whispers and stifled mirth coming from somewhere in the bushes that lined the paths, and a female figure darted out onto the path just ahead of Gabriel, her skirt still tucked up at her waist, showing an expanse of goose-fleshed white thigh before she yanked it down again. A minute or two later, a well-dressed young man emerged, fastening his britches.

It was a cold and inhospitable spot for such business, Gabriel reflected, but judging by the women hovering in clear invitation along the path, the weather didn't deter customers. He turned onto the path along the canal, a pair of swans sedately keeping pace with him through the water below. And then he heard it, that unmistakable voice. She was talking softly, but he knew that light, musical voice. How many times had he heard it in his mind since that hasty parting an eternity past? The voice came from behind him in the gathering dusk, and instinctively he pulled his hat down low over his forehead, ducking his head as he stepped swiftly off the path and into a screen of bushes.

Ariadne, her husband, and a maid were walking from the palace along the canal. The maid walked slightly behind the other two. But Gabriel couldn't take his eyes off Ariadne. He hadn't had a close look at her in the palace, only at her husband. Her hair was elegantly coiffed, jewels winking against the lustrous black curls, and her small figure was clad in the first style of elegance, her damask skirts swaying gracefully as she walked, her arm tucked into her escort's. She was smiling up at her husband, and Gabriel felt a deep, cold shaft in his chest that *his* Ari should look at another man like that.

Ivor Chalfont, the man she had sworn she had no desire to marry. Something had happened to change that. Could it be possible that once he himself was out of the picture, he was banished from Ariadne's mind? How could it be possible after all they had shared, all they had promised each other?

They had passed him now, and he stepped out onto the path behind them. He walked behind for a few minutes, feasting his eyes on Ariadne, noting every movement of her shoulders, the easy swing of her hips beneath the rich rustle of damask, listening to the murmur of her voice without being able to distinguish the words. She turned her head to say something to the maid walking just behind her, and he gazed at her profile, the straight nose, the firm jut of her chin, the sweep of her cheekbone. And then, abruptly, he struck off across the grass, away from the path, walking quickly, keeping his hat lowered.

Just as she turned to speak to Tilly, Ariadne felt the strangest quiver down her spine, creeping up her neck into her scalp. Someone was walking over her grave, she thought, but then, out of the corner of her eye, she saw the cloaked figure hurrying across the grass. It was Gabriel. She would recognize his figure anywhere: thin, almost reedlike, the slight stoop of his shoulders, the stance of a man who spent long hours hunched over pen and paper.

Gabriel was here, in the middle of St. James's Park. He must have been following her, she realized. After he'd seen her in the piazza, he must have followed them home, so he knew where she lived. And that meant, at least, that she would not have to go in search of him. If he was close by, she would find the opportunity to meet him in secret. The logistics for the moment defeated her, but she felt her spirits lift a little with the knowledge that she was in charge of the situation now. Now that she knew where he was, she could act.

✦ ✦ ✦

Gabriel Fawcett stood in the shadow of a doorway on Dacre Street, looking at the house into which Ariadne, her maid, and her husband had just disappeared. It was such a grand house, and Gabriel couldn't really imagine Ariadne, *his* Ari, with her disheveled curls and hiked-up skirts and sandaled feet, living in such magnificent style. And yet that very afternoon, he'd glimpsed her, every inch the noblewoman, being received into the Queen's apartments. And when she had come out, she had seemed to walk upon some cloud, above the mere mortals like himself, cowering unnoticed in corners, folk who did not have the credentials to move beyond the royal antechambers where they hung about, hoping to draw the attention of someone of influence.

He felt diminished, rudderless. He had expected to find her overjoyed to see him, eager as ever, hot for his kisses, filled with plans for their escape into the future they had imagined for themselves. Instead, she was someone quite different, always in the company of her husband and seemingly perfectly happy to be with him.

Ivor Chalfont was her husband. A distant cousin who had grown up as she had in the rough-and-tumble world of outlaws. How did two such outcasts fit into these surroundings? And yet they did. Whatever lay beneath the surface impression, Chalfont and Ariadne fit their new surroundings as if they had been born into them. And Gabriel was so out of his depth that he was close to drowning.

The more he looked at the house, the more hopeless it all seemed. Ari had talked so blithely of their being able to meet in secret in the midst of the metropolis, but he had nothing to offer her to compete with Dacre Street. Even if she were still willing, even if it could somehow be managed, he had little enough to spare to fund a clandestine liaison, let alone a life for the two of them away from the world.

He was still watching the door five minutes later when it opened and the maid appeared holding a small dog. Gabriel retreated further into the shadows. The girl looked around before carrying the dog down to the pavement. She set the animal down and stood with arms folded against the cold, waiting for the puppy to relieve herself. Then she picked up the dog again and, before entering the house, glanced around once more before bending and slipping something underneath the winter-bare flowerpot on one side of the door. Light showed for a moment as she opened the door, and then it closed, and darkness fell again.

Gabriel waited, but the door did not open again. He darted across the street, bent, and lifted the flowerpot. A glimmer of white showed. It was a scrap of tightly folded paper with a large G scrawled above the fold. Ari always wrote his initial on her missives. Bold and black, with no frills of curlicues. Without opening it, he tucked the note into his breast pocket and hurried back into the park, out of sight of the house.

He was lodged in the house of a shoemaker in Shoe Lane. His father's merchant friend had sent him there, to a cousin of his, promising a fair price for a clean room and a decent dinner. He smelled roasted mutton as he let himself into the narrow hallway and raced up the staircase to his own chamber before his inquisitive landlady, a motherly soul with a nose for gossip, could poke her head out from the kitchen regions and quiz him on his daily doings.

Only when he had shot the bolt on the door did he open the note. Just one line: *Gabriel, meet me in St. James's Park, just inside the gate from Dacre Street, at mid-morning the day after tomorrow.* A large A ended the short missive. He stood looking down at it. There was no salutation, no tenderness, no promise of any. None of the usual soft and loving sentiments that had accompanied her communications in the past, those hasty, love-filled notes hidden under the stone on the cliff top above Daunt valley.

But he would see her, speak to her. Convince her again of his love, remind her of her promises. And surely all would be as it used to be between them.

✦ ✦ ✦

Ari fought her distraction throughout the evening. Had Gabriel picked up the note? Tilly said she had seen no one on the street when she'd gone out to put it under the pot. If it was still there in the morning, Ari would find a way to remove it and wait for another opportunity. Tilly had looked askance at being given such a strange errand, but she never questioned Ari's actions and if asked to keep a secret would do so without demur. Ari didn't like to burden her with deception, but just this once, she had reasoned. If Gabriel had been watching them in the park, then it was not unreasonable to imagine that he had followed them home.

Fortunately, Juno provided diversion and, after a visit to the kitchen where she had been plied with chicken scraps and generally petted by the maids, recovered her courage and her spirits. When Tilly brought her into Ari's small parlor where she and Ivor were having supper, the puppy's antics were sufficient to exasperate Ivor and entrance Ariadne, who quickly forgot that dogs were supposed to be working animals.

"Oh, Ivor, don't look so disapproving," she chided as he separated Juno for the umpteenth time from the fringe of the Turkey carpet. "She wants to play."

Ivor merely frowned and cut into his meat. He was not fooled for a moment by his wife's appearance of normality. She was not really herself, despite the effort she was so clearly making. So what was she hiding? And why? The woman who had given herself so wholeheartedly to him was now withholding something from him. And it was beginning to make him very uneasy.

In bed that night, Ari was as warm and passionate as ever, and yet still he felt something holding her back. But there was nothing he could confront her with, nothing he could put his finger on. And when, afterwards, she turned on her side with a sleepy murmured good night, he kissed her turned cheek and lay looking up at the flicker of firelight on the tester above, racking his brains for something that could sound an alarm.

Ari felt his wakefulness as she tried to breathe deeply,

rhythmically, hoping that if Ivor thought she was asleep, he would sleep himself. She felt, absurdly, that even thinking about Gabriel while Ivor was awake might somehow alert her husband to thoughts he would consider treacherous. It had been such a hard-won battle to get him to accept the past and accept that it didn't affect their present that she was terrified if he had the faintest inkling she was even thinking of Gabriel, he would feel betrayed.

And her thoughts of Gabriel hitherto, which she had always confined to when she was alone, had been more curious than longing. She wanted to know he was safe and well, that perhaps he, too, had found happiness outside their own passion. But seeing him, feeling his presence as a physical reality, had shocked her out of a pleasant oblivion.

She wanted to see him, to talk to him, not just to bring things to an end between them but also to find out how his life was, how he was feeling, what poetry he had written. She didn't love him as she had thought she had, but she still had his best interests at heart. But she knew that Ivor would not accept that. He would never be convinced that what she wanted did not imply a deeper want. Any contact she had with Gabriel would be seen as a betrayal. Even if she knew it wasn't. And the unhappiness they had endured to get to their present equilibrium had been too intense to risk again.

She rolled onto her back and became suddenly aware of a faint mewling sound from somewhere below her in the darkened chamber. It was a pathetic whimper that she could not resist. She rolled onto her side again and peered over the edge of the bed. A pair of soulful eyes gazed pleadingly up at her from the shadows beside the bed. She listened for a moment to Ivor's deep, regular breathing. He seemed to be sleeping soundly. She leaned down over the edge of the bed and scooped up the puppy, tucking her under the covers in the crook of her arm.

"Don't get used to this," she murmured into one long, floppy ear. "Our lord and master will not be happy to find you here." A wet tongue licked her cheek, and she smiled in the darkness, her eyes closing as Juno settled against her.

✦ ✦ ✦

Christmas Day dawned to the sound of church bells ringing throughout the city and a heavy, glistening frost under a weak sun.

Ivor came awake as he always did, instantly alert. He put a hand out to touch Ari's turned hip and instead encountered a soft, warm, furry shape that moved under his hand.

"What the hell?" He sat bolt upright in the dim gray light of dawn and stared at his other bedfellow. Juno wriggled with pleasure, her brown eyes fixed worshipfully upon him. "Ariadne, what is this dog doing in the bed?" he demanded in outrage as Ari rolled onto her back, blinking sleep from her eyes.

"Oh, how did she get over there?" Ari exclaimed. "She was sleeping on my other side well away from you."

"That does not answer my question. *What* is it doing in the bed?"

314 ♦ JANE FEATHER

"It's a she, not an it, Ivor, and she was so lonely down there on the floor. I couldn't leave her to cry all night. She's probably missing her mother and her litter mates." Ari scooped the puppy against her breast, tickling her under her chin.

"Put her down at once," Ivor commanded in tones of revulsion. "I will *not*, now or at any time, sleep with a dog in the bed. Is that clear, madam wife?"

"Oh, look, you're scaring her," Ari accused, not in the least put out or surprised by her husband's outrage. "I expect she needs to go out now, anyway." She swung her legs over the edge of the bed, still cradling the puppy, and padded to the door that opened onto the small parlor. "Tilly . . . Tilly, are you up?"

"Of course I am." Tilly was on her knees, rekindling the parlor fire. "I'll fetch up your hot water."

"Thank you, but first, will you put Juno out in the backyard?" Ari held her out as Tilly clambered to her feet. Lowering her voice to a whisper, she said, "See if the note has gone." And then, raising her voice to its normal pitch, she continued, "Ask one of the maids to give her some breakfast, please."

Tilly nodded without comment and carried the animal away.

"Merry Christmas, wife." Ivor's tone had lost its acerbity as he came up behind Ari, circling her waist, drawing her back against him. "Shall we begin the day again?" His lips nuzzled her neck, and she turned in his arms, reaching up her own to circle his neck.

"Merry Christmas, husband." She kissed him with the swift upsurge of desire that could still surprise her as it delighted her.

He ran his hands down her back, caressing the swell of her backside, pressing her loins against his hardening erection even as he drew her back into the bedchamber, kicking the door closed before tumbling with her onto the bed.

"Tilly will be back in a minute," she protested without conviction, moving sinuously beneath him as he leaned over her on his elbows. Ivor ignored her protest.

Tilly, returning with a jug of hot water, noted the closed door and, with a shrug, set the jug down and returned to tending the fire.

TWENTY-FIVE

*A*riadne found the palace much less intimidating on the second visit. Tilly's relief at being left behind to organize the Christmas feast for the household in Dacre Street had been obvious, but Ari was no longer overawed by the sheer size of Whitehall or the numbers of liveried flunkies and equerries. She felt that she blended quite easily into the crowd of splendidly robed courtiers and their ladies thronging the antechambers.

"The Duke and Duchess will attend mass in the Queen's Chapel," Ivor said quietly. "Anyone in that chapel will be presumed to belong to the Catholic faith. The King and his wife will attend the Christmas service in the Chapel Royal."

"But the Queen is also Catholic."

"True, but she cannot be openly seen at a mass. I believe she celebrates privately with her ladies. In public, she is at the King's side."

Ariadne nodded. "So I will join the celebrants in the Queen's Chapel. Where will I find you afterwards?"

"The revels will be in the Banqueting Hall immediately after service. Follow the Duke and his retinue, and I will find you there." He lifted her hand to his lips, brushing a kiss across her knuckles. "Courage, my sweet."

At that, she put her chin up, retorting, "I have that aplenty, sir. Look to yourself."

He laughed softly. "I will. Your way lies yonder." He gestured to an arched door at the far side of the courtyard, where a steady stream of courtiers was passing through.

Ari nodded and slipped into the procession. In the antechamber to the Queen's Chapel, she stood with the crowd, forming an aisle in front of the chapel doors that stood open onto the candlelit, incense-fragrant interior. His grace of York and his wife, Mary of Modena, made their appearance within a few minutes, their personal retinue following. Ari curtsied with the rest as they passed.

"Why, it's Lady Chalfont, is it not? You are of our persuasion, madam?"

To Ariadne's confusion, the procession stopped just beside her as the King's mistress, the Duchess of Portsmouth, addressed her. Ari felt the eyes of the Duke and his Duchess upon her as she curtsied deeply.

"Lady Chalfont." The Duke of York spoke pleasantly as he took her hand and raised her from her obeisance. "My brother was talking of you only last evening. I gather he gave you one of his puppies. A signal honor, indeed."

"One I am truly sensible of, your grace." Ari smiled.

"So you celebrate the Christmas mass with us?" He nodded, his hooded eyes in his rather florid complexion grazing over her countenance, the luxuriant locks of his peruke swinging gently with the motion. "And what of your husband?"

"Sir Ivor is worshipping in the Chapel Royal, sir."

He inclined his head in acknowledgment. "Ah, well, it is not unusual in these times for husband and wife to hold to different faiths."

"No, your grace."

A swell of organ music from the chapel caused the royal procession to move forward again, leaving Ariadne aware of curious glances, not all of them particularly friendly, which did not surprise her. Her grandfather had described the court as a competitive place, its members constantly jostling for royal notice and favor.

She followed the throng through the doors into the chapel. The Duke and Duchess were seated in a boxed pew a little apart from the main body of the small church. It became quickly apparent that there would not be sufficient seats for the entire congregation, and Ari kept herself close to the rear, near the doors, where any mistakes she might make in the order of service would not be too noticeable. Paradoxically, in the midst of this throng, she felt a sense of privacy. She could indulge her thoughts without worrying about Ivor's searching gaze.

Tilly had found the note gone, which must mean that Gabriel had picked it up. What was he doing on this Christmas Day? Was his family in London? It seemed unlikely. West Country folk, insular as they were by nature, rarely ventured out of their own three counties. The journey was too long and hazardous for casual travel. Perhaps he was with friends. She didn't like to think of him on such a day alone and friendless in some anonymous lodging in this hostile and anonymous city. She had only managed a glimpse of his face in the piazza, but she thought he had looked thinner, frailer somehow. The journey to London would have taken its toll—she knew its hardships well enough herself—and Gabriel had never struck her as tough and capable of much physical endurance. It was part of what had drawn her to him, that ethereal quality, so different from the rough-hewed, raw physical power of the men she had grown up with. How was he managing in the hurly-burly of London? It was definitely not a city for the faint of heart. But perhaps he was with family friends. His parents would not have sent him alone and friendless into the city to make his way for himself.

✦ ✦ ✦

Gabriel was, in fact, standing opposite the house on Dacre Street, looking up at its impenetrable front, windows and doors firmly closed. He didn't know what he was doing here. He would see her tomorrow, as arranged. Instead, he was jeopardizing everything by standing here in the open, gawking at her house. What if her husband were to find out? Ivor Chalfont was, to all intents and purposes, a Daunt with the same bloodthirsty inclinations of the whole tribe, if Ari was to be believed, and he had no reason to doubt her. She had sent him away for his own protection when she was officially unattached, but it would be so much more dangerous to seek her out now that she was actually married, another man's legal property. Gabriel had no wish to die on the end of Sir Ivor Chalfont's sword.

But he had to admit that the gentleman he had seen did not look in the least like a bloodthirsty outlaw. His features were refined, his figure elegant, although the strength of his frame beneath the magnificent clothes was unmistakable. And he showed a tenderness towards Ariadne that no one could mistake.

As Gabriel stood there, the front door opened, and the maid he had seen yesterday emerged onto the street. She set down her burden, which turned out to be the very small spaniel puppy. As soon as its paws touched ground, it darted forward with an excited yelp, only to be brought up short by the ribbon around its neck.

The maid reined the dog in and started walking along the street, keeping the puppy at her heel. Gabriel hesitated for barely a moment before he started to stroll across the street towards her. "Excuse me, mistress."

Tilly stopped to stare at her accoster, surprised and wary. "Sir?"

"Forgive me, but I believe you work for Sir Ivor Chalfont and his lady." He smiled with what he hoped was reassurance. He couldn't believe what he was doing, but he couldn't seem to help himself. He had come so far in his search for Ariadne that nothing seemed too risky anymore.

"And what if I do?" Tilly demanded cautiously. He struck her as a rather shy and harmless young man, but appearances could be deceiving. She jerked the puppy back to heel.

"Pretty little thing," Gabriel observed, bending to scratch between the puppy's ears.

"Present from the King 'imself," Tilly declared. "Gave it to my mistress." She continued to regard him with the same wariness.

"Your mistress must be quite a favorite at court."

Tilly nodded. "Aye, and she's there this minute, if you must know." She frowned. "And just what d'you know of Sir Ivor and Lady Chalfont?"

Gabriel hesitated before saying, "I used to know Lady Chalfont once, back in Somerset . . . before she was Lady Chalfont."

Tilly looked astounded. "You wasn't of the valley," she stated.

"No. I saw her once or twice when she came up to the cliff." He offered a placatory smile, improvising rapidly. "She once rescued me from a spring trap. Foolishly, while I was hunting, I wandered across the boundary of my father's farm and strayed onto Lord Nesbitt's land. I didn't know where his gamekeepers set the traps." He gave a rueful shrug. "I don't know what I would have done if Lady Chalfont, Ari as she called herself then, had not come along."

Tilly reflected. She knew that Miss Ari frequently stole away from the valley, up the cliff path, despite orders to the contrary. The young man's story was quite plausible and his Somerset accent true enough. She regarded him with her head on one side, her considering gaze shrewd. "Was it you my lady left the note for?"

Gabriel nodded. "I saw her at the theatre the other night, but we weren't able to speak properly, although she did see me. I followed her here, and that's when she left the note. She wanted to know if I needed anything, if I was new to London and needed any help."

That sounded like Miss Ari, Tilly decided. If she saw someone she had once known in need, she would offer help. But why was she doing it in secret? It didn't smell right to Tilly, and perhaps, she thought, it would be wise to keep this young man under her own eye. If Miss Ari was getting herself into deep waters, she might need a hand to pull her out. One thing Tilly knew for sure, Sir Ivor would stand for no nonsense if his wife was up to her tricks, however well-meaning. Sir Ivor was not a man to deceive, however innocent it might be.

"And do you need help?" she demanded.

Gabriel shook his head. "Not really, but back in Somerset, I didn't have a chance to thank her properly. She said she had no time to talk and ran off before I could discover anything but her name. Her note said to meet her in the park tomorrow." He offered a hesitant smile. "I own it will be pleasant to see a familiar face, to talk with someone from back home. London is a big place."

"That it is," Tilly agreed. Her eyes were on the puppy, rooting happily in the cracks between the cobbles. She could quite understand what the young man must be feeling. She was homesick herself often enough.

"I know I should wait until tomorrow to see her," Gabriel said with disarming frankness. "But 'tis Christmas Day, and I miss my family. I thought perhaps if I could just hear a familiar voice, like yours, mistress, I might find it easier to . . . oh, foolish nonsense." He cut himself off with a shrug. "I daresay you'll be celebrating Christmas with much merriment. Roast goose, perhaps?"

Tilly nodded. "Oh, that an' all the rest," she said. "Pies and puddings. Once they come back from the palace, the feast will begin." She stopped as the puppy squatted on a scraggly patch of grass to relieve herself. "That's a good girl," she said approvingly, turning back to the house. "I'd best be getting along now, sir. Still a lot to do in the kitchen."

"Yes, of course." He half turned to leave. "A Merry Christmas to you, mistress."

Tilly lifted her hand to the door latch. "And a Merry Christmas to you, sir." She stood for a moment with her hand on the latch, then said abruptly, "If you've a mind to take your Christmas dinner in the kitchen with us, you'd be welcome, sir. If you've nowhere better to go."

Tilly was naturally warmhearted, and the man was lonely and homesick and far too thin and pale. He was a Somerset lad, a farmer's boy, although, judging by his raiment, he came from well-to-do farming stock, and whatever his connection with Miss Ari, it gave him the right of Somerset hospitality. There was more than enough to go around in her kitchen. And maybe, Tilly thought, she might pick up some enlightening information as the wine flowed freely at the table.

Gabriel heard himself thanking her, introducing himself, and accepting the invitation, even though his rational self screamed that it was madness. He was walking into the proverbial lion's den. But the temptation to be under the same roof as Ari was irresistible. She was at the palace right now, and even after she returned, if he stayed in the kitchen, there would be no danger of them meeting. Grand ladies, as Ariadne so clearly was now, did not frequent kitchens. But he might be able to catch a glimpse, maybe even get some inkling of what her life with her husband was like. The servants might talk a little or respond to a gentle prod.

"Come you in, then, Master Gabriel," Tilly said briskly. "There's a seat by the range and a cup of sack."

Gabriel followed her into the square hall and through a door at the rear leading down a narrow flight of stairs to the kitchen, filled with the aromas of roasting goose and apples and steaming puddings and a constant mist of flour rising from the long table, where a young girl in cap and apron was rolling pastry for mince pies. For a moment, he was overcome with a wash of homesickness, for the life he had once led in the square Somersetshire farmhouse, where talk of war and rebellion was generally muffled in the tankards of scrumpy and October ale.

✦ ✦ ✦

Ariadne wondered how long this interminable service in the chapel could possibly continue. The incense was making her head ache, and the monotonous chanting made her want to sleep where she stood, shifting from one foot to the other. But finally, it came to an end, and the Duke and his wife moved out of their box and processed, their retinue behind them, out of the chapel. The rest of the congregation followed suit, all as relieved as Ariadne, as far as she could tell from the renewed buzz of conversation and the haste with which they pushed through the chapel doors.

The crowd crossed the large central courtyard to the Banqueting Hall. The brisk chill air awoke Ari and banished her headache. A young woman came up beside her and said, "I haven't seen you here before."

"No." Ari turned swiftly. "I am but recently arrived in London." She gave a self-deprecating smile. "Indeed, I know no one but my husband."

"Oh, you know his majesty well enough to receive one of his prized puppies as a gift, and you know her grace of Portsmouth, it seems, which means you have made your curtsy to her majesty," the young woman responded. "I would say you've done rather well for such a newcomer."

Ari looked for the sting but couldn't find it. She laughed. "If you put it like that, madam, then I would have to agree with you. But in truth, it doesn't feel like it." She tilted her head in inquiry. "I am Ariadne Chalfont . . ." The question mark hung in her voice.

"Madeleine Covington, a very junior lady of the bedchamber to her grace the Duchess of York." The girl grimaced. "A *very* junior attendant on her grace."

"A thankless task?" Ari hazarded, reading between the lines. Ladies of the royal bedchambers were always of noble families, but the younger ones were often treated worse than lowly kitchen maids.

Her companion laughed. "You could say that, but you'll keep it to yourself if you're wise. I am to count my blessings and hope for a rich and noble husband."

326 + JANE FEATHER

Ari smiled her comprehension as they entered the vast Banqueting Hall. The King and his consort were already seated on a raised dais at the far end, and the Duke and Duchess took their places with them. Musicians played in the galleries above, and the long tables in the body of the hall were piled with platters of roast meats and baskets of bread.

Ari looked around for her husband, but it was almost impossible to see anything in the crowd. Velvet, damask, silk, fur brushed past her as she stood at a loss, once more alone. She managed to make out Madeleine Covington standing behind the Duchess of York's chair, but there were no other familiar faces. People were surging to the long benches at the tables, somehow seeming to know where they should sit. Ariadne knew there would be a hierarchy; the salt cellars were very prominently displayed two-thirds of the way down the table. Was she elevated sufficiently to sit above the salt?

Fortunately, before she had to think about testing her position, she felt Ivor behind her. He placed a hand on her shoulder, murmuring into her ear, "Come, we have done sufficient duty for today. No one will look for us in this mob. Let us go home to our own table."

"Oh, can we?" She looked over her shoulder at him, relief clear in her eyes. "I don't think I can bear another minute of this."

For answer, he cupped her elbow and eased her out through the clamoring throng to the doors. They edged through the constant stream of servers bearing huge silver platters above their heads, as they dodged and weaved through the crowd to the tables, and finally reached the blessed cool air of the courtyard.

"What a nightmare," Ari breathed. "I don't think I could face coming back here, Ivor."

"You can, and you must," he responded steadily. "But enough for one day. We're going home."

TWENTY-SIX

*A*riadne went into her bedchamber as soon as they reached home and discarded her cloak, gloves, and muff, dropping them on the bed. "Ivor . . . Ivor, could you help me, please?" she called over her shoulder through the open bedchamber door.

Ivor came in at once, unclasping his sword belt. "What do you need?"

"Unlace me and help me out of this gown, please. Tilly will be busy in the kitchen." She tugged at the front lacing of her bodice. "We're not going out again, and I can't eat in these clothes."

He laughed. "It would be a pity to drop goose grease on them, I agree." He moved her hands aside and unlaced her bodice. She shrugged her shoulders, shaking her arms, and the overgown fell to the floor, the rich emerald damask puddling at her feet. She stepped away from it, kicking off her heeled sandals as she turned to give him her back so that he could unlace the underdress.

Ivor took his time, unthreading the laces one by one, enjoying the way her body seemed to slip from its casing, her pale skin with its faint pink tone glowing beneath the fine muslin of her chemise as he eased the apple-green silk underdress away from her. He placed his hands on the rounded tips of her shoulders, feeling the warmth of the flesh beneath, then moved his hands down, molding the fine material to her shape so that her body was clearly outlined.

"We don't have time for this, Ivor," she murmured in faint and unconvincing protest as his flattened palms pushed up beneath the chemise to caress the smooth, silky roundness of her bottom.

For answer, he propelled her two steps forwards to the bed, bending her at the waist so that her hands were flat upon the coverlet. Ari felt cool air laving her heated skin as he pushed the chemise up beyond her waist, moving a knowing hand around to caress her sex, a finger slipping into the warm and moistening cleft. His free hand released his penis from the laces of his britches, and his loins pressed hard against her as she thrust her hips back, her thighs parted to receive his length.

He drove deep and fast, and her hips moved with him, her breath coming in gasps, her head thrown back as the speed and power of his thrusts brought them to an orgasmic peak that made her cry out as her head fell forward. She felt his teeth graze her bared nape in a little nibbling kiss of possession that brought a soft moan of pleasure to her lips, and she slid forward until she was lying half on and half off the bed, her chemise rucked up around her waist, her bare legs dangling in an abandoned sprawl.

Ivor looked down at her, his eyes filled with a deep masculine satisfaction, born from his own fulfillment and the knowledge of hers. "What a glorious wanton I have taken to wife," he declared, bending over her to turn her onto her back, taking her hands and hoisting her to her feet. He kissed her mouth, hard and then gently, his lips lightly brushing hers, his tongue dipping into the corners in a warm, moist caress.

"Come, now, that little exercise has left me sharp-set, and I can smell roast goose from here."

Ari laughed, an exultant laugh redolent of the heated excitement of the last minutes. She shook down her chemise and went to the armoire for a lavender velvet morning gown edged with Brussels lace. It was a comfortable garment for wearing in private, fastened down the front with pearl buttons in black velvet loops, but it was certainly elegant enough for receiving visitors, not that they were expecting any this Christmas Day. She sat at the dresser to tidy her hair.

Ivor refastened his britches and glanced at his image in the mirror, standing behind his wife. His hands rested for a moment on her shoulders. "Happy?"

She nodded, covering his hands with her own before rising from the stool. "Very, but also very hungry."

Smiling, he followed her out of the bedchamber. Tilly was in the salon when they entered, setting out a decanter of Canary wine with some savory tarts. "Thought you'd like a little something while we get dinner on the table."

"A good thought, Tilly. We're famished." Ivor reached for the decanter. "Praying makes a man hungry." He poured wine into two goblets and passed one to Ari. She took it with a smile of thanks, inhaled the sweet aroma, and promptly sneezed . . . and sneezed . . . and sneezed. Her eyes were streaming as she reached blindly for the side table to get rid of her full glass before it spilled everywhere.

Ivor was quite accustomed to Ari's sneezing fits. Anything could bring them on, inside or outside, it didn't seem to matter, and they were unstoppable. Deftly, he rescued her glass and without a word hastened from the room to the bedchamber for a handkerchief and lavender water.

He burrowed through the drawers in the dresser for the pile of handkerchiefs, and his hand encountered a smooth vial. Curious, he took it out and held it up. It was unmarked, just a green glass vial with an oiled stopper. He twisted out the stopper and smelled the contents, his nose wrinkling. Vile, sulfurous stuff. He'd never seen Ari take any of it and wondered why she kept it buried deep under her undergarments. Probably some female potion, he decided with a shrug, picking up the lavender water and a couple of handkerchiefs and hurrying back to the salon, where Ari, nose and eyes streaming, was poised for another sneeze.

"Here." He handed her the handkerchiefs, and she buried her face in them, pressing the bridge of her nose tightly, which sometimes worked. The lavender water under her nose finally did the trick and Ari leaned back against her chair, dabbing at her eyes and nose.

"Let me try the wine again, Ivor." Her hand reached out for her glass.

"I hope that's wise." He passed her the glass somewhat warily.

"It's all right, it's over." She took a relieved sip of her wine, and her bright color died down. "Forgive me, I don't know why it happens."

He shrugged. "At least I'm no longer afraid you're having an apoplexy. The first time I saw that happen, I was convinced you'd been possessed by a fiend." He laughed and picked up the decanter again. "I must have been about ten."

"Dinner is served, sir, my lady," Tilly announced formally from the door. "I thought you wouldn't mind if we didn't serve the boar's head, seein' as 'tis only the two of you."

"Of course not, Tilly. We'd hardly expect it," Ari reassured her. The full ritual of the boar's head and its accompanying carol was all very well for the royal feast in the Banqueting Hall but somewhat out of place in the more modest accommodations of Dacre Street.

"No, time enough for that when we have a quiverful of children to grace the festivities," Ivor said with seeming casualness as he led the way to the dining salon.

Tilly glanced back at Ari, who pretended she hadn't caught the glance and took her seat at the long table. "I wish you and the men would join us at table, Tilly, just as you would have done in the valley," she said, diverting the subject.

"Oh, no, miss, 'tis different here in town. The servants

all eat together in the kitchens, and it'll be a right jolly party, I'm sure," Tilly returned with a complacent smile. "We're not short of good victuals and sack, thanks to Sir Ivor." She bestowed a special smile upon him. "You just settle in to the goose and ring that bell when you need me." She bustled away, her tawny woolen skirts swinging about her with the energy of her stride.

"It does seem rather an indulgent feast for just two people," Ari said, regarding the laden table, the golden roasted goose surrounded by baked apples, a glistening pink ham, a raised game pie with red currant jelly, dishes of artichokes and mushrooms and buttered salsify.

"We've earned it." Ivor carved the goose.

✦ ✦ ✦

In the kitchen below, the levels of sack in the flagons went down steadily amid general merriment. The food was demolished, baskets of bread disappearing as fast as the little kitchen maid could replenish them from the bread oven. Gabriel sat at his ease in a place of honor at the top of the table, one hand negligently around his sack cup, feeling relaxed for the first moment since that afternoon on the cliff when he'd escaped from the Daunt men.

Although why he should feel relaxed he couldn't imagine, sitting there as he was in the heart of enemy territory, drinking his rival's wine and eating his food. But a full belly could do wonders for a man. He was perfectly at home in this company of working men. His father, for all that he bore the title of squire, did not disdain the company of his own farm workers at the farmhouse table on high days and holidays, and Christmas was always a big family feast.

Juno was playing tug-of-war with his boot, and he indulged the puppy idly, flicking his toes against her little teeth.

"Oh, give over, you little menace," Jeb said, pushing the puppy to one side with his foot. "Don't let her pester you, master, even if she does come from the King's own bitch. No good spoilin' 'em."

"True enough," Gabriel agreed, but he bent and scooped the puppy onto his knee and gave her a morsel of goose from his trencher. "She's a pretty little thing, though."

"Indeed, she is," a light and oh, so familiar voice chimed from the doorway. "And she shouldn't be down here pestering you. We came to wish you all a merry Christmas and to th—"

Ariadne stood in the open kitchen doorway, Ivor just behind her, smiling at the company. She had spoken as she heard the exchange between Gabriel and Jeb on the bottom step of the kitchen stairs, but the words died on her lips. She stared at the man sitting at the kitchen table surrounded by Daunt men, and her hand flew to her throat. A fleeting gesture as she wrestled for some semblance of control over her face and voice. Her gaze flicked to Tilly, who was stirring something in a pan over the range. The girl did not turn to greet the newcomers, but Ari could see by her stiff back that she was rigid with tension.

"Yes, indeed, a merry Christmas to you all," Ivor

chimed in, giving Ari a precious moment to gather herself. "And we wanted to thank you all for your loyal service this last year. There have been some difficult times, I know." He smiled around the group, and then his eye fell upon the newcomer. "Ah, a stranger in our midst?"

He directed a raised eyebrow at Tilly, who, still concentrating on her stirring, muttered, "I found the young man on the street, Sir Ivor, all alone on Christmas Day and new to the city. 'Tis our Christian duty to make all welcome on this day of all days." It wasn't a lie, she told herself. It was exactly how it had happened.

There was no reason to question such a statement. Ivor inclined his head in acknowledgment. "As you say, Tilly." He turned to Gabriel. "I bid you welcome, sir. Where are you from?"

Gabriel half pushed himself up from the table, and Juno scrambled down from his lap. "From Dorset, sir." It was the neighboring county to Somerset, and the hint of a Somerset accent in his voice could be easily explained by that proximity. His heart was pounding as if it would burst from his ribcage, and he fought to keep his eyes away from Ariadne, who had stepped behind her husband, standing slightly in the shadow of the doorway.

"Ah." Ivor nodded. "Of what family?"

"My name is Maitland, sir. My father has a small holding . . . nothing much but sufficient for our family's needs."

"And what brings you to London? It's an inhospitable place for country folk."

"I've an uncle in Cheapside who said he'd find work

for me if I made the journey, but when I got here, he'd gone, taken by the typhus."

Ivor frowned in sympathy. "So what do you plan now?"

"I have a little money, sir, enough to keep me in simple lodgings while I look for work." Gabriel found the lies tripping off his tongue with the ease of practice, except that he was not in the least practiced at the art of deception. Ari was so close to him that he imagined he could feel the heat of her skin, inhale her own particular fragrance, but he dared not even look in her direction. The air seemed to crackle between them, and the sensations were so intense that he couldn't believe others in the kitchen were unaware of them.

"Well, I wish you good fortune," Ivor said with a friendly nod before turning again to Jeb. "An expression of our thanks, Jeb. Will you see it distributed?" He held out a heavy purse.

Jeb took it with an appreciative nod. He was a man of few words, and Daunt men knew what was owed them.

Ivor turned to Ariadne, surprised by her long silence. It was unlike her to be backwards in offering her own appreciation. She managed a smile, but as she took a step forward, she bent and clicked her fingers at Juno, who came bundling across to her. She picked up the puppy, cradling her against her cheek to obscure her countenance as much as possible, and murmured her own thanks before, with a reiterated "Merry Christmas," turning and hurrying back upstairs.

Ivor followed more slowly, frowning. Something had

happened yet again to disturb his wife's equanimity. But what? She had been all smiles and merriment as they went down to greet and thank the household who had stood by them through so much danger and discomfort. In fact, it had been Ari's idea to go at that moment, but then it seemed as if she had been struck dumb by something.

Back in the dining salon, she took her seat at the table again, still holding the puppy, who seemed to be occupying all her attention. Juno licked her face with extravagant adoration, and Ari murmured nonsense to her, playing with her ears and stroking the back of her neck.

"Ari, put the dog down," Ivor said after a moment. "The table's no place for an animal."

Ari gently set the puppy on the carpet and picked up her wine goblet. "You're right, of course. She's just so pretty." Her voice sounded strange to her ears, almost without expression, and she could only hope that Ivor would notice nothing.

It was a vain hope, of course. Ivor noticed everything where she was concerned. He was looking at her far too intently, a frown in his blue eyes. "Is something the matter, Ari?"

She shook her head vigorously. "No . . . no, what could be? It's Christmas Day."

"Mmm," he agreed. "But for some strange reason, Christmas Day now seems rather different from Christmas Day half an hour ago. Something upset you in the kitchen." It was a statement, not a question.

"Don't be ridiculous, Ivor. We were only there five

minutes. What could have upset me in five minutes?" She could hear the slight note of desperation in her voice and feel the color fluctuating in her cheeks. She took a deep draught of her wine and steadied her breath.

"I really don't know," he said. "But something did." Anything else he'd been about to say was forestalled by Tilly's reappearance with the maids, carrying a flaming plum pudding and a platter of mince pies. "There's a good brandy sauce there, too," she declared, keeping her eyes down as she set the jug on the table. "And some sugared almonds with ginger and orange peel."

"It smells wonderful, Tilly." Ariadne felt her composure return as she seemed to step back from the edge of the precipice. If Ivor had continued to press her, she would have betrayed herself somehow, but now the brief respite had given her control again. She could be her old self and hope that he would forget all about that strange interlude.

How could Gabriel possibly be sitting in her own kitchen? She was only just getting her head around the idea that he was in London, that he'd come to find her. She was still trying to find the right words to tell him the next morning that their dreams of a future together could never be more than that, just the dreams of a pair of idealistic young lovers. If she had never seen him again, she thought, she could have lived her life remembering him with love, treasuring her memories of their time together, of the way they had felt about each other, and that would have been the end of it. It would not have been a betrayal of her life with Ivor, simply a part of her own past that made her who she was. The woman whom Ivor loved.

But now Gabriel was here, flesh and blood. The man she had once loved to distraction was sitting in her kitchen, and she could still remember what that love had felt like. The memory now brought an acrid wash of guilt, although she had no reason to feel guilt. It was all in the past, before her commitment to Ivor, and yet the guilt became more intense the longer she sat opposite her husband, trying to behave as if nothing untoward had occurred.

She could not wait until the morning to bring an end to it, she realized. She would break down long before then. "Would you excuse me a moment, Ivor?" She pushed back her chair with an apologetic smile. "I have a need . . ." She gestured vaguely and hurried from the room, crossing the foyer to her bedchamber. Ivor would assume she had need of the commode situated behind a screen in the corner of the chamber. She opened the secretaire and hastily scribbled a few words on a scrap of parchment, folding it tightly, enclosing it in her fist. Then she slipped from the chamber, crept past the dining-room door, and ran down the stairs to the kitchen.

The company was still assembled at the table, and Gabriel, to her relief, was still at his place. "Don't let me disturb you. I came to get a few scraps for Juno," she said brightly. "She's pestering Sir Ivor for plum pudding." She brushed past Gabriel at the end of the table on her way to the scullery.

Gabriel's hand closed over the tiny scrap of paper on the table beside his plate as she disappeared. When she returned with a bowl of scraps for the puppy, he was engaged in conversation with one of the kitchen maids.

Ariadne returned swiftly upstairs, reentering the dining salon. "I am sorry for being so long, but I thought to get something for Juno." She set the bowl on the hearth and then took her place at the table again, reaching for the jug of brandy sauce. "So, is Tilly's London plum pudding up to Daunt valley standards?" She poured sauce over her pudding and smiled at Ivor over her spoon.

$\mathcal{G}$abriel excused himself from the kitchen and headed for the privy at the rear of the backyard outside the kitchen door. He stumbled slightly as he fumbled for the door latch. "Take the lantern, man, you'll end up in the midden otherwise," one of his dining companions advised with an inebriated hiccup.

Gabriel unhooked the lantern from the wall and stepped outside. The cold air made his head spin, and he cursed his stupidity in drinking as deeply as he had. Sir Ivor's house was hardly a safe place to let down his guard. He crossed the yard to the noisome lean-to in the far corner and went in, holding his breath against the stench. Holding the lantern high, he unfolded the paper with one hand and looked at the single scrawled line.

Meet me at the entrance to St. James's Park across the street at ten this evening.

Short and to the point. He dropped the note down the reeking black hole into the midden beneath, relieved himself, and headed back to the brightly lit kitchen. Voices were raised in raucous laughter, and singing spilled out into the yard as he unlatched the door.

He slid into his chair again, picked up his tankard, and tapped the rhythm of the song on the table with his fingertips. His companions were too far gone in drink themselves to notice that the level in his tankard did not go down for the rest of the evening.

Just before ten, he pushed back his chair and rose with feigned unsteadiness to his feet. "Good people . . . good friends . . . thank you for your hospitality, but I must seek my bed before 'tis much later. Your kindness overwhelms me, and Mistress Tilly, never have I eaten such a magnificent Christmas feast." He stumbled across to her and kissed her heartily on both cheeks.

Tilly, deeply regretting her invitation and now anxious to see the back of him, said gruffly, "You're welcome enough, but now you'd best get along with you before the hour grows much later. Even on Christmas night, the streets are not safe."

"My thanks, mistress." He wrapped himself tightly in his cloak and, with a final farewell wave, let himself out again into the yard. The fresh air this time merely increased his clarity, and he climbed the steps unerringly to the street above. It was dark, with only the faintest glimmer of a moon beneath scudding clouds, and the night smelled of snow.

The dark shapes of the trees and bushes in the park seemed menacing in their silent presence as he stepped through the narrow break in the screening shrubbery onto the thin gravel pathway within the park. Ari had said to meet her there, at the entrance. He wouldn't miss her if he stood just inside the hedge. The lights of the palace across the park still blazed, and the sounds of music drifted over the canal. There were people still in the park, hurrying along the pathways, cloaked shapes moving along the canal, and Gabriel felt somewhat reassured. He stepped away from the shadow of the hedge to stand full square on the path, where he didn't feel so isolated.

✦ ✦ ✦

Ariadne toppled her king with her finger. "I resign, well played."

Ivor frowned at the chessboard. "You didn't have to resign. You could have played to a draw. Why didn't you?"

"Could I?" She looked surprised. "I didn't see how." Her eyes darted to the clock on the mantel. It was almost ten o'clock.

"I'll show you." He righted her king and moved a couple of pieces. "This is where we were three moves ago."

Ari controlled her impatience with difficulty. She remembered the position well enough, and she had chosen to bring the game to a rapid conclusion rather than a drawn-out endgame. But Ivor mustn't know that. It would never occur to him that she would deliberately throw a game away in normal circumstances.

"If you had moved your bishop to rook four at this point, that would have prevented my check with my knight . . . like so." He moved the piece and looked across at her for confirmation.

"Yes . . . yes, I see," she said hastily. "I must not have been thinking clearly . . . oh, I think Juno needs to go out. I'll just take her to the street for a moment."

"Not alone, you won't," Ivor stated. "She doesn't seem anxious to go out." He looked down at the puppy, who was lying across his feet in perfect contentment, her rounded belly evidence of a good dinner.

"No, but she needs to. She's not properly housebroken yet." She got to her feet, bending to lift the puppy. "I'll take her to the kitchen. One of the men can take her out."

Ivor let her go, busying himself with putting away the chess pieces. Whatever was wrong, he would find out soon enough. Ari had never been able to keep a secret from him, and he was beginning to think he'd been patient enough, waiting for her to confide in him.

Ariadne fetched her cloak and tied a ribbon around Juno's neck, then took the backstairs to the kitchen, but instead of going out through the kitchen, she took a side door that opened into a narrow alley alongside the house.

She only dared to be away a few minutes this time and ran to the end of the alley, peering into the street. The light from the salon shone through a crack in the curtains, but she would only be visible to someone standing at the window, looking down. She ran across the street, Juno galloping at her heels, and slipped into the shadows between the hedges.

"Ari." Gabriel sprang forward, sweeping her against him as she appeared on the path.

"Gabriel . . . Gabriel, no, please, let me go." She pushed

against him. "I haven't many minutes, and there's so much to say."

"I don't want to say anything, I just want to hold you." Gabriel buried his mouth in her hair as he pressed her head against his chest. "Please, just let me hold you. It's been so long."

Ariadne pushed her head back and straightened upright. She spoke with desperate haste. "Gabriel, my dear, please. Listen to me. This has to be over between us."

"No," he exclaimed in a fierce undertone. "No, it cannot be. I came all this way to find you, Ari. We will go away together—"

"*No.* No, Gabriel, we will *not.*" She looked at him with desperation in her eyes. He *had* to understand. "Everything has changed. Oh, we can't talk properly now. My husband will expect me back any minute. I will meet you here tomorrow morning, as agreed. Ivor will be attending the King's morning audience, and I will explain everything then."

She pressed her fingers against his lips and then was gone, a fleeing shadow through the gap in the hedge, leaving Gabriel wondering if she'd even been there at all. But he could feel the imprint of her body against him, and her fragrance lingered in the cold night air. She was no figment of his overwrought imagination.

She was real, in his world again. She could not mean what she had said. There was no way all could be over between them. He had come to find her, to take her away. Nothing must stand in their way. She just needed reminding of all they meant to each other. Her life was

346 ♦ JANE FEATHER

so different now, but she just needed reminding of their past. When he kissed her, when there was time for the long, languorous kisses they used to share, then she would remember.

♦ ♦ ♦

Ivor heard Ari's swift step outside the salon door, and then she came in, Juno at her heels. Her cheeks were pink, and her hair was escaping its pins.

"What have you been doing?"

"Oh, it's cold and windy outside," she said, bending to warm her hands at the fire. "I think there's snow in the air. I decided to take Juno myself. I walked a little way with our neighbor's boot boy. I thought that would be safe enough, and all our people are practically under the table now."

"Well, you're safe enough, obviously," Ivor observed. "Although I would prefer you to have a rather more obvious bodyguard than a scrap of a lad. However, no harm's done." He stretched and yawned. "Let us to bed. I must attend the King in the morning."

He moved around the room, snuffing the candles and tamping down the fire. "Go ahead and get ready. I'll be along in a moment. I'll just check that the doors are locked."

Ari went into the bedchamber, carrying the puppy. The fire was low in the grate, and she threw fresh logs on it and drew the curtains at the windows. Ordinarily, Tilly or one of the maids would have already set the room ready for the night, but in the circumstances, it was not surprising that it hadn't been done. She undressed and pulled her night shift over her head, then took out the little vial from the bottom of the drawer. She took a quick gulp, no longer bothering to measure it out by the spoonful, and screwed the stopper back in. The door opened behind her as she did so, and with careful, unhurried movements, she put the vial back into the drawer, smoothing undergarments over it.

"Is all well?" Her voice sounded normal as she pushed the drawer closed and turned to the door, her backside resting casually against the dresser.

"Seems so." Ivor looked at her closely as he shrugged out of his coat. Her swift, almost guilty movement with the dresser drawer had not escaped him. "What's in that little bottle that you keep in that drawer?"

Her heart seemed to jump into her throat, and she felt her cheeks warm. There was no point pretending she didn't know what he was talking about. If he'd found it, she could hardly deny its presence.

"Oh, just some potion of Tilly's. Why?"

"I was curious. I've never seen you take it. What's it for?" And now, although his voice was evenly pitched, sounding only mildly curious, his blue eyes were as penetrating as a diamond blade.

"Oh, something for the headache." She shrugged and turned away from that intense gaze and picked up her hairbrush. "I get them sometimes . . . with the flowers," she added for good measure.

348 + JANE FEATHER

348 + JANE FEATHER

348 + JANE FEATHER

348 + JANE FEATHER

348 + JANE FEATHER

348 + JANE FEATHER

348 + JANE FEATHER

348 + JANE FEATHER

348 + JANE FEATHER

"Don't lie to me," Ivor said, his voice still even, but there was no mistaking the steel beneath. "You're a hopeless liar, Ariadne, and always have been. What's it for?"

It seemed to Ari as if the whole house of cards was falling about her ears. She had to keep Gabriel from Ivor at all costs, and the prospect of keeping two secrets from him was suddenly overwhelming. Why should he mind that she had been taking this precaution against conception? It had been only a minor deceit, only ever intended to be temporary. She was probably ready to stop taking it now, ready to have Ivor's child if he so wished. Surely she could make light of this, shrug it off as if it were of no great matter.

She pulled the brush through her hair and said casually, "Before we left the valley, I asked Tilly to make me up a medicine that would prevent pregnancy . . . just for a little while . . . only a little while, Ivor." She risked a glance at him, and her heart filled with dread.

"You did *what*?" His voice was very quiet, and he didn't move from his position by the door.

"It was only for a little while, Ivor, just while we were on the journey. I couldn't face being pregnant while we were traveling, and if you think about it, it would have been horribly inconvenient, and the journey was dangerous and uncomfortable enough as it was." She injected a note of defiance in her voice, facing him directly now. "It was my decision to make," she added.

"It was not your unilateral decision to make," he stated, still not moving from his station by the door, but Ari could feel the willpower that was keeping him there.

He was furious, and when Ivor was truly angry, he was not a comfortable person to be around. He was holding himself back from unleashing the power of his fury, and she debated swiftly whether it would be better to provoke him and get it over with or try to placate.

"Forgive me, I didn't think it would be of any interest to you," she tried, and instantly realized her mistake.

"You didn't think it would be of interest to me whether you conceived or not?" he demanded incredulously. "Don't play me for a fool, woman. You knew all along that it would matter to me. Otherwise, why didn't you consult me in the first place?"

There was no answer to this. Ivor continued into her silence, "I can't trust you, can I, Ariadne? *Can I?* The one thing I have said all along, is that I have to be able to trust you, as you must be able to trust me. I have done nothing to forfeit your trust, but you have treated mine as if it meant nothing to you. All these weeks, you have been deceiving me in the most fundamental way. Not only have you been denying me the right to a child, to an heir, but you have used the most despicable, deceitful trick to do it."

Ari shook her head, too distressed for coherent words. "No . . . no, Ivor, please, it's not like that."

"Then what is it like, Ariadne? Tell me, pray, enlighten me." His voice dripped sarcasm, which in some ways she found harder to bear than his anger. Anger was at least a pure emotion, a pure response. "Do you even know what's in that filthy stuff? What kind of poison have you been drinking? It could render you barren, did you think of that?"

She shook her head again. "Tilly would never—"

"What does Tilly know?" he interrupted. "She's an ignorant country girl, well-meaning enough, but she knows nothing."

"Her mother . . ." she began, and then gave up. There was nothing she could say, no defense she could produce.

"For God's sake, Ariadne, maybe, just maybe, in the early days of our marriage, when things were not right between us, maybe I could understand how you might have been reluctant to conceive, but since then . . . since we put matters right . . . since I *thought* we had put matters right, you told me you loved me, in God's name." He pushed his hands through his hair in a gesture of helpless incomprehension. "*How* could you say those words, knowing all along that you could not possibly love me?"

"That's not true!" she exclaimed. "I love you, Ivor. I meant it, of course I meant it."

"And yet you deceived me in the most despicable manner. Could you only bear to carry the child of your lover, your poet?" he demanded. "My child was not worthy. Was that it, Ariadne?"

"No . . . no, of course not," she cried, her voice filled with distress that he should think such a thing. "Oh, please, Ivor. Never have I thought that. I will be proud to carry your child. Gabriel is gone from my life . . ." The untruth choked her, and she turned her head away from his gaze. She felt as if she were swimming through quicksand. She hadn't invited Gabriel back into her life, he *wasn't* back in her life. She would send him away, once and for all, in the morning. But until then, every word she spoke was a lie.

Ivor looked at her for a moment, then shook his head in disgust. "I can't be in the same room with you, Ariadne. I can't bear to look at you." He turned on his heel, and the door slammed behind him. Juno whimpered and ran to the door, sniffing beneath it, her tail waving frantically.

Ariadne stood still, her hairbrush poised above her head. A wave of nausea rocked her, and she stumbled behind the screen to the commode. When she emerged, drained, purged, filled only with a deep sense of loss, she crept shaking under the covers and lay curled on her side, trying to shut out the world, praying only for the amnesia of sleep. Juno yelped, and she reached down and scooped her up, tucking her under the covers with her. The puppy's body warmth was some comfort.

She awoke at some point in the night and knew instantly that she was alone in the bed. Ivor's side was cold and empty. Where was he sleeping? Or had he left the house altogether? She sat up, swinging her legs out of the bed, and listened. The puppy jumped to the floor and looked up at her with an air of expectation.

The fire still glowed, throwing a feeble light around the chamber, but Ari could see no hint of light from beneath the door leading to the small parlor. And she could hear no sound apart from the usual scratchings and creakings of a house at night.

Ivor wouldn't have gone out, not in the middle of the night. There was nowhere for him to go. She slipped

352 + JANE FEATHER

to the floor and crept barefoot to the door, opening it a crack. The room was empty. She stepped back, closing the door softly again, and climbed back into bed with the puppy.

She hadn't the strength to confront Ivor again that night. In truth, she didn't know how to defend herself from his accusation of deceit. She *had* deceived him, by omission if not commission. But she hadn't seen it as such. She'd done what she'd done for her own benefit, certainly, but she hadn't thought it would hurt Ivor. She had always made decisions about herself for herself. She had reasoned, if she had thought at all, that what Ivor didn't know couldn't harm him, and when she was ready to bear a child, then she would stop taking the precaution.

But of course it had something to do with him. Of course he had a right to know. Even if they had disagreed, he should have been able to state his own point of view. And what if he was right about the medicine? What if the potion had made her barren? If she could never give Ivor an heir, then she had caused irreparable damage. A man was entitled to a child. It was a wife's duty to give him one. He would be entitled to cast her aside and take another wife if she had deliberately made herself infertile. The church would grant him an annulment without question.

The panicked thoughts raced across her brain like a raging fever, and she forced herself to think calmly. Surely Ivor would never go to such lengths to revenge himself? He was capable of anger, but he was not a vengeful person. He was a much finer person than she was, Ari decided, on a little sob of self-disgust. He had grown up in the valley just as she had, but he hadn't emerged twisted and selfish and thinking only of his own comfort.

She flung aside the covers again and got up, hurrying to the dresser. She took out the vial and went to the window, opening the latch. A gust of windblown snow blew into the chamber, rattling the door in its frame. Ignoring the icy blast, Ari unstoppered the vial and leaned out, pouring its contents into the night, the sulfur smell making her nose wrinkle. She shook the last drops out and closed and latched the window again. A dusting of snow had settled on the floorboards beneath the window. She left the empty bottle on the dresser and jumped back into bed, chilled to the bone, her teeth chattering.

She was just shutting the stable door after the horse had bolted, but in the morning, maybe, she would find the right words to convince Ivor that she had not set out to betray his trust.

Not in this, at least. But the abyss of her assignation with Gabriel yawned at her feet. And there were no two ways of looking at that. She was most deliberately deceiving her husband. If he ever discovered that, then his accusations of untrustworthiness tonight would be strengthened a thousandfold.

But what if she told him the truth? It was too late for that now. She had met Gabriel in secret once, and she was planning a second assignation. She had known for two days that he was in London, following her. And she had said nothing. She was condemned by her own

TWENTY-EIGHT

Ivor came into the bedchamber just after dawn. Ariadne woke instantly from a fitful doze and sat up, holding the covers beneath her chin. "Good morning." It seemed a ridiculously normal greeting in the circumstances, but she didn't know what else to say.

Ivor did not return the greeting; neither did he look at her. He bent to make up the fire. He was still dressed as he had been when he'd left her the previous night, and Ari guessed he had slept in a chair in the salon. If, indeed, he had slept.

He straightened from the fire, and his eye fell on the vial on the dresser, its stopper lying beside it. He picked it up and turned at last to the bed. "So, you got rid of this poison." His voice was without expression, his face a mask.

She nodded. "You *must* forgive me, Ivor. Truly, I meant no harm . . . I know I was only thinking of myself, and it was selfish and underhanded, but I didn't think of it as a betrayal." She twisted the covers in her fingers, frowning fiercely as she tried to think of something to say to banish the anger and contempt in his eyes. "In the valley, it was different," she said, feeling for words. "When this started, we were in the valley. I had to plan for the journey not as your wife but as myself. We were sent to accomplish something, and I was thinking only of how best to do that . . . and . . . and it seemed to me that if I became pregnant quickly, it could be a complication." Her voice trailed away. There really was nothing else she could say; that was the truth as she knew it.

Ivor stood deep in thought. She had planned for the journey not as his wife but as herself, Ariadne Daunt, who, all her life, had had to think for herself, plan for herself, react on her feet. Somewhere in there, he could catch a glimmer of understanding. Ariadne of the valley was not this Ariadne, his wife and partner. She had acted then without thinking of him, because she was accustomed to making decisions for her own protection.

"I might be able to see some excuse in that," he said. "But these last weeks, since we arrived in London, still you did not confide in me, did not consult me. Why not?"

"Habit," she said simply. "I've been swallowing the stuff every night for so long I didn't stop to think about it."

"I don't believe you." His voice was sharp again. "Of course you thought about it."

"Not very much," she responded stoutly. "I continued to take it because if I thought at all, it was that we should get properly established before we had a child, and then . . . well . . ."

"Well what, Ariadne?" he prompted when she had fallen silent.

"Well, I thought it was probably too late to consult you about it, since I'd been taking matters into my own hands for so long. I thought . . ." She took a deep breath. "I thought if I told you, you'd react exactly as you are reacting, and it seemed easier just to brush it under the carpet."

She opened her hands in a gesture of resignation, letting the coverlet fall, and looked at him with a bleak smile. "Cowardly, I know, but that's the truth, Ivor. Every word of it. I did not intend to betray your trust. I did so, and I am deeply sorry for it."

"Sweet Jesus, what an impossible woman you are." He exhaled noisily. "I don't know how I am supposed to live in harmony with you. You blithely follow your own primrose path, offering ingenuous explanations for the most outrageous actions, and expect me to accept your wildest extravagances with a smile and a pat on the head."

"I don't expect a pat on the head," she ventured, not daring yet to hope that the crisis was over.

"No, you'd do better to expect your ears boxed," he stated. "I can't talk about this anymore. Go downstairs and find me some hot water and some breakfast. I've had a miserable night, and I have to put in an appearance at court this morning."

"Yes, husband." Ari slipped to the floor, reaching for

her dressing gown, trying and failing to hide her relief. "Is there anything you would like especially for breakfast?"

"Surprise me," he said sardonically, unbuttoning his shirt. "It appears to be a particular talent of yours."

Ariadne hurried from the room, the puppy on her heels, and sped down to the kitchen. One of the kitchen maids was riddling the ashes in the range, looking as green as grass. Ari let Juno out into the yard, where the snow was thickening. The puppy leapt forwards and then jumped back with a surprised yelp, shaking her paws.

"Oh, go on, don't be a baby," Ari scolded, toeing her back out into the yard. "Hurry up, and you shall have bread and milk."

"Lord, Miss Ari, what're you doin' down here at this hour?" Tilly asked, coming into the kitchen from her sleeping quarters. She tied a kerchief around her head as she spoke. "Eh, Ethel, get those ashes riddled. We need hot water." She took the kettle over to the water cask in the scullery. "Sir Ivor wantin' to break his fast, then?"

"Yes, and quickly, Tilly." Ari went into the larder. "What can I give him?"

"Got a sore head, I shouldn't wonder," Tilly commented from behind Ari. "Supped some stuff, we all did. A good Christmas that was."

Up to a point. Ari took a breath and said, "I have to thank you for keeping my secret, Tilly. Master Gabriel means no harm, I promise you. He won't come here again."

"Aye, that would be for the best," the girl stated. "Felt right sorry for him, I did, but if Sir Ivor's not to know of 'im, then I want nothin' more to do with it, Miss Ari."

"I understand," she said swiftly. "And you shall not, I promise."

Tilly made no reply, and Ari decided to leave the matter well alone. She surveyed the slate shelves of the pantry. She was ravenous herself, having lost everything she'd consumed during the Christmas feast in her purge over the commode. "Kidneys, bacon, mushrooms, fried bread, and eggs. D'you think that will suffice, Tilly?"

Tilly looked somewhat awed. She was feeling rather the worse for wear herself. "Aye, if you think so, Miss Ari. I'll get on with it now."

"My thanks." Ari went to let Juno back into the kitchen. The puppy tumbled in, shaking her damp coat and shaking out each paw in turn. She fell on a bowl of bread and milk that Ari set by the range for her. "I suppose his majesty will want a report of your progress this afternoon," Ariadne muttered, half to the puppy and half to herself. "I hope he doesn't expect me to carry you around all the time."

"Lord, miss, are we to go back to that palace today?" Tilly sounded less than enthusiastic as she broke eggs into a skillet.

"I'm afraid so, Tilly. But I hope we won't have to stay long."

"Hope not." The girl threw some bacon rashers into the skillet.

Ari filled a jug with hot water and carried it upstairs for Ivor. He was in the bedchamber, standing naked at the washstand, rubbing salt on his teeth. "Good, put it there. I need to shave."

Ari set the jug down by the basin, her eyes lingering on the long sweep of his body. But she knew this was a strictly look-but-don't-touch moment. Ivor seemed oblivious to his nakedness, and he still seemed to have an invisible fence around him. She was not going to endanger the possibility of a return to equilibrium by taking a premature initiative.

"Tilly will be bringing breakfast shortly." She backed out of the bedchamber and went to mend the fire in the small parlor. They weren't out of the woods yet, but there was a glimmer of light on the horizon.

Except for her meeting with Gabriel. For a moment, she toyed with the idea of not keeping the assignation. There was no reason she couldn't avoid Gabriel altogether. He could hardly force himself upon her. She was a married woman. Eventually, he would simply leave her alone and go away. But she knew she could not do such a cowardly thing. She had loved him once, and she owed him a definitive ending. She had to see him one last time, to see him on his way, knowing that he was safe and without expectation. And then it would be plain sailing. No more secrets, *ever*.

✦ ✦ ✦

Ivor brushed a speck of lint from the dark blue velvet sleeve of his coat. Silver lace edged the deep cuffs and was matched by the extravagant lace fall of his cravat.

" 'Tis snowing quite hard," Ari observed from the window. "Perhaps you should take the sedan chair."

"A little snow never hurt anyone," he said carelessly.

"You're getting soft. You used not to think twice about plowing through a drift up to your waist."

"Not dressed in velvet and lace," she retorted, stung.

He merely shrugged and slung his cloak around his shoulders, turning up the collar. "I'll be back for dinner sharp at two o'clock. Make sure you're ready to go to the palace afterwards. You'll use the chair."

He was simply issuing orders, his tone curt, and she had to bite back a swift retort. But she said only, "If you can walk, I can," and stalked out of the chamber. Ivor was punishing her with unfriendliness, although she could detect no real anger anymore. She bit back a sigh. Maybe he was entitled to his revenge, but it was very depressing. However, in light of her upcoming assignation, maybe it was best if he kept a distance between them, just until she had a truly clear conscience.

Ivor picked up his hat and gloves. He wasn't quite ready yet to put the whole wretched business behind them. He was still hurt and angry at the idea that she could make such a major decision without even considering his feelings, and it seemed small recompense to let her feel the sting of his displeasure a little longer. But it really went against the grain. He was not one to harbor ill feeling, most particularly where Ari was concerned. He'd put things right properly when he returned from the palace.

He left the house and crossed the street into the park. It was snowing quite briskly, and the path was covered in white. There were few people about; it was not good weather for the park's less salubrious trading.

He walked briskly towards the canal and didn't notice the cloak-wrapped figure standing in the trees edging the path.

Gabriel watched the tall, powerful figure of Ariadne's husband walk by, his feet crunching in the snow. His hat was pulled low, concealing his features, but there was no hiding the man's muscular power and energy. He had a sword at his waist and swung a silver-handled cane as he strode past. Gabriel guessed it was a sword stick, easier and quicker to employ in an emergency than a sheathed sword beneath the folds of his full-skirted coat. Obviously, Sir Ivor was alert to any possibility of attack even on a simple stroll through the park.

He would be no match for the man, Gabriel knew. He could handle a small sword with some competency, but he knew instinctively that he would be unable to put up an adequate defense against Sir Ivor Chalfont. He hadn't been educated in the arts of the warrior. *The pen is mightier than the sword*, he told himself, watching Sir Ivor stride into the snow. But he couldn't derive much comfort from the aphorism.

He stepped out from the tree, looking towards the gap in the hedge that gave entrance to the park. Ariadne would appear as soon as she was certain her husband was safely away.

She appeared in a few minutes, swathed in a hooded cloak. She stepped through the hedge and stood for a moment looking around somewhat uncertainly.

"Ari . . . Ari, over here."

She turned at the urgent whisper. Gabriel had moved

back off the path as soon as he'd seen her and now beckoned from the trees. She hurried over to him, her pulse racing, the blood thudding in her ears. Ivor was long gone. No one would recognize her even if they saw her, but there was hardly anyone around and no one on the path. Even so, she was afraid. So much was at stake.

"Ari . . . Ari . . . how I've longed for you." Gabriel caught her against him, pushing the hood from her face, bringing his mouth to hers.

Ariadne felt suffocated for a moment. Memory washed over her, of all the kisses they had exchanged all those months ago in the innocence of that burgeoning summer love, but they hadn't been like this. This kiss threatened to engulf her. It was dark and heavy and held no promise.

She wrenched her head free of his hands and pushed him away, breathing fast. "Gabriel, no. You must stop it. We can't do this."

He stared at her. "Can't do this . . . can't do what? I want to kiss you, Ari. I *must* kiss you. I have dreamt of this moment for so long. Is it the snow? Are you cold? Of course you are . . . where can we go to find shelter?" He looked wildly around as if shelter would miraculously materialize.

Ari shook her head. "No, 'tis not that, Gabriel. I am not cold. Please, just listen to me. We cannot do this . . . it is over, my dear friend." She placed a hand on his arm. "Please try to understand. I am married now. When you left and I married Ivor—"

"You were forced into that marriage," he interrupted, putting his hands on her shoulders. "Ari, we agreed you would escape from that bondage as soon as you were able. We will be together. I have a plan . . . I know it will work. We will go far from here, across the sea. I'm sure I will find some employment."

Ariadne stared at him as if he'd taken leave of his senses. "What in heaven's name are you talking about, Gabriel? Across the sea? Where? Why?"

"France, Italy, there are so many places . . . and that way, we will be safe," he said. "Your husband need never know where you are. We will start anew, set up as a married couple, and I will—"

"Oh, what a dreamer you are, Gabriel." She shook her head helplessly. "I know we had a fantasy that we would be together in the end, but things have changed. I cannot go with you. Gabriel, my dear friend, I do not *wish* to go with you. I love my husband." She took a step back, out of his grasp, and her own hands fell uselessly to her sides as she saw the devastating effect of her words.

"You don't *wish* to go with me? You don't love me anymore?" He looked blankly at her as if she were speaking a foreign language. "You don't mean that."

"I do." She spoke firmly and clearly. "I love my husband. I feel deeply for you, Gabriel, and will always cherish the time we had, the love we shared, but we were children playing at love."

"*No,*" he said vehemently. "I was not playing at love, even if you were. I have thought of nothing else the whole time we have been apart. All these weeks of journeying, you have been in my thoughts as I tried and tried to think of how I would find you again." He shook his head in bewilderment. "How could it not have been the same for you, Ari? How could you cast me aside so easily?"

His words cut her to the quick. She stepped closer, grasping one of his hands between both of hers. "It is not like that, Gabriel," she insisted. "I *care* for you, truly I do. I want only your happiness, but it cannot lie with me . . . not anymore." She reached for his other hand. "Indeed, we were foolish ever to think that it could. We are such very different people. I am so sorry, my dear. I would not hurt you for the world."

He shook his hands free of her clasp and just stared at her, his eyes blank. "How could you be so faithless?" he said after a moment. "I kept faith with you all these months, while you . . ." He turned away from her, his shoulders hunched.

Ariadne stood uncertainly. She wanted to put her arms around him to comfort him, to kiss him at least in farewell, but she did not dare touch him again. She had said what had to be said. She could only keep faith with one man. She took a step towards his averted back, laid a hand tentatively on his shoulder, then let her hand drop. "Forgive me," she murmured, and turned away, hurrying out of the park and back to the house.

Gabriel stared down at the snow-covered ground. He didn't know how long he stood motionless, but he started back to awareness when something hit his head. He looked up to where a squirrel sat chattering in agitation on the bare tree branch above him. A nutshell lay on the ground at Gabriel's feet. Obviously, the creature had dropped it. Gabriel shook his head and stepped away from the tree.

He would not give her up. He *could* not give her up. What else was there for him? He could not stay in London, hanging aimlessly around the court, hoping someone influential would notice him. He wasn't made for that life. That was Ariadne's new life, her new married life. And he could not endure seeing her with her husband. Smiling at him, bestowing upon another man the soft looks, the sensual touches, that belonged to *him*. It would be sheer torment to see her so happy, so at home where he himself was so ill at ease. And he could not go home with his tail between his legs, not when his father had spent the proceeds of an entire harvest on providing him with what he would need to find advancement at court.

No, he would not accept her rejection. He would keep vigil on the house. She would have to come out again, and he would make her see then that she could not do this to him. She owed him her love. It was not something you could take away once bestowed.

He would make her see how wrong she was to think she could abandon their love.

TWENTY-NINE

*A*riadne stood for a long time in her bedchamber, her fingers unmoving on the clasp of her cloak, as snow dripped onto the floor from its folds. Why had she assumed that Gabriel would make it easy for her? She should not have assumed that he had gone on with his life the way she had gone on with hers. But what else could she have done? There were no convenient lies she could have told to soften the blow. The truth, brutal though it was, had to be told.

He would go home now, back to his family in Somerset, and he would forget about Ariadne now that he knew there was no future in remembering her.

But she still felt soiled in some way by that encounter. In fact, she was beginning to feel she could do nothing right anymore. She had run afoul of her husband, and she should have known better, and now she had caused a deadly hurt to a man who had been her lover and her friend. And the worst of it was that she could not think how to change either of those things.

"Miss Ari, should I put out your gown for this afternoon's audience at the palace?" Tilly came into the bedchamber. "Lord love us, miss, you're dripping all over the floor. Standing 'ere like a statue. What's the matter?" She pushed Ari's hands away from the clasp and unfastened it herself, drawing the cloak away and bundling it up. "I'll put this to dry in the kitchen. I didn't know you were going out this morning."

"Oh, I just wanted to smell the snow, Tilly." Ari pulled herself together. "I wanted to see if London snow was different from Somerset snow."

"'Tis a lot dirtier, that's for sure." Tilly grimaced at the black snow water puddling on the floor. "I'll send Ethel up with a mop." She took the wet cloak away, and Ari sat by the fire, warming her damp feet on the fender. The clock struck a quarter to two. Ivor would be back for dinner in fifteen minutes, and she hadn't dressed for the afternoon. But a lassitude filled her. Maybe she could escape the ritual, just this once. A headache, perhaps.

No. She sat up abruptly. There'd been enough untruths. She would feign nothing ever again. She got up and went to the armoire to choose a suitable gown for the Queen's audience.

Ivor returned as she was brushing her hair. And this time, he came in smiling, bending to kiss his wife's cheek as if nothing had ever happened to disturb the smooth equanimity of their marriage. "It's almost stopped snowing."

Ari shot him a tentative look. Was it over? Was she forgiven? She felt relief seeping into her and for the first time understood how tense she had been all morning as her shoulders released the strain. "Then we can walk to the palace. I am in need of fresh air and a little exercise." She smiled. "Tilly has prepared a mutton stew for lunch, humble fare but good for this weather. How was the King's audience?"

"Tedious as ever." Ivor tossed his damp cloak over the arm of a settle. "Everyone was rather bleary-eyed, and his majesty seemed somewhat irritable. His color was very high, choleric almost." He poured himself a goblet of wine from the bottle on the sideboard. "Wine?"

Ari shook her head. "No, thank you. I need to keep my wits about me in the Queen's audience chamber. Her ladies have sharp tongues."

"No one has enough to do, that's the trouble," Ivor observed. "By the way, the King said he expects a report on the puppy when he visits her majesty later this afternoon."

"Oh, I'm sure I can give him a glowing one, although I shan't tell him how nasty you are to her."

"I am not in the least nasty to her," he protested. "I just don't believe in dogs in the bed or on the dinner table."

"Dinner is served, Miss Ari," Tilly announced from the door. She frowned. "Why didn't you send for me to help you dress?"

"Because, Tilly dear, I can manage myself," she said, smiling. "I've been dressing myself since I was three years old."

"Not in those clothes," Tilly retorted. She bustled over and began to adjust the set of the neckline on Ari's gown of bronze damask. Ari submitted patiently until the maid pronounced herself satisifed.

Ivor gestured that Ari should go ahead of him to the dining salon, saying, "Oh, by the way, Tilly, there's no need for you to accompany Lady Ari this afternoon." He filled a bowl with the richly fragrant stew in the deep tureen in front of him. "I will be there myself."

"You're invited to the Queen's audience?" Ariadne was relieved at the thought of Ivor's presence at her side.

"At the King's bidding," he responded, passing her the bowl. "The formalities are always less rigidly observed once one is accepted into the royal entourage." A slightly sardonic note was in his voice. He had no more time than his wife for the ceremonial observances, pointless as they were. But they had to be honored when necessary.

It had stopped snowing when they set out for the palace. As they entered the park, passing the place where Ari had met Gabriel just a few hours earlier, she couldn't help a covert sideways glance, dreading that he would still be there, waiting to confront her again. But she could see only the bare shapes of tree trunks in the gray light.

She heaved a sigh of relief as they entered the outer palace courtyard. Tedious though the afternoon promised to be, at least she didn't have to hide anything, except, perhaps, her boredom, from anyone.

The Queen greeted her graciously enough, and his majesty entered a few minutes later, accompanied by his brother, the Duke of York, and a group of lesser gentlemen, including Ivor, who kept slightly to one side of the group, his blue gaze alert as it rested on Ariadne.

The King addressed Ari as soon as he'd greeted the Queen. "So, my Lady Chalfont, how is my little bitch doing? Does she please you?"

"Oh, more than I can say, sire." Ari rose from her deep curtsy at his majesty's signal.

"Is she behaving herself?"

"Beautifully, sire." Ari tried to think of some sparkling piece of witty repartee, but her brain seemed mired in sludge. It had been such a long and stressful day, all she wanted to do was crawl into bed and forget it altogether.

"Glad to hear it," he said, sounding bored. He turned his attention to his wife, and his air was far from benign. "What of you, madam wife? How is it with you?"

"Well enough, sir," Catherine replied, looking at her husband with a slight frown. "You seem overly flushed, your majesty. I trust you are not feverish."

"Pah! I'm as fit as a flea. Ask the leech." The King dismissed his wife's concern with a flourish. "You, Buckingham, bring me wine. I've a camel's thirst on me." He turned back to Ariadne. "So, madam, I understand you prefer to worship with my brother York than attend our Christmas services in the Chapel Royal."

Ariadne couldn't tell if there was an accusation in the statement. His majesty was looking at her with a rather predatory air, which put her on her guard. She curtsied. "I was brought up to worship in the Catholic fashion, sire. I trust I did not offend your majesty."

He gave another dismissive gesture. "Hardly. My own

brother goes his own way in such matters. I don't know why the country takes it all to heart so. There's that wretched bastard of mine trying to drum up support . . ." He shook his head with exasperation. "I wish I knew what to do with him."

"Perhaps an accident could befall him, sir." The Duke of York wafted a perfumed handkerchief beneath his nose as he spoke. "Simpler all around, if he were out of the way."

Charles looked at his brother. "It would certainly be a weight off *your* mind, sir," he declared with more than a touch of malice. "You won't want to fight Monmouth for your throne, I'm sure."

His majesty looked around the circle. "You're all dull as ditch water this afternoon. I don't know why I waste my time in your company. Nell . . . Nelly, my sweet . . . you shall entertain me." He beckoned to his mistress, who was standing beside the Queen's chair.

She came forward instantly, dropping a curtsy. "Your majesty, I am at your service as always."

He laughed and drew her to her feet, kissing her hand. "My dearest Nelly, my life would be insupportable without you. Come, we shall play some backgammon. I have in mind some amusing forfeits." He tucked the lady's hand into his elbow and sailed from the Queen's presence without a glance at his wife.

Catherine appeared unperturbed. She took a sip of her tea and set down the cup. "Shall we have some music? Marianne, my dear, will you play for us?"

The lady rose with a curtsy and took her place at the harp.

✦ ✦ ✦

"Sweet heaven, I thought we would never get out of there." Ariadne walked swiftly through the antechamber as the guards closed the doors to the audience chamber behind them. "I thought the woman would play forever."

Ivor grimaced. "I've heard better harpists in my time, too. But we're clear now. And we won't have to return until the New Year festivities."

"Five whole days." Ari gave a little skip of pleasure. "Perhaps we can go to the theatre again. Or maybe go for a ride if the ground is not frozen. I haven't been on Sphinx for an eternity."

"The horses are eating their heads off in the stables," Ivor commented. "Maybe tomorrow we'll take them out." They emerged into the bitter cold of the early winter evening. The snow had stopped, but the ground was freezing, the snow cover glittering under a crystal-clear star-filled sky. "We must hurry. It's not safe in the park after dark." He set off rapidly, clasping Ari's elbow firmly. "I should have told Jeb to meet us here."

"But 'tis still early," Ari protested.

"It's dark nevertheless." He directed them out of the palace into the courtyard. There were a few people around, and the space was lit by flickering torches.

"Chalfont, a word with you."

Ivor turned at the voice. A stocky man, resplendent in gold and turquoise silk, a luxuriant peruke curling on his shoulders, was waving imperatively at him. Ivor frowned, recognizing the Lord Chancellor, Lord Jeffries.

Not a man to be ignored if one wanted recognition in this court of favorites. He said quietly to Ariadne, "Stay in the light while I talk to the Lord Chancellor. His favor is well worth courting."

"Why won't he come to you?" she asked with a touch of indignation.

"Because he doesn't need to," Ivor said succinctly. "I won't be a moment." He walked across the courtyard to where the imperious Lord Chancellor stood waiting.

Ari grimaced. It was hard to accept the supplicant position when one was accustomed to being the commander. She found it hard, and she could understand that Ivor probably found it even harder to swallow his pride. But she had little doubt that he would soon enough make his mark, and people, even as lofty as the Lord Chancellor, would come to him. He radiated a natural authority.

She was cold standing still and began to walk around, staying as instructed under the safety of the torch lights, her feet crunching on the crisp snow as she stamped them to keep her toes from freezing in her thin sandals.

A slender figure emerged suddenly from the shadow of an arch. "Ariadne."

She stopped, her heart thumping against her breastbone. "Gabriel?"

"Aye, 'tis me. Did you think I would take my congé so easily, Ari?" He came up to her, his face white and tense. He had been waiting for this opportunity to catch her alone since he'd shadowed her and her husband across the park into the palace earlier that afternoon. The long hours of waiting in hiding had taken their toll, and he was filled with a reckless determination.

"I cannot give up my love so easily, and I don't believe, Ari, that you mean it when you say you don't love me anymore." He put his hands on her upper arms, pulling her towards him. "You cannot mean it. I could not feel as I do if you didn't have the same feelings for me. Remember how we loved, how we kissed, the promises we made." He was speaking in a low, rapid voice, desperate to say what he had to, desperate to convince her. His fingers tightened on her arms, and she made to pull away.

"No, Gabriel. Let me go. This is madness. I told you how it must be. You *must* accept it." She tried to jerk her arms free.

"No, be still," he demanded. "Please, Ari, be still. Let me kiss you just once, and you will see that it is as it always was . . . how it must always be." He reached for her mouth with his own, and she squirmed, kicking out at his shins, wrenching her head aside.

"Take your hands off my wife."

Each word was like a drop of ice-cold venom. Gabriel gasped, his hands falling from Ari's arms, and slowly, her heart battering against her ribs, she stepped away from him. The point of Ivor's sword stick flashed between them and pressed into the hollow of Gabriel's throat. A bead of blood welled around the blade's tip. She saw Gabriel swallow convulsively, and the blade moved not a fraction of an inch.

"Ivor . . . no," she heard herself whisper.

He didn't look at her. "Be quiet."

She didn't dare say anything, just stared at the bead of blood, at Gabriel's complexion growing more ashen by the moment. And then Ivor said, "It is a capital offense to draw blood within his majesty's walls. We will continue this beyond the walls of the palace courtyard. You will walk through the gate into the park."

The point of his sword slid away from Gabriel's throat, moved against his ribs, and the young man took an unsteady step in the direction of the arched gateway that would take them beyond the palace walls and into the park. Ariadne followed, frantically trying to think of something she could say, anything that would turn this terrifying Ivor into some semblance of the man she knew.

Gabriel was trembling like a leaf as he walked through the gate and out onto the path that ran beside the canal. He looked around, desperately hoping to see help somewhere, but no one paid them the least attention, everyone hurrying, intent on finding sanctuary from the crystal-clear cold of this star-filled night.

Ivor's sword point pricked Gabriel's side as he directed him off the path into a shrubbery on one side.

Gabriel felt vomit rise in his throat as he saw the lonely darkness of the place. He had meddled with the dangerous men of the valley, and all the old horror stories his nurse had told him as a child about the bloodthirsty Daunts came back to him in vivid color. He swallowed the nausea, struggling not to break down, to remember that he was a Fawcett.

Behind the shrubs was a small clearing, bathed in the

sky's silver light. He could not die in this brilliant star-light, Gabriel thought. Surely that could not happen. But the sword point had moved again, back to his throat.

"So, not content with sitting at my table and making free of my hospitality, you wish to take my wife also." Ivor's tone was almost conversational. "I am assuming I have the pleasure of addressing Master Gabriel Fawcett, the poet?"

Ariadne closed her eyes for a moment. She had never heard Ivor speak in that deadly tone before, but for the first time, she understood the real danger to Gabriel. Her hand moved infinitesimally into the secret slit in her wide, swinging skirt.

"Well?" Ivor demanded, so fiercely that Gabriel jumped and the sword point dipped into his skin. "Answer me, sir."

Gabriel swallowed again, hesitantly raised a hand as if he could push the sword point from his throat. "Yes . . . yes, I am Gabriel Fawcett."

"And not content with taking my wife's virginity, you would now cuckold me in the marriage bed." It was not a question. Ivor's eyes were blue stones, his expression hard as granite. "I cannot allow that."

"Ivor, please," Ari said softly. "Let him leave. It is over. I told him this—"

He turned his eyes towards her for second, and she fell silent, shriveling under the burning fury they contained. "Go home. *Now.* I have work to do. You and I will do our own work later."

Ariadne's fingers closed over her knife. In her wildest,

most horrific nightmares, she could not have imagined doing what she was about to do. She moved suddenly, knocking Ivor's sword hand to one side and stepping instantly in front of Gabriel, her own knife gleaming in her hand, before Ivor could move his arm back to where it was.

"I cannot let you do this, Ivor." Gray eyes met blue ones with as fierce a determination. "I will not let you kill him." She was silent, watching his face, and then said with soft insistence, trying to make every word penetrate, "You don't want to kill him, Ivor. You know you don't."

"And you would kill *me* to save your lover?" he queried, an eyebrow raised in sardonic disbelief. "Put the knife away."

She knew the danger had passed, or at least the extreme danger. Her astonishing challenge had surprised him enough to break the concentrated power of his rage. She lowered her knife hand, feeling Gabriel quiver behind her sheltering body. She stayed where she was, still holding Ivor's gaze.

"Move aside," he said finally, lowering the sword stick and sheathing it. "You have played your part, Ariadne, and now you will go home and wait for me. We have a long night ahead of us."

Still, she hesitated, and he said very quietly, "Do not compel me to move you aside."

Ari stepped away from Gabriel, hearing his sharp, fearful intake of breath as he found himself facing Ivor unshielded once again.

"Go back to the house. *Now.*"

"I'll go. But you won't . . . ?" She left the question hanging.

"This is *my* business now, and you will leave it to me," he stated. "You've made enough unilateral decisions for one lifetime. Now, get out of here before I really lose my temper."

She looked at him askance, hearing herself say absurdly, "You mean you haven't?"

"Oh, wife of mine, you do not want to be in my vicinity if I ever really lose my temper," he assured her, his eyes still on the silent and quivering Gabriel.

She took him at his word, but with a final touch of stubborn defiance, she first turned back to Gabriel and lightly grazed his ashen countenance with her fingertips. "Farewell. You will find someone more worthy of your love, Gabriel. I know you will." And then, sensing Ivor move behind her, she pushed through the shrubs and hurried back across the park, alert to the dangers around her, her knife in her hand, her ears stretched to catch every rustle and crackle of the frosty ground.

The lights of the house shone as she emerged from the park, and she ran up to the front door and banged the knocker. When Tilly opened the door, Ari ran past her upstairs, her eyes blinded by tears of exhaustion and the fearful knowledge that her marriage hung in the balance. What was said and done in the long hours ahead would determine whether she passed the rest of her life in lonely unhappiness or safely in the arms of the man who held her heart, the only man she could ever truly love.

THIRTY

*I*vor stood unmoving until he was certain Ariadne was out of earshot. Then he said almost conversationally, "So, Master Poet, how long have you and my wife been consorting behind my back?"

Gabriel shook his head. "Consorting? No, no, I beg you to believe me. We have been doing no such thing. I came to London to find her. I saw her at the theatre . . ." He put a hand convulsively to his throat, where the bead of blood still welled against his lace collar.

"Here." Ivor handed him his own handkerchief. "You'll not die of blood loss, I can safely promise you." He regarded his erstwhile rival with a touch of puzzled contempt. What on earth had Ari seen in this whey-faced creature? He was her very opposite in every respect. But perhaps that was his answer, he thought. He waved away his bloody handkerchief as Gabriel tried to return it to him.

It was long past time to unravel this treacherous thread that had entangled his marriage from the beginning. Ari's lone efforts had clearly not been successful. They had simply tied more knots in the thread. "Do you love her?"

Gabriel scrunched the handkerchief into a ball in his fist. "I have loved her since I first saw her on the cliff top," he muttered. "She is perfection."

Ivor gave a sharp crack of laughter. "How little you know her, my friend. *Perfection* is the last word I would use to describe my fiercely independent, headstrong warrior of a wife. Believe me, you and she would not suit. She would trample you into the dust, without meaning to, I grant you, before you knew what had hit you."

Gabriel was beginning to sense the truth in these words as he thought of Ari with her knife drawn, facing down her sword-wielding husband, but he held his tongue. The acute danger seemed to have passed, but he felt that his wisest course was simply to answer this terrifying man's questions as truthfully as he knew how and venture nothing of his own.

"So, does she love *you*, do you think?" Ivor asked, his expression revealing nothing as he waited for an answer to this all-important question. He thought he knew the answer, but his own belief wasn't sufficient to convince him. He needed confirmation from the only other person who would know the answer.

"She says not," Gabriel admitted. "But she *did* love me. We loved each other." Finally, he risked looking his interlocutor in the eye. "She says she does not love me anymore."

"And do you believe her?" Ivor still spoke without expression.

Gabriel wanted to shout to the heavens that she *did*

love him as he loved her, she just needed to be reminded, but his tongue was still as those intense blue eyes seemed to bore into his skull.

"Answer me." The rasped command was enough to bring his fear flooding back.

Slowly, Gabriel nodded. "I believe her." It was said in an undertone.

"Very well." Ivor concealed the surge of joy he felt at this simple statement. He had thought it, but he hadn't *known* it absolutely. He took Gabriel by his thin shoulders and looked down at him, fixing him once more with his penetrating, intense blue gaze. "You will not show yourself at court again, Master Fawcett. I care not what you do or where you go, but if I ever see you in the vicinity of my wife again, I will not be so gentle with you. Is that understood, sir?"

What would constitute an *ungentle* Ivor Chalfont? Gabriel wondered. He was still trembling inside from the supposedly *gentle* treatment over the last half hour. He took a deep, steadying breath and slowly nodded, finally relinquishing the dream that had informed his life for the last weeks. Ariadne Daunt was not for him.

"Go home, Master Poet," Ivor said with a note of compassion now. "Ariadne is too bright a sun for you. She would have singed your wings long since." He turned away, leaving Gabriel still standing in the little clearing, and walked back to his wife.

✦ ✦ ✦

Ari heard the front door bang shut. She heard his footsteps and saw the latch lift on the door to the small parlor, where she waited. She stood with her back to the fire, feeling its warmth against the backs of her legs.

Her husband came in, closing the door behind him. Deliberately, he turned the key in the lock and then looked at her as he unclasped his cloak, tossing it aside. "So, madam wife, we will have some truth spoken at last. How many times have you spoken with Master Fawcett since we arrived in London?"

She shook her head. "Just twice."

"I am to believe that?" He sounded incredulous. "You have been as jumpy as a scalded cat for days, and you expect me to believe that had nothing to do with your lover's presence?"

"Gabriel is not my lover," she declared. "You have to believe that, at least. Yes, I have known he was in London for a few days. I saw him for the first time in the piazza when we went to the theatre. He has been following me ever since. I did send him a note, asking him to meet me, but I have spoken to him only to tell him it was over and he must leave."

"And you chose to keep this a secret," he said flatly. He walked to the sideboard and poured a glass of brandy from the decanter.

"I thought . . . oh, dear God, I no longer know what I thought," Ari said helplessly. "I know how you felt about him. You haven't exactly kept it a secret. And I thought it best to deal with it myself. I would see him, end it, and you would be none the wiser, and we could continue in harmony."

"I accept that your feelings have changed for your poet, but that is no longer the issue. In fact, it ceased to be many weeks ago." He spun around to look at her. "*Why*, Ariadne, did you not confide in me? If you had told me that he had entered your life again, we could have dealt with it together. If you truly had no feelings for him any longer, there was no reason to keep his reappearance to yourself. Can't you see that? Instead of honesty, you chose to creep around behind my back, violating my trust again." He took a draught from his goblet and turned to refill it.

She spoke to his back, but she felt as if her words simply slid away, and they began to sound meaningless to her own ears now. "I didn't think it should involve you, Ivor. It was *my* muddle to clear up."

"It was *not*," he stated. "It was a situation that affected both of us. And instead of telling me, you conduct hole-in-the-corner, secret meetings and correspondence with the man who was once your lover."

"No," she exclaimed. "No. I did not . . . or not exactly." She subsided. If he insisted on looking at it that way, then there was nothing she could do or say to persuade him otherwise. "I have never betrayed your trust, even though you don't believe it. I love you, Ivor. Why can't you trust in that above all else?"

There was a long silence. The fire crackled, the candles flickered as a gust of wind rattled the ill-fitting glass of the window. Ivor had turned to face her again, his goblet in his hand. His gaze seemed to look beyond her as he spoke. "*Trust*. A word you bandy so lightly, Ari. When I was six years old, my mother woke me before dawn, dressed me, and took me to the stables. My father put me on a horse to ride pillion behind one of his household and told me to remember that I was a Chalfont. Nothing more was said, and that was the last time I saw my home or my family, and three days later, I found myself in a strange land, surrounded by strangers. Hard, unfriendly strangers, and no one thought to explain to me what I was doing there or why. It was at least a year before I finally gave up hoping to see my father ride into the valley to take me home again. And several more years before I understood that I had been sold, abandoned by my family and sold for the family's interests."

He drained his glass, setting it down. "I understood then that trust was a fool's game. I do not give my trust lightly, Ariadne. You are one of the very few on whom I have bestowed it. And you have violated it."

"Oh, no, Ivor." She looked at him, shocked and horrified. "My dear love, I have never violated your trust. Not truly. I have never faltered in my love for you, not for one second since we declared our commitment. I have never faltered in the deep and abiding friendship I have had for you since you first arrived in the valley."

She crossed the small space between them, taking his hands in both of hers, carrying them to her lips, kissing his knuckles, holding his hands against her cheek. "Please, you must understand. I have never thought to betray you in anything. I trust you completely, and I never fully understood how you could doubt me. Please, Ivor, trust me, trust my love for you. Trust that I will never knowingly betray you. Oh, I'll make mistakes. I have made so many in the last days, but they were made out of my love for you."

Ivor looked into the great gray pools of her eyes. He read only love and truth there and a passionate plea for belief. And slowly, he understood. Deep down, he had been frightened that he would lose her. He had not had faith in the honesty that he knew was so much an essential part of the Ariadne he had loved since childhood. She had told him the truth at the beginning, that she could not love him as she loved her poet. And then, as that had changed, she had told him a new truth, and he had been unable to trust in her truth.

It was as if a great, all-encompassing shadow had finally dissipated. "We have both made mistakes," he said gently. "And I ask you to forgive me mine, my love." He cupped her face between his hands and brought his mouth to hers. It was a kiss of healing, of promise. The unspoken promise of trust unbroken.

And when he finally raised his head, Ari leaned back in his arms to look up at him, a little glimmer of mischief in her eyes. "I think mutual forgiveness probably requires more dedication, husband."

"Oh, do you, indeed?" He ran his finger over her lips, and she sucked it into her mouth in a wicked little movement that made him catch his breath. He lifted her against him and moved closer to the fire, setting her down in the circle of warmth. He undressed her, slowly lingering on each garment as he removed it, and Ari felt the heat of the fire lave her bare skin as her muslin shift fell away from her, and she stood naked, her eyes never leaving his.

"Lie down on the rug," he instructed, his hands now moving over his own clothes. "I have a most powerful need of my wife."

Her skin prickled at the imperative power of his desire, the urgent thrust and throb of his penis as he stripped away the last of his clothes. He came down to the rug beside her, moving over her, a hand sliding between her thighs, probing the soft folds of her sex, teasing the little nub of flesh that rose hard against his touch. Her hips shifted of their own accord, then lifted to receive him as he entered her with one smooth movement that seemed to drive his very self into her core. She seemed to lose her self in his eyes, under the force of his body, possessing her, joining with her as one whole.

And when it was over, when the world shattered around them in a million starry pieces, he stayed within her, their bodies still joined. He caressed her cheek, brushed his lips across her eyelids in butterfly kisses, and she encircled him tightly within her arms, binding him to her.

"I didn't know it was possible to love someone so much," Ari murmured into the damp hollow of his shoulder, linking her fingers behind his back, delighting in the knowledge that this rock-solid body belonged only to her. "You are mine."

"I am your shield and buckler, my sweet. I will hold the world at bay for you," he murmured, smiling at the strength of her encircling arms, their rounded softness concealing their muscular firmness. "And I will be all the stronger knowing that you are mine, that your strength is as mine."

It had been a long and hazardous journey to reach this safe harbor, Ari thought. A harbor where the shared passions of love and desire were secure behind the banner of one small word: *trust*. She tightened her arms around him once again, stretching her body against his length, secure in the knowledge that nothing could come between them again.

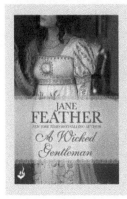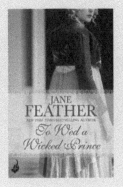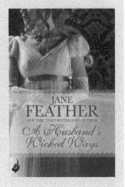